Julian Mitchell

Julian Mitchell was born in 1935. He was educated at Winchester and Wadham College, Oxford. In addition to five other novels written before *The Undiscovered Country*, he has written successful plays for the stage, including *Another Country*, for which he also wrote the screenplay, and many other scripts for television and film, including *Wilde*.

Margaret Drabble, born in Sheffield in 1939, read English Literature at Newnham College, Cambridge. Her 17 novels include, most recently, *The Sea Lady* (2006). She has written biographies of Arnold Bennett and Angus Wilson and a memoir, *The Pattern in the Carpet* (2009). She is married to the biographer Michael Holroyd.

The Undiscovered Country

The Undiscovered Country

Julian Mitchell

FOREWORD BY MARGARET DRABBLE

CAPUCHIN CLASSICS

CAPUCHIN CLASSICS
LONDON

The Undiscovered Country

© Julian Mitchell 1968
This edition published by Capuchin Classics 2010

2 4 6 8 0 9 7 5 3 1

Capuchin Classics
128 Kensington Church Street, London W8 4BH
Telephone: +44 (0)20 7221 7166
Fax: +44 (0)20 7792 9288
E-mail: info@capuchin-classics.co.uk
www.capuchin-classics.co.uk

Châtelaine of Capuchin Classics: Emma Howard

ISBN: 978-0-9074290-5-7

Foreword

Julian Mitchell is a writer of many talents and much wit. He began his literary career by publishing poetry and editing a poetry magazine while still at Oxford, produced several successful novels during the 1960s, and then abandoned fiction for the theatre, screen-writing, film and television. He suffers from an embarrassment of riches, and those of us who enjoyed and admired his fiction were sorry when he gave it up. He has given various reasons for this decision, and it may be that in his last novel, *The Undiscovered Country*, which appeared in 1968, he felt that he had explored the limits of the genre to his own satisfaction. He has always had a restless and enquiring mind, and has been more eager to move on than to look back and rest on his laurels.

The Undiscovered Country is a startling and innovative work, quite unlike anything he had written before, and unlike the experimental fiction that was being written at that time. It is original both in form and in content. The first half of the book appears to be a first-person memoir which opens with a description of the author's days at prep school, where he forms a close, admiring and entangled friendship with his hero and 'alter-ego', a boy called Charles Humphries, a child unusually blessed, we are told, with 'four living parents' – a characteristically intriguing phrase. The story moves on through public school to Mitchell's National Service as a submariner, studies at Oxford, an Aldermaston CND march, travels in America, work at the BBC, and the beginnings of a successful literary career, punctuated by occasional sightings of Charles, who has taken a somewhat different path. The narrator, 'Julian Mitchell', speaks in his own voice, mentions real people (some famous, some tangential), and describes experiences recognisable, historically, as his own, yet we sense that his friend and creation Charles inhabits a different realm of reality. The resultant mix of levels and identities is challenging, entertaining and disconcerting. The documentary aspects of the memoir go far beyond the playful postmodern tricks of writers who more recently have introduced themselves as characters or commentators in their own work: this is a wholesale, thorough deception, done with all the conviction of a faithful keeper of a diary. This is a circumstantial account of the 1960s as they were, and as we remember them. (It also manifests Mitchell's exceptional gift for puns, both good and bad.)

But the events of the 1960s are not the subject of the book. The second half of it, written in a completely different tone and key, is allegedly the transcription of an unfinished and fragmentary novel left by Charles to Julian after his death by suicide. This is based on the *Satyricon*, an extravagantly homoerotic classical text by Petronius dating from the decadent reign of Nero, which is also fragmentary in the form in which we know it. In this section, Mitchell ventures into another world of the surreal, the pornographic, the carnivalesque, as Charles describes his picaresque wanderings through a mysterious Kafkaesque hotel in a mysterious country (is it America?) in search of an ideal, beautiful, ever evasive and sex-changing lover. Events in Petronius are mirrored, and so is his wildly various style, which ranged from plebeian prose to mock heroic to verse, and was larded with *doubles entendres* and puns: Mitchell uses, as did his model, pastiche, parody, encapsulated short stories (including a sad one about extinct ducks) and comic-satiric onslaughts on contemporary art and literature. It is a bravura and inventive text. But it is more than that.

The theme of identity and gender came to prominence in the 1960s, both in literature and legislature, as women's groups and the Campaign for Homosexual Equality fought to redefine who we were and who we thought we were and who we had a right to be. Charles's sexual encounters in the underworld, and his fantastic confrontations with both mother and father figures, take us on an exotic journey in search of the self, as Mitchell travels through a succession of styles of living and writing. We recognise the Beatniks, the political activists of the barricades, the dramaturges of Peter Brook's *Theatre of Cruelty*, and, in a parody of Aristophanes' *Lysistrata*, the pioneers of what came to be called Pink Power. Abraham and Isaac and Oedipus also play their part in the cavalcade.

Homosexuality had been partly legalised in 1967 by the Sexual Offences Act, following the Wolfenden Report and a long public campaign, and this material was topical, although still highly controversial – we were a long way from the freedoms of Alan Hollinghurst's *The Swimming Pool Library* (1988), towards which some of Mitchell's subterranean sequences seem to point. It is relevant to note that in 2007 Mitchell wrote a highly-praised documentary TV drama called *Consenting Adults*, which dramatised the relationship between Wolfenden and his gay son Jeremy. Mitchell's own father thought homosexuality a crime, and did not speak to him for two years after he got wind, at his club, of the contents of *The Undiscovered Country*. Times have changed.

But this is not a campaigning work, nor even a reflection of the zeitgeist, although it serves as both. (Fellini's great film, the *Satyricon*, appeared a year after Mitchell's version, in 1969, and I cherish the probably erroneous view that he was prompted to it not wholly by Petronius, but also by being alerted to Mitchell's novel, which would then have been doing the rounds of the screen agencies. Both are very much of their time, as well as lasting works of art.) It is also an attempt, through multiple refractions, to arrive at an inner truth of the divided self. Mitchell has often said that irony is a danger to writers as well-read and as aware of the ridiculous as he is, but here, through excess of parody, he reached a mysterious equilibrium and a poignant sense of the human quest.

There is one image in this book that haunted me when I first read it, and does still. In a trout stream in Gloucestershire at the end of his parents' garden, he tells us, lived a solitary goldfish. No one knew how it got there, and the young Julian hoped it was happy there. Perhaps it thought it was a trout. 'Nature', says Mitchell the novelist, 'provides me with a thousand metaphors each day. And there was a goldfish in the pool below the bridge.' I could not resist asking him, when I met him, whether there really was a goldfish swimming amidst the trout. 'Of course', he said. But of course, to this day, I do not know whether to believe him or not. I do not know whether the goldfish and Charles were real. And that, to me, is a sign of the book's ongoing life.

Margaret Drabble
London, May 2010

PART ONE

A Friend in Need

1

Charles and I met for the first time in January 1944 when we were new boys together at a prep-school in the Midlands. We were almost exactly the same age.

I remember nothing of the journey from King's Cross that terrible afternoon except the schoolboy noses pressed against the window of our compartment and the schoolboy eyes gloating over the two miserable new bugs. I'm sure the master in charge of us was kind, the other boys merely curious, but only one thing in my life had ever frightened me as much as those threatening, flattened nostrils and sly, calculating eyes, and that was the grinning circle of long-trousered boys in the Essex village where my family lived. My mother used to make me wear a tweed cap when I went bicycling. One day the gang pushed me off my bicycle and threw the cap into a bed of fresh green stinging-nettles. Those nettles were vividly before me all the way to Nottingham.

The only thing that gave me any courage at all was that I hadn't, like Charles, actually broken down. He sat opposite me, screwing up his green and white striped cap in his hands, the tears endlessly falling. I had never seen anyone look so utterly desolate, so wholly abandoned to sorrow, and I was both frightened and a little scornful of him. The previous night, allowed for the last time in my life to sleep in my mother's bed, I had cried myself out. Having no more tears to shed, I felt superior.

Later that evening we sat together in the junior boys' common-room, both of us so miserably at a loss about our surroundings that his ability to continue dredging up tears seemed the only sure thing in the universe. The common-room had white-painted lockers along one wall, a long, broad table at which we ate and did our lessons, a letter-rack next to the empty fireplace, and a large bow-window which looked across a patch of brussels sprouts and cabbages and over a low stone wall to the playing fields. It was wartime, of course, and no doubt flowers were meant to fill the view rather than those drab, rotten-smelling vegetables, but even with roses the outlook would have been meagre. It was a flat, sandy piece of country, and where the football fields ended a tall row of evergreens sealed off the outside world like a prison wall. Charles and I preferred to gaze hopefully at the letter-rack. The five minutes which the school butler spent sorting the letters each morning keyed us to a pitch of anxiety and excitement which was scarcely endurable. After they were over – five days out of six we were, inevitably, disappointed – I had to run down the corridor against the school rules to reach the lavatory, and Charles was usually racing at my heels.

That first evening, of course, the letter-rack was empty, and the green oil-cloth black-out blinds were down. Miss Graham, an ample, patient woman who seemed to me far older even than my grandmother though she was, I now suppose, only about forty, kept order without offensive strictness. She must have decided that Charles and I would be best comforted by being left alone. We sat side by side on a sofa. Charles hadn't yet said anything at all that I was aware of, though we had already had our high tea. I was and still am very bad at remembering people's names on first meeting, and I don't think I was even sure what he was called – at times I had felt that I must pull down my socks and look at my blue Cash's name-tapes to see what my own name was. But I felt I knew him as intimately as it was possible to know anyone, and that I would never forget his face whatever might happen to him or me.

He had black, curly hair, brown eyes, very small ears, and a long, strong nose. His cheeks had no colour at all. As he grew older, the nose became less dramatically prominent, but it was always the main feature of his face – even when he didn't wear glasses and his eyes, skittering nervously from face to face, seemed to be signalling for attention. They were never easy eyes to meet, so one tended to look at the bridge of his nose instead. When I think of him, I always think first of the way his eyebrows met there, thick and black: my grandmother always used to say that if your eyebrows met it meant you'd die by hanging.

The other boys were demonstrating model cars and aeroplanes, swapping stamps and cigarette cards (their rarity in 1944 made them highly prized), reading or writing home. I hadn't dared bring my own stamp collection to school in case stamps might be thought cissy, and I was relieved to see that there was at least one thing I understood in the otherwise inexplicable world about me. I summoned a pale courage to ask Charles if he, too, was a collector. The question seemed to appal him, to make the ultimate, impossible demand of his dreadful day. The tears surged forth again, and he glared at me through them with unutterable reproach. Strangely, this didn't frighten me. Instead it made me feel that his suffering must be so infinitely much more agonizing even than my own that I must do something to comfort him.

All my life I have had strong, usually impertinent and useless, impulses to help people. Often I have managed to suppress them. But this time, almost in spite of myself, my arm found its way round his shoulder. He leant his head against me. And there we sat, wordless, till cocoa-time.

If I felt superior to Charles that first day, the feeling did not last. Since we were the only new boys, we had been automatically placed together at the very bottom of the school in every class. After a few days, during which Miss Graham gauged our abilities, we were moved up to higher forms for the subjects whose elements we seemed to have mastered. We could both read and write, for instance, unlike some of our seniors. I was particularly proud of my spelling, but Charles could actually say things in French, which put him far above my head, and he had even started Latin. The only subject at which I could beat him was maths, for which he showed complete indifference. While I thoroughly enjoyed elementary algebra, he regarded it as beneath his interest and made only a token effort to solve even the simplest equations. His attitude amazed me. I was a vigorously competitive child, determined to be top of every form I was in. I never questioned the intrinsic value of a subject, simply tried to know more about it than anyone else. The composure with which Charles got nought for algebra day after day seriously lessened my pleasure at getting a regular ten out of ten. I couldn't understand it, any more than I could understand his French. Nor could Mr Yorke, the Maths master, who had watery eyes, red hair and a bristling moustache like a bright patch of autumnal bracken. One day he lost his temper and gave Charles half an hour's extra work for slackness.

After the class, I said, 'You asked for that, Humphries.'

Charles pulled his cap on roughly and said, 'Corky's stupid to get in a bate like that. It's not my fault I don't like rotten old maths.'

'What have you got to do?'

'Just today's equations over again.'

'I'll help you, if you like.'

'Don't be daft, Mitchell. You can't go into extra work with me.'

'I'll show you how to do them. They're awfully easy. Honestly.'

'Oh, I know they are,' said Charles grandly. 'But it's all such a bore.'

After lunch, when we were left to ourselves for a few minutes before going to change for football, Charles came up to me as I was reading *We Didn't Mean To Go To Sea* for the fourth or fifth time and said, 'If you're so jolly clever at maths, you show me, then.'

Eagerly I explained what I knew, demonstrating on a piece of scrap paper. He frowned at my workings and said nothing for a minute or two, then took the pencil from me and said, 'You mean, is this all I have to do?'

He copied some examples from CV Durrell's *Elementary Algebra* and began to work them out. He wrote left-handed, in a neat script. When I offered to help, he told me to shut up. After five minutes he showed me what he'd done. There was no mistake that I could see.

'I told you it was easy,' I said, rather crestfallen. I'd hoped we'd emerge flushed and triumphant together from our joint intellectual effort, but though I was slightly red in the face, he was as pale as ever.

'It's an awful bore all the same,' he said. 'Thanks.'

Later, during his half-hour's extra work, he faultlessly completed Durrell's next three chapters of exercises, ones which Corky hadn't even explained to us yet. Corky immediately assumed that he must have got hold of a master's copy of the book and cribbed the answers from the end. He went to the headmaster and told him that Charles was not only a cheat but a liar, too, as he insisted he had done the equations by himself, which simply wasn't, on past evidence, possible. Charles remained very calm, and asked how Corky supposed he'd done all the workings, then? They weren't in the masters' copies, were they? Corky was baffled. After I'd been summoned to give evidence for the defence, Charles was let off with a caution. Captain Nichols told him that if he hadn't been a new boy he'd have given him a black mark all the same, for cheekiness and showing off. From then on, Charles's progress in maths was spasmodic. When he roused himself, he could outshine everyone, but he did so only about once a month.

It was the same with football. While I was rather a dogged player and ran vigorously after the ball wherever it went, an earnest trier, Charles was more brilliant but less reliable. He could dribble better than anyone in the fourth game (we were only eight or nine a side down there, the number fluctuating with the patients in the sickroom). But dribbling was considered a form of showing off, especially by a new boy, and anyway Charles wasn't usually paying attention when the ball was passed to him. When he did get it, he preferred to keep it to himself. So either he would be a hero for dribbling past everyone and scoring, or a selfish clod who'd ruined everything by failing to pass at the crucial moment. He quite enjoyed games, I think, but his mind was mostly elsewhere, probably on one of the novels of Percy F. Westerman.

Percy F Westerman wrote, if I remember right, mainly about the heroic British soldiers of the heroic British first world war, and Charles and I for a time read almost nothing else, except an occasional Biggles. Mr Anderson, the French master, perhaps because he had lost his right leg in the war Percy F Westerman so buoyantly celebrated, did missionary work on behalf of Rafael Sabatini, reading him aloud every evening for twenty minutes before prep in the school library, but for some reason we scarcely ever attended – perhaps we thought it babyish to be read to – so Sabatini is still only a name to me. But then so now is Percy F Westerman, though I devoured his complete works. Books absorbed me, but I didn't, I'm afraid, absorb books. I couldn't, at the beginning of a school term, remember which Westermans I'd read only a couple of months before, and when I eventually graduated to detective stories, I frequently read the same one twice, only realizing at the end that I actually did know who the murderer was all along. Certainly, though we were both good at English, neither Charles nor I showed any literary leaning in those days, though I'm inclined to blame the school's unthinking philistinism for part of our backwardness.

The library looked into the back of a huge sprawling rhododendron and smelt of damp and tedium, though on winter Sundays there was sometimes a fire. Photographs of school teams took up almost as much wall space as books, though Victorian editions of the English classics were there for anyone who dared to lay hands on them. Few boys dared. I vividly remember the Waverley novels, for instance, untouched by generations of schoolboys, exuding a really poisonous air of boredom; and I know it's that set (bound in blue like Captain Marryat whom I equally neglected) which has prevented me to this day from ever opening a book by Sir Walter Scott. Westerman, Ransome (whom I adored), Henty (Charles's favourite), WHG Kingston, Captain WE Johns – these were accessible, the pages not crammed with bleak type, their length not beyond our own estimates of our powers. But Dickens, Thackeray, Scott, Harrison Ainsworth (how could we tell the difference?) were out of the question. Charles once got a hundred and fifty pages into *David Copperfield*, but gave up, saying that the plot was too complicated to follow. I actually finished *Vanity Fair*. But that was when we were senior boys, near to leaving, and even then the headmaster, who used to walk round the dormitories once or twice a week, looked at me suspiciously when he found me reading it in bed.

He was a direct man. 'Are you reading that because you like it?' he said. 'Or because you want to make an impression?'

I didn't honestly know, though I naturally protested I liked it better than any book I'd ever read.

'Are you quite sure?' he said. He smelt, as always after dinner, of whisky, which reminded me of home and my father's goodnight kiss. It was a reliable, comforting smell, though confusing on Captain Nichols where it could lead to mercurial switches of mood.

I think I was genuinely puzzled by the way he looked at me. He had a very big, creased forehead, which seemed an infinity of wrinkles, and as he frowned his eyes, which were grey, seemed to be pleading with me to own up like a good chap. I was frightened, but I held my ground.

'Yes, sir,' I said.

He continued to stare at me, the whole dormitory silent, wondering if he was going to burst out with one of his famous explosions of wrath, accusing me of insolence, lying or something equally unimaginable in his presence. But all he did was pat me on the shoulder and say, 'Well, it's a good thing you're going to Winchester, Mitchell. You're much too brainy for us here.'

The dormitory sniggered. After he'd gone, quite a junior boy called me 'brainy' to see what I'd do. Still quaking from what had seemed a terrible ordeal, I pretended to be too deep in my book to hear. It was a great relief when the lights were turned out and I could safely put Thackeray aside for the night.

Captain Nichols's suspicion was typical of the man and the school. His military rank was perhaps a pip or two lower than his upright, clean-shaven appearance suggested, but it concealed the fact that he hadn't seen any actual fighting in the war he often referred to. Someone discovered, goodness knows how, that though Captain Nichols had been in Palestine with Allenby, it was only in the catering corps. (Our abominable food was naturally attributed to this. The rissoles which recurred again and again in our diet were known as camel splats.) He was a tall man, with a passion for rowing and social climbing which took him, once the war was over, to Henley every year, where boys' parents were always impressed by Mrs Nichols's flowery manners and hats. The school had a snobbish side – it boasted no less than two honourables, both of whom went on to Eton – and I was astonished by the number of boys who, like Charles, had four living parents.

Though the Captain was a formidable figure to a small boy, he was not sadistic and corporal punishment was reserved exclusively for those who ran away or were caught smoking. He was very fond of cricket and spent hours coaching any boy who showed talent. Often he would make the younger masters bowl to him in the nets after dinner, and we would hear him exhorting them to 'pitch it up' long after we were supposed to be asleep. Most of his pupils went on to Uppingham, Repton or – his own old school – Shrewsbury. He was, I suppose, something of a schoolboy himself, a bad teacher, but a kindly man. But he lacked any intellectual interest, and on the false principle that stupid men were the mental equals of bright boys – or perhaps on the correct assumption that most of the boys weren't in the least bright, either – he chose masters like himself, either too old or too physically incompetent for the minor army messes in which they and he might have been happier. One or two of them, it's true, were quite capable teachers within their limits, perhaps because they actually liked boys. But if any of them had secret designs on our bodies, they kept their hands to themselves, with one exception, and they never attempted to seduce us by going a page beyond the syllabus. Such masters were what most parents wanted. It was only Charles who made me realize that what most parents wanted wasn't necessarily what was right for their children.

The one master who couldn't control his hands was, as seems to be common, the one who by his eccentricity encouraged us to use our minds – Mr Bradley. He was short, bald, and had had his nose broken, he claimed, playing rugger for his college at Cambridge. I now rather doubt whether Mr Bradley ever went to Cambridge or played rugger, but the claim enabled him to treat our soccer with such disdain that Captain Nichols eventually had to relieve him of the chore of refereeing it. Instead he ran the rifle-range, and teaching us the correct prone position for firing he managed to spend a satisfactory amount of time prone himself beside us. His head shone, and he had large, surprisingly hairy hands, one of which would clasp pupils breathlessly to him while the other corrected exercises. If one had done well, he would give one a smacking kiss on the brow and send one back to one's desk with an equally smacking slap on the bottom. If one had done badly, he squeezed one even harder against him and groaned dramatically. We were all quite ignorant of ordinary sex, let alone its sophistications, and we accepted our smacks and squeezes with resignation. Our only real criticism of Mr Bradley was that he licked the point of his indelible pencil, so that his lips were always stained with purple, as though he had impetigo. We didn't like the way the purple was passed on when he kissed us.

He always directed the school plays, and it was during rehearsals that he had his greatest opportunities for kissing and smacking. 'What a pretty girl you'll make,' he would say, hugging some furiously blushing boy. Yet the boy would feel obscurely pleased, too, because Mr Bradley's compliments, though ambiguous, were always offered with his own enormous blush, a fierce crimson from ear to ear across his pate. He was musical, too. Sometimes he would play for his own pleasure on the piano of the school assembly hall, and though no one was allowed in, the sound would be so intriguing that boys would gather at the door to listen. He liked loud music best, sometimes so loud that other masters would send boys to ask him to play more quietly or not at all. Once, sent by Captain Nichols, I found him with tears pouring down his cheeks as he thundered out the music, his right foot scarcely lifting from the loud pedal. I was halfway down the hall before he saw me, but then he jumped up, slamming the lid of the piano. 'Go away, boy, go away!' he shouted. 'Get out! I never want to see you again!' And he threw open one of the French windows behind him and banged out into the masters' garden. I think he'd been playing Brahms. Charles said he played very badly.

Charles knew a lot of things like that. Both sets of his parents lived in London and took him enviously often to the theatre and to concerts. I was staggered to learn, too, that they were on the best of terms and frequently dined with each other. With stepbrothers and sisters on both sides, Charles, I suspect, never quite belonged to either. Moving regularly from South Kensington to St John's Wood and back, he had plenty of opportunity to compare everything from their styles of dress to their methods of showing affection, and he did so all the time, with a quite unnatural detachment.

Although they always took me out when they came to visit him, I never got any firm impression of his parents. His mothers were continually altering their hairstyles, which was baffling, and his fathers seemed virtually interchangeable – big, jolly men, clean-shaven, fair-haired, smelling of exotic London hair-oil. I don't think, with my permanent difficulty with names, that I was ever quite sure which pair was which until I saw their cars. Charles's real father had a Bentley, his stepfather an Armstrong-Siddley. In these we used to drive to Newark and Grantham for blow-out hotel lunches and teas. Sometimes in the summer term we went boating on the insipid Trent. Prep-school boys are always very ashamed of their parents, but Charles was not so much ashamed as indifferent. When he spoke of them, it was rather disparagingly, as of people who weren't very sure what they were doing. I daresay he was a trying son to have about the house, especially if he was only half one's own. His objectivity certainly bewildered me. I found it almost sacrilegious the way he talked about his parents as though they were masters and matrons at the school. Now I see his critical stance as the key to his whole character. It is ironical and unfair, but I'm sure that it was, in part, his parents' friendliness after their divorce which led to much of the confusion in Charles's later emotional attitudes.

In any case, he was far more sophisticated than I, and not only about the arts. He knew things about life which my own parents kept rigidly from me. For instance, when pictures and stories about the Nazi concentration camps were published in the daily papers, they were either cut out from the copy we had at home or the paper 'didn't arrive' that day. Captain Nichols applied, I think rightly, the same censorship to *The Daily Telegraph* which was all we boys had to read in the library. (Its thin, close columns of type successfully discouraged us from taking any interest in political news; it was only in the summer, for its cricket scores, that it was eagerly queued for.) But Charles knew no censorship and had seen some of the Belsen and Buchenwald photographs at home. They affected him for the rest of his life.

One day, during the long break, we went together into the bare, rambling spinney where boys were allowed to build themselves huts known, it now seems to me oddly, as 'blue heavens'. We had shared a blue heaven since our third term – boys in the junior common-room weren't allowed them, so it must have been in the following summer, 1945, when we were ten. I remember we were very thrilled at last to have leaves to fill some of the holes in our leaky roof.

Snugly inside, we began to speak in a private language which now mostly escapes me, but which involved some simple kind of inversion. Its privacy, in any case, was shared by the entire school. I was very indignant because a boy called Ford, who used to wet his bed, had been beaten for running away, and I thought this was dreadfully unfair. I only thought it, I must admit, because Charles had told me that Ford was a very unhappy boy whom we shouldn't rag because his father had been killed in the war, and that was why he wet his bed. Even Charles wasn't so sophisticated as to have read any psychology yet, but something he had once overheard his mother saying to a woman friend convinced him that boys like Ford weren't unhappy because they wet their beds, but the other way round.

'It's cruel,' I said. (Or perhaps, 'Sit lucre' – we were very anagrammatic.) 'After all, he only got to the bus-stop.'

'People are cruel,' said Charles.

'But why? Why should they be? Captain Nichols must know it's not Ford's fault.'

'Oh, he only cares about what the parents think. It's jolly bad for the school's reputation if boys run away all the time.'

'But they don't,' I said indignantly. 'Ford's the first boy to try since we've been here. Gosh, if I got beaten for running away, I bet it'd make me run away again as soon as I jolly well could.'

'You've never been beaten. You don't know what it's like.'

'Nor have you. So there.'gh

Charles was uncrushed. 'I think,' he said, 'I *think* what happens is that it hurts a lot, and as well as that you feel everyone loathes you. That's the idea of it.'

'What are you blithering about?'

'Well, you know how you blubbed when Mr Anderson gave you a bad mark for throwing that book at Tomlinson?'

'I didn't blub.'

'Yes you did.'

'I did not.'

'Well,' said Charles, 'you went through the motions of blubbing, anyway.'

I consented to be amused by this parody of Mr Anderson's excuse for giving extra work to a boy whom he suspected but could not prove was chewing gum in class. 'So what?'

'You weren't blubbing because you knew you were wrong and were sorry about it, were you?' said Charles carefully. 'You were blubbing because everyone always turns against anyone who's punished whether he's actually done anything wrong or not. And it's beastly when people do that, and so you blubbed.'

'I did *not* blub.'

'That's where people are so cruel. They do what everyone else does without thinking. That's how the concentration camps happened, Daddy says.' I had, of course, heard of the concentration camps, even though I knew nothing more about them than that they were somehow too awful to be mentioned. 'What is all this piffle?' I said, fascinated.

'Well, what he says is, if people weren't very cruel by nature, they just couldn't have done all those things, could they?'

'What things?'

'Oh, you know.' He frowned down at the furrows his fingers were rubbing in our dirt floor.

'I don't, Humphries. Honestly. What did they do?'

'It doesn't matter.'

'Yes it does. I want to know. Come on.'

'They tortured people,' he said unconvincingly, though I was almost ignorant enough to be taken in.

'Well, even I know that. How, though?'

He shuddered, then said in a very small voice, 'They made lampshades out of people's skin.'

I looked at our bare arms, my heart thumping. 'Why?'

'Because they – I don't know. But they did.'

'But lampshades are made of paper, aren't they? I mean, usually? Or that white china stuff? How would the light shine through skin? You couldn't see anything, could you?'

'Perhaps they didn't want to see,' he said.

'But why not?'

'I don't know, Mitchell.'

'Yes you do, or you wouldn't have said.'

'Don't be silly.'

'I'm not being silly.'

'Yes, you are.'

'No, I'm not. You're just trying to avoid telling me.'

'Oh, shut up.'

'I'll ask Mr Bradley. He'll tell me, I bet.'

'You mustn't do that,' said Charles. 'There'd be the most awful row. We're not supposed to know about the concentration camps.'

'Then how did you find out?'

'I read about them in the papers.'

'Tell me. Please tell me.'

'You won't want to know when I have told you,' said Charles unhappily.

'Oh, come on. Or I'll jolly well go and tell Captain Nichols you told me about the lampshades.'

Charles knew perfectly well that I'd do nothing of the sort, but he decided all the same to share with me what he knew. It wasn't very much, but it was more, I suppose, than he could bear to know by himself. Certainly, however much we share it, it will always be intolerable.

He pulled his wallet from his hip-pocket. It was a beautiful, envied thing, of what we firmly believed to be crocodile skin, and it had many folds and pockets and secret flaps. From the most secret of all, one which even I, who had been privileged to examine the wallet in detail, had never found, he produced a very crumpled piece of newspaper. He smoothed it out slowly, keeping the important part face down on his thigh. Then, without a word, he handed it to me.

It was a photograph, but for several moments I couldn't make out what it was of. Though there were recognizable Nissen-type huts in the background, the foreground was almost abstract, a jumble of black lines which I couldn't read.

'What – ?' I began. Then the lines jumped into shape and I saw.

It was a picture of a mass grave, of a great pit of dead men, dead women and dead children. They were heaped up like a bonfire, limbs jutting out like old pea-sticks. There was no one in the photograph who was alive. All the dead people were naked.

After the first shock, I began, hardly conscious of what I was doing, to turn the photograph round and round, squinting at it closely, trying to make out the naked details of the bodies. I couldn't, of course; the editor had seen to that. But I went on peering at the white blanks between the rigid thighs as though nothing else in the picture mattered. I had read about death in the newspapers, but had no knowledge of it. I had eagerly noted the enemy casualties after a battle – ours were always light, of course, and unspecified – but the figures meant nothing to me. Was this what they meant? I couldn't believe it, and stared and stared at the censored nakedness, the only parts of the photograph whose truth had been whited away.

Then Charles took the photo away from me, and put it back in its secret place. We neither of us said anything for a long time.

'Swear you won't tell anyone,' he said, as we went in for lunch.

'Of course I won't.'

'Swear.'

'I swear.'

I mention this incident because I'm sure that the photograph haunted and appalled Charles all his life, even more than it has haunted and appalled me. He once told me that although he was horrified when, much later, he first saw photographs of the victims of Hiroshima and Nagasaki, his horror was not so much at the unspeakable deaths that were being died in front of the camera as at the fact that 'our side' was responsible. He had been able to endure his knowledge of the death-pit so long as he felt sure that 'we' didn't do things like that. The discovery that 'we' did led to a brief flirtation with religion. The doctrine of original sin seemed temporarily irrefutable.

The day we heard about the atom-bomb he was as thrilled and excited as anyone else. He was staying with me at the time in Gloucestershire, to which my family had just moved. My father was still in the Navy, working on the Joint Planning Staffs in London, and he rang up to tell my mother the news and that it meant the war was at last virtually over. Charles and I were playing croquet when my mother called out to us in great excitement from the house. We dropped our mallets and ran in.

There were some flags in the nursery cupboard, and we hung them out of the windows as if Sapperton were London, though the house was nowhere near a road and the only person who could possibly see them was Betty Allen, who fetched the cattle in from the big field above us. We didn't know what to do after that. Quite soon we went back to our croquet, from which we could look up and appreciate the flags ourselves. The official end of the war didn't come till several days later, and was something of an anti-climax.

Charles often came to stay with me, though I never went to stay with him. This wasn't because I wasn't asked, but because my parents didn't approve of London for young children. Though my brothers and I visited it regularly to see the dentist, and were often taken to a matinee to make up for a morning's drilling, we rarely, if ever, spent a night there. This was one reason why Charles seemed so enormously privileged. For many years I used to think of him swaggering through the streets on his way to huge lunches at the Trocadero and exotic teas at Gunter's. My small country skills were no compensation for all the things I thought I missed.

I used them, though, for what they were worth. Charles was terrified of horses, for instance, and refused even to be led up and down the drive on my younger brother's immensely passive pony, Teddy. I made a point of calling out to him from my great height on Flicka every time I went riding, but he never even looked up from his book. When it came to damming the small stream at the bottom of the valley, though, or climbing trees, or even chopping them down, he was as enthusiastic as I. We spent timeless, idyllic days simply exploring the great beech woods which hung on both steep sides of the valley, scaring ourselves silly at grass-snakes, lying for hours in never-gratified expectation outside what we thoroughly convinced ourselves was a badger's den. One year he almost won the bowling for the pig at the Frampton Mansell fête, and got a consolation prize of a dozen boxes of matches, which pleased him absurdly. They all had dreadful jokes on the backs, which he repeated for days. And once he actually won a ten-shilling note at the hoop-la stall.

He liked staying with me, I know. We used to spend hours during term-time planning what we'd do when he came. But, having two families between which to share his time and affection, he could never come for long, and for me the week or ten days of his visit would pass intolerably quickly. After he'd gone, I would mope about, imagining him living his swell's life in London, gaining knowledge on which I'd never be able to catch up. When we met again at school he would always be vague about how he'd spent the rest of his holidays, but he'd drop remarks about the American musicals he'd seen (it was the era of *Oklahoma!* and *Annie Get Your Gun*) and make his queer, detached criticisms of films I'd never even heard of. I daresay he usually went to bed at the same time as I did, but he managed to give the impression of night after night spent sitting up into the small hours. He was far more than simply my best friend; he was also my intellectual, social and aesthetic guide; my *alter ego*; my hero.

And I worshipped him – not with the frenzy of adolescence, but rather with the sort of earnest devotion boys usually reserve for masters, made up of awe, liking, puzzlement and perfectly innocent love. I don't think Charles ever reciprocated this feeling, but our closeness was recognized by the other boys, and he was surprisingly tender to me – surprisingly because boys, though tender themselves, are often savage towards tenderness in others. He took my griefs and grievances to heart, I mean, and if I had extra work to do or was punished in some other way, he didn't go off and play without me, but waited in the library, sullenly glowering over *Encyclopaedia Britannica* or old volumes of *Punch*. Though we naturally had friends among the other boys, neither of us would have dreamed of doing anything important without the other. Though we sometimes quarrelled with a terrible verbal violence, we never, I think, actually struck each other or imagined having anyone else as best friend. At least, I never did. And if Charles ever imagined it, he – tenderly – never did or said anything about it.

It's hard not to make it sound as though we were lovers, but though we certainly discussed sex together when Charles found out about it (needless to say he took it very calmly, while I was simply astounded that babies were not born through women's tummy buttons), we never made even the usual experimental advances boys do make towards each other. And though I was openly devoted, there was a reserve about him – that critical detachment – which I could never break down. In our intimacy I was always totally frank, saying what I really felt and thought. Charles was never spontaneous like that. He could receive love, but not give it. The immediate trust and openness I longed for were never granted, to me or anyone else.

There are two incidents from our prep-school life which I think shed significant light on Charles's later life, the first apparently minor, the second more obviously, to our sex-obsessed age, important. I'm not sure that the first didn't, in fact, reveal more of Charles's character.

It happened after we'd been at the school some two or three years – when we were eleven or so. The old dormitory-master, Mr O'Neill, presumably chosen for his strong heterosexual drive, had succumbed to it and married the clothes matron, to our amazed disgust. They moved, doubtless with considerable relief, into a cottage on the edge of the school grounds, beyond the evergreens. In Mr O'Neill's place we had Mr Aitken, a very lanky master with a green tinge to his face for which he was known as 'Cheesy'. Cheesy's looks accurately represented his inward physical state, and after a few weeks he developed some serious illness – kidneys I think. For the rest of the term the other masters took it in turn to supervise us eighty-odd boys as we dressed and undressed, washed, took a cold bath every morning and two hot ones a week, changed our handkerchiefs when dirty and emptied our chamber-pots. One night, by what I can only imagine to have been an oversight, Mr Bradley was in charge. (Perhaps Captain Nichols simply didn't want to see the truth about his proclivities.) Nothing untoward occurred, though, and none of us saw anything odd about his fat figure lingering in the doorways as his eyes ate up the sight of our pink bodies, stripped to the waist for washing.

However, next morning, as we lined up along the corridor to go down to prayers and breakfast, something very strange happened. Mr Bradley was standing outside the dormitory-master's room, a whistle in his hand. He called for silence, and silence of a sort slowly came. He looked up and down the corridor. Now was the moment he should have blown the whistle for the long lines of boys to march off down the stairs. But instead of blowing, he just stood there. Everyone looked at him.

Suddenly, amazingly, he leant back against the wall. Then, very slowly, he slid to the floor and lay there, a small white froth on his lips. For a moment we simply stared at him.

Then – 'He's drunk! He's drunk!' someone yelled, and we took up the cry in panic and excitement, bewildered by the inconceivable collapse of authority. 'He's drunk! He's drunk! He's drunk!'

I was in a dormitory very close to the master's room, and I saw very clearly as Mr Bradley fell and the boys came rushing towards him. I can see it now. To my everlasting shame, I hear myself shouting with the others, shoving and screaming and milling round poor, bald, froth-flecked Mr Bradley. We are a mob without a leader, pure anarchy. A boy is knocked down and I feel my foot treading on his thigh. I hammer my elbows into my neighbours' ribs. The yelling goes on and on, more and more frenzied.

Then Charles is at my side. I am screaming at the top of my voice, 'He's drunk! He's drunk!'

'Stop it!' Charles shouts. He is terribly angry. 'Stop it! Stop it!' And he pulls me roughly out of the mob into the calm of a dormitory doorway.

It must have been just at that moment that Matron came flying down the corridor, scattering boys left and right, furiously blowing her whistle.

'Line up! Line up!' she ordered, cuffing everyone within reach, still moving rapidly towards Mr Bradley, who lay where he had fallen, eyes glazed. She bent quickly down to him, felt his pulse then stood up again. The noise had utterly ceased.

'Off you go!' she said. 'Prefects! Take charge!' She blew her whistle, then flew back to her surgery past the gaping boys.

Slowly, ashen-faced, some even sobbing, sure something dreadful had happened, we began to move. Just as my dormitory reached the head of the stairs, I saw Matron come dashing out of the surgery again, carrying a glass of something, stirring it busily as she ran. She looked miraculously cool and white, starched to a perfect self-control. I longed to run to her and bury my head in her breast, but of course that was impossible.

Nothing was said at the beginning of prayers, but as we got up off our knees Matron brought Captain Nichols a note. He stood at the lectern, slowly reading it. Then he looked at us over his spectacles for what seemed eternity.

'Matron tells me,' he said at last in his gravest voice, 'that the reason for the simply disgraceful noise from the dormitories this morning was that Mr Bradley was ill. Mr Bradley is a diabetic. That means that he has to give himself an injection of insulin every morning or he would die.' He let the last word echo, and it did. 'Mr Bradley left his insulin behind in the master's house last night. Bravely, he attempted to do his duty before going to fetch his life-saving medicine. For your sake, and for the sake of the school.'

We were all, I'm sure, quite convinced by this time that Mr Bradley was dead.

'What a way to behave! Taking advantage of a master's illness! Shouting and yelling and stampeding! I'm ashamed of you, of all of you!' He looked as though we had indeed broken his heart. One boy – I think it was Ford – began to cry. I held my breath, appalled at myself, not daring to look at Charles beside me.

'I'm glad to say,' went on Captain Nichols, in a more normal voice, 'that thanks to the prompt action of Matron, Mr Bradley has already recovered.' There was a sigh of relief. 'But no thanks to any boy in this school!'

We jumped again. Captain Nichols let his furious eye rove over the eighty heads all bowed in shame. Then he snorted with disgust and abruptly left the lectern and went to the door. There he stopped and turned dramatically towards us. 'The Red Mark treat is cancelled!' he thundered, and vanished through the curtains.

We were a very subdued school that morning, even though Mr Bradley, apparently none the worse for wear, took all his classes without comment. In the long break I went off to our blue heaven, rather hoping Charles wouldn't follow. I had been very frightened by the sudden eruption of violence and my own unexplained part in it. I wanted to think about it quietly.

I was hugging my knees and trying to remember exactly what had happened when Charles crawled through the doorway.

'Comewel,' I said.

He nodded, but didn't answer, as he should have done, with, 'Bad to glee here.' I stared at the scar on my right knee.

After a long silence he said conversationally, 'You're jolly lucky I didn't slap your face this morning, Mitchell.'

'It was awful, wasn't it?'

'Hysteria is always awful,' he said, as if he were thoroughly used to it. 'The only way to stop it is to slap the person's face. It shocks him out of it.'

"Was I hysterical?' I was glad to have a word for it.

'Yes.'

'I'm sorry, really I am. I didn't understand what was happening. Everyone was so – so –'

'Mob violence is disgusting,' said Charles, with sudden violence himself. 'Daddy says, never get in a big crowd, in case it loses its head.'

At once I saw a crowd with a dragon's head, shooting out flame like a flame-thrower.

'Is that what happened this morning?'

'Yes.'

Now that I knew, I wanted to be forgiven, to be told that it was somehow all right to have yelled and screamed with the rest, although, of course, it couldn't ever be.

'How can you stop it?' I said. 'I mean, it just *happened*, didn't it? Weren't you in it, too?'

'Of course I wasn't. How do you think I could have dragged you out otherwise?'

'I'm terribly sorry. I didn't mean to.'

'Of course you didn't *mean* to,' he said with the same sudden violence. 'No one ever does *mean* to. That's what's so disgusting. People don't have any self-control. Daddy says, a mob is always much more powerful than the people who make it up.'

'Gosh, yes. It was just like that this morning.'

'It was the people shouting about how he was drunk which was worst,' said Charles. 'I bet no one in the school, not even the prefects, has ever actually even *seen* a man when he's drunk.'

My heart bounced with guilt, and there was a ringing in my ears.

'I – I – I think I was saying that, too.'

'Of course you were. You were bawling it. I saw you. It made me absolutely furious. You at least should have known better.'

'How?' I said miserably. 'I didn't know *what* I was doing, I told you.'

'But you should have done. I did.' And he refused to forgive me.

What now strikes me as most extraordinary about this genuinely terrifying episode is that Charles must have been the only boy in the school who didn't lose his head in the general panic. None of the rest of us could explain or understand what had happened. But Charles, uncannily for a small boy, was able to judge the experience from outside and to point the moral to be drawn. His rigorous attitude made it all much worse for me. To this day my confidence in democracy can be utterly shaken by the sight of an angry football crowd or a fervent religious or political meeting, and I can get very near to hysteria in the jostle of rush-hour on the London Tube. But Charles – Charles never lost his head.

He didn't even lose it when he had every excuse. Several terms after Mr Bradley literally fell down and foamed at the mouth he fell in another sense. The school play that term was a wildly unsuitable romantic melodrama about the English Civil War. I was a gaudy Cavalier in love with a loyal serving wench, and my old mother, Lady Lovelace or Locket or Lucy, saved us for love by sacrificing herself to the blood-lust of the vile Roundhead Charles. Mine was a rotten part, during which I had to kiss a boy I didn't like very much called Foster. I had to carry him bodily offstage to a waiting coach, both of us disguised, pretending   I
was a man who'd come for the body of a plague victim. No line was memorable, so I can't quote the play at all; indeed, its dialogue was so banal and pish-tushery that I had unusual difficulty in learning it. Such resounding lines as there were

belonged to Charles and the old aristocrat, both of whom had good opportunities for expressing hate, fear, rage and revenge, while Foster and I were stuck with the clichés of royalist passion. This meant, mercifully, less talk about kissing than about the king, but some embraces were unavoidable.

One afternoon, shortly before the performance, Mr Bradley was rehearsing us in the school hall. The stage, though small, was perfectly adequate for our limited range of emotions. Mrs Nichols sometimes attended rehearsals, urging me to be more romantic and cavalier, but today she was absent, and Foster and I were embracing with our natural tepidity. I always took my acting very seriously, even when the play was as uncompromisingly silly as this one, and so, though my kisses shunned actual physical contact, I was trying to convey ardent passion through dramatic facial and vocal contortions.

Suddenly Mr Bradley leapt from his seat below us, groaning. 'No, no, no, no, Mitchell. I've told you a hundred times, *kiss* her. *Him*. Foster.'

I did my best, letting my lips rest chastely on his ear.

Mr Bradley bounded up on the stage. 'I said, *kiss* him.'

'I *did* kiss him, sir.'

'You did *not*. You don't call that little peck a kiss, do you?'

'Well, sir, what –?'

'Dear, idiot child, have you never seen a man kissing a woman? Does your father never kiss your mother?'

'Of course, sir. But they're married, sir. And Foster and I aren't, sir, are we? I mean, in the play?'

This was true, and Mr Bradley was briefly disconcerted. He put his hands on his hips and jutted out his lower lip.

'No,' he said. 'But as soon as you get to France, you're going to be, aren't you? You're going to have the banns called. You're engaged. You should kiss as *though* you were married, because you want to be married so much. Got it? What does having the banns called mean, Foster?'

'I don't know, sir.'

'Yes, you do. What happened at church last Sunday?'

'At church, sir? Last Sunday, sir?'

'Tell the child, Humphries.'

Charles, who was reading a book in the wings, said, without looking up, 'It means announcing there's going to be a wedding between a bachelor and a spinster, and if anyone objects they're supposed to say so.'

'Very good,' said Mr Bradley. 'Now for the ninety-ninth time of asking will you two lovebirds try and look as though you do actually love one another?'

'But, sir,' said Foster unexpectedly, 'we don't.'

'That has nothing to do with it. Acting means portraying feelings you don't really feel. Kindly act.'

'You mean, like not showing an animal you're afraid, sir, when you jolly well are? Sir?'

'Dear boy,' said Mr Bradley, giving Foster quite a loving kiss, 'when you grow up, *if* you ever grow up, you will find that you will have to do far more acting before *people* than you are ever likely to have to do before *animals*.'

'That's what politeness is really, isn't it?' said Charles from the wings.

'Ah, the cynic Humphries speaks. Yes, Humphries, politeness is largely a question of artful simulation.'

'What's simulation, sir?' said Foster.

'Simulo, simulare, simulavi, simulatum. Get on with the play.'

'But, sir, what is it?'

'I said, get on with the play.'

'Yes, do,' said Charles from the wings.

'Thank you, Humphries,' said Mr Bradley. 'You may proceed, Mitchell, with your simulation of passion.'

I proceeded, but however much Foster and I simulated, we failed to convince either our producer or ourselves. We came to quite like each other through our total inability to kiss with conviction.

'Oh, for heaven's sake,' said Mr Bradley at last, leaping up on the stage again, 'like this, boy, like this.'

He seized Foster in his arms and smacked kisses all over him. Foster stood there resignedly, then, when Mr Bradley had stopped back, took out his handkerchief and wiped his face. Charles laughed loudly.

'Humphries, come here.'

Charles ambled out.

'What amuses you so much?'

'Your demonstration, sir. It was *meant* to be funny, wasn't it, sir?

'Are *you* trying to be funny, boy?'

'No, sir. Of course not, sir.'

'Are you quite sure?'

'Yes, sir. Sir, were you ever engaged?'

'That's none of your business. Go back and read your book.'

'But were you, sir? I mean, were you showing us how engaged people kiss then, sir?'

Mr Bradley was blushing furiously, and his eyes were watering. 'Insolence,' he muttered. Then a curiously embarrassed yet cunning smile came over his face. 'If you know so much about kissing, Humphries, perhaps *you'd* care to give us a little demonstration on your friend Mitchell here.' He pointed at me sharply. I backed away. 'Come on. Kiss him. Show us how you do it.'

'Why can't he kiss Foster?' I said. 'We're both men. Let him kiss one of the women.'

'You're all *boys*,' said Mr Bradley. 'I want to see him kissing you. I want to see how the heavenly twins make love to each other.'

We didn't like being called the heavenly twins. Charles shrugged and gave me a look which meant it was better to do the stupid thing we were asked to do and get it over with than to argue. But I hated the idea. Charles and I weren't soppy. We occasionally rested arms on each other's shoulders in our blue heaven, or punched each other on the arm, but kissing was strictly for new bugs and girls.

'But, sir, I need to see how it's done, don't I, sir? And I can't do that if he's kissing me, sir, can I?'

'Do as I say!' shouted Mr Bradley.

I was profoundly embarrassed, with Foster, Mr Bradley and the other boys all watching, but I stood my ground and allowed myself to be kissed. Charles did it very dryly, on the cheek.

'On the lips, please, Humphries,' said Mr Bradley, still bright red in the face. He seemed to be straining every muscle not to move. 'On the lips.'

Again, Charles shrugged. But he did what he was told, and it wasn't too awful, after all. It didn't last long, anyway.

'Thank you, Humphries,' said Mr Bradley, relaxing. He gave Charles a brisk kiss on the top of his head. 'You may go back to your book now.'

And the rehearsal continued.

The whole thing is clear to me now. Mr Bradley had himself under more control than we suspected. He took his pleasure indirectly, where it did us no harm.

In fact this particular indulgence helped Charles and me to get over a quarrel. By then our relationship was securely manic-depressive. Either we were intimate and exclusive allies, or we didn't speak to each other at all. The other boys ignored our hysterical ups and downs and regarded us as a fixed twosome, the heavenly twins; after all, we were never enemies for more than a week, though a terrible week that was for both of us.

The afternoon of the rehearsal we weren't speaking to each other because of a particularly bad quarrel over car catalogues. A craze had swept the school that term for writing to garages and motor manufacturers for 'literature' about their latest models.

Charles had taken a rather reluctant part in this, maintaining that it was pointless to know about the outside of a car unless you also knew how the inside worked, which none of us, of course, did. Typically, he got hold of a book on the internal combustion engine, and decided to find out. Then, whenever I showed him some particularly proud acquisition, a glossy brochure for an Alvis or a Lagonda, he would make incomprehensible remarks about bore and brake horse-power. Finally, over the Humber Pullman Limousine catalogue which I had swapped for a Lea Francis with another boy whose father actually owned one, Charles had gone too far. He had disparaged not only the car but the catalogue, which had stiff covers and was therefore particularly opulent and desirable. We had come very near to fighting, and snatching, I had torn it. We hadn't spoken for two whole days.

Now, as soon as the rehearsal was over, Charles came over to me and said, 'I'm sorry.' Generously, I understood him to include the torn catalogue in his apology.

'Oh, it's all right.' I was always very moved when we made up again after a quarrel, and I felt a lump rising in my throat.

'We had to do it,' Charles explained, 'or he might have started foaming again. He's not quite all there, you know.' Then, abruptly, he changed the subject. We were walking towards the spinney. 'Do you think we've been happy here?' he said.

We had another term and a half to go before we left, but he was always projecting himself backwards and forwards in time to see how the present looked. He would say things like I'm glad I wasn't a new boy with Greene,' when to me the fact that Greene *was* a new boy and we were prefects made the imaginative leap unthinkable.

'Well, do you or don't you?' he said.

'I suppose so.' Anything that reminded me of the passing of time and the irreversibility of clocks brought tears to my eyes. I hated New Year's Eve. I couldn't understand why anyone should want to celebrate the fact that the old year would never, not in all eternity, come again. When Mr Yorke pointed out to us on March 12th 1945 that it wouldn't be possible to write the date as 12/3/45 again for a hundred years, I was broken-hearted. Now that Charles forced me to realize that this was the last Wednesday afternoon in November that I would ever walk with him in the school grounds, I choked with the sadness of it all.

'Why do you suppose so?' he said in his most ruthless manner.

'Because – because –'

'You don't know. I knew you didn't. Shall I tell you why?'

'Oh, yes. Please.'

'Because we haven't been happy. I've been thinking about it. We're only boys. You've got to be grown-up to be happy. Until you're grown up you're not free. Young people are always having to do things they don't want to, like going to school and eating porridge.'

That was true enough. 'But all the same,' I said, 'we're not actually unhappy, are we?'

'I'm not sure. We'll know later, when we know what it's really like to be happy.'

'Aren't you happy at home, even?'

'No,' he said. 'People make you do things at home just as much as they do here. You have to have meals when they say and brush your hair and wear the awful clothes they choose. To be happy, you have to be absolutely free.'

He already wore glasses by then, and his eyes glowed behind them at the thought of his freedom. He made me long to be grown-up. But I wanted to have been happy at school, too, so that I could look back on it as a golden time.

'Haven't we been as happy as we could be, though, under the circumstances?' I asked hopefully.

'I don't think so. This is a bad school. I've been thinking about that, too. If it was any good they'd've made us work harder and try for scholarships.'

It was an astonishing new idea, even for Charles.

'Are you potty or something?'

'It's true, isn't it? The masters are all stupid, except Mr Bradley, and he's so peculiar. As a matter of fact, I think he's jealous of us.'

'Barmy,' I said. 'Completely barmy.'

'We leave this place when we're thirteen, don't we? But he can't leave. He's stuck here for ever.'

'But,' I said with unusual lucidity, 'if he's a grown-up, he can be happy, you just said so, and if he's not happy, why doesn't he leave?'

'You don't understand the first thing, Mitchell. You're such a clot, it's so sad.'

'You can't answer, that's why you say that.'

'Of course I can. Mr Bradley can't leave because he isn't free.'

Being grown-up began to seem less attractive.

'Why not?'

'I don't know,' said Charles. 'I think he probably fell in love with the wrong woman. Perhaps she broke off the engagement. Gave him the ring back and everything. I've always thought it must be something like that.'

'Gosh! Poor Mr Bradley!'

'Well, it may not have been that exactly, of course. But you can see he isn't happy. It's obvious. I'm really very sorry for men like that. They miss so much.'

From that moment, Mr Bradley ceased to be an alarming and stimulating eccentric and became simply pitiable. His hugs and kisses and slaps were those of a sad, thwarted, small, bald, lonely man, living out his life in a terrible emptiness.

Such was Charles's power over my imagination. I saw everything through his eyes, and remembering Mr Bradley now, it is still Charles's thwarted lover that I first see. My apprehension of reality was a jumble of unrelated, often nonsensical impressions; Charles related them, organized them, explained them to me. Everything I have written about our school is really what Charles taught me. He made me feel inferior, it's true; but I felt, also, privileged. That sense of privilege has never left me.

When we left school at the end of the spring term, we swore solemnly that we'd write regularly and that we'd be friends till the day of judgement. Rather self-consciously, as in the holidays, we called each other 'Charles' and 'Julian'. We felt very grown up. My father had written to me, putting 'Esquire' after my name on the envelope, and Charles had been told the facts of life by both his fathers as well as by Captain Nichols. Comparing the different versions, we felt we were armed at all points for manhood.

For some reason Charles couldn't come and stay with me those holidays. After the first three weeks at Winchester, where I'd been made to feel impossibly young and far from the maturity I'd imagined myself already to possess, I wrote him a letter. It didn't seem quite right as I read it through. I couldn't explain the immense complexity of my new life, though it was all I could think of, and I didn't want to admit how much it frightened me or that I had to sweep the house hall every evening. Nor could I explain that in spite of everything I was really quite enjoying myself without him. There seemed only the old school, Mr Bradley and Captain Nichols, to write about, and they were no longer quite real.

I never got a reply. I think I'd have been embarrassed if I had.

2

I next saw Charles, to my amazement, on a cricket-field. It was in the summer of 1954, at Portland in Dorset, and HMS *Maidstone*, depot-ship to a squadron of submarines, was playing the naval school of Russian. Quite why I, a national service submariner, was chosen to play for *Maidstone* I don't remember, though it can hardly have been on merit. I liked cricket, but my best performances were two for twenty-three against a local village called Plush, and eleven not out against Tolpuddle. I was probably picked because *Maidstone* was away being refitted and the squadron sports officer had only thirteen or fourteen names to juggle with. Or perhaps I was ordered to play. My captain liked his ship to be represented on every possible occasion, and as the midshipman I was the obvious 'volunteer' for sailing, Sunday morning chapel and games.

As I went up the pavilion steps, I saw a man in white flannels bending down with one foot on a bench to do up his laces. It was Charles. I recognized him instantly, and my first instinct was to flee to the safe, windowless fug of the ward-room of my submarine.

Nothing embarrasses a middle-class English youth more than to meet someone from his prep-school. The rest of his education has been a covert but systematic effort to control and conceal the naked emotions which that first merciless barbarity exposed in him. He loathes the memory of the place for his own innocence in it, whether he was happy there or not, and he will never admit that he could have been. I was no exception to the general rule, and carefully nurtured a cynical aloofness to things, scared silly by my own possibilities. Charles's sudden appearance threatened the whole painfully constructed carapace of suave, sophisticated manhood. I turned away, passionately hoping that he hadn't seen me, that I would have time to prepare a face to meet him.

But if I was foolishly tangled in my youth and class, Charles, it appeared, was not. I had hardly taken two steps before he called out, 'My God! If it isn't Julian Mitchell!'

I turned round with an elaborate surprise which can't have deceived him for a moment. He was taller, of course, and thicker; he shaved, obviously, and his black hair was cut very short; but his face was as pale as ever, and his eyebrows still met in a lush tangle above the bridge of his nose. He wore dark glasses clipped over ordinary ones.

'Charles!'

'What the bloody hell are you doing here?' he said, smiling broadly.

I explained about my submarine.

'Really?' he said. 'You mean you go under the water and everything?'

'Oh, we just chug out into the Channel every morning, dive for a few hours and chug back in again. It's very dull. We're just a tame mouse for the asdic boys.'

'And you personally stand there, looking at the dials and pumping water in and out and everything?'

'Practically by hand,' I said. 'My ship was supposed to have been scrapped in 1947.'

'I'd never have thought it of you.' He bent down to go on lacing up his boots. 'But I suppose you always were something of an outdoor type.'

'Oh, we never go out of doors. It's too wet.'

He grinned. 'Ah, a joke! You make jokes. I don't remember you doing that in the old days.'

'I don't remember you being much of a cricketer.'

'Oh, I'm not. I can't see, for one thing. But one has to do something not to go mad with boredom.' He stood up and stamped his feet. 'Why aren't you on the Russian course like everyone else?'

I simply didn't know, and even now I can't think why I never applied for it. It seems to have been the All Souls of national service, a sort of junior college for intellectuals whose bodies had let them down by obstinately passing all the physical examinations for conscription. The life can't really have been as high-powered as I like to imagine it, with everyone either arguing furiously about Trotsky or reading *Anna Karenina* in the original for the sixth or seventh time, but it can't not have been a good deal more stimulating than my own, which was spent mainly under water, playing cribbage with my captain and letting him win.

'Oh, I quite like the sea,' I said. I liked it very much, actually, but I was afraid to say so, in case Charles might be scornful.

'Really?' he said. 'On the bridge in a storm, with the waves breaking across the bow and everything?'

'Exactly. Except we're mostly under the waves, of course. I wish we weren't.'

'God, I'd be scared stiff,' he said.

I was heartened by his ordinary reaction. Submarines weren't frightening at all, but it was gratifying the way people thought they were.

'Do you like the Russian?' I said.

'It passes the time. And at least I'll have the language when all this nonsense is over.' He seemed to be looking round for someone.

'You have the advantage of me there,' I said. 'I don't expect anyone in civvy street will want me to drive a submarine for him.'

The captain of our team, an Instructor Lieutenant-Commander, came out of the dressing-room. 'Get your finger out, snotty,' he said. 'We're fielding.'

'See you later,' I said to Charles.

He nodded. As I went in to change I heard him calling to someone. 'Brian! Guess what! I've just found my long-lost brother!'

My heart gave a quick skip of relief. We were over the first meeting, the carapace uncracked.

It was a typical Portland day, the sun hot between the high clouds which the wind bundled across West Bay and over Chesil Bank into the harbour. The steep sides of the Bill gave no shelter to the sports ground, and two sweaters were recommended for the fielding side. I had only one, and shivered at cover-point and mid-wicket as soon as the sun went in. It was clear, though, that the Reds, as our opponents were known, weren't going to keep us in the field very long. Our opening bowler, Petty Officer Stoker Mechanic Croxley, was adept at exploiting the damp Portland air, and his medium-pace inswingers occasionally swung so far that they defeated both batsman and wicket-keeper. By the time the score was forty-one for six Croxley had taken five for eleven, there had been fifteen byes, and only one batsman had yet scored a run in front of the wicket.

He was one of the openers, a tall blond man with a technique which belonged to a rather higher class of cricket. His left elbow was always beautifully pointed, and he kept the bat absolutely straight. If he hadn't scored very many runs, it was more, one felt, because a defensive game gave him greater technical pleasure than an attacking one. He glanced and deflected and drove with precision and elegance, and he was quite imperturbable. Croxley, a great stump of a man, had an appeal like a drill-sergeant which often terrified the fielders quite as much as the batsmen and the umpires it was meant to impress, but even his tremendous bellows for lbw lacked conviction in the face of the batsman's masterly indifference. He seemed quite happy to carry his bat and to ignore the feeble efforts at the other end.

Forty-one for six soon became forty-four for seven, and then, after a couple of fours over slip's head by the Reds' wicket-keeper, fifty-seven for eight. Charles came in at number ten. The captain called the field in to crowd him. I moved to silly mid-on. Charles gave me a lordly wave of the bat before taking guard.

'I wouldn't stand quite so close, if I were you,' he said. 'My pad may come off and hit you in the balls.'

The other batsman came down the wicket towards him. 'Remember, play down the line,' he said. 'Left elbow up.' He demonstrated, then went back to his crease.

Charles looked round the field, then settled down with his left elbow self-consciously pointed.

Croxley's first ball was short outside the leg stump and Charles simply stood there and let it go past to the wicket-keeper, who managed, for once, to stop it.

'Well left,' said the good batsman.

Charles acknowledged this with a flourish of the bat and walked down the pitch to remove a piece of grass, as though it were a test match. The next ball was on a length, starting outside the off-stump and swinging across the wicket to hit him on the thigh. Croxley appealed prodigiously, but since Charles was clearly standing outside the leg stump and had again not moved the umpire gave him not out.

The last ball of Croxley's over was straight and didn't swing. Again, as only hopeless cricketers do, Charles simply stood there. The ball hit the edge of his bat and sped along the ground straight towards gully.

'Yes!' Charles called, and ran.

His partner, taken completely by surprise, also started to run, then, realizing the folly of it, shouted, 'No! Get back!'

Charles, however, went on blindly running. Gully fielded the ball and threw it hard in to the wicket-keeper, who missed it. The good batsman was still calling 'Get back! Get back!', but Charles had now completed his run and the two of them stood together at the bowler's end while the overthrow was chased. The good batsman decided to make the best of things and started to run. Charles, at last aware that something was wrong, began running with him, then stopped. So did the good batsman, completely bewildered. By the time Charles had gone back again the good batsman had been run out. He was furious.

'I'm terribly sorry, Brian,' said Charles. He looked very crestfallen.

Brian glared at him, then walked stiffly back to the pavilion.

'Good work,' I said.

'He'll never forgive me,' said Charles. 'He takes his cricket terribly seriously. You've no idea.' He seemed genuinely upset.

That was the end of Croxley's over. Rather belatedly our captain decided the Reds hadn't made enough runs to make a decent match of it, so he put me on to bowl at the other end. Charles adjusted a pad as I set my field. When he saw it was me he had to face he said, 'Good heavens, insult bowling to injury.'

I measured my brief run, whirled my arms round once or twice to loosen my shoulders, then bowled. Even at the best of times the power of my spin depended rather more on the wicket than my fingers, but I did usually keep a tidy length. My first ball went straight through outside the off-stump. The second did the same, only it was rather short. Both times Charles attempted no stroke.

'Pitch it up,' said the captain.

I did. I bowled an agonizingly slow straight full toss, so slow and so straight that even Charles had to try and hit it. He missed and was bowled.

'Sorry,' I said, even though his wicket gave me the best bowling analysis of my life – one for nought.

'Very well bowled,' said Charles gravely.

We walked off together, neither of us quite sure what to say next.

'I thought your batting lacked aggression,' I said. 'Most people think the idea is to hit the ball with the bat, not just to stand there.'

'Do they?' he said. 'Yes, I suppose they do. I haven't played cricket for years. At school you could avoid it by playing tennis instead. I only took it up again this summer.'

'Frankly, it looks like it. Do you bowl?'

'Don't be silly, Julian.'

Clearly Charles was present only at the whim of another short-handed sports officer.

'Your friend Brian's pretty good, isn't he?' I said.

'Oh, he's one of those natural all-rounders. His father put him down for the MCC at birth.'

'He has real style.'

'I dare say.'

It was tea-time. I sat next to Charles, who introduced me to Brian, to whom I took an instant dislike.

'Julian admired your style,' Charles said. I thought I detected a mocking tone, but I couldn't be sure.

'Well, all you have to do is keep your head down on a wicket like this,' said Brian. 'If you keep the bat straight and don't play back, you should be all right. It's all a question of technique.'

He was a great admirer of Peter May, it turned out. I expressed my intense admiration for Gloucestershire's Tom Graveney.

Brian shook his head. 'It's an awful pity, but he just hasn't got the temperament. Very few professionals have. You see, for them it's just a job. An amateur has the psychological advantage every time. He just wants to do his best. He isn't worrying about getting the sack while he's out there in the middle. All the best players are amateurs, and they always will be.'

I protested sharply, and quite soon we were arguing about the House of Lords. Brian thought it was in every way superior to the Commons.

'It's only in the Lords,' he said, 'that you get a really good debate. In the Commons, it's just points of order and party politics.'

I was a passionate advocate of the abolition of the Lords at that time, on the grounds that there was no evidence whatever that those who inherited title and wealth also inherited wisdom or even intelligence, and that since 1832 the Lords had been deliberately and exclusively destructive of all positive and ameliorative legislation. I had not then studied modern history, so I argued this view with more vehemence than telling examples.

Brian listened impatiently, then accused me of wanting a single autocratic chamber, and ultimately a one-party state. The House of Lords, he said, represented Britain better than the House of Commons, because it was non-party.

'Non-party!' I said. 'It's ninety per cent fascist and proud of it.'

'Ah,' said Charles, who had listened to us with a rather anxious smile, 'the Moscow line. Coroneted hyenas, the lot of them.'

'Of course, if you're going to talk like that,' said Brian, 'there's no point in continuing the conversation.'

'All right, I withdraw "fascist". But you'll have to agree that the Lords is ninety per cent reactionary and conservative.'

'Certainly not. I don't even know what you mean.'

'I mean they're a lot of backwoods old bastards whose sole object in life is to preserve as much as they can of the status quo, and if possible to put the clock back without anyone noticing.'

'Oh, really. How childish!' Brian bit into a chocolate bun with lordly disdain.

'Of course, you're both wrong,' said Charles. 'The Lords is a valuable institution precisely because it *is* party political. It's the only place you can send the utterly useless men from the Commons. How else are you to get rid of them?'

Brian choked. 'It isn't like that at all,' he said indistinctly. He drank some tea. 'I deplore as much as anyone the abuse to which some politicians have subjected the Honours' List. But the political peers, I think I can say in all fairness, are in the long run less important, less significant, less, one might say, ultimately influential than the hereditary ones.'

He wasn't looking at us at all. His hands crept towards the lapels of his blazer. I suddenly imagined him in twenty years' time, a junior minister, leaning forward over the dispatch box, in love with himself and his easy flow of words, tipped as a future prime minister.

'After all,' he was saying, 'there is no substitute for wisdom in government, and by the very nature of their upbringing, their training, their inherited responsibilities, the peers – and I mean the ordinary, hard-working, landowning ones – are better equipped to make the unprejudiced, detached judgements on which the nation depends for its well-being. Political parties are necessary and good in a democracy, but for the –'

'Come on, you lot,' shouted his captain. 'You can't sit on your arses all afternoon. Get out and field.'

We were the only people left at the table. Brian jumped to his feet and went out.

'What a bloody stupid, pompous man that is,' I said.

'Well,' said Charles, 'it's not for his virgin mind that we all love him.' He checked himself, as though he'd been disloyal. 'And you'd be amazed how good he is at Russian. He has a photographic memory.'

'For that,' I said, striking hopefully for a witty comeback, 'the mind has to be a blank plate.'

'Good, good,' said Charles. He smiled unhappily. 'You really should be on the course. We could use a quick comic intelligence like that.'

'Oh, it's nothing. All there is to do in a submarine is think up jokes. I've got several more. Do you want to hear them?'

'Later,' he said.

It began to rain before *Maidstone's* innings was finished. Everyone sat in the pavilion, listening to the drumming on the roof. Charles and I chatted self-consciously, still unsure of each

other. Brian played darts. At a quarter past five the match was
called off.

I suggested to Charles that we went to Dorchester for dinner.
There were some pretty villages we could drink in on the way.

'All right,' he said. 'I'll see what Brian's doing.'

'Oh, Christ, do we have to take him?'

'If he's not otherwise engaged.' Charles turned away before
I could ask why.

To my relief, Brian was going to see an Etonian friend of his who
had failed to get a commission and was a writer at *Osprey*, just up
the hill. Charles seemed sad when I said 'Good.'

'Brian's really very nice when you get to know him. He can't help
his views – he just repeats what he's heard every day since he was
born. And anyway, he may be right.'

'The only way he's right is right-wing.'

Charles groaned. 'Oh, dear, another submarine joke. How am I
going to sink so low?'

'You won't have to. My car just doesn't go under water,
I don't know why.'

It was a 1943 Ford Tudor (for 'two-door') saloon, with mock
leopard-skin upholstery, and I shared it with another submarine
midshipman who was away on an exercise. We'd seen it advertised
in the Weymouth paper. It stood in a field – had stood there for
many years, to judge by the rings of rust – and if we hadn't bought
it it would have declined into a hen-coop. The petrol-gauge didn't
work, it sometimes boiled over even going along the flat, and its
tyres were paper-thin; but it only cost twenty pounds and it could
still labour up to forty-five miles an hour in a high wind. We called
it Oscar, after Wilde. Later, it died on the way to Portsmouth. A
scrap-dealer gave us two pounds ten for the carcass.

Charles got in without a word. I cranked vigorously and we set
off. Now we were alone together, there was an almost palpable
constraint between us. I fiddled with the choke and made myself
busy with the windscreen wipers. Charles just stared straight

ahead. Halfway along the isthmus which connects Portland to the mainland speech was forced upon us. Smoke began to pour out of the bonnet.

'Damn,' I said, pulling up. 'I should have checked the radiator before we started.'

'That's not steam,' said Charles. 'That's smoke.'

He was right. We leaped out, expecting an immediate explosion, and ran up the pebbles of Chesil Bank. There was nowhere to hide but the sea. Charles looked furious at having his life put in danger.

'God, I'm sorry,' I said. He didn't answer. The smoke grew thinner, then died away. The rain had put out the fire.

Pretending a fearlessness I did not feel, I started back to the car.

'Don't be a bloody fool,' said Charles. He stayed where he was.

The bonnet was very awkward to open. The handles were almost rusted away, and had to be forced with great gentleness. I struggled with them for what seemed minutes before they yielded. Smouldering on top of the engine was the old sack which we used to keep the salt sea air away from the fitfully sparking plugs. I threw it into the road and stamped on it, cursing myself for an idiot. Charles came back and watched me, then we both stared at the engine. It didn't look damaged, but I knew nothing about internal combustion. It was a matter of some pride; I was a seaman, a navigator, not an engineer.

'Do you suppose it's all right?' I said.

'How should I know? I study Russian.'

'But you used to know about engines. Don't you remember? You had a book about them.'

'Did I? Well, if I ever understood it, I've forgotten what I knew.'

We shrugged at each other. Then Charles gave a sudden delighted crow of laughter. 'So much for your Humber Pullman Limousine!'

'You do remember!'

'Oh my God, how could I forget? Those dear dull days beyond recall!'

We began to laugh, nervously at first, then hysterically.

'Captain Nichols!' I said.

'"The Red Mark treat is cancelled! And for heaven's sake, boy, pitch it up!"'

'Mr Bradley!'

'"Dear child, when you grow up, *if* you ever grow up, you will learn that life is *not* just a bowl of cherries."'

'"One hour's extra work for going through the motions of chewing in class!"'

We leant against Oscar for support, then crumpled up on the running-board and leant against each other. 'Mr O'Neill! Corky! Cheesy!' We were light-headed with relief, drunk on the shameless admission that we had once been undying friends, innocently happy, children, knowing each other better than we were ever likely to know anyone again. It was a dreadful strain, being the sophisticated young men we acted even to ourselves; now we were two helplessly giggling schoolboys in the rain. It was like a sudden long break from serious life. We revelled in our release.

'Bliss was it in that dawn to be alive,' I said. 'But to be dead was very heaven!'

'Stop it!' said Charles. 'For God's sake, stop it!' He beat the side of the car.

A bus swished by, and an old man on a bicycle dismounted on the other side of the road and stared at us as though we were mad. We didn't care, but we were getting absurdly wet.

The car started again at once, and we drove on, misting the windows with sudden spasms of laughter, at ease at last. I decided to take Charles to Maiden Castle, the ancient British camp near Dorchester. As we went inland, the rain stopped and everything began to look lush and fresh under a soft, rinsed sky.

'How can a castle be maiden?' said Charles, as we left Oscar by the roadside.

'When it's impregnable, of course.'

'Oh, no,' said Charles. 'Oh, God help us all!'

He broke off a long stem of cow parsley with a head like a cauliflower and beat me with it every time I made a bad pun. I made many. We searched our memories for dreadful old jokes, for what made the fly fly and the owl 'owl, and we argued fiercely and pedantically over whether the lobster blushed because it saw the salad dressing or Queen Mary's bottom. The sun came out and made the puddles steam, larks soared and sang above us, the rich earth smelt wet and sweet.

And then, suddenly, there was a rabbit sitting in the path. It made no move as we came closer, but crouched there, trembling slightly. Its head was swollen, its eyes glazed.

'Oh, God,' I said, and my stomach turned over.

Myxomatosis was rampant all over England then, and crouched, slightly trembling, mortally sick rabbits were a common sight. But each time I saw one, I felt the same guilty nausea.

I looked for a stick or a large stone, but the path was chalk and mud and all I could do was wrestle a stake out of the bedraggled wire fence. Charles watched me curiously, then with horror. All our euphoria had gone.

'What are you going to do?' he said.

'I'm going to kill it.'

'You can't! You mustn't!' His face was so white it might never have circulated blood. 'It may recover!'

'It won't.' I lifted the stick. The rabbit just crouched there, trembling, very near to death.

Charles seized my arm. 'How can you?' he almost whispered. 'You mustn't kill things, ever.'

'Look, I don't get any pleasure from doing this, I promise you. If you don't want to watch, go on ahead. I'll catch you up.'

'Leave it. Let it die in its own way.'

'I can't,' I said, and I couldn't, any more than I could explain why not. I had been brought up in the country, with the countryman's unresolved ambiguity towards all animals, loving what I killed and killing what I loved. I might shoot rabbits for sport, but I couldn't bear to see them dying a lingering, paralysed death. If I saw one crouching and trembling, I had to kill it. 'Go on – it only takes a second.'

Charles turned abruptly and walked on up the path. I watched him go. Then I hit the rabbit as hard as I could on the back of the neck. The stake was rotten and broke. The rabbit fell over on its side, but wasn't dead. Its nose twitched. Small insects fed on the glaze of its eyes. I found a lump of chalk and killed it properly, messily. I hated touching diseased creatures with my hands, so I bundled the oozing body off the path with the toe of my shoe, then carefully wiped my feet on the wet grass.

Charles was waiting for me. He had thrown his cow parsley away, and he looked very remote behind his dark glasses. 'Why did you do that?' he said.

'Because I had to.'

'That's no answer.' I vividly remembered our 'blue heaven' and Charles's ruthless exposure of my blundering false logic. But we weren't boys now.

'Well, I did. Myxomatosis is a terrible disease. The only thing you can do is put the poor bastards out of their misery.'

'I suppose you think they're grateful.'

'Don't be stupid. It's only being humane.'

'Humane! The only time people use the word is in "humane killing".'

'Listen, even if I were a vegetarian, which I'm not, I'd still kill rabbits in pain and misery like that one.'

Charles said nothing. I'd shown him a side of my nature, perhaps, that he'd never expected.

'If you live in the country,' I said, 'these things look quite different. There are dead and dying animals everywhere, and other animals waiting to eat them, and foxes killing chickens and hawks eating mice and – hundreds of things living off each other. You just can't pretend life isn't like that if you live in the country.'

'What's that got to do with anything?'

'Well, you obviously think it's wrong to kill a hopelessly sick rabbit, and to me it's quite obviously right.'

'When you picked up that stick, you looked like a caveman.'

'Cavemen wouldn't have deliberately introduced a filthy disease. Only civilized men could dream up a thing like that.'

'What do you mean?'

'What I say. Myxomatosis was deliberately introduced to destroy the whole rabbit population of the British Isles, so that farmers could get an extra bit of yield to the acre. Don't talk to me about cavemen.'

'Is that really true?'

'Of course it's true.' I felt quite angry. 'I don't care what you think. I don't care if I am just trying to make up for the fact that they've got the disease from us in the first place. It doesn't make any difference to the rabbits what my motive is.'

'I had no idea.' Charles stared back down the path. 'Don't you sometimes feel dazed,' he said after a moment, 'just thinking of the things men do? To animals, to the earth, to each other?'

'Yes. Sometimes.'

'We're not humane,' he said. 'Just human.'

He was following some private thoughts of his own. I remembered the creased, incredible photograph he'd shown me all those years ago. Maiden Castle was just ahead of us, up a steep slope. Charles shook his head, as though to stop himself thinking.

'Is that where we're going?' he said.

'It's the first bit of it.'

'All right.'

We started walking up the slope, rather apart from each other. Then Charles suddenly said, 'The reason I wanted Brian to come is that I'm in love with him.' He walked very fast, his eyes on the path. It took me a moment to catch up with him; and with myself.

'Are you serious?'

'Utterly.' He spoke precisely, dryly, rapidly. 'He's beautiful, awful, everything I'm not, my opposite in every way. We're made for each other. My thighs ache every time I look at him.'

'For heaven's sake!'

'There is no heaven. It's hell.' His mouth winced in a sort of smile. He kept striding on.

'Aren't you – aren't you a bit old for this sort of thing?'

He stopped and swung round on me. 'For falling in love with the captain of cricket? Yes, much too old. Too old, too blind, too intelligent, too odd, too ugly. Do I hideously shock you?'

He did. 'Everyone goes through it,' I said.

'Ah, the voice of the countryman! But does everyone come out the other side?'

I had myself. I'd spent my spring leave in Paris doing so, triumphantly overcoming my well-bred shyness with girls, demonstrating my virility as far as my purse allowed. Sex, I was confident, would be easy from now on; the first great mystery was over. But Portland offered few opportunities for the fastidious; if you gave a lift to an escaping Borstal boy, said our engineer officer, he might give you a quick one, but that was about it. Quite soon, though, I told myself, I would leave the Navy's obscenities behind and go to Oxford, where the girls would form an orderly queue to enjoy the embraces of a mature amorist who also wrote some of the most passionate love-lyrics of his or any other time. Till then I was reduced to strolling along the front at Weymouth, mentally stripping the prettier bathers, and counting the sexual symbols on the four-foot scale-model in sand of Worcester Cathedral. People aimed pennies at it, slicing off spires, humbling pinnacles. Every morning its architect had to rebuild from the foundations after the ravages of the night tide and frustrated holiday-makers. That daily re-erection pleased me as a primitive emblem of the masculine sexual life.

'Do you realize,' I said, 'that this is the first time in my life that I'm actually one jump ahead of you?'

'Congratulations. Do they have special brothels for officers, or do you have to share with the men?'

'Really, Charles –'

'My father warned me to be very careful with tarts. My real father, I mean. The other one pretended not to know about them. When I refused to be confirmed everyone thought it was all due to masturbation. So they made my father put on the face he uses for talking about his life-insurance, and he lectured me for an hour on venereal disease and the absolute necessity of wearing French letters.'

'That was thoughtful of him.'

'Are they comfortable?' he asked with what seemed genuine curiosity. 'Do they stay on all right?'

'I believe the percentage of failure is very low.'

'Perhaps if I persuaded Brian to wear one –' He laughed harshly.

I didn't find it very amusing. 'Why don't you ask him and find out?'

'Oh, I couldn't do that. I'm in love, castratingly, hopelessly in love. If my object were attainable I would cease to love it.'

'It doesn't sound very satisfactory.'

'There are compensations, like sitting next to him in class. I only play cricket so that I can be in the same changing-room with him.'

'I thought there must be some reason.'

'Cruel, cruel,' he said. Then, 'Have I ruined your day? I'm so sorry.'

'I'm sorry you're unhappy, if you really are.'

'Are you?' He undipped the dark glasses, and I saw his eyes for the first time. The whites were pink. I'd forgotten how deep the brown was; the irises were almost as black as the pupils. I looked away.

'I'm sorry for anyone who's still stuck in – in that sort of thing. You'll soon grow out of it.'

'But what if I don't? What if I'm queer for life? Perhaps I am.'

'I doubt it very much.' My shock had worn off. Now I was quite angry. 'And why the hell do you have to tell me all this?'

'I have to tell someone. I go mad telling myself.'

'Why not try a doctor?'

'Doctors cure bodies, not minds, not personalities. And if I went to a psychiatrist he'd have me dishonourably discharged from the Navy in two minutes. And then I'd never see Brian again.'

'I can't imagine why you want to see him. He struck me as singularly unattractive.'

'Not under a shower.'

'Oh, for God's sake, Charles! Your perversions don't interest me. Just shut up about them.'

'I don't have perversions. I have *a* perversion.'

'Well, for God's sake, shut up about *it.*'

I glared at him, then looked away again. His eyes were too demanding or mocking or sad, I didn't know which.

'I kissed you once,' he said. 'Do you remember?'

'Yes, I do. And I hope for your sake that you don't end up like Mr Bradley, that's all.'

'Oh, I shan't do that. I'm not interested in boys.'

'Can we change the subject?'

'If you'll tell me why you're so frightened of looking at me.'

I tried again to meet his eyes, and again failed. I stared instead at my shoes. There was still some blood on them. I had a sudden, stabbing suspicion that I might be jealous of Brian. I'd thought that Charles was still, in a sense, mine; we'd laughed and leant against each other, remembering. Perhaps he'd never been mine. The idea of jealousy was far more shocking than anything Charles had said.

'If you like, we can just go quietly back to Portland.' He spoke wearily, as though I'd failed him, but it was no more than he'd expected. 'Or I can catch a bus.'

'Don't be ridiculous. I'll race you up the hill.'

I set off at once, not waiting for him, glad to be running, to feel the rough ground jarring my feet, the sweat beginning, the violent pumping of my heart. I wanted to run up the hill for ever. It was steeper than it looked, with molehills and thick tummocks of grass. I stumbled and struggled, willing my legs to go on, panting, the blood booming in my ears, drowning out that terrible thought. I reached the top of the first great ditch of the camp, and threw myself down on the wet grass. Then I rolled over and stared at the sky. It wasn't true, it couldn't be. My heart thundered.

When I looked for Charles, he was still toiling halfway up the slope. He couldn't have done much running. He looked rather pathetic, picking his way with an old man's care.

'You're not in very good condition,' I said, when he at last arrived.

'What is there to be in condition for?'

'Oh – life, love, literature. The passing scene. I don't know.'

He sat heavily down. 'Life is all very well in its way, I suppose, but it's hardly what it's cracked up to be, is it?' He puffed a little. 'And love is merely a sophisticated name for certain physiological compulsions, unless you mean the incestuous psychological drives which wreck every attempt at rational human conduct. But enough of that.' He felt the seat of his trousers with his hand and stood up again hurriedly. 'As for literature – surely it's over? We're in the post-literary age. So there seems nothing whatever to be in condition *for*. I think the only tolerable approach to the human situation in our time is that of the wholly, devotedly, unfit man.'

'Good God, you still talk the same old crap.'

He smiled down at me. 'You'll get pneumonia, lying on that wet grass. Where do we go from here?'

I got to my feet. The larks still sang and Dorset spread luxuriously below us and the sky dreamed of holidays by some other sea, all sun and wine and laziness. But we were here and now and I wasn't sure where that was. Charles put his dark glasses back on.

'Well,' I said, 'there are some more of these ditch things, and then nothing very much in the middle.'

'Then we'll ignore it. Let's walk along the ridge. I've seen this bit of view now.'

Charles was never very interested in views. As he walked along he looked carefully where he was treading. 'Life, love and literature, you said. Why literature?'

I've kept nothing of what I wrote in those days, and the loss is not likely to be regretted. I read all the modern verse I could find and wrote poems with the firm conviction that I was a serious apprentice to literature, destined for major achievements. The result was a lot of clumsy imitations of Auden and Spender and Pound and Eliot, full of rusting anchors and decaying dockyards, though I had only to open my eyes to see a busy naval dockyard in perfectly good order. I preferred an imaginary melancholy world to the real one, and I thought, 'I have been faithful to thee, Cynara, in my fashion,' was one of the greatest poems ever written.

At the same time I was going to be a very great actor indeed. I read James Agate's *Ego* with devotion, and sent for all the little magazines I saw advertised in other little magazines. It was one of my greatest ambitions to edit a little magazine myself. Somehow, though, I neglected the classic English writers – perhaps wisely. I remembered little of the novels I read in my hammock on *Maidstone*, and when I re-read them now they come quite fresh and new. Those whom I did read – Lawrence and Forster and Hemingway and Fitzgerald – went the way of Percy F Westerman. There was a literary tapeworm inside me, avaricious for print, but it swallowed prose whole, leaving me only the poetry for nourishment.

'I write,' I said.

'What do you write?'

I decided to hide nothing. I recited my latest melancholy poem, about a lighthouse whose lamp was no longer lit.

'Good,' said Charles, when I'd finished. 'Not bad at all.'

'Do you really think so?'

'Oh, yes. You have no voice of your own, of course, but your influences speak through you, you have a certain ventriloquous gift.'

'Have I?' I wasn't sure whether to be pleased. I thought probably not.

'It's the best thing for a young poet, parody. You can learn far more from imitation than from trying to write things of your own. It's a terrible mistake to try and be original. If you ever do have anything of your own to say, it'll find a way of saying itself.'

'You don't feel the poem does say something?'

'Good heavens, no. Only that you've read with some intelligence. You don't *imagine* it says anything, do you?'

'Well, I had rather hoped so.'

Charles ignored the resentful tone in my voice. 'I've stopped writing poetry myself. It seems to me that unless one's a very gifted lyricist, it's wisest not to put one's pen near paper till one's – oh, forty. Besides, television's the new medium. We should all be thinking in visual terms, not verbal ones.'

'What about your eyesight?'

He stopped, surprised. 'What about it?'

'You look at the world through tinted glass. Television is very black and white.'

'Actually, it's a sort of bluish grey. But it'll be coloured one day. It probably already is in America.' He strolled on. 'I suppose you think my glasses are an affectation.'

'I didn't say that.'

'Most people do. They're not, though. I have to wear them, or I get the most frightful headaches. I'm diseased, like your rabbit.'

'Charles, how awful!'

'Oh, my disease isn't mortal, of course. And medicine being so on the ball these days, they'll probably find a cure before I'm totally blind.'

'How bad is it?'

'It gets worse.'

'But why did the Navy accept you?'

'Oh, I wanted to do Russian at someone else's expense, and I can see enough to get by. There was a bit of a fuss about the dark glasses, of course. They won't let me wear them on parade. But we do very little parading, thank God.'

I was astonished at his coolness. He looked briefly at the view and said, 'It's all much the same, the country, isn't it?'

'No. Not when you get to know it.'

'But it's still just grass and trees and cows and telegraph-poles, if you live there a hundred years.'

I looked at it. There seemed more to it than that. 'What bothers you so much about it? It's only nature.'

'And what is more frightening than that? You said yourself it was nothing but animals killing and eating each other.'

'They all go back to the earth in the end. Nothing takes what it doesn't return. Didn't you do the nitrogen cycle at school?'

'Oh, yes, and the indestructibility of matter. Now there's a *really* terrifying thought. Doesn't it frighten *you*, that you're just part of some meaningless process, hideously unchangeable? That you have a mind and a heart and – well, what for lack of a better word we'll call a soul – and it really doesn't matter in the slightest? It scares the shit out of me, I don't mind telling you.'

It didn't frighten me. Perhaps I hadn't yet felt it as affecting me personally.

'You don't believe in God, do you?' he said, and for a moment he put galactic space between us.

'No,' I said, and he came back again. 'I don't think I ever did, did you?'

'I tried to once. If anything, it made the nitrogen cycle seem slightly worse, as though the universe was a bicycle-wheel spinning by the roadside, while God had a slash in the ditch.'

'Yes! Exactly! But – I don't know. I don't mind being part of a process. I'd be much more frightened if I wasn't. I don't mind the idea of dying – when I'm old, I mean. I'd be simply furious if I died now.'

He laughed. 'You feel you belong, then, to all this?' He waved towards Dorchester. 'You don't mind living, begetting, sickening and dying, while mindless things like stones and trees survive you?'

'Not really. Do you?'

'Christ, yes. Sometimes I'd like to get my hands on the bloody atom that started the whole ridiculous mess that's ended in me, and personally split it over the head.'

'That's no good,' I said. 'You have to make what you can of things as they are.'

'You don't believe in positive and ameliorative legislation, then, after all?'

'Of course I do. I mean – you can change laws and social structures and even the whole natural environment, but you still only live for a bit, then die. You can't change that. And if you let it get you down, you're just wasting what little time there is.'

'You're a pure hedonist, then?'

'No. Well, perhaps I'd like to be. But I don't think anyone can be a pure anything, and it's a terrible mistake to try.'

'I see. So you're just the usual English empiricist. How nice for you.'

'Well, what do you believe?'

'I don't know. I wish I did. Half of me agrees with you, that we should relax and take things as they come, be flexible and open and all the rest of it. But the other half – I *can't* accept that that's all there is to it. There *must* be some point.'

'There isn't.'

'But if you say that, you're dismissing so much, you're side-stepping so many real problems.'

'Perhaps they're not really real.'

He thought for a while, then he said, 'It's no good. It's too safe, your way. Too limiting. Life isn't that simple. Even if you're right, *why* are you right?'

I didn't know, but I thought I *was* right. I felt light-headed again, moved by our conversation, as though I'd discovered something profound and satisfying. I rarely knew what I thought till after I'd said it; then it moved me deeply.

There was an old tree-trunk not far ahead. We walked towards it, then sat down.

'Good old Julian,' said Charles. He seemed moved, too. 'If you can face life, why shouldn't I? We're blood-brothers. On the other hand, why *should* I?'

'It's like killing the rabbit. You have to.'

'A categorical imperative?'

'I don't know what that is.'

'Nor do I, really. I've only read about it. I wish I didn't talk quite so much bullshit.'

'Talk as much as you like. It's just – marvellous, hearing your voice again.'

'My dear old fellow!' said Charles, mocking me, and yet not mocking me, either.

We sat in silence. I could feel stones through the soles of my shoes, and ridges of bark digging into my bottom, and I stopped thinking and gave myself up to feeling, pure, tear-starting, inexplicable emotion. When I was a child, I used quite often to experience extraordinary moments of exaltation, when I became one with the garden, the fields beyond, the valley, the whole earth and sky and sun, dogs barking, tractors ploughing, pigeons calling, and I understood, effortlessly, utterly, the whole shape and meaning of life, because it was in me and I in it, and everything was as it should be, and it always would be, whatever happened, world without end or beginning. I never feel such moments now. But I remember them almost with agony, because I can only remember that I did feel, not how I felt. I'm sure there aren't any words for it, but listening inattentively to music I sometimes surprise myself recalling what it was like.

One of those moments – one of the last – came to me as I sat there with Charles. It was not a vision or a hallucination, and I don't know how long it lasted – a fraction of a second, perhaps. And then I was myself again, on, not of, the earth, the exaltation vanishing like ice-cubes in a furnace. I felt shaken, happy, sad. I wanted to tell Charles, to share it with him.

'Do you ever feel – swept up by the universe?'

'Never. Only swept under.'

'Haven't you ever felt – in touch with everything?'

He looked at me gravely. 'No. I couldn't. Some people are sports – outcasts – mistakes. I'm one of them. An animal with my eyes would have been dead years ago.'

'But you aren't an animal, so you wear spectacles and live.'

'If it were only my eyes!'

His confession didn't worry me nearly so much now. I felt very tolerant, having just been part of the universe. 'You don't think you're really queer, do you?'

'I don't know. I hope not. But that's what I mean about being a sport. I don't seem to feel or think like the others. Their amusements and interests and motivations just don't ever coincide with mine.' He frowned. 'They honestly enjoy dirty jokes, for instance. I can't even remember the beginning of one by the time it's ended.'

'I wouldn't worry about that if I were you.'

'But you aren't me.'

'No.'

We got up and walked back down the hill to Oscar. I thought sadly as we went that we would never again laugh together like schoolboys in the rain.

At the hotel in Dorchester, Charles drank nothing before dinner and only two glasses of wine with the meal which he said was an outrage. The vegetables, he said, were tinned, and tinned vegetables in the middle of Dorset in June were grotesque, disgraceful and insulting. He spoke loudly, so that the waitresses couldn't pretend not to hear.

Afterwards, as we went to the car, he said he was sorry, but he wasn't used to drinking.

'Christ, you ought to try the executive branch. Do you know how much we pay for a bottle of brandy? Six and six. Some people are drunk the whole time.'

'Very enviable, I'm sure.'

We set off back to Portland. Oscar's headlights were feeble, but I liked to pretend that he knew the road. Charles didn't speak. I hadn't at first believed that he could be fuddled on so little, but now I saw that he was. He replied very oddly to my questions.

'How are all your families?'

'I have no family. I'm an orphan.'

'Surely not?'

'Always, always, always.'

A mile or two later I tried again.

'Are you going to the university when all this is over?'

'Yes. No. What's the point? I know everything already.'

I laughed.

'I do,' he said thickly and angrily. 'What is there worth knowing that you can't learn by yourself?'

When we arrived at the dockyard gate, two men in civilian clothes were showing their passes. They were Brian and his friend from Eton.

Charles sat up. 'Where can we all go?' he said, wide awake again. 'There must be somewhere, isn't there?'

'We can go down the boat, if you like. How late is it?'

It was nearly eleven o'clock. And then I remembered that Brian's friend might be an Etonian, but he wasn't an officer. It was absolutely against regulations to entertain ratings in the wardroom.

Charles was already introducing himself; then he introduced me. The Etonian was called Neil Ross.

'Julian's invited us all down to his submarine for a drink,' Charles announced.

'That's very decent of you,' said Brian.

Neil and I looked at each other. He was tall, dark and aristocratic, and in ordinary life I would have felt distinctly his social inferior. But it wasn't ordinary life, and we lived by the Naval Discipline Act. Practically anything one did could be called prejudicial to good order or conduct unbecoming to an officer.

'I'm afraid I shall have to decline,' said Neil. 'We don't want you court-martialled, do we?'

'What's the matter?' said Charles.

'I'm not an officer. You all are.'

'Oh, don't be so bloody feeble.'

'Neil's right,' said Brian. His voice rang with a proud tradition of friendships sacrificed to discipline. 'Hard cases make bad law. Neil and I should really have separated before we came back to the dockyard.'

'If you'd been on a bus,' said Charles, 'one of you could have gone upstairs, the other down. But it might have been safer to make Neil wait for the next one.'

'Don't be silly, Charles.'

'We shouldn't have met at all,' said Neil. 'Except for me to salute and for you to tell me to polish my buttons.'

'That's not a very intelligent attitude, Neil. You shouldn't be bitter about failing your CW Board. You know very well that there's good sense behind these regulations.'

'You silly little twit,' said Neil. '*Sir.*' He doffed his hat in a fierce, unsubmissive salute and walked off.

'Come back here!' Brian shouted. Neil paid no attention.

'Leave him alone,' said Charles.

'I've a bloody good mind to put him on a charge,' said Brian. He was furious. 'What a ridiculously childish way to behave.'

I was frankly relieved to see Neil disappear round a warehouse.

'Well, you'll come and have a drink, Brian, won't you?'

'Thank you very much, Mitchell, I will.'

Tom Barnes, the navigating officer, was on duty that night. He was putting corrections on his charts in the control-room. He was always months behind with them.

'Hello,' he said. 'Party, party?'

'Just some cricketers. Won't you join us?'

'No thanks. And curfew's at midnight tonight. I've got to get some kip, you know. And so have you. We're doing a CASEX Nine tomorrow morning.'

'What the hell's that?'

'Christ, Snotty, how long have you been in this ship?' He handed me the key to the wine-locker.

'Too long. How far have you got with the corrections?'

'I'm up to March.'

'This year or last?'

'Bugger off.'

Brian wanted to see all over the ship, but the fore-end was full of hammocks with sleeping sailors, and with Tom in the control-room there wasn't much to show except the engines. Then I took them up the conning-tower and explained that we didn't have torpedo tubes any longer, because we were only used for training.

'You haven't been on any big exercises, then?'

'No. We do mock attacks, of course.'

'Not much of a preparation for the real thing, is it?' said Brian.

I knew that some submarines, more modern than mine, went on secret expeditions into the Arctic. We all suspected that they were spying, though we didn't know how or on what. On the Russian course, they probably knew much more about it than we did, chugging out to sea every day on simple exercises. My main job was being the captain's secretary, writing letters and making monthly returns. Brian managed to make it sound as though his work would be much more valuable and interesting, when he got to it.

'Of course there have to be people just running the ships,' he said when we were back in the ward-room. 'I see that.'

'So you'd bloody well better,' said Tom from the control-room.

Brian looked startled, and accepted his whisky in silence. Charles drank ginger ale. The ward-room was tiny, designed to sleep four, when the bunks were up, and to seat six when they were down. It stank, as the whole ship did, of diesel-oil, hydrochloric acid and cigarette smoke. An orderly confusion of pipes and wires ran overhead. I had thought it snug; now it seemed simply squalid.

Charles sat next to Brian across the narrow table from me. He didn't seem to notice the smell. His eyes moved back and forth between Brian and the wire-fronted locker over my head which held the ship's six pistols.

'Those are my guns,' I said. 'I'm gunnery officer. We have so many rounds a month we're supposed to practise with. We shoot at empty bottles on our way out to the exercise areas. No one's managed to hit one yet. It's bloody difficult, shooting a pistol, especially when both you and the target are wallowing up and down.'

Brian frowned. 'Don't you ever get out on the range?'

'Never. I don't even know where it is.'

'Really! I must say, the more you tell me, the more I feel that, whatever the incidental excitement of sea-going life, the real work of the Navy is increasingly being done ashore.'

'You mean all the nice girls love a sailor?' said Charles.

'Do be serious, Charles.'

He allowed a sad smile to flit across his face, then relapsed into silence. Brian and I briskly discussed the future defences of Britain. As far as I remember, Brian believed in the Nato umbrella; I don't think I believed in anything very much, except that it might be as well to be a couple of hundred feet under water when the bombs started dropping.

'Going to the varsity?' Brian said, when defence was exhausted.

'Yes – Oxford. Wadham.'

'Oh. I believe it's quite a good little college, considering.'

'Considering what?'

'Well, it's not exactly one of the most social places, is it?'

'Perhaps Julian is going there to work,' said Charles. 'Not to be President of the Union and go beagling.'

'I don't even know what I'm going to read yet.'

'But you know you're going to write, don't you?'

'Everyone says that Oxford and Cambridge aren't what they were,' said Brian. 'In some colleges you can't even get lunch in your rooms any longer.'

'Where are you going?' I asked.

'Trinity.'

'Oxford or Cambridge?'

He smiled indulgently. 'If I'd meant Oxford or Dublin I'd've said so. There's only one Trinity which is just called Trinity.'

'It's the one in three, you see, rather than the three in one,' said Charles. 'I'm going to King's. Brian and I will be freshmen together. I like the idea of being a fresh man at twenty, don't you? As though you've exhausted one adult self already.'

'I expect we will be worn out by then,' I said. 'What are you going to read?'

'I don't know. History, philosophy. I haven't decided.'

'I shall read Classics, of course,' said Brian. 'There's really no substitute, especially if you're interested in writing, I should have thought. The best English prose is classical prose.'

'I couldn't agree with you less,' said Charles. 'The written language must be based on the spoken language. No one's spoken in classical rhythms since – who? Burke? And no one ever will again, either.'

'My dear Charles, there's no better model than the classical style.'

'There most certainly is. People who write it nowadays look and sound ridiculous. There's nothing behind it, no real living language. It's like Georgian poetry – the form has lost all touch with the content.'

Brian considered this. 'There may be something in what you say. But I still think a classical education is the best.'

Charles flushed with pleasure at winning his small concession. He leaned forward, clasping his hands between his knees, as though he was afraid they might fly out and do something he'd regret.

'You see,' he said to me, 'Brian can listen to reason when he wants to.'

'It all sounds like a load of old balls to me,' said Tom, appearing for a moment in the doorway. He shook his head, then went away again. It was rather unnerving having him both there and not there.

Brian said, 'The trouble with you, Charles, is that you don't have enough respect for the real things which matter. You don't appreciate your cultural inheritance.'

'Oh, you'd be amazed how much I love old-fashioned things. And people. Don't you, Julian?'

I felt we were on dangerous ground. 'I think I prefer the things, actually.'

'You're wrong, all wrong. It's through the people that you can understand what's happened to this country. They're dotted about all over the place, stuck in the attitudes of 1900, 1914, 1920, 1937 – 1945, come to that. They're living embodiments of whole periods of history. That's their charm. Like Brian – he's a carefully bred, elaborately nurtured specimen of – what would you say? 1890?'

Brian frowned. 'There's no need for personal abuse.'

'But it's not abuse! It's love, appreciation, genuine enjoyment!' Charles was trembling, pressing his hands between his legs. 'I love you for being what you are.'

'That seems a pretty dubious compliment,' I said. Charles made me more and more uneasy.

He grinned unhappily. 'Perhaps it's not love. Perhaps it's just nostalgia.'

'Really,' said Brian, 'this is all very childish.'

I decided to change the conversation. 'When does your course end?' I asked.

'In September,' said Charles.

'Yes,' said Brian. 'Then we'll be scattered about and start putting what we've learned to some profitable use, I hope.'

'Oh, I expect we'll both end up at Cheltenham,' said Charles. He didn't look as though he really believed his luck could be so good.

'I certainly hope not. There are plenty of much more interesting places than that.'

'Oh, Cheltenham's very nice,' I said. 'It has lovely balconies and things. And there's the steeplechasing in the winter, too.'

'I don't approve of gambling,' said Brian.

'I do,' said Charles. 'My whole life is a fearful betting against the odds.'

'Nonsense. Everything is on your side. You're intelligent, well-bred, not badly off. You're part of the nought point one per cent of people who really count.'

'I believe there are rather more of us than that.'

'Well, why quibble? You're extremely fortunate.'

Charles smiled at me, full of self-pity. I didn't honestly feel very sympathetic. It seemed to me that he was indulging himself with tiresome fantasies which he ought to try and grow out of as quickly as possible. My thought must have shown in my face, because he sighed and said, 'It's time we went to bed.'

'Have they given you decent rooms?'

'No; we're in a sort of dormitory.'

'It's a disgrace,' said Brian. The nought point one per cent weren't supposed to sleep in dormitories, apparently.

We said good night to Tom and then I walked with them up the gangplank and along the jetty. The dockyard looked in the moonlight almost as deserted and decayed as I liked to make it in my poems.

We parted outside the harbour-master's office. Then they turned left to go up the hill to *Osprey*, while I went right to leave the dockyard for the Portland Roads Hotel, the pub where some of the less affluent submariners were putting up while *Maidstone* was away.

'Goodbye,' said Charles. It was obvious how pleased he was to have half a dockyard mile of Brian to himself. He was fretting to go.

'Very nice to have met you,' said Brian.

I nodded and left them. Charles had always been full of surprises, I thought; it was annoying, though, that I was never prepared for them. It was nonsense, of course, that I was jealous of Brian; I couldn't imagine why I'd ever thought I was. It was typical of Charles to make me feel something idiotic like that. He had changed utterly and not changed at all. I wondered about myself. My head began to run with odd phrases, to fiddle them into lines and rhythms; a poem was coming on. I didn't know what it was about, but then I never did at the time.

3

A week or two later I sent the poem, much revised, to
Charles. It had turned out to be a celebration of my
moment of identification with the universe, if that is what it
was, on Maiden Castle. I thought it very beautiful. Charles
didn't. He complained of abstract ideas unconcretized,
rhythmical slackness and verbal dullness, and I daresay he was
right. But the poem started a vigorous correspondence which
survived Charles's posting to Cheltenham and my unchanging
Portland routine. Brian went to Germany. 'He's very excited,'
Charles wrote. 'He feels he's going into the front line of the cold
war.' He never mentioned his crush – that, I'd decided, was what
it was – and I had no adventures of my own to describe, but we
advised each other at length about the nature of physical and
spiritual love. Our letters were full of the exuberant certainty of
the very young, of fine phrases and unalterable judgements. But
though we were voluble about art and love, about actual life we
were strangely silent, and wrote only of what we'd read and
seen. Charles developed a craze for the ballet and Italian films,
deplored the dreariness of Cheltenham, and denounced
Richard Burton's Hamlet which he'd recently seen at the Old
Vic. I'd seen it, too, and admired it extravagantly. Burton had
stood in the middle of the stage for one of the soliloquies and
made the sweat break thrillingly out on his forehead. I longed to
know how he did it. Charles dismissed it as an actor's trick, and
for three letters running attacked my critical intelligence. He
accused me, too, of praising the production just because I'd

been taken to see Claire Bloom, the Ophelia, in her dressing-room. It's true that it was my first visit to an actress's dressing-room and that I had been extremely impressed. I was still going to be a very great actor, really quite soon. Our leaves never coincided, though I went over from Cirencester once to see him. There was nothing much to do in Cheltenham, so we went to a film, then had dinner. Afterwards we strolled up the Promenade and he pointed out a coffee-bar where you could get Russian tea. The constraint we had felt at first in Portland lay between us again, and this time we failed to break through it. It showed in our letters, too, in what we left out.

And then, astonishingly, the long tedium of national service was over, and the day I got home there was a letter from Stephen Spender at *Encounter*, accepting one of my poems. It was an auspicious start to civilian life. I wrote and told Charles, who replied with some scathing remarks about Spender's own poems, but congratulated me all the same. 'There are no amateurs in poetry,' he wrote, 'only those who write bad poems.' I was impressed, and used the remark myself until I discovered that he'd adapted it from something Manet once said to Gauguin. Perhaps he'd expected me to know that. His range of reference was much wider than mine; I still only read poetry.

The correspondence stopped as soon as we went to Oxford and Cambridge. As has often been said, undergraduates spend their first year making and dropping new friends; they hardly have time even to consider old ones. And there are other preoccupations, like one's work. By a series of accidents and misunderstandings I was doing PPE, and like many national servicemen I discovered that my brain had lost the habit of academic application and that I was quite incapable of following the simplest economic argument.

Not that I spent very much time turning the baffling pages of Hicks and Samuelson. There was an immense amount to do, and terrible decisions had to be made; if one joined all the clubs, one would never go to any of them, but they all sounded tempting. And there were so many people to meet and parties to go to and poems to read and poems to write – everything was a great muddle. The stage called imperatively. But I discovered with shock and chagrin that I suffered such agonies of stage-fright that I'd never make an actor. I couldn't understand it – at school I had always relished the tension before a performance. Now I struggled with my nerves for a couple of terms, but after I failed Prelims I had to deny myself any further torture. My frustration foamed into free verse. *The Spectator* accepted a poem, but *The Isis* was largely unimpressed, and I was singled out for bathetic incompetence by a critic in *Cherwell*. I made friends with other and better poets – Peter Levi, the dashing Jesuit, and Richard Selig, the American who died so young, and Bernard Bergonzi, who was in my college and impressed me enormously by having published two slim volumes already. My first year flashed by in a brilliant kaleidoscope of faces and books and talk, and I still had no idea where I was. Sometimes I wondered vaguely about Charles. But Oxford was difficult enough to comprehend, I couldn't cope with Cambridge as well. Perhaps he was as bemused as I. In any case, neither of us made any effort to get in touch.

In September 1956, just before the start of my second year, William Donaldson, who had been in submarines with me and was now at Cambridge, came to stay at South Cerney, where my family was then living. If Charles had had a craze for the ballet, Willie had had an all-devouring passion. Night after night he had gone up to Covent Garden from his base at Portsmouth, coming home scarcely in time for his ship's sailing in the morning. Once he even persuaded Svetlana Beriosova to come to a party on his submarine, thus getting himself a reputation for eccentricity and high life. Now he was reading English at Magdalene, and shared some of my views on contemporary poetry. We both thought the existing magazines of Oxford and

Cambridge were unsatisfactory, cliquish and dull, and we decided to start a new magazine of our own, to reveal hidden talent, to link the two universities and to get outsiders to take a sharp look at our self-enclosed worlds. We spent weeks trying to think up a name for this paragon of little magazines and after rejecting *Foetus, Trend, Bifurcation* and a hundred others, settled on *Gemini*. It never occurred to us, I'm afraid, that the reason why other magazines were disappointing was that there just wasn't very much undergraduate talent around. (There never is.) But we launched into the project with missionary enthusiasm and, to our amazement, perhaps, we suddenly discovered that we had actually put a first number together. Published the following March, it had poems by Sylvia Plath, Elizabeth Jennings, C Day Lewis, Peter Levi, CA Trypanis and Richard Aldridge; Stephen Spender wrote on undergraduate poetry, and there were articles by Bernard Bergonzi, Andrew Sinclair, Ronald Bryden, George Wightman and Hugh Bredin. We even had three advertisements, one for Wright's coal tar soap. It seems rather an impressive list of names to me now, but we were quickly called *Junior Encounter* which annoyed us very much.

Towards the end of November I took the interminable train to Cambridge to see Willie about the final arrangements for *Gemini's* first number, and at a party in Magdalene I suddenly saw Charles grinning at me from across the room. I hardly recognized him at first, because the outside of his dark glasses was silvered over, reflecting the room, and his hair was extremely long, covering his ears and lapping over the collar of his coat. He wore a pink shirt with a silky yellow tie and a white jacket of some rough, nubbly cloth. He might have been an ostentatiously incognito film-star.

He pushed over towards me and said, 'It's not true, is it?'

'What's not true?'

'You haven't really persuaded Willie to sink his whole capital into some funny little magazine, have you?'

'Well, not all of it, I hope. How are you?'

'I'm all right. Do you like my glasses? Do you think they suit me?'

'Are they good for your eyes? That's what matters, isn't it?'

'Don't be so dreary, of course it doesn't matter. They're gay, they're plumage, they're display. And simply marvellous for making love, you've no idea – pure narcissism for your partner. Two of you in your lover's eyes – imagine it! What could be lovelier?' I made an effort not to look startled. I had never imagined him like this, foppish, twittering, camp.

'What if you're both wearing them?'

'Infinite reflection, total defence! Pure abstract loving!'

'I think I probably prefer to keep my eyes closed anyway.'

'You *would*,' said Charles. 'Oh, dear, you haven't changed. Change and decay in all around I see, Oh thou who changest not, away from me! But perhaps it's a change to be using someone else's money to start a magazine, so all is not lost.'

'Well, I have none of my own, and someone has to pay for these things, you know.'

'Why haven't I been asked for a contribution?'

'You once told me you weren't going to write till you were forty.'

'Well, I'm not, of course. But a little article? Something on Ronald Firbank? A tiny snide critique of a few clay-footed charlatans?'

'I think we'd prefer the latter. Have you anything in mind?'

'Dear, no. But if you asked me very nicely, I could probably think up something absolutely delicious.'

Willie had come up behind us. 'If you accept one word by that ridiculous pouf Humphries,' he said, 'I resign. I resign anyway. Oh, Charles, didn't see you there. How are you?'

'You can't come between my oldest friend and me,' said Charles, putting his arm round my shoulder. 'He was Castor to my Pollux before your scruffy little magazine was even thought of.'

'Castor sugar on your bollocks?' said Willie. 'Well, it's all a matter of taste, I suppose. Can't say I'd fancy it myself. And *Gemini* will *not* be scruffy, it will be printed on the finest handmade paper and designed by my friend, your friend, everybody's friend, Graeme McDonald. Julian, meet Graeme. Graeme, meet Julian. Charles, go away. Let these two great contemporary minds clash without distraction. Where's that long-haired tart of yours?'

'Which one?' I heard Charles saying as Willie led him away. 'I have so many.'

For the rest of the party which, like all undergraduate parties, went on much too long, I kept hearing Charles's voice, shriller than I'd ever heard it, making silly, incomprehensible remarks. Many of them were greeted with equally silly and incomprehensible laughter. Once again Charles had managed to astonish me. The crush on Brian, it seemed, had been a beginning, not an end.

'I never thought Charles would turn out like that,' I said to Willie. 'He was always rather serious.'

'Oh, he still is. He's supposed to be going to get the most brilliant first of his year in History. King's has a fellowship all lined up for him.'

'It seems hard to believe.'

'Oh, everyone's like that in the Footlights. You can't get in unless you camp it up the whole time.'

'Charles acts?'

'You could call it that, I suppose. They all do at King's. It's a tradition. Ask Dr Leavis.'

It was a bewildering evening. When one's young one always imagines that the group of friends one hangs out with is the most brilliant of its generation. But one has only to cross a quadrangle, of course, to find another group equally sure of its brilliant superiority. In order not to disillusion each other these groups mutually avoid direct challenge or confrontation. But an Oxford undergraduate thrown suddenly into a Cambridge party is challenged at every turn. He doesn't know the signs and code-words, he blurts out the wrong names, scathes the wrong gods, ignores the right ones. In his perplexity he drinks too much, which makes his blunders worse. He ends the evening feeling the whole thing's been a deliberate and successful attempt to make a fool of him. That, anyhow, is what I felt after receiving the pitying looks of Willie's friends. I had even managed to say the wrong thing about Scott Fitzgerald to Andrew Sinclair. Willie himself just giggled at my confusion, increasing my sense of persecution. He regarded Cambridge as a lunatic charade, anyway, and undergraduate parties as the chattering of monkeys in a zoo. He never drank very much, and confined his love life to London girls. The more I think of it, the more extraordinary it is that he ever agreed to start *Gemini* at all.

Eventually a college porter arrived with the Dean's compliments and an order for the party to cease forthwith. People upended bottles over their glasses, swallowed their dregs, and began to leave. Charles came to say goodbye. With him was a small blonde girl with big blue eyes and a tiny waist luxuriously squeezed by a wide black belt with a horse-brass fora buckle. Charles didn't introduce us, but he asked me to come and see him next morning about noon. I said I'd love to.

'On second thoughts, some absolutely ghastly people are coming for drinks before lunch. You'll loathe them and we won't have a moment to be *intime*, so come earlier.'

'All right.'

'I wouldn't go if I were you,' said Willie. 'He burns the most repulsive Indian incense. It chokes you to death, honestly. You'll never be the same again.'

'Oh, Julian's always the same. Aren't you, love?'

He went away, taking the girl with him. I asked Willie who she was.

'No idea, I'm afraid. He always trails a girl like that about with him.'

'For show, you mean?'

'Simply can't tell you. If you start worrying about other people's sex lives, you have no time for your own, so I don't.'

University towns are at their loudest on Sunday mornings, all the churches and chapels competing for the up and coming, and when I woke with an evil hangover I decided I disliked Cambridge very much indeed. It was cold and raining, and I thought of the murderous fen barons of King Stephen's civil war, and the undrained marshes before the Dutchmen came. Cambridge always seems likely to vanish in a cold fog, swallowed up by the past, especially in November.

When the bells stopped I was walking along the Backs, too early to go and see Charles or wake up Willie. The sudden silence was eerie. The trees dripped so much they seemed to be leaking. I had nearly gone to King's instead of Wadham. Now I was very glad I hadn't. The thought of Oxford cheered me considerably. I decided I'd go and see Charles at once, even if he was still in bed. It was a meeting I wanted to be over with.

Charles's room was in the splendid Gibbs building, facing the river on the second floor. I knocked loudly and he shouted, 'Who is it?'

'Me. Julian.'

'OK. Just a minute.'

I waited. In Oxford I always walked straight into my friends' rooms, but you could never tell in Cambridge; or with Charles. I'd never been in any room of his before.

After a minute of shuffling noises he said, 'Sorry, I can't find the bloody key.'

'Do you always lock yourself in at night?'

He didn't reply, and I heard more shuffling, before the key went into the lock and turned. The door opened, but Charles was invisible behind it. 'Hurry up,' he said.

He shut the door quickly behind me again and locked it. He was stark naked except for a pair of dark goggles pushed on to his forehead. The only light in the room was the violet glow of a sunlamp, perched on a pile of books itself balanced on a chair. It pointed down like arc lamp in a prison camp at the sofa.

'Sit down. I've only just started,' said Charles. 'I hope you don't mind. I give myself ten minutes each side every morning.' He went back to the sofa and stretched himself out on his back. 'You'd better put on some goggles – this thing is very bad for the eyes. There's a spare pair on the desk.'

I found them and put them on. Everything became very dark and green. It was like being deep under water; or in the sort of opium den illustrated in children's stories about slant-eyed heathen Chinese. It took me several moments to see anything at all.

'How long have you been on this fad?' I said.

'Oh, not long. I had some spots on my back which wouldn't clear up, so I bought this thing and fell in love with it.' As my eyes began to make out the details of the room I saw that he had covered his face with a sheet of some glittering material.

'Whatever's happened to your face?'

'It's so pretentious, walking about looking sunburnt in the middle of the English winter. I hate people who do that.'

'But why tinfoil?'

'Well, in summer, when it's all right to look tanned, it concentrates the rays by reflecting them. So in winter I use it to deflect them.'

'But for heaven's sake, if your body's tanned, why not your face as well?'

'It's just not my style,' he said.

It felt really very odd to be looking at Charles with a blank shining head and no clothes on, everything dim except the glistening tinfoil. My hangover seemed suddenly much worse.

'Besides,' Charles went on, 'I show my body only to a very select few. In fact only to my doctor.'

'The golden body doesn't symbolize a sun-baked sex-life, then?'

'No. And you?'

'A blank.'

'Quite. We all live like monks, resorting from time to time to a little bell-pulling.' He was quite unlike the Charles of the party. There was no shrillness in his voice, and when he made a joke, he did so dryly, as though not wanting any response. 'It's a good thing, really. You get much more academic work done in an asexual community.'

'I'm told you're going to get the most brilliant first of this or any other year.'

'Well, I'm trying. These twenty minutes of womblike darkness every morning are a marvellous mental discipline. I lie here and go systematically over everything I've read in the last twenty-four hours. There's usually five minutes over for general contemplation, too. I'm becoming quite a mystic.'

'Shouldn't you have your left leg over your right shoulder for that?'

'It makes for an uneven tan.'

Though I tried not to stare at Charles, I didn't succeed. The light and the goggles gave his spread limbs a greenish, corpse-like tinge, as though we were in a morgue. There were bookshelves, I could just make out, which might be slabs, and dull glints from the walls, which might be brass coffin-handles, though more probably reflections from the glass on pictures. But apart from his sinister colour and stillness, Charles looked young, alive and well. He was neither thin nor fat, solidly built but not over-muscular. Though his legs were hairy, above the navel he was smooth all the way up to the decapitating tinfoil. He was uncircumcised, well hung, but not so brilliantly as to cause admiration or envy. I hadn't realized what a good body he had. One so rarely sees one's friends naked, one tends not to think of them as physical specimens. I hadn't seen Charles naked since our prep-school, and then he'd been thin and bony; perhaps that's how I'd subconsciously imagined him ever since.

'Charles, I don't think there's been a single occasion on which we've met when you haven't somehow or other astonished me.'

'I know,' he said simply. 'It's my function in your life, just as your function in my life is to be always the same.'

'That doesn't sound very amusing.'

'It's just as necessary. I've often thought about you, lying here. I'll tell you something that's been puzzling me. We don't see each other at all, hardly, do we? Yet we do influence each other, don't you think?'

'I'm afraid you've become much too mystical for me if you think that.'

'I don't mean anything occult. I mean, I often think, What would Julian say about all this? And then I see whether what you would think alters what I think myself. Sometimes it does, sometimes it doesn't. But you're always there in my head to be consulted. It's usually about how to treat someone, I think. Am I in your life like that?'

I thought about it. 'No. You see, you always surprise me, and if I could imagine what you'd say, then you wouldn't, so I can't.'

'Now say that in English.'

'If I could imagine what you'd say, then you wouldn't be able to surprise me. But you always do. If you're in my head, it's as an unknown quantity. A threat, almost. You're "Mr X".'

'Who's he?'

'I don't know. God, perhaps.'

'I see. How interesting. Yes, I suppose you must feel like that. Very interesting indeed.'

'Isn't it time you turned over?'

'Almost. What I was going to say was, granted that we are what we are in each other's lives, do we actually like each other, do you think, or not?'

'Of course we like each other.' I didn't understand the question. 'How else would we have got these places in each other's lives – if we do actually have them?'

'Oh, we have them all right. But I think you're wrong.' An alarm clock went off. Charles sat up, silenced it and set it for ten minutes later. Then he turned over and lay on his stomach. 'I don't believe our relationship is a matter of choice,' he said, as though there had been no interruption. 'If we are as necessary to each other as I think we are, choice doesn't enter into it, and as liking is a matter of choice, then it doesn't, either. So though we *may* like each other, and we probably do, there has to be something more basic, something deeper, to explain the necessity.'

'I don't think we *are* necessary to each other. We may have been once, years ago, at school. But not now. If you have an imaginary me in your head, it's probably that dirty little schoolboy whom I hereby totally disown.'

'You weren't dirty,' he said. 'You were rather clean, actually. And I've known you since then, briefly but deeply. You are a developing personality in my imagination, not a static one.'

'Thanks. I suppose you're going to tell me that we're madly in love.'

'Well, not madly. But definitely in love. I don't mean erotically, of course – erotic love is very much like liking, a matter of choice. And lovers are often quite unnecessary to each other, except physically. Though it would be dangerous and silly to deny that there is an erotic element in all relationships.'

'I, too, have read paperback Freud.'

'So you agree that we are in love?'

'Oh, come on, Charles.' I was beginning to need air in that submarine gloom, and my head was throbbing painfully. 'There must be lots of people in both our lives who have had the same sort of influence on us as you say we've had on each other. Our parents, for instance – masters at school – dons. It's pure chance who you model yourself on.'

'Oh, I agree. But once someone has become necessary to you, then the effect is permanent. If you don't want to call it love, you needn't, though it's just English prissiness not to. But I still want to know – do we actually *like* each other? Because I've decided that I don't want to be in love with people I don't like, and I'm going to root out their influence on me and find new heroes to replace them.'

'I think you're talking utter balls.'

'Tut, tut,' he said, with a sudden reversion to his camp manner of the previous evening. 'You're not in the Navy now, you know.'

I didn't know what to say. Any two undergraduates with a smattering of logic could and did define their way into and out of love at the slightest opportunity. I had done so myself, often. But there was something more to it than the usual abstract word-spinning. There was a tension between us, a feeling of something literally in the air. It wasn't the Indian incense Willie had mentioned – there was no trace of that. I felt Charles meant more than he was actually saying and I didn't know, or want to know, what it was. I began to feel frightened. My head throbbed and throbbed.

'I see myself,' said Charles after a long pause, 'as a neurotic philanderer, always returning to the one great love of my life, who refuses to accept my love, who doesn't even believe in it, because my life is so patently disgraceful and unloving.'

'I thought you showed yourself only to your doctor.'

'And you, now. You've got to admit it's significant that you arrived at ten-thirty when I wasn't expecting you for at least another hour. That you *chose* to find me in this naked, if unerotic state.'

'I didn't choose it. I always wake up early when I have a hangover. I didn't know where else to go.'

'It's enough to make mystics of us both. You do love me, of course, much more than you know. But your idea of love is so wildly different from your experience that you've never recognized the experience for what it is.'

'You always bloody well know when you're in love, for heaven's sake.'

'Erotically, yes. Otherwise, almost never.'

'Balls.'

'Of course you must think it's balls. You daren't admit the truth. You daren't admit, for instance, that you subconsciously *wanted* to get here early enough to catch me in bed. You got an extra bonus there, didn't you?'

'Think what you like,' I said. Could he be right? Of course he couldn't. The room was beginning to move about. I felt like a diver struck with the bends. There was something dreadfully wrong with the pressure, and things were swimming which should have been still.

'You probably even drank too much last night to give yourself a hangover so that you'd have a cast-iron excuse for getting here early.'

'Oh, of course! And that was my parents' whole idea when they conceived me! What utter crap!'

'Don't panic, Julian. There's no need to get excited.'

'I'm not panicking!'

The alarm-clock went off again. It was the opium. The den was a terrible hallucination. I jumped up from my chair. Charles switched off the bell and pushed up his goggles, then unplugged the lamp. For a moment the room was in complete darkness. I would have screamed if I could have found the air, but my diaphragm seemed paralysed. Then Charles pulled back the curtains and let in the cold grey Cambridge light. I pulled off the goggles, and the mysterious green morgue, the opium den, the shadowy submarine world disappeared. Instead I saw a high, handsome room, with abstract prints on the walls and over the fireplace a Francis Bacon painting of a caged, shrieking Pope, his scream as paralysed as my own. I couldn't take my eyes off it.

'It was a twenty-first birthday present from my stepfather,' said Charles. 'He nearly had a stroke when he saw what he'd bought me.'

I turned towards him. He was silhouetted against the window, his face still invisible. He came slowly towards me. 'I'm really even more naked than I look,' he said. 'I haven't got my contact lenses in.' He came very close. His eyes looked blind and strained, as though the light caused them actual physical pain.

'Dear Julian,' he said. 'How little you know about either of us.' He stepped forward, kissed me lightly on the mouth, then stepped back again. He contemplated what he'd done, his head slightly on one side, his hands on his hips, his legs rather apart. Then he said, 'I must go and cover my nakedness. Excuse me a moment.' He went into his bedroom, leaving the door ajar.

This is too hard to write. Charles is dead. I am a minor novelist, telling the literal truth. I am a character in one of my own books. Yet I feel I am really a character in one of his. He never wrote it, and I don't know what to do or say.

Why do you torment me? Why do you make me do this? Must the dead bury their living?

There are no answers. I am in my grave and the earth is over me, wet and sweet as it was in Dorset. I would rather lie here, scratching my name on the coffin walls. Why do you force me to push back the lid, to heave through this sweet, wet earth? What shall I do for air?

You said we were necessary to each other. How can I survive, then, without you?

I am no Orpheus. It is my own ghost I must bring back to life, staring into its eyes every step of the way. I hear your mocking laughter and feel your love. I am writing this only for myself. You made me. So it is for you, too.

Yet still it is hard to tell the truth. Not to admit that, had you asked me, I would have followed you into the bedroom; not to confess that I was throbbing and aching with hope and fear. I have read the books and believe them; there are many genders, but only one sex. I am past guilt and shame for that, and so should we all be.

No, it is not the sexual temptation that is hard to tell, but the remorse. I cannot forgive myself. I can think only of how I might have saved you, so easily, following without a word and accepting whatever you did, we did, giving of my own accord what you could not ask. You would have asked it of anyone else in the world, I know; and often you did ask it, and got it, and it was not what you wanted. Only I could give it, but I must give it freely. And I stood in your room, staring at your half-open door, unmoving, unable to move, hearing the picture's silent scream behind me and the stillness from beyond the door. And I can never forgive myself, because I might have saved you. And afterwards it was too late.

How long I stood there I don't know. When Charles came out of the bedroom again he was wearing a dark blue shirt with a plain green tie and a pair of black corduroy trousers. He went straight to his desk and put on the silver-coated dark glasses.

'Would you like a drink?' he said.

I mustered my senses together and marched them back to normal life, if it was normal, if it was life. 'Yes, please.' I was astonished how natural my voice sounded.

'Gin, sherry, whisky?'

'Gin, please.'

'How are things going at Oxford?'

'All right. I failed my Prelims in PPE and switched to History.'

'A good thing too. It's better to do one thing properly than several things in bits and pieces. Tonic or French?'

'Tonic, please.'

He handed me my drink, then poured the rest of the tonic into a glass and sat down with it.

'It's not quite what one had imagined, university life, is it?' he said. 'We all read *Brideshead Revisited*, I suppose, and now we can't understand why we're disappointed.' It was a formal, social, distant, dressed Charles now, relaxed, consciously making himself agreeable. I was grateful for the distance and the dress.

'We're two years older than Waugh's characters, of course. National Service sobered us up.'

'Well, it certainly didn't make us giddy with happiness, did it? Do you remember the cricketer, Brian?' He mentioned him as though he'd just been a casual acquaintance. 'He's Secretary of the Union now – and certain to be President. He's about as nasty a politician as the Tory Party can hope for from this generation.'

'I didn't like him very much the only time I met him.'

'No, nor you did. Do you remember that silly scene we had about his friend who wasn't an officer? Well, Neil Ross reports the Union for *Varsity* now, and every week he has something nicer to say about Brian. Can you imagine it? He's Brian's chief henchman. They cook the votes together in the Conservative Club elections. One day he'll be Brian's PPS in the Commons, I suppose. Then a peer.'

'Good God!'

'People never do what you expect of them, do they? When you and I are famous novelists, we'll be able to use little incidents like that to show how much we understand about human weakness.'

'You think we'll be novelists?'

'Almost certainly. Not full-time, of course. But everyone writes at least two novels nowadays.'

'I think I shall stay as a poet. Novels are so long.'

'You'll never be a poet, I'm afraid. I've seen odd things of yours here and there, and you just haven't the gift.'

'Well! Thanks a lot!'

'But you probably write quite decent prose, don't you? And what about plays? Have you ever thought of them?'

'Yes. But I think of myself as a poet first.'

'Well, you're too young for extended dramatic work, of course. But please, when you do turn to plays, don't write them in verse, will you? How's the acting?'

'I've given it up. How's yours? Willie says you're in the Footlights.'

'Oh, it's not acting, it's family charades. I'd hate to act. Anyone can do a turn, though.'

We chatted on in this insipid way for half an hour or so, Charles occasionally denouncing my stupidity in his old authoritative way, while I refused to get cross. It was mild, friendly, forgettable talk about nothing that mattered. Though I never felt precisely at ease, I felt very much easier.

Then someone knocked at the door and rattled the handle. A girl's voice called 'Charles? What are you doing in there?'

Charles let her in. It was the girl I'd seen him with the night before. Her waist was just as tiny this morning, though the belt was white with a jet buckle. I thought she was very pretty. Charles kissed her.

'Antonia, this is Julian Mitchell – I've been telling you about him for thirteen years. Julian, my sister Antonia.'

'What's he been telling you about *me* for thirteen years?' she asked.

Though I knew Charles had half-brothers and -sisters, he had almost never spoken of them. 'He was always very discreet,' I said.

'Thank God for that. And what were you both being discreet about behind locked doors, may I ask?'

'We were making up for lost time,' said Charles. 'He's at Oxford, you see.' He was slightly flirtatious with her, I thought; perhaps the camp was for her amusement.

'Actually,' I said, 'he was sunbathing. It was very dull.'

'You thought so?' said Charles. 'You're not very courteous this morning.' It was the only reference he ever made to the tension of forty minutes earlier.

Antonia wasn't listening. 'Oh, goody,' she said, 'you're drinking already.'

'Now, listen,' said Charles, 'I promised your mother not to let you do anything likely to bring discredit on your family name. You can have one glass of sherry before the guests arrive, and one while they're here, and that's all.'

'Isn't he a pig? I've been drinking gin for two years.'

I was trying to work out which side of Charles's family she came from. I asked for enlightenment.

'Oh, that's just Charles's piggishness. We both have the same mother, but he always says *your* mother, as though she had nothing to do with him. It's just one of his million and one ways of making people furious.'

'I forgot to ask you yesterday,' said Charles. 'How are *your* brother and *your* sister?'

'Tell him to stop it, will you, Julian?'

'Charles, stop it.'

'Thank you. Bruce and Caroline are very well, as far as I know. They're both at school, thank God.'

'So should you be, too,' said Charles. 'I'm a passionate believer in equality of education, aren't you, Julian? Who wants to marry dumb blondes like this one?'

'Lots of people, I should think.'

'There, Charles, now shut up.' She stuck her tongue out at him. 'You're just a pig.'

'I didn't ask you to come for the weekend, you invited yourself. I'm frightfully busy. And you insist on me giving a party for the nastiest people in Cambridge. I think I'm really incredibly nice.'

'Perhaps you are, then,' she said. She kissed him on the nose. Then she turned to me and said, 'Were you at that dreadful party last night? Wasn't it awful? All those people *talking*.'

'He was only the guest of honour, say whatever you like about it.'

'Gosh, were you? I'm frightfully sorry.'

'That's all right. I didn't enjoy it much, either, as a matter of fact.'

'Wasn't Charles just *terrible*? I was ashamed of him, really ashamed.' She looked at him with great fondness. He smiled and patted her cheek.

'Do you want your sherry or not?'

'Can't I have gin?'

'Not before lunch, you know how weak your head is, and you've got to be hideously respectable for Mrs Bowman at tea.'

'It's an awful long way away, tea-time. And you have a rotten head yourself, and you're having gin, so why shouldn't I?'

'It's not gin, it's plain tonic water.'

'You're a pig,' she said. 'All right, sherry.'

It was very uncharacteristic of Charles to have a weak head, I thought; it was about the only thing in which I was actually superior to him. Yet, permanently afflicted as I was with self-doubt when it came to any comparison with Charles, I wondered whether it really was superior of me to be able to hold my liquor. Perhaps his weakness meant that it was only by a tremendous effort that he kept control of himself, that he couldn't afford to relax his vigilance for a moment. While my strength could mean only that I didn't have any great internal pressures to withstand; and that somehow seemed inferior, especially in a poet.

Antonia and he smiled at each other as he gave her the sherry. It was strange to see him as a member of a family, he was so independent, so self-sufficient. And now here he was with a teasing affection for a sister which I'd never even suspected. Yet I suppose that if I'd ever thought about Charles's sisters, I should have been able to guess what they'd be like and how he'd treat them. Antonia was very young, sweeter than she'd be again for five or six years, with a London season coming up, and I could easily imagine myself falling in love with her. I watched them, fascinated and obscurely pleased by their pleasure in each other.

Antonia mentioned a man she'd met at Willie's party. Charles frowned.

'I'd give him a miss, if I were you. He's not really very – nice.'

'Nor are you, Charles. Nor are most of your friends.'

'Sweetheart, my oldest, dearest friend is in the room. Do think before you speak.'

'Oh, I know Julian's nice – he must be to have put up with you all these years.'

'He's certainly much nicer than that smooth bastard you fell for last night.'

'What's the matter with him?'

'He doesn't tell the truth or eat his porridge.'

'Oh.' Antonia nodded. 'That bad.'

'What does that mean?' I asked. 'Do I eat my porridge? Do you?'

'It's just an old family phrase,' said Charles. He looked slightly embarrassed. No one likes to be caught using nursery language in public. He put his arm round Antonia and said, 'I'm in charge of her. I can't let all the shits in Cambridge ask her out for drinks, can I?'

'How did you know he'd asked me for drinks?'

'So he did! I promise you, he's absolutely not for you, sweetheart. And you will not go to drinks with him.'

'All right.' She seemed delighted by the sternness in his voice. I couldn't help smiling. Charles as the protector of young maidens was an entirely new idea. He was quite right, I now realize; without knowing it, I was already observing people like a novelist.

Other people began to arrive, and I left to go and wake up Willie Donaldson. We were going to have a serious business lunch with all the Cambridge people involved in *Gemini*, to discuss policy and future issues. When I said goodbye to Charles he shook my hand quite formally and said, 'See you again soon, I hope.'

'Do you ever come to Oxford? You know where to find me.'

'Perhaps,' he said. 'Perhaps.'

'And you will write something for us?'

'Perhaps.'

I helped to edit five numbers of *Gemini* altogether, but nothing of Charles's ever appeared there, because he never submitted anything and I was too cowardly or too stupid to ask him to do so. New names added to the magazine's apparent success – Allen Tate, Harold Hobson, WH Auden, Dom Moraes, Quentin Stevenson, Ted Hughes, Stevie Smith. We conducted a poll of the two universities, we printed an up-to-the-minute account of the Algerian situation, we considered ourselves important. Willie Donaldson lost an undisclosed amount of money. I went on writing poetry and started on short stories. I fell in and out of love. I worked hard.

In the spring term of 1958 I read in the papers that Charles had been sent down from King's for having a girl in his room at an improper hour. As usual the undergraduate press made a big fuss about it, but it wasn't until I saw Charles again a year later that I learnt the truth.

By that time I had surprised myself and my tutors by getting a first. Bewildered by my success and having no clear idea of what, if anything, I wanted to do, I decided to try academic research. What I most wanted was to get to America on a fellowship. I felt I must get out of England, out of the predictable pattern of life my abilities suggested. In spite, or perhaps because, of the Suez debacle, it seemed as though nothing would ever change in Britain, that the Conservatives were in power for the rest of my natural life, that a tedious complacency would slowly smother all imagination and ambition. I swallowed the myth of America whole. There, where life was real but not too earnest, I would find a liberation from the strictures of my upbringing and country. And I was lucky. I was awarded a Harkness Fellowship of the Commonwealth Fund, to begin in September 1959.

Meanwhile I had to justify my transatlantic research. My subject was political poetry under James I and Charles I, and I spent long hours transcribing crude pornographic libels in hideous seventeenth-century handwriting in the Bodleian and the British Museum. Whatever it may seem, it was no more peculiar a topic for a thesis than most others, and I know exactly why it appealed to me. I had been taught the period by

Lawrence Stone, an outstanding alchemist of dross to gold among Wadham history students, and it fascinated me; I was, I still thought, a poet; and all my friends at Oxford were, since Suez and Hungary in 1956, obsessed with the question of committed literature. We read Brecht and Camus and, some of us, Sartre; we desperately searched for merit in communist novels; we fell on Pablo Neruda with joy and relief. Dennis Potter, then editor of *Isis*, inflamed us to left-wing protest. Under the circumstances the political frustrations which led to the English Civil War seemed important and relevant. The frustrations and idealism of my own generation, meanwhile, was being neatly channelled into the Campaign for Nuclear Disarmament. Over the Easter holidays of 1959 I went on the Aldermaston March.

I was, I'm afraid, a sceptical marcher. I had been deeply affected by an exhibition of photographs of Hiroshima victims at the Oxford Town Hall, and I felt passionately, indeed I still feel passionately, that the use of atomic weapons should be unthinkable, and since it isn't, that there should be effective international agreement to prevent them being used. But I wasn't a member of the CND or at all sure what its policy was, an uncertainty shared by many others who were generally sympathetic. I don't think I ever believed for a moment that British renunciation of the bomb would actually do much good to anyone, even the British. In my heart of hearts I may even have been against unilateral disarmament, as I felt that Britain was withdrawing more and more into an indifferent affluence which alarmed and depressed me. Though I had my beautiful and impracticable ideals, the real reason I went on the March was that I was temporarily in love with a fiery disarmer. Perhaps there's nothing shameful about that, really; if one is ashamed of being in love, one might as well let the bomb drop anyway.

We spent the first night of the March in Reading, footsore but not refractory. Local schools were made available to us as dormitories. We all felt rather exalted. My companions seemed basically reasonable and intelligent people, and my usual horror of political crowds was allayed. (Perhaps the rationality and intelligence of its supporters was what led to CND's failure as a political movement; the fashionable view, I know, is to blame the irrationality of the leadership, but other political movements have thrived on that.) My love-affair had reached the stage where each of us held one pole of a banner. (It never got further.) Only some militant Trotskyites, who persistently shouted for industrial action against the bomb, marred our general satisfaction with the day's work. But the night was less satisfactory. Few of us were properly equipped for the floor of a gymnasium, and sleep was difficult. The moon threw huge girders of shadow across the lines of humped, exhausted marchers, till, restlessly dozing, I dreamt we were in a vast expressionist theatre, actors in some urgent but incomprehensible drama by Ernst Toller.

By about three in the morning I was wide awake, and no amount of hopeful gazing could induce the bundle next to me even to show the face I thought I loved. (There was no sexual segregation among the marchers, but there was no sign of licentiousness, either. I was rather disappointed.) Somewhere under the duffel-coat, perhaps stifled in one of its thick sleeves, snuggled the reason for my march, the core of my protest. I was really demonstrating, I told myself, in the sense of showing off, I wasn't protesting anything except love. Under the influence of Samuel Beckett's novels I was a fitful nihilist; now his bleak contempt for human ideals began to seem the only rational view of life that was possible. Pleased with the grimness of my mood, I got up, put on my own duffel-coat, and went out to smoke a cigarette on the school playground. There I came on a couple kissing between two goalposts painted on a wall. They parted as I stepped out of shadow into moonlight, and the man asked me if I had a match. It was Charles.

'Hello!' I said foolishly.

'Well, well,' said Charles. We grinned at each other, highly embarrassed. Then he said, 'So you've graciously stepped down from the editorial chair to slog along with the rank and file, have you?'

'That's right. What are you doing here?'

'Throwing in my lot with the working-class movement, of course. Aren't you?'

'I thought I was protesting against nuclear weapons.'

'You were always a political innocent,' he said. The girl took his arm. She, too, wore a duffel-coat – everyone did, I seem to remember, though it can't really be true – but the hood was up, and all I could see were two points of light, flickering from Charles's face to mine and back again. 'How about the match?' said Charles.

I handed him my box and he lit two cigarettes, then gave one to the girl. 'Go back to bed, baby,' he said to her. 'I'll be along in a minute.'

She went off without a word. Charles watched her go, then said, 'A duffel-coat does nothing for a woman, does it?'

'It depends on the woman. Some girls look lovely in their pixie hoods.'

'I don't agree.'

'Who is she?'

'Just a girl.'

We stood in silence for a time, smoking. Then I said, 'What are you up to these days?'

'I'm in the movies.'

'Acting?'

'No. I'm assistant assistant to the producer's assistant. I answer the phone and say, 'Mr Schatz is not in, I'm afraid, can I take a message?' And they say, "No, thanks."'

'Don't film producers have girls to do that?'

'Yes. But some people are too important to be fobbed off at the switchboard. They're put through to me to fob off. The more stages you go through to be fobbed off, the more important you are. It's a fascinating creative life, the movies, you've no idea.'

'Is that *all* you do?'

'Oh, no. Sometimes I'm allowed to go off with the second unit and watch them shoot a few locations. Then I'm called assistant to the assistant director. That's fun.'

'Well, we all have to start somewhere.'

'We do? And what about you? I hear you got a first.'

'Yes. Who told you that?'

'Oh, I keep my tabs on you. I suppose you're doing research, you couldn't resist it.'

'Well, I am, actually, yes. I'm going to America in September.'

'How nice for you. You'll find it very peculiar if Mr Schatz is anything to go by. And they won't like you. You talk too much and too fast, like me. Americans only like listening to themselves.'

'Have you ever been there?'

'No, but Mr Schatz says the phone service is terrific.'

'I thought he spent most of his money avoiding the telephone.'

'Oh, yes, but over there you can dial direct, you can get fobbed off much more quickly. I wonder how you'll find the wide open spaces. They should suit you, I think. Or are you staying safely in New England?'

'I'm going everywhere. I have a car on my fellowship. It's terribly grand.'

'Good, good. All Englishmen need to get out of England for at least three months in every two years. The same applies to New Englanders, Mr Schatz says. He was born in Riga, himself.'

'Does he know you're on the Aldermaston March?'

'Oh, yes. I told him it was an anti-American demonstration and he quite understood. He's quite anti-American himself. He asked if he could come, too, in his Rolls Royce. I said I thought he should save himself for Trafalgar Square.'

'He wouldn't march, I suppose?'

'I shouldn't think he's walked more than a hundred yards since he was twenty. He must have walked a bit then. He says the only way to get ahead is to hustle, and he hustled. Now he's fat. It might not be good for him. Are you very anti-American?'

'Not at all.'

'Oh, I thought that was the point of this thing. To assert little England's right not to be protected by the USA!'

'Some of us have slightly more elevated motives.' I didn't like the anti-American element on the March; it seemed dangerously stupid, while the Trotskyites were just very noisy.

'Yours may be,' said Charles.

We fell into silence again. We had been talking in very low voices, of course. Now someone suddenly screamed in a nightmare and we could hear people grumbling and turning over and groaning.

'Where are you sleeping?' I asked.

'In the masters' common-room. They have easy chairs, you see. I met a man who says he's been on every march since 1929, communist, fascist, striking, strike-breaking, the lot. He says it's essential to be first into the masters' common-room if you want a decent night's sleep. Otherwise it's the floor.'

'I wish I'd thought of that.'

'Well, now you know for tomorrow. He has special boots and a knapsack equipped like a coach-built Cadillac – there's practically a cocktail cabinet.'

'Is that quite right for marching?'

'There's no need to be uncomfortable just because you're protesting – that's a very puritanical idea. I'm all for sit-down strikes, myself, if I have to strike. Would you like some whisky?' He produced a flask.

'I thought you didn't drink.'

'It's purely medicinal. And Barbara likes it.'

So did I. I held the whisky in my mouth for a moment, then let it trickle down my throat. It was just what I wanted.

'Charles, whatever happened at Cambridge?'

He screwed the cap back on the flask. 'I was sent down.'

'I know. But why?'

'Because I got a silly Girton girl pregnant, and after the abortion she turned melancholy and religious and confessed herself to her moral tutor who lived up to her name and was extremely moral and angry about it. More about the abortion than the pregnancy, I think. Anyway, it was established that intercourse had taken place in my room in College contrary to all the regulations and – well, the whole thing was ridiculous and unpleasant.'

'The intercourse or being sent down?'

'The intercourse was so-so. The rest was impossible. They wanted me to feel guilty, I can't think why. One of my fathers insisted that I marry the girl, but the other insisted I didn't, so I was spared that in the end. You can imagine the row.'

'I am sorry. You were going to be a fellow and everything, weren't you? And now you're in the movies.'

'I wouldn't have stayed on at Cambridge. I'd had quite enough of that. Academic life is for those who can't find satisfaction in the world as it is.'

'And I take it you can.'

'No. But there are so many stone walls in Cambridge, and iron bars. It's not true that they don't make prisons. They do.'

'But at least you would have got a good degree.'

'Yes. And there's always pleasure in knowing when you're good at something. But I got a first in Part One and they can't take that away from me.'

'No.' We stood in silence again for a while. Then I said, 'Well, at least it was a girl.'

'They don't send you down for boys. You can't get them pregnant, you see.'

'And you'll stay with Mr Schatz?'

'Good heavens, no. Schatz is a schitz.'

'What will you do?'

'God knows.'

I yawned. 'It really is odd the way we keep running into each other, Charles.'

'No, it isn't. Given our narrow social world it's only odd that we don't see each other more often.'

'Well, see you tomorrow. I think I'll try and get some sleep now. Who are you marching with?'

'Barbara.'

'Aren't you part of a group?' As I said it, I realized what a silly question it was.

'Me in a group? Really, Julian. I'm not a conformist nonconformist – you should know that.'

'Well, see you tomorrow, anyway. I'm exhausted.'

'I'm not. I never sleep much. I think I'll go for a walk.'

'Don't get arrested. The police are terribly suspicious of us.'

'Frankly, I don't blame them. Good night.'

'Good night.'

I went back to the gymnasium and lay down. Charles hadn't been wearing dark glasses, I suddenly realized; but then, it was the middle of the night. I felt very happy, I couldn't think why, as though a great weight had been lifted from my mind. As I drifted off to sleep, I thought how right Charles had been to say we were always in each other's thoughts. I'd been so sure he was queer, and now it seemed he wasn't after all; I must have been worrying about it all those months, that's why I felt so relieved.

When I looked round for him in the morning I couldn't find him. There were several thousand of us, so it wasn't very surprising. I stood by the roadside as the March left the town and headed towards Maidenhead, watching everyone troop by, sure I'd be able to pick Charles out. But I missed him somehow. I kept up the search on and off all morning, dropping back through the columns or surging ahead of them, but there was still no sign of him. After lunch I again stood by the roadside and watched the whole procession go past, but again there was no Charles. It was most mysterious. I decided he must have got disenchanted. As he'd said, he wasn't fond of groups. I hastily rejoined my love-affair; there was a sinisterly good-looking rival on my end of the banner, and everyone was singing, 'Free beer for all the workers.' I joined in, singing, as far as it was possible, sceptically.

4

After that night in Reading I felt that there might perhaps be some truth in Charles's suggestion that we hadn't ever simply liked each other, and that the tensions and dramatic revelations of our recent meetings were caused by some emotional entanglement which went back to our schooldays. Whatever that entanglement had been, I now felt free of it. My sense of relief persisted beyond the gymnasium, and I thought that Charles's absence on the following day perhaps meant that he too felt we had no further need to meet. He had always been an alarming figure in my life, even in the days when I'd worshipped him. He'd been so much cleverer than I, so much older for his age, so much more sophisticated. And later he'd seemed to threaten me with my own lack of assurance, had suggested possibilities within me which I didn't wish to recognize. Now I felt that he couldn't threaten me again. He had been mild, amusing, quite unalarming in the moonlit playground, and we had talked as equals. After all, I had succeeded at something; the chronic sense of inferiority which he had always inflicted on me had given way to a first small confidence in myself as myself. If my life had been nothing but preparation, a series of schools, training camps and colleges, now it had begun to have some purpose. In the summer holidays before I joined the Navy I had written a terrible verse play, a farewell to childhood; in the year before I left for America I wrote two dreadful novels, farewells to a protracted adolescence. Neither, mercifully, was published.

I might not have much to say yet, I realized, but I had the will to say it and I trusted myself to do so competently. I could guess what Charles's reaction would be to anything I wrote, but it worried me much less than it once would have done. When I came back to England, it would be as an experienced, travelled, educated man. And perhaps America would even show me what I was going to do with my life.

It didn't quite do that, of course, but it did show me much else. The social class from which Charles and I came puts a very high value on self-control. It considers the inhibition of inconvenient feeling to be the mark of a civilized man. Perhaps it once was – at least, not of a civilized man so much as of an empire-builder or an administrator. In America I came to realize that I was neither, and that most of the values I'd grown up with were irrelevant to me. Further, the intellectual class to which I belonged – which read the weeklies and taught and discussed books and politics and went to plays and had opinions – this class, too, was inhibited, by a coterie smugness which created an ennervating imaginative timidity. I began to see both the hothouse academic life of Oxford and the refrigerated literary life of London as extraordinarily provincial. Not before time I realized that there were other standards of value besides those of All Souls and the *New Statesman*. (I had failed to get into the first, though the second had published a poem.) Excellent though both these were in many ways, they were also distinctly and depressingly parochial.

I didn't, of course, see all this the moment I stepped off the *Queen Elizabeth*, and America was not all exhilaration and universality. A friend at Yale once said that what he liked most about England was that it was possible there to have privacy without loneliness, which it wasn't in the United States. He was right. I soon found that loneliness is one of the concomitants of the freedom America gives its visitors; and I suspect that everyone has moments when the self-discovery which America encourages (at least in foreigners) turns to self-disgust. But I usually had only to drive out of the town in which I was staying to feel better. The landscape enthralled me, the size of it, its variety and splendour. I travelled widely; I went from New Haven to Cambridge, Massachusetts, to Washington; through the South to Austin, Texas; through the West to California. And there, for a summer, I stopped. First, there was work to do at the Huntington Library in San Marino; then – well, it was time I stopped somewhere and took a long look at it. Why not Los Angeles?

I could not, I suppose, have chosen a worse American city to observe. Los Angeles is too big for anyone even to try to comprehend, and I knew virtually no one to whom to turn for guidance. The sun shone daily, but the smog filtered out its goodness. There was the beach, it was true; but I grow very bored on a beach by myself. There were the movies; but I could see them anywhere, and conducted tours through the studios didn't appeal to me. Eventually I settled into a stupid, bar-drifting, semi-Bohemian semi-campus life, where people said 'Man!' to each other a good deal and did no work. A new novel, written in Washington and revised in Austin, was accepted for English publication, which gave me a certain minor status in this world, but I was extremely bored most of the time, and I cannot now think why I didn't leave. Perhaps I thought I ought to loaf about for a bit to find out what loafing was like. I took a summer school course at UCLA to see what that was like, too; the teacher was splendid, but I felt like one of the housewives in the class who confessed that she was taking the course to keep herself busy. America had expanded my horizons all right, but Los Angeles did nothing to help me fill them with purposeful life. The sheer size of the place made me shrink further within myself; my poems became very formal, full of conceits and private references. I longed each day for the mail, lived only in letters.

One evening I was invited to a party given by two graduate students from the University of Southern California. She was writing on Smollett, he was 'in' Physics. They lived in a small apartment in Venice West. At that time Venice was full of beatniks, bearded, self-consciously dirty men and carefully sloppy women who talked without humour about the horrors of the American way of life and quoted cryptic Zen Buddhist injunctions in the translations of Allen W Watts and DT Suzuki. Poets and novelists were their heroes – Ginsberg, Corso, Kerouac, Burroughs – and they smoked marijuana almost on principle and were extremely pleased when people made offensive remarks about them in the street. Their refusal to join in conventional American life was, I suppose, theoretically admirable; but the beats I knew were too muddled or lazy to enunciate anything approaching an alternative philosophy. They seemed to be sleepwalking through life, to be living only as symbols of revolt, never as revolutionaries. America is full of contradictions. In a curious way these people were utterly conventional, conforming nonconformists, predictable in thought, word and deed. Their life was just as sterile and stereotyped as the one they vilified. I sometimes felt that they'd been invented by *Life* magazine for the convenience of its moralists. A livelier beat life, everyone said, could be found in San Francisco. I could believe that, without wanting to find out whether or not it was true.

Irma Jean and her boyfriend were not beats, but they lived on the fringes of the beat world and used to boast about the pot they smoked and the sexual freedom they permitted each other. Both were dutifully bisexual, solemnly making it outside the conventional postures and then reporting proudly back about how great it was. They claimed that they were never jealous, but jealousy might at least have demonstrated that there was some real feeling between them. There was sadly little sign of that. I felt they lived together only because they wanted to appear emancipated, but that may have been unfair. They were college students, after all, and one apartment is cheaper than two; perhaps the real basis of their *ménage* was like that of any primitive marriage, simply economic. In any case, they were friendly, and I knew few enough people who invited me to parties, even if they did expect me to bring my own 99-cent jug of Gallo wine.

The evening was sedate to begin with and grew only mildly more animated as it progressed. There were twenty or thirty people there, all connected with one or other of the local universities, and we danced and drank and occasionally argued about the deterioration in Ernest Hemingway's novels or John F Kennedy's chances of carrying California in November. Then several things happened quickly.

First, there was a loud report from the street, followed by screams. We rushed to the windows and saw, by the street-lights, a policeman putting his gun back in his holster and a youth in jeans and a T-shirt sitting on the pavement clutching his stomach.

'My God!' said Irma Jean. 'They've shot him!'

The policeman went up to the boy and stood over him, holding off the excited crowd which came running up. 'Pulled a knife on me,' we heard him explaining. Within two minutes a police car arrived, followed by an ambulance. The boy was lifted into the ambulance, the doors were shut. The ambulance and the police car drove away, wailing. In five minutes all trace of the sudden violence had gone.

Speculating wildly about the incident, we came away from the windows and got on with the party. Some people argued fiercely that the cops were trigger-happy; others said the crime-rate in Los Angeles was the worst in the world. Without anyone quite noticing, new guests arrived. They were bearded and sandalled and wore dark glasses, and Irma Jean's physicist said, 'Christ, who asked those crumb-bums?' No one, it seemed;

but one of them had once slept with Irma Jean and she felt it wouldn't be polite to ask him to take his friends away again.

'Man!' said this beat. 'We heard the gunfire and figured that's where the action was, so here we are, Irma Jean, baby.'

'Fix yourself a drink,' she said sourly.

One of the new arrivals, I thought, was looking at me in a definitely hostile manner. His beard was only about a month old and he wore a motorcycle cap pulled over his eyes, but I was sure I'd not seen him before. I supposed he was irritated, as people sometimes were, by something reproachably English in my appearance. It was extraordinary how sarcastic people could get about my accent, too; it was almost as annoying as being asked to repeat orders to waitresses because they thought I sounded so like Ronald Colman, a film star I wasn't sure I'd ever actually seen.

I glared back at the hostile beat, then turned to the television set. Irma Jean, who had fantasies about being avant-garde, said she hated television as it was, but that it had great potentiality as a purely abstract art-form. If you turned off the sound and just left the picture, she said, it was like having a two-dimensional mobile in your room. In the mobile a man was angrily thumping on the bonnet of a 1956 Buick. Then he moved to a 1957 Pontiac and thumped on that. His mouth opened and shut, opened and shut. I didn't think much of Irma Jean's new art-form, but I could see at once that the man was selling used cars; he looked exactly like the Republican candidate for President.

When I looked up for someone to tell this to, I saw the beat was still looking at me, though now he seemed more contemptuous than angry. As I caught his eye, he gave me a big wink. Then he began to shoulder over towards me.

I was still as bad at putting names to faces as I had been when I first went to school, and the beard, cap and dark glasses combined to make almost no feature recognizable.

Possibilities flashed through my mind; another Harkness fellow, gone native? An acquaintance from the ship? Someone from Harvard or the Folger? And then, suddenly, the nose stood boldly out from all the paraphernalia of the face, almost nude in its self-assertion. It was Charles.

'Pussy cat, pussy cat, where have you been?' he said. 'I've been looking all over America for you, man.'

'What on earth are you doing in that absurd outfit?' I said.

He looked furious. 'Don't bug me, Julian. Don't you try to put me down.' The beat language sounded ludicrous in his English accent, even though he'd obviously tried to modify it. It was the first time in my life, I think, that I'd ever said something which put him out. I wasn't surprised that he was sensitive, though. He looked wholly unconvincing. He wore the obligatory levis with a thick leather belt, motorcycle boots, and a leather jacket open to show that he had no shirt or vest beneath it. His thumbs were in the belt, and he stood with his legs apart, glowering through his dark glasses. His beard was uneven; there was quite a thicket on his lips and chin, but almost nothing on his cheeks. I thought he looked absolutely grotesque, like someone got up for charades in someone else's clothes.

'If you wanted to find me,' I said, 'all you had to do was write care of the Commonwealth Fund.'

'Find you? Why should I want to find you? Why should I ever want to set eyes on you again?'

'You said you'd been looking for me.'

'Christ, I was only being friendly. And all you can do is try to bug me. Right off. Why the hell do you have to keep cropping up in my life?'

'Well,' I said. 'I was invited here, actually. Were you?'

I thought for a moment he was going to hit me. Then he suddenly relaxed and said, 'Man, you sure have been growing confidence out here in the Californian sunshine, haven't you? Do you still have your navel?'

'No, they made me hand it in at the state border.'

'Wisecracks, yet! How's the thesis, Mr Oxford?'

'Broody. No sign of hatching. How's your pretty sister?'

That threw him completely. I enjoyed watching him flounder. 'She's OK.' He looked round, then he said, 'We can't talk here. Where's your pad?'

'My apartment's on Sawtelle. It's not far.'

'I know where Sawtelle is, thanks.'

'Want to come over?'

'Sure. This scene has nothing, but nothing. Let's split.'

I thanked Irma Jean for a nice party and for the impromptu cabaret in the street; the 'happening' hadn't yet been invented, or we might all have been congratulating her on her originality.

Irma Jean thought I was callous. 'I hope that poor kid'll be O.K., that's all.' She was a wife and mother at heart. 'But what's the rush? The party's only just getting going.'

'I have to go, I'm afraid. I mean, I have to split.'

'Well, take care of yourself.'

When Charles and I were out in the street I said, 'Where's the motorbike, then?'

'I haven't got one.'

'Oh. Then we'll take my car. You can sit in the back seat and pretend you're riding pillion.'

'Listen,' said Charles in his natural English accent, 'I have not come halfway round the world to be mocked by you or anyone else. I don't give a shit what you think about my clothes, but if they bother you so much, let's just say good night and go our ways, shall we?'

'Get in,' I said. 'I promise not to come *The Tailor and Cutter* over you if you don't like it.' He got in, slamming the door loudly. 'What *have* you come halfway round the world for, may I ask?'

'I haven't the faintest idea.' He switched on the radio and found a station playing cool jazz.

'Did you ditch Mr Schatz?'

'No, he ditched me. I was sent out here on a fool's errand to look at some starlets for a movie he had no intention of making. Really he was about to switch studios, and the new studio had all sorts of new assistant assistants lined up for him – they were part of the deal. But he liked me, he said, so he got the old studio to take me on temporarily, so I'd be on their books, not his, when he quit. Of course, as soon as the news broke, they fired me.'

'I remember you saying what a fascinating, creative life it was in the movies.'

'Oh, I was properly named, a right Charlie. I should have realized something was wrong when he started being so goddam nice. All movie producers are crude, dishonest, insensitive, corpulent, ulcerous bastards, and strictly incredible.'

'Ah, well, you have the satisfaction of knowing you'll give them what they deserve in your novels, when you write them.'

'No one would ever believe me. The critics would say it was all dated satire and that I lacked the ability to draw convincing, lifelike characters. There's no one like a novel reviewer for ignorance of actual life.'

'You sound bitter.'

'No. I just happen to have met several novel reviewers. I've even reviewed a few novels myself. It's not a career for anyone who wants to do any living.'

I thought, in my innocence, that it would be rather exciting to review novels, but it wasn't the time to say so. We drove in silence for a while. I wanted to know why Charles was dressed as a beatnik, what he thought he was doing, where he was living, everything. But I also wanted him to tell me himself. I wondered why he'd been so anxious for us to be alone together.

'Who were your friends?' I said at last.

'Who were yours?'

'Academic epigoni.'

'What's that supposed to mean?' Before I could answer, he went on in a sudden rush: 'Don't be clever with me, Julian, for God's sake. I've had all I can take of people being clever, including myself.'

'Is something the matter?'

'Of course it is. When isn't it?' Then he muttered something I didn't hear.

'What did you say?'

'I said I should have got the hell out of that party the moment I saw you.'

'I'm glad you didn't. I'm sick of LA. I admit I didn't recognize you at first, but when I did, I was honestly more pleased than I've been for months.'

'Is that on the level?'

'Yes. You're awfully suspicious tonight.'

'You didn't exactly show you were pleased.' He sprawled back and put his feet up against the windscreen. 'You want to know why I'm here, don't you? You want reasons for everything, right? You got a first from Oxford, so you think there always has to be a rational explanation for even the most irrational act. Well, I'll tell you. I'm here because this is where I got fired, and I didn't see any point in running home to mother. In any case my mother – the real one – is dead.'

'Charles, I am sorry. Really I am.'

'Why? You didn't know her. You don't even know if I liked her. I'm not even sure myself.'

I tried to remember what she looked like, and failed. I never had got his parents straight in my mind.

'When did it happen?' I asked.

'Last September. My stepfather's already thinking about marrying again. So that my little stepbrother can have a mother-substitute, of course, only for that. Bruce is fourteen.'

'Your mother must have been very young.'

'Fifty-two. She smoked too much – forty cigarettes a day. Everyone told her to cut down, but she couldn't. Or wouldn't.'

'Will you allow me to say that I'm sorry if you're sorry?'

'There's no point in being sorry. People die. There's nothing so very awful about it. Anyhow, forget her. I was telling you why I'm here because you wanted to know, though it's none of your business. I was fired in May. Where are we now?'

'July the twenty-third.'

'Really? I thought it must be getting on for October.'

'Charles, what *are* you doing here?'

He shifted his feet slightly. 'Nothing. I don't mean negatively nothing, but positively nothing. I've been trying to stop thinking.'

'About anything in particular?'

'Don't be *clever*, damn it!' He crashed his feet back down on the floor of the car. 'That's exactly what I'm trying to get away from, that kind of quick, slick answer, that easy payments attitude to life. Anyone with the right IQ can be clever like that, anyone.'

We came to my apartment house in West Los Angeles. I had two bedrooms, a living-room, bathroom and kitchen, which belonged to an Italian professor at UCLA who'd gone away for the summer. The second bedroom meant I could have friends to stay, I thought. So far none had come or shown any signs of coming.

'Are you still not drinking?' I asked as we went in.

'Do you have any milk?'

I went to get him some and fix myself a bourbon on the rocks. My passion for America didn't allow me Scotch. Americans couldn't understand that at all, and now, neither can I. When I came back into the living-room with the drinks he was pacing up and down. He took the milk and put it down at once on top of the TV set. I worried a lot about the professor's furniture, so I put a newspaper under the glass. Charles watched me with a pitying smile.

'What am I doing here?' he said.

'I don't know. You were telling me.'

'I shouldn't have come. You're exactly the kind of person I don't want to be – satisfied, conventional, successful – none of that interests me. You think you're contented, so you are. But what do you feel?'

'Feel?'

'You see! You don't even know what the word means. You keep your milk in the ice-box so it won't taste real, and you don't leave rings on the furniture in case it might look as though someone actually used it!'

'Don't be ridiculous. It's eighty every day here. The milk'd turn sour if it wasn't kept cool. And it's not my apartment. I don't want a large bill for damages when I leave.'

'Reasons! Reasons! What do you think actually matters in life? What's it all about? What's it for?'

'I don't think it's *for* anything. The question is meaningless.'

'Great! It's meaningless. So it doesn't exist, and you don't have to answer it. You've taken out your slide-rule and it doesn't measure up. You've defined it away. You live behind glass like a – like an abstract picture. You have two dimensions and you hang on a wall. You're a family portrait and you'll marry another family portrait and you'll have lots of pretty miniatures for children and they'll grow up to be family portraits just like you. Wonderful!'

'I don't see how I can be both an abstract and a family portrait.'

'Good, good, you jump on inconsistencies! Excellent! Man, you've had a great education – the best! IBM will love you, they'll give you fifty thousand dollars a year to programme other people. You're sound, reliable, solid, you have common sense, you'll go a long way.'

'Charles, do sit down and stop ranting.'

'Ranting! Now there's a very good word, a beautiful word. People who rant aren't sound and reliable, are they? So you don't have to listen to them, do you? Isn't life simple!'

'Not very. Do sit down.'

'I don't like to sit, I like to move around. Movement, that's what keeps me going. I know, I know! It's illogical, it's contradictory, I don't use words correctly. But I don't *care*, baby, I don't care. It's true, that's why I say it. I *feel* it, so it's true.'

'It's perfectly all right by me. I'm not a modern philosopher.'

'Oh yes you are! Don't kid yourself. You're swathed in all that logic and reason, you're wrapped in it like a mummy, you can't move they've swaddled you so tight, so you won't have to feel. Rich people have money to protect them, you have intelligence. One day perhaps – probably, in fact – your intelligence will make you rich, and then you'll be able to afford double-glazing, two thicknesses of window between you and the stink and bellow of reality. You'll be able to watch it in comfort, take notes on it, invent theories, write books and publish them – oh, it'll be a lovely life, a marvellous life! And you'll never have lived for one single sensitive moment! Great!'

He sat down abruptly, then leapt up again and took his glass of milk. He drank half of it and shuddered. 'Cold milk, cold heart,' he said.

'When did you start on all this anti-reason?'

'When did I see reason for what it is, you mean? I don't know.' He sat down again. I was relieved. It had been like watching a tennis match while he paced up and down. 'I suppose I've known all along that people were holding back on something – I mean, masters at school, parents, dons, all the people who were supposed to prepare me for life. They were teaching me things they didn't really believe themselves, though they didn't know that. They thought they believed them. But their own behaviour was so different from what they expected of me that I got suspicious. *They* could be bad-tempered for no reason, *they* could say things I wasn't allowed to – they punished me if I said them. So there was something about life I wasn't being let in on, something which scared people, only they wouldn't admit to being scared. When I found out about sex, I thought it must be that. It was, too, up to a point. But it wasn't *just* sex – that's where this whole crazy century's gone wrong. It was the depth of feeling sex reveals, the whole irrational, blind, driving bundle of forces which make us love and hate and kill and protect – all the battery of violent instincts. They're what frightens people. So they don't talk about them, they don't let children know, they tell them to wash their hands after shitting, instead. Very wise, very sanitary. And it makes a natural act seem dirty, unmentionable. Good, good, we've built in another automatic defence against feeling.'

'I don't see why you shouldn't enjoy your shitting *and* wash your hands afterwards,' I said. 'And anyway, toilet-training's psychologically much more important than that, it –'

'I don't want to know. Man has a soul as well as a mind and a body. You live by the mind alone, with an occasional ten minutes for the dirty business of the body. You've abandoned your soul because it scares you.'

'There was a time when you thought the word "soul" wasn't very useful.'

'True, true. But I'm not afraid to use it now. Or of being sentimental. I used to dread being sentimental. You think sentimentality's a crime, don't you?'

'Not a crime, no. But it fuzzes the outlines of things. I like things to be clear, not distorted.'

He jumped up again. 'But that's exactly it! You want things to be clear, so that you can understand them, pin them down like safe, dead butterflies. But sentimentality, being sentimental, having feelings at all – they *all* distort things. They muddle them up, they're not rational. But they're *real*. They're the only reality we have!'

'If you're simply saying that we can't be certain that anything exists outside our own consciousness, of course that's –'

'I'm not simply saying anything! I'm feeling!'

We argued for hours that night, though it wasn't exactly argument. Charles refused to argue, he said it simply entangled him in a lot of artificial ways of thinking. He asserted, sometimes explaining why he felt it right to assert, but to any protest I made he just said I was refusing to let myself feel.

There are few things more irritating than to be accused of inadequate feeling, even when one suspects that one may perhaps, on a certain subject, feel less than other people. At that time I was very bored with my life, and boredom can often be caused by the absence of anything to feel strongly about. That, I think, was my condition. It wasn't that I didn't have strong feelings, only that I had nothing with which to engage them. Sometimes, at night, they came howling after me, demanding their release, and I struggled to put them on paper. But they wanted to be free, not caged. I would sweat and strain with them, weep with frustration, tear my notebooks in half, even shout and throw things. I would force myself to get drunk to shut them up. Next morning I would gather the notebooks together again and wonder what had hit me. But mostly, in Los Angeles, a lotus-eating indifference kept me quiet and my feelings lay like after-dinner dogs in a kennel of idleness. So, while I denied Charles's caricature of me as a hand-sewn, hidebound, English digest of other people's opinions who said nothing but 'It all depends on what you mean by feeling' – although I knew I wasn't this fantastic projection of what he disliked in himself, I sympathized with some of what he said, and was fascinated by the spectacle of his deliberate revolt. I told him I thought his was an intellectual rebellion against intellect, which he almost admitted, and that given an intellect like his it couldn't succeed, which he naturally denied. But I didn't tell him what I most strongly felt; that I thought he would go mad if he kept it up.

He told me a few things about his life. He slept wherever he was invited, having no place of his own; his visa allowed him to stay in the United States for several more months; he had enough money not only to get by but to get back to England when he had to. His mother, he said, had left him a thousand pounds, none of which he had touched.

'I'm thinking of going East.'

'To New York?'

'No, the Far East. West from here. I want to go to Japan, of course, and see this Zen business actually working. And I have a thing about the Siamese. They're so brown and small and sexy. I want to have lots of Siamese sex. Have you ever had a Siamese?'

'Not so much as a cat. Or a twin.'

'That was a terrible magazine you ran,' he said. '*Gemini*! Twin punks!'

It became very late, but he showed no sign of leaving, rather the opposite. He looked round the apartment as if he'd like to move in with me. After his first assault on me and everything he claimed I stood for, he seemed pleased to see me again. He said so several times. I was amused, and reminded him that he'd said he had no reason ever to set eyes on me again. That gave him the chance to hold forth about the necessity for having contradictory feelings. To stop him talking I asked him if he wanted to stay the night. He said he did.

The second bedroom was the Italian professor's children's nursery, and it had ducks and rabbits and other animals printed in bright colours on the washable wallpaper. Charles was delighted and quoted Wordsworth. I left him clucking at the hen above his pillow.

When I woke next day at noon, he had gone, leaving no message. Only the milk-stained glass and the rumpled bed proved that his appearance had not been one of the violent fantasies with which loneliness sometimes assailed me. I assumed he'd been moved by some sudden, insistent 'feeling' to get away, and I wondered, as I drank my frozen orange juice

(I was too lazy to squeeze my own, and I was glad Charles didn't know that), whether I would see him again in Los Angeles. I thought probably not.

But I was wrong. For the next few weeks, before I left for San Francisco and then went back East for the winter, I saw Charles irregularly but often. He arrived one day with his suitcases and asked if I'd look after them for him. From time to time he came and took away clean socks and underpants and left dirty ones. Without saying anything, I took these to the launderette with my own. He seemed to need my company, too. The beat life he had adopted obviously failed to come up to his expectations, whatever they may have been, but I was there for him to come and berate for an outlook I didn't actually hold, and attacking me he was able to persuade himself that his way of life was superior. Also, perhaps, he came simply for respite. He was driving himself by pure will-power to submit to a freewheeling, haphazard, sadly rather pointless existence and he found it, I think, mentally more exhausting to suppress his natural intelligence than he would admit. I played the role he assigned me, watched, evaluated, drew my own conclusions. I admired his perversity. I knew I would never be able to keep up a self-deception like that even for twenty-four hours, and I couldn't help envying the stamina which had kept him going for almost three months. And it wasn't simply self-deception, I decided. Though I was critical, I could see that Charles was involved in something necessary to him, that the funny hats and conscious attitudes were the decor of a genuine drama. He, who complained how everyone else sought protection from reality, had some inner reality from which he was trying to protect himself. I didn't know what this could be, and facilely attributed his confusion to the death of his mother.

Occasionally he took me into the beat world. There were parties and orgies and a lot of pot-smoking and bad verse; but it wasn't my kind of life and I was soon, in any case, having an affair within my own world, a skirmish with love which I took very seriously and which precluded, I felt, involvement in orgies. Charles said I was much too rational about it, and he may have been right; but I still preferred to love one person at a time.

It will not come as a surprise to anyone who has read a novel called As Far As You Can Go that the character there called Eddie Jackson was based at some distance on Charles, or that some of the book's scenes of looseish Californian living are fairly faithful accounts of the society in which he moved. It was Charles for instance who first took me to the Watts Towers, then little known, now something of a cult among admirers of the primitive. Eddie Jackson became, in the writing, less and less like Charles and more and more fascinating to me as an imaginary character, until he began to upset the whole balance of the book and I had to make him drive on to the wrong lane of a freeway to a spectacular death. I discussed a similar, real death with Charles one day and he said he thought no one ever did things like that unless he wanted to, and that it was a great way to go. I argued for the possibility of genuine error, but he said I didn't understand how people worked. Perhaps I didn't. I certainly found him baffling. But then he was trying to baffle himself. Like Irma Jean and her boyfriend he made such a strenuous point of his indifference to the gender of his lovers that I began to wonder if he had any real sexual impulse at all – if his sex wasn't, in fact, hysterical or factitious or narcissistic, a way of communing with himself. Remembering what he'd said at Cambridge about the advantages of mirror-glasses, I asked him whether or not he kept his eyes open these days. He looked suspicious and said he didn't know, he was too caught up in the total self-commitment of the act to notice. I continued to wonder if it might not really be self-containment. I always knew when my eyes were open, and I have always been thoroughly sceptical of men who talk about committing themselves in the sexual act. They make me think of people committing themselves to God through some devotion-monger like Billy Graham. My own sex is never like that, and I distrust all intermediaries, preaching or silent.

Charles and I were both twenty-five then, and it was exactly half our lifetimes since we'd last seen so much of each other. I couldn't help reflecting on how our roles had changed. At school, Charles had been my leader, I his disciple; he had been the man of the world, I the innocent. Now I felt that he was trying to regain an innocence that perhaps he'd never had, while I acted as his corrupt, worldly advocate of compromise for happiness. Sometimes he made me feel like a mother who believes in letting her child find out for himself the harshness of the world and the spuriousness of its panaceas. I was the home to which he could return to nurse his wounds. I didn't mind playing mother, knowing I was nothing of the sort, and I let him talk without paying very much attention to what he said, believing that what he most needed then was a listener, someone who would accept his experiment as necessary for him and who wouldn't nag him to conform. When I refused some of his invitations to participation in beatnik rites, I think he was relieved; when I did accompany him, I felt he was constrained, that my presence prevented him from letting himself go. He was trying to force himself to be free, and I made him self-conscious.

At the end of August I told him I was leaving for San Francisco on September the fifth, and suggested he came with me. He seemed tempted, but then declined, saying he was all right where he was, thank you, he dug the LA scene. I asked him in that case to please remove his suitcases before I left.

'Sure,' he said. 'There's plenty of time.'

Then he disappeared. I have a maddening habit of being a day or two ahead of myself, and by the morning of September the fourth I was ready to go. I planned to take the coast road through Santa Barbara and Big Sur, a long, winding drive. An extra day would have been welcome. But I still had to give Charles his cases.

I telephoned round the few friends of his I knew, but they were unhelpful. In any case, many beats refused to have the telephone, either because they couldn't afford it or because they objected to it on principle; in some cases, I daresay, the telephone company had equally strong principles about them. I pinned a note for Charles to the door of my apartment and set out to find him.

Venice was built as an early twentieth-century folly, complete with baroque hotels and bridges and canals. It was in a sad state of decay by 1960, however, inhabited mainly by old people on small pensions and the beats, its grandiloquent architecture crumbling, the paint flaking, the whole bombastic enterprise exposed as a rickety piece of commercial speculation. I tried everywhere I knew, and some places I didn't know – the bars, normal, queer and lesbian (the ladies played pool), the beach, the few apartments I remembered. Only the beach was attractive; everything else smelt of poverty, pretension and failure. No one had seen Charles for days. I took a last dip in the Pacific, watching the roller-coaster's heave and swell from the heave and swell of the ocean. Then I went back to my apartment. The note was unopened.

By ten o'clock that evening I was furious. It was not, I felt passionately, the act of a friend to leave me in this awkward position – I trusted none of *his* friends to look after the cases for him. I had half a mind to dump them outside the door, where they would almost certainly be stolen. But I knew perfectly well that Charles knew I wouldn't do that, and was probably trading on the fact, just as he knew that I would now be furious and was probably laughing at me somewhere. I was, he'd say, the complete bourgeois, who worried about property instead of yielding to my true feeling and letting the bags look after themselves. Recognizing that there was some truth in this made me angrier still.

I went to bed, meaning to get up early next morning and leave the cases with Irma Jean, whether she wanted them or not. Another note on the door would explain what I'd done. It was an obvious solution, easily achieved, and yet I still felt furious, as though Charles had deliberately let me down. Naturally I couldn't sleep. It seemed an unusually hot night and I kept imagining footsteps which might be Charles's. The previous night I'd ended my affair – or rather, said a tentatively temporary goodbye. Now there was no reason why I shouldn't have luxuriated in the tragedy of farewell for another twenty-four hours. I could, crudely, have been having sex right that minute. I fumed and fretted under the sheet, knowing that now I'd be certain to start late, probably with a headache.

At last I got up to take a cold shower, but as soon as I switched on the water I thought I heard the doorbell. I hadn't, of course, but the thrumming of the water *might* cause me to miss it, so I abandoned the idea of a shower and looked for something to eat or drink. There was nothing left in the apartment but orange juice and milk. I wanted bourbon; I even began to hanker after Scotch. Finally I bored myself back to bed and went to sleep.

The doorbell rang at four in the morning. When I saw what time it was I almost decided to let it ring, but of course I didn't.

'You took a hell of a long time to answer,' said Charles.

'Here they are,' I said, thrusting the cases at him. 'And why in God's name didn't you collect them earlier? I wanted to leave this morning.'

'Well, it's not even dawn yet.'

'I mean yesterday morning.'

'You said today.'

'And can't I be inconsistent too? Do you have a monopoly on instinctive behaviour and changing your mind?'

'You should have gone if you wanted to.'

'I know I should. I wish I had. Do you realize what time it is?'

He shook his head vaguely. He didn't care about the positions of the hands on clocks, he said once, unless they were aesthetically pleasing. He pushed past me, saying, 'Mind if I come in for a minute?'

'Yes, I do mind,' I said, banging the door furiously. 'I was asleep. I want to go back to sleep so that I can start at seven o'clock without feeling completely washed out.' I was too angry to notice that he looked even paler than usual.

'I wanted to talk to you about that.'

'Have you changed your mind? Do you want to come with me?'

'No. Have you got any milk?'

'You know where it is.' I spoke automatically. Then my anger came boiling back. 'No, damn it! That's my breakfast milk! You bloody well can't have it.'

'Is something bugging you?' he said, surprised.

'Look, Charles, I'm tired, I'm getting up early in the morning. Unless you have something very important to say, I'd be grateful if you'd kindly remove your cases and yourself.'

'Oh, but I do. That's why I'm here. I don't want you to go. I want you to stay here.'

'I'm honoured, flattered, thrilled. But I'm afraid my plans are made. I'm a square, a fink, a terrible bore, but I'm not changing them for you or anyone else.'

'I wish you would,' he said. He started pacing up and down. 'Hell, what do you want to go fart-arsing about in San Francisco for? Why be a tourist? Stay here and get to know something about the place.'

'I know all I want to, thanks.'

'You don't know anything. You don't even know what happened to that boy who got shot the night I found you.'

'Well, do you?'

'Yes. He's still in hospital.'

'What's that got to do with anything?'

'You should take a deeper interest in the life around you.'

'Jesus Christ,' I said, 'for God knows how long you've done nothing but tell me to explore myself.'

'I felt for that kid, so I found out what had happened to him. You saw he was shot, but you didn't even feel enough to wonder whether or not he was still alive.'

'Well, thanks for telling me, and I'm glad he is. But I didn't know anything about the case. What *I* feel is that the Los Angeles police shoot altogether too many people every day.'

'Good, good – you worry about an abstract number, not about individuals.'

I was too weary for another harangue. 'I'm going to bed. If you want to sleep here, you're welcome. I left the sheets on the bed, in case you turned up. But you'll have to go when I go in the morning. Good night.'

'Wait a minute. I haven't finished.'

'I know you haven't. But I've heard it all before and tonight I just don't want to hear it again.'

'But I must talk to you – seriously.'

'I'm sorry, Charles. You should have come earlier. I spent the whole bloody day trying to find you.'

'Someone said you'd been looking for me. He thought you were from the FBI. I was in Pasadena.'

'That shows how clever your friend is, him and the rest of that bunch of paranoid schizophrenic layabouts you hang around with. Now I really am going to bed. Good night.'

I went into my bedroom, shut the door and hung up my dressing-gown. I had barely got under the sheet when Charles came in.

'Julian,' he said, 'if you leave me tomorrow, it will be the greatest betrayal of your life.'

'Oh, will it? Too bad.'

'You just can't do it.'

I pulled the sheet over my head and groaned. 'Charles, we are old and dear friends, and in the name of our friendship, will you please let me go to sleep?'

He sat on the end of the bed. 'You must listen. I need you. I need you desperately. I can't go on without you.'

I have said that I thought Charles might drive himself mad if he kept up his beat charade too long. Now I sat up and looked at him, wondering if the crisis had come.

He smiled and said, 'Don't you wear pyjamas? I always imagined you did.'

'Well, you were wrong. Now what is all this?'

'I want you to stay, to help me see this thing through. You're the only person who understands me, who knows why I *have* to see it through. I can't do it alone.'

'Then why are you doing it at all?'

'Because – because, because. When I found you that night I was about to chuck the whole thing. But then you were there, and it was worth going on after all, to show you. I couldn't just show myself.'

'But you have shown me. I admire your perseverance, even though I think the whole idea's crazy.'

'It's not crazy. It's never been crazy. I'm finding things out all the time – about myself, I mean. That's why you've got to stay. I'm getting scared. I don't trust myself not to panic and – I have to have someone I can – You're like a stone I can come and touch to make sure I'm still alive and that it isn't all hallucinations.'

'What isn't?'

'Everything.' He was twisting and plucking at the sheet. 'Julian, I'm violent, I want to hurt people – torture them – kill them, perhaps. I – I dream about the concentration camps.' He pulled open his leather jacket and bared his chest. Round his neck he was wearing a silver chain; on the end of it hung a swastika. 'There's a – a gang in Pasadena. They have initiations

– torture – beating – branding. I *like* it, Julian, I *like* it. And I keep dreaming about Auschwitz – about stripping all those – those people, and pushing them into the gas-chamber – I'm laughing and beating them in with the butt of a pistol and – I'm hard and – all those naked bodies – I –'

He began to cry. The swastika bumped on his chest as the sobs shook him. Then he buried his face in his hands. 'You mustn't go,' he whispered. 'Don't leave me.'

I hadn't then read the since-fashionable Marquis de Sade, and I knew nothing of the logic of anti-reason which allows the individual to do anything he wants because he wants it and denies the right of society to interfere with him in the pursuit of his pleasure. Now that I do know something of those inanities, I see, or think I see, how Charles came to the apparent revelation of his sadism. He had been pursuing a notion of pure feeling, of pure response, of action taken only at the prompting of desire. There can be no doubt that there are sadistic impulses in all of us. In his deliberate attempt to strip himself of all inhibitions, Charles inevitably discovered these impulses in himself; and felt obliged, by his principle of feeling, to let them drive him to their fulfilment. All of which sounds very pat as I reason it now. At the time I could only think of one thing – the newspaper photograph he had carefully smoothed on his thigh in our 'blue heaven', fifteen years before. Since then I had read many accounts of Auschwitz and Belsen and Dachau, and they had left me feeling, always, as I felt now – utterly helpless before the evil and madness in mankind. I believe that it was one of my deepest terrors that I, too, could be capable of such evil – a terror which I never acknowledged even in my dreams. Or if I dreamed it, at least my waking consciousness refused to let me know.

Now I stared at Charles with a dismay so profound that it moved him to forget his own. He raised his head from his hands. He had taken off his dark glasses. He tried to smile.

Then he put one hand on my leg and patted it several times. Neither of us said anything for a long time.

'You'd better come with me tomorrow,' I said at last. 'You'd better get away from here.'

'No. I can't run away.'

'It wouldn't be running away.' But I saw that for him it would.

'You see,' he said almost dreamily, 'I wanted to be the cop shooting that boy. That's why I went to the hospital to check up on him. I felt I'd done it myself.'

'That seems to show,' I said, trying to keep my voice normal, 'that you're not really a sadist at all.'

'You don't understand. Sadists torture till they feel tender towards the person they're torturing. It's their way of showing love.'

'Charles, the guards at Auschwitz didn't love the Jews.'

'They did, in a way. The Jews became necessary to them. Oh, I know it's crazy, but we're all crazy, one way or another, even you. What is love? No one knows. It's what binds people together. So the guards loved the Jews.'

'It's not true. It's just not true. And I don't believe you're a guard, or could ever be one.'

'I could. So could you.'

There was a long silence.

'What do you want me to do, Charles?'

'I want you to stay here. I don't know what I might not do if you went away.'

'For heaven's sake, don't you think this nonsense has gone on long enough? Don't you see what harm you're doing yourself? You can't make sense of your life by following every casual impulse – you have to choose between feelings, to do one thing and not another. We live in time and space. We can't do everything at once, we have to take account of other people. You can't carry on as though no one else exists.'

'I know all that. I'm not as stupid as you think. That's one of the things I've discovered – that I'm not happy living for myself.'

'Well, then, why go on? Where do you think you're going?'

'Nowhere.' He looked at me bleakly. 'Do you know what I sometimes think? That I have no feelings. There's a silence I can hear, a total, wonderful, absolute silence at the heart of all this chaos. That's where I'm going, that's where everyone goes. It's death. And I long for it.'

'Death? Two minutes ago you were –'

'They're all stages on the way, these feelings, violent or tender. When I was in Pasadena – before you can join, they make you undergo an initiation. They were childish in a way – the things they did to me, I mean. But I submitted. And it felt terribly – I mean terribly – restful, lying there, chained up, helpless, yielding. It was luxurious. I could hear the silence then. I wanted to go on hearing it for ever. I wanted to die.' He suddenly stood up and undid his belt. He pulled his trousers down and showed me a livid scar high up on his thigh. 'That's my death mark. I have only to look at it to remember how sweet the silence was.' He buckled himself up again.

'You should see a psychiatrist.'

'I knew you'd say that, sooner or later.' He sat down on the bed, closer to me. 'I want to – I've got to face the silence and come back again alive.'

'You'll kill yourself.'

'No – well, I may. It's the risk I run. But it's worth it. We hide death away these days, don't we? It's not nice, it's not decent. But how can we live if we don't face it? It's a fact of existence, like the circulation of our blood or the laws of thermodynamics. We shouldn't hide it, we should love it.'

'You're using your mind again,' I said, at a total loss.

'Yes. When I'm – when I saw the fear in – I've seen people looking at it, loving it. And that made me love them. I wanted to share their love.'

'I don't know what you mean. Love?'

'Yes, love.'

We stared at each other. His contact lenses were in, making his pupils unnaturally large. In the light of the bedside lamp his face was cavernous, the bones stark beneath the skin.

'Stay,' he said.

'I can't. Come with me.'

'No. This is where everything's happened. I shall go west from here, if I go anywhere.'

'I won't do any good by staying,' I said. 'I think you should see a doctor. You're not mad yet, but you're going mad. I can't do anything to help you.'

'You're here. That helps.'

'You're asking too much. You've done nothing for weeks but tell me how safe and unadventurous and afraid I am. Well, you're right. I am afraid – for myself. I won't stay.'

'I need you.'

'Your saying that only makes me feel more afraid. Fear is just as demanding a feeling as wanting to torture someone.'

'That won't last,' he said slowly, frowning as though at a discovery. 'I've been trying anything and everything. It's only a stage. There's nothing left to try except the silence.'

'That's absurd. You haven't tried life.'

'I can't do that till I've tried death. Don't you understand that?'

'You're mad! For God's sake come to San Francisco with me and give up this whole crazy nonsense.'

'No.'

I meant what I'd said. I was intolerably frightened. Watching him pondering his life and death on the edge of my bed, I felt almost violated, as though I was one of his masochist partners. I resisted him, I resisted the idea. I wasn't a masochist, I refused to be hung with his chains and swastika, to be branded with his mark.

I got out of bed and began to dress. He watched me with a curious smile.

'Where are you going so early in the morning?'

'San Francisco.'

I fetched my razor and toothbrush from the bathroom and shoved them into my open case. I looked quickly round. I'd forgotten my hairbrush and my bedside book. It was *The Naked Lunch* by William Burroughs; I'd bought it in Mexico. Charles caught my arm and looked at the title.

'You're really getting with it, aren't you?'

I pulled away from him and put the book and the hairbrush in the case and shut it. 'Are you coming or not?'

'No.'

And I left him there, and I left him there. I couldn't stay, it wasn't in me to stay. It was not a betrayal. I could not help myself. I did not believe I could help him. But I should have stayed. It would have made no difference, but I should have stayed.

I write this in Gloucestershire. It is a fine late September day. The leaves are just beginning to turn. I have only to lift my head to see the polled Hereford cattle browsing in the water-meadow below the house. The garden runs down to the River Colne. It is full of trout, slowly waving over patches of clear gravel in the sunlight. A few yards downstream from the end of the garden there is a low iron bridge. Below the bridge, under the shadow of a willow, lives a goldfish. You can see it at once. Even when it hides under the green weed, imagining itself invisible, you can spot its swift flickers of red and gold. No one knows how it got there. Perhaps it was a goggle-eyed prize in a clear plastic bag at a fairground, and the winner gave it its freedom. It could be a sport, a mutant. I like to think that it believes itself to be a trout like its neighbours in the pool. One day, in an excess of imitation, it may rise to a cunning fly and be caught. If not, it will go on imagining itself to be what it is not, till it falls victim at last to old age or an otter. Unless someone introduces another goldfish to the river, it will never be able to mate.

Charles had no children either.

When I arrived in New York at the beginning of October I went to the Commonwealth Fund headquarters on Fifth Avenue to pay my respects and collect my mail.

The girl who handed me my letters said, 'Did you sell your book to the movies, Mr Mitchell?'

'Alas not. It's not exactly a cinematic subject.'

'Oh, what a shame! We were all so excited, we thought you had it made.'

'Why? I wasn't in Los Angeles for movie-making, you know.'

'You mean they never got in touch with you?'

'I'm afraid I don't know what you're talking about.'

'You don't?' She seemed flabbergasted. 'But they called us all the way from Hollywood to ask for your address!'

'Who did?'

'Just a minute, I've got a record of it somewhere.'

My heart thundered with anticipation – could I be famous before I'd even been published? And with *Imaginary Toys*? It didn't seem possible.

'Perhaps I'd already left Los Angeles when they called,' I said hopefully.

'Oh, no, this was way back at the beginning of summer. Here we are – it was May sixteenth. A Mr Charles Humphries called from Twentieth Century Fox. He wanted to know where he could find you. We thought you'd hit the big time for sure!'

'No. No, it wasn't that. He was just a friend working there.'

'Are you feeling all right?' she said.

'Yes, thanks. You raised my hopes there for a moment. But thanks for telling me. Sorry we've both been disappointed.'

When Charles said he'd been looking for me, he actually had been. But why hadn't he come to find me? I was, by a fluke, in Los Angeles, he had my address. I didn't move my apartment. Why had he bothered to call coast-to-coast if he wasn't going to follow it up?

I worried about this on and off for months. Eventually I decided that he didn't, really, want to see me – only to know I was there. It was like him wanting me to stay in Los Angeles – I was a touchstone, someone to reassure him as to his own reality. My solidity, my reliability, were not, it seemed, as contemptible as he'd made them out.

Just after Christmas I got a postcard from Japan. It showed a picture of Hiroshima after the atom bomb, but on the back it said only, 'Mickey Mouse is a Jew'. I didn't know what it was supposed to mean, but I assumed Charles was more or less all right.

5

I had several more postcards from Charles; one from India, showing a complicated sexual posture from a temple sculpture, one from Egypt, a propaganda photograph of the destruction caused by the British in 1956; others from Siam, Malaya, Persia, Israel, Cyprus and Gibraltar. All were laconic, none gave an address. I took it that he had looked at death and decided against it, and I was glad if that was so.

I finished my second novel, *A Disturbing Influence*, in New York. Back home again, I took up Alfreda Urquhart's offer of a cottage in Amberley, Sussex, and started on my third. I also began to review books for *The Spectator* and to fancy myself as a literary figure, even though I was going back to Oxford in the autumn to finish, I hoped, my thesis.

I hated England for those first few months. The slowness, the indolence, the inefficiency drove me wild with frustration. Nothing worked properly, neither people nor things. The road-system was medieval, if that, the government Victorian, the rich stupid and the poor servile. I'd forgotten how stifling and sterile the class obsession was. In America I had felt free of all that; perhaps I exaggerated and romanticized my freedom, but even with its accompanying loneliness I infinitely preferred it to the studiously demarcated social life of home. There I felt I had been judged by what I said and did; here that people listened not to what I said but to how I said it. My accent was Oxford; certain people accepted and others spurned me on the basis of that alone. American equality might not be what Rousseau had in mind or Marx, and it had grave limitations of race and (sometimes) wealth; but within those limits it was a living reality. In England no one seemed interested in equality at all; everyone wanted to feel superior to someone else, and the monarchy was cherished because it capped the whole structure and let people feel inferior when they wanted, too. I hated the whole business, became querulous, angry, rude to shopkeepers and waiters, blaming my ill-temper on the country's decadent smugness. Perhaps it would have been fairer to blame some of it on myself. I had to decide quite soon whether to be a don, or to try to live by writing, or to take a job. I'd had two years of freedom from such basic decisions, and I resented my return to the mundane. I even became quite picky about the Commonwealth Fund.

Charles, I soon learnt, had also come home. He had astounded his friends and relations by staying one week in London, then taking a job on a farm in Suffolk. Apparently he was doing simple labouring, though as far as I knew he could scarcely tell a sheep from a goat. He'd been brought up entirely in London, and apart from visits to such friends as myself, he knew the country only from train windows. Neither Bodmin nor Cheltenham nor Cambridge could have given him much taste for rural life, and whatever he'd got up to in Los Angeles I was quite sure it wasn't milking cows or sowing corn. I remembered his indifference to the view from Maiden Castle; the nearest he'd come to a hen, I thought, was the one he'd clucked at on the wall of the Italian professor's nursery. I wondered whether his on-the-spot researches into Zen Buddhism were responsible for this latest aberration. If I hadn't known him better, I would have been tempted to call it a stunt.

I wrote to him care of his family, but got no answer for several months. It wasn't till that autumn when I was at St Antony's, Oxford, that I heard from him again. It was a short letter, thanking me for mine, and saying how busy he'd been with the harvest and ploughing and getting the winter wheat in; it said nothing whatever about his feelings or his object in taking up agricultural labour.

In December I had to go to Cambridge for a few days to check some manuscripts, and while I was there I thought I'd go and see how Charles was doing. I wrote well in advance, asking him to let me know a suitable time to call. I got a rather agitated answer, saying that he didn't really want to see anyone at the moment, but that he'd make an exception for me provided that I came alone on a Sunday and promised not to stay for more than two hours. He gave me elaborate directions on how to find his lodgings.

I got there at twelve-thirty on a cold, grey day. Suffolk is beautiful at any season of the year, though, and the long, gently sloping ploughed fields and the thick leafless woods heartened me, lifting my depression from the crabbed obscenities of the reign of James I. The village was not far from Bury St Edmunds, and the house was a 1930s semi-detached red-brick cottage. Charles's landlady, a bosomy, smiling woman in a flowered apron, said he was in and showed me upstairs to his room. He heard us coming and opened the door.

The first thing that struck me was how well he looked. He'd given up contact lenses and dark glasses for green-tinted spectacles with gold rims – his eyes were getting better unexpectedly, he said, and he had a stouter pair for fieldwork. The new glasses made him look much less aggressive than usual. But the real change was in his colouring. He had shaved his beard, and instead of the characteristic pallor, his cheeks had a dull, olive-brown glow which made him, for the first time in his life, I thought, almost handsome. His hair was short. His hand, as he shook mine, was strong and calloused, the nails short and cracked but not bitten. He was wearing his old leather jacket over a thin blue roll-neck sweater and grey flannel trousers.

'It's very good of you to come,' he said.

'It's good of you to let me come.'

His room was small and tidy, with no personal mark on it whatever. A coal fire burned in the grate which was surrounded by buff tiles in the shape of a sub-cubist sunset. On the mantelpiece were several ornaments – a glass deer with red eyes, an ashtray from Pwhelli, a brass bell in the form of a thatched cottage (you rang it by its central chimney) and a glazed figure of a kneeling African woman, exaggeratedly thin with bulging, elongated breasts. There were two armchairs covered with a dark brown nubbly material, the antimacassars stitched with lupins and other cottage flowers. The bed, with a shiny teak headboard, stood in a corner, making no pretence of being a divan. A wardrobe with another splintered sunset for a mirror was at its foot. There were two pictures on the walls; one of fishing-boats in perhaps Concarneau, perhaps St Ives, the other of a red-sailed barge. The wallpaper was of a small, nondescript abstract pattern, white scratches on brown, and the frieze of orange and yellow was not designed to match it. The whole place reminded me strongly of the digs a friend of mine once had in Rose Hill, Oxford, and I marvelled at the ubiquity of such extraordinary taste.

'I can't offer you anything to drink, I'm afraid,' said Charles.

'That's all right. I said I'd take you out to lunch. There's a pub in Bury, isn't there?'

'I'd rather not go there,' he said. 'Someone might recognize me. I know it sounds silly, but –' He was very nervous, twisting his rough fingers, shifting his feet. I looked away, thinking my obvious curiosity was embarrassing him. I noticed with a shock that there wasn't a single book in the room.

'Well,' I said with an effort, 'how's farming?'

'It's all right.'

'What are you planning? Are you going to get a place of your own?'

He looked sad and said, 'Don't be bright and cheerful, Julian. You make me feel like a patient in a mental hospital.'

'Sorry. But it is visiting day, isn't it?'

'You're the first person I've allowed to come here. You mustn't mock me.'

'What do your parents say about it all?'

'They've given me up as a bad job. They say I'm old enough to go my own way. They think I *ought* to be in a loony bin.'

'There've been times I've thought it myself. But you look extremely well.' He shrugged.

'Let's go and eat,' I said.

'All right.' He got slowly out of his chair. All his movements were slow, with the steady purposefulness of a man who spends his life at hard labour. It was an extraordinary change from the jumpy, pacing Charles of eighteen months ago. As we were about to leave, he stopped and put a hand on my arm. 'Tell me truthfully, what do you think of this room?'

'I think it's absolutely hideous, an insult to the beauty of the countryside around it.'

He looked pleased and relieved. 'Good, good,' he said, with something of his old manner. 'Excellent.' I think he meant it was good that I'd spoken as truthfully as he'd asked.

He chose to be taken to Stowmarket. 'No one will know me there,' he said.

'What are you afraid of? Or is it whom?'

'I don't want people to think I'm a phony, that I'm patronizing them. They're so suspicious. They think I'm either mad or an ex-convict. They gossip about whether I was jailed for fraud or rape – they're sure it couldn't be anything ungentlemanly like grievous bodily harm. The word got round that my godfather arranged the job for me. He's a trainer at Newmarket, and they respect that very much. They're always asking me for tips.'

'Perhaps they think you were really put away for doping.'

'Maybe. It's no good, of course.'

'What's no good?'

'Pretending I'm a labourer. I'm only doing it to prove that I can work with my body, if I ever have to. It's so exhausting, you've no idea. I'm completely worn out every evening, utterly stunned with fatigue. People of our sort always say how nice it is to feel physically tired, but it's not, not day after day. And it's quite untrue that physical labour leaves your mind free to think. It doesn't. I haven't had a single thought since I've been here.'

'Perhaps it was time you gave your mind a rest.'

'Yes, that was part of the idea. It's been an unqualified success, that part.'

'You couldn't have chosen a lovelier part of England. I love Suffolk.'

'Yes. It's very English. I've begun to notice things like – well, things about nature. Obvious things, like the relation between the shapes of trees and the prevailing wind. You probably know all about that already.'

'I did once. I've forgotten it all again, though.'

'I'm sorry to hear that. I hoped that once you knew those things without having to think about them, you knew them for ever.'

'Ah, but I never worked on the land. I've always really been just a visitor in the country. I used to know a lot about horses once, though.'

'We don't have any, of course. We're a farm.'

'Exactly. Riding is for visitors.'

'I'd like to ride. I think you might get a better sense of the landscape from a horse. I scarcely know what's growing in the next farm's fields.'

'And all this is another experiment? How did the last one end?'

He didn't answer for a few moments. Then he said, 'You were right not to stay. I never did hear the silence. I only imagined it. After you'd gone I had a sort of nervous breakdown. It was very good for me. I took a slow boat to Japan. It took weeks and weeks. I looked at the sea, day after day. It was like thinking about one of the nonsense phrases in Zen – you know, "What is the sound of one hand clapping?" Because they're nonsense, eventually you go into a sort of trance, defeating your own reason. Well, I concentrated on the sea, only reason reasserted itself.'

'I'm glad to hear that.'

'I thought you would be.' He gave a ghost of a smile. 'I'm extremely sorry about that performance I put on in Los Angeles.'

'There's nothing to be sorry about.'

'Yes, there is, but never mind. I'm still not sure what all that sadism was about. It's – I'm not even remotely tempted that way any more.'

'Perhaps it was a form of purgation.'

'Perhaps. It seems now as though it all happened to someone else. People always say that after something has changed them. I'd been having nightmares about the concentration camps since – oh, since before I went to school.' He frowned. 'I don't know how I knew about them – I probably didn't, actually. I read stories about heroic officers in prisoner of war camps, of course, and later it all got mixed up with the Jews and the gipsies, I suppose. My parents – my real father, that is, and my stepmother – were terribly irresponsible. They took all the Sunday papers and left them lying around the house for anyone to read. I remember a story in one of them about the Japanese using people for bayonet practice. I dreamed about the bayonets going in – in all sort of strange places. Children have much more imagination than adults. They feel the bayonet when they read about it. I did, anyway. And then, getting mixed up with all those psychopaths in Pasadena –' He sighed. 'Well, it's all gone now. I shan't dream like that again. Though I shall have my scar for ever.'

'It's better to have a scarred body than a scarred mind.'

'I knew you'd say that. How nice you are.'

'Very. I astound myself.'

We drove on in comfortable silence, or rather in as much silence and comfort as my dilapidated car allowed.

'Are you going to keep it up?' I said as we came into Stowmarket.

'No. But I shall stay in the country. Towns are impossible – the noise and the traffic and the endless social life and the bloody telephone. I shall never have a telephone again as long as I live. I'm going to rent a cottage and just live in it till my money's gone.'

'I'm amazed it managed to survive your journey home.'

'Oh, I worked here and there, getting enough in one place to take me to the next.'

'Did the Zen people come up to expectation?'

'Sort of. By the time I got there I wasn't so interested any more. It's not for us, that kind of thing. It doesn't work outside a particular society and culture. It can't.'

'Like wine, you mean. It doesn't travel.'

'I don't know,' he said. 'I haven't tasted any wine for years.'

We had a filthy lunch, but Charles ate hugely, spooning potatoes on to his plate till I felt quite embarrassed. Afterwards there was only just time for coffee if I wasn't to overrun my allotted two hours. I asked him if he really meant me to stick to them.

'Yes,' he said. 'The limit isn't on you but on me. I don't trust myself not to be tempted.' He wouldn't say what by or to do what.

When we got back to his village, though, he stayed in the car for a few moments. I was impressed by his obvious weariness, but also by his calm. He seemed to be back on possible terms with the world and himself. Yet he still seemed to have no clear plans for the future.

'Charles,' I said, 'what are you going to *do?*'

'I think I shall become an architect. I think I'm an artist, really, and none of the pure arts attracts me. Painting these days is all about painting, about how you put paint on the canvas and let colours arrange themselves. Music is all about intervals and the way you hit a note. Writing is in the doldrums. I don't think I'm capable of breaking out of all that aestheticism and cautiousness. It's the best art we have, the aesthetic art, but I think it's pretty trivial, ultimately. I don't believe in pure beauty. The beauty I most admire moves me because I can relate it to something in myself. I can't do that with beauty that exists just for its own sake. So I'm really only interested in applied arts, like architecture.'

'Won't it mean an awful lot of training?'

'Yes. But I probably won't be an architect in the end. It's most unlikely, really. It's just the idea of it which appeals to me.'

'Well, the best of British luck.'

'Thanks. And the same to your thesis.'

He got out and stood waving beside the road as I drove away. I thought he was right, that it was extremely unlikely that he'd ever become an architect. But then it was hard to imagine what he'd do. He had spent so much time devotedly exploring himself that I couldn't see him ever finding anything else quite so interesting and absorbing. He had dismissed the arts as too pure for him, but I wondered whether he might not end up as a poet. Literature can never be pure like music. And poetry certainly needed a new vision, a fresh approach. I'd heard him reciting some of his verse at a beat party in Los Angeles, so I knew he wrote it. I hadn't been very impressed, but then I can never concentrate on poetry being read aloud, especially not to jazz. Perhaps there might have been something worth listening to.

I thought continually about poetry at that time because I was just ceasing to write it, overcome at last by the depth of the chasm which gawped between my ambition and my performance. In prose I could get a much closer correspondence between design and achievement. Yet it was hard to admit to myself that I was no good. Everyone always says that poetry is the highest form of literary art, and though I now believe that that was never necessarily so and is certainly not even remotely true for our own time, yet it felt like the end of an ideal, a dreadful surrender, when I faced the fact that years of earnest trying hadn't produced enough poems of sufficient interest or technical accomplishment to fill even a pamphlet, let alone a slim volume. Though I felt this was equally true of most of the poets who did publish slim volumes, it was no consolation to be as bad as they. Perhaps I was only wishing on Charles a career that I'd myself abandoned through sheer lack of talent, when I felt that if anyone could achieve a momentous break with the tedious complacency of English verse it might be he. But when I wrote and told him that I thought he should go on writing poetry he didn't reply.

After Christmas I moved to London to complete my work at the British Museum and the Public Record Office. Ronald Bryden, who was then literary editor of *The Spectator*, asked me to fill in for him while he went home to Trinidad for a month's holiday. So I continued to do the splits between literature and scholarship. I spent my days on the thesis and at *The Spectator*, my evenings on *As Far As You Can Go*, which didn't seem to be going nearly far enough. It was the first time I'd ever spent several months at a stretch in London, and I found it both exciting and depressing. My thesis seemed to get more and more boring, the research to proliferate far beyond my intention. I treated it with growing disdain, and preferred to sit in Ron's office in Gower Street, chatting with Bernard Levin and David Cairns. *The Spectator* was publishing Dr Leavis's celebrated attack on CP Snow, and that made me feel in the thick of the cultural battle.

I heard of, but not from, Charles. He had taken his furnished cottage, apparently, soon after Christmas, and he was busy filling it with girls and *objets trouvés*. Friends were allowed to visit him now, though they were not, as far as I could gather, very old friends. Occasionally he appeared in London to change his girl, as he might a library book, then retired again to Suffolk. I met him on one of these expeditions at a party in Kentish Town. He was just leaving. He had a girl on his arm, and in his free hand he was carrying a large, rusty cog.

'Hello,' he said. 'Do you like my cog?'

'Quite. Is it part of anything important?'

'No, no. It's for my garden. I shall put it on a pedestal. Don't you think it's beautiful?'

I had, once, before I'd gone to America, had a brief flirtation with the relics of industrial England, but that was a long time ago. 'No,' I said.

'Oh. Julian doesn't like it, darling. What shall we do?'

The girl, who was dark with long black hair and an air of tolerance towards the world's absurdity, said, 'I don't think we need do anything, need we?'

'But he's my oldest friend, my alter ego, my doppelganger, my secret sharer, my –'

'You'll make me jealous if you go on,' she said, giving me a smile so friendly that I was smiling back before I knew what I was doing. I almost never liked my friends' girlfriends till they became their wives, but I liked her already.

'If you like it,' I said, 'that's fine by me.'

'Thank you,' she said.

'Goodbye,' said Charles. 'Sorry we can't stay. But the last train to Stowmarket leaves in twenty minutes. Come and spend a weekend.'

'Do,' said the girl.

For various reasons I didn't. When Ron Bryden came back I retired to Oxford and battled with variant readings all through the spring and summer. Rumours reached me of Charles's rapid progress through progressive liberal girls and careers. He was going, I heard, to be a publisher; a teacher, even though he had no degree; a social worker; a folk-singer; a foreign correspondent for *The Observer*. I, I decided, was not going to be a don. I left Oxford and went back to London, renting a basement flat in Olivia Manning's house in St John's Wood. By the sort of coincidence which makes people believe in a critical conspiracy, we were both reviewing novels for *The Sunday Times*, week and week about. Upstairs and down, the novels poured off the endless conveyor-belt of the publishers' autumn lists, till they threatened to fill the house, like the furniture in a Ionesco play. I quickly came to see what Charles meant about novel reviewers knowing nothing about life; they simply don't have time to do anything but read.

One day I received a bulky envelope through the post and tore it open expecting yet another novel. But it wasn't, it was Charles's poetry. 'I have taken your advice,' he wrote, 'and written a great deal of verse. What is it like? Come for a weekend and tell me. The money has almost run out, so come soon.' There was a PS: 'If you want anything to drink, bring it.'

The poems were dismayingly bad, full of the sort of abstraction he'd once scathed in my own work. They were full of words like 'beauty', 'love', 'joy', 'ecstasy', 'vision' and 'history'. There was no feeling for language, no striking imagery, only a poor sense of rhythm. I wondered whether they might not be the work of one of his girlfriends. Only the general message of the poems was unexceptionable; it was that life was good and that love between man and woman made it better. Ella Wheeler Wilcox herself would have approved.

I wrote and said I'd come and stay the following weekend. He sent a postcard by return with the one word – 'Good'.

I arrived after lunch on the Saturday. He hadn't given me any directions and I had to ask the way several times. The cottage was a mile and a half from the nearest village down a meandering lane. It was tiny, with a thatched roof, and it stood on the edge of a wood, so well concealed by an untrimmed hedge that I almost passed by without seeing it. There was no other house in sight.

Charles wasn't in, but a log fire was burning, and I could see from the various pieces of junk which lay around indoors and out that I'd come to the right place. Unlike his last Suffolk home, this one was full of books and magazines, and I browsed through his shelves, waiting for him to show up. Other people's books are always much more interesting than one's own, they suggest the limitations of one's imaginative world, they mock the gaps in one's knowledge, they make one want to sit down and start catching up immediately. Eventually I became oppressed by the range of Charles's reading – psychology, history, politics, literature, sociology – and I explored the cottage from top to bottom instead. There wasn't much to explore – two bedrooms upstairs, the one with the unmade double bed presumably his, the sitting-room full of books, a large kitchen with a big wooden table. That was all. The garden was unkempt, though someone had scythed the grass under the apple-trees. Bits of cast-off machinery were all over the place, balanced on tree-trunks, dangling from branches, under my feet like man-traps. Pigeons called from the beechwood, and there was the occasional hysterical tocking of a pheasant, like someone turning over an old car on a cold morning.

I was rather irked by Charles's absence, but I assumed that he and his latest girl were in the town shopping. As there was no sign of a bicycle and I knew he had no car, this seemed the most likely explanation. I had lots of novels to review, so I resisted the temptation on the shelves and sat by the fire to start reading. There wasn't much light in the room from the small windows and I looked about for a switch. There wasn't one. Charles had no electricity. I began to feel quite angry. It seemed ridiculous to light a lamp at half-past three in the afternoon, and anyway I wasn't at all sure how to do it. I went and sat outside in the thin sunshine, wrapping my coat around me for warmth. The novel

I'd chosen seemed peculiarly dull; like a hundred others which come out every year, it dealt with the struggles of a decent working-class mother to bring up her family in an industrial town in the 1930s. It was a worthy subject that had been done to death, and this particular version seemed to do little to resuscitate the corpse. I tried to be fair, but my fingers became increasingly numb. I felt that if the lovable mother washed her front step again I would scream.

Finally it became too cold to stay outside any longer, and I went back in. The fire was dying, and I had to go and find where the logs were kept, then bring some in. Charles's bellows, like his sculpture, belonged on a scrapheap; perhaps that's where he'd found them. They were liberally punctured, and the fire took a long time to revive. I wished very much that I hadn't come. I started to drink the whisky I'd brought, and emboldened by it I risked lighting a lamp. With my tenth match I got one going. It smoked like a power-station till I learnt how to adjust it, but then it gave a warm, yellow light, and I felt a sense of tremendous achievement. I sat down by the fire and got on with the novel. It seemed better indoors.

When Charles arrived it had been dark for an hour and I'd almost given up on him. Hearing a noise outside I went to the door and looked out.

'Is that you?' I called.

'No,' he said from the blackness, 'it's me. Is that you?' He wheeled his bicycle up to the door, then threw it down on the grass. 'Bloody thing. The chain came off *four times*.'

'Where the hell have you been?'

'Doing a Betjeman. There are some beautiful churches round here – wonderful roofs.' He came in and shut the door.

'Surely you can't see them in the dark?'

'No. True. Well, actually, I met a terribly nice girl – an art student from Ipswich. She was sketching in a churchyard – they still do, you know, the tradition never dies – and we got to talking and looking in each other's eyes and so we bicycled off down a lane and found a haystack, and then I thought it was only decent to buy her a cup of tea – and then she was rather hard to get rid of, I'm sorry to say. Have you been making yourself at home?'

'For about four hours.'

'Sorry. But it would have been wrong to pass up an opportunity like that, wouldn't it? I think I'm going to have a bath, I'm cold. You can come and talk to me while I'm warming up.'

'I didn't know you had a bath.'

'Of course I have. It's through the kitchen.'

What I'd taken for the larder door in fact led into a tiny space, the length and little more than the width of a small bathtub.

'How do you heat the water?'

'Calor gas. It's very good. Sit down. No, you'll have to go out for a moment, there isn't room for two in here unless one's in the bath. I've tried it often. You can get two in the bath, of course, but the one underneath usually drowns.'

I went out while he ran the water, undressed and got in. Then he shouted for me to come in. The room was full of steam – there seemed to be no ventilation whatever – and my glasses misted up at once. I wiped them, but it did no good. Charles said, 'You'll have to take them off. One of the things you can't do in this place is read in the bath. Are your eyes bad?'

'Not very.'

'Are my poems?'

'Well, yes, Charles, I'm afraid they are. I'm sorry, but there's no point in not telling you they're really no good at all.'

He raised his knees and slid under the water till only his eyes and nose showed above it. Then these, too, disappeared, and he bubbled for a moment or two. Surfacing, he said, 'That was me consigning my poetic talent to the deep.'

'Quite honestly, you surprised me.'

'I've told you before, that's my function in your life. But this time you've surprised me, too. I thought you'd go out of your way to find something to console me with. I was hoping to show you how wrong you were, to prove to you that I was an even worse poet than you thought. Now I can't, can I?'

'Not really, no.'

'Well, at least we're agreed that yours was an absolutely rotten idea, a putrefied fantasy, a wish beyond any posibility of fulfilment. You're one stage nearer seeing me for what I am.'

'Oh, I know you by now, thanks.'

'Do you really think so?' he said curiously, almost eagerly, as though I'd said something of extraordinary interest. We were both half-blind and in a vaporous gloom, so I don't know what expression he had on his face then.

'Yes,' I said. 'Not absolutely, of course. I can't predict what you're going to do next, ever. But once I know what you're doing, I usually have a pretty shrewd idea of how you'll do it.'

'Poor you,' he said gaily. 'What a lot you've had to put up with.'

'I'll tell you something else that's surprised me. Everyone says you keep quite a harem down here. Where are all the girlfriends?'

'I sent them away for the weekend. I wanted you all to myself.'

'Is there no special one?'

'No. The latest had to go and see her parents. They were getting worried – she's supposed to be taking a diploma in cooking somewhere.'

'Ah, you were jealous, you sent her away.'

'Good God, no. You're welcome to her. She's only a scrubber.'

'A what?'

'It's the new word for "short-term sexual partner".'

'Oh. You go in for those, then?'

'It usually turns out that way, I'm afraid. It's quite convenient. Why didn't you bring one of your own?'

'Novel reviewers are terribly unloved.'

'Deservedly,' he said. 'Can you cook?'

'A little.'

'I can't. That's another reason for having scrubbers – they all want to fatten me up. It's delightful. I can only do steak and peas. Why don't you go and see what you can do? There's masses of stuff out there, if you're clever with saucepans.'

The kitchen was well-stocked, and I found some veal escalopes in the meat-safe. I decided to do them with my special mushroom sauce. It was fortunate that I'd brought two bottles of red wine with me, as well as the whisky.

When Charles came out of the bathroom, he sniffed and said 'Christ, *cuisine française*, is it?'

'Sort of.'

'Where did you put the poems?'

'They're in my case.'

'Right.'

He went into the sitting-room. As I peeled the mushrooms I could hear him opening the case, then the crackle of paper as he crumpled the poems up, then the whoosh of flame from the fire as he burnt them. He didn't pause to read any of them. When he'd finished he came back into the kitchen and said, 'My talent is taking its revenge. I think the chimney's on fire.'

We went out to look. Nothing seemed to be wrong. The stars were bright and it felt like frost. Charles peed on the grass, and we went back in again.

Every evening I take the two dachshund bitches for an hour's walk over the fields on the other side of the valley. The old dog's heart is failing; he stays behind. Beyond the pastures where the dachshunds disappear in the long grass, visible like dolphins only in leaps and bounds, there are fields of stubble. The harvest has been in for a fortnight. Already they are ploughing and harrowing for the winter wheat. The freshly turned earth is a rich chocolate, with a fringe of purple. On these hazy, beautiful late

September days the sound of the tractors carries for miles. I can hear one now. It is seven o'clock in the evening.

When I was young, we used to go gleaning after the harvest, gathering corn for the hens. Now the stubble is often burned. The only really autumnal look about the hedgerows is where the fire has singed them prematurely brown. Pheasants rise under our feet, furiously gobbling; there are partridges, too, as we go down the lane, ripe, sweet blackberries on one side, wine-dark elderberries on the other.

Yesterday I saw a hare, leaping like a miniature gazelle across a field; then freezing; then leaping again; then freezing. Today I found some scarlet poppies. And coming round the corner of a field, where some bushes grow against a dry-stone wall, I saw a rabbit. They are creeping back, the rabbits; no disease ever kills all of a thing.

The bitches have good noses, but they see nothing. The rabbit was away and gone before they found the scent. Then they gave tongue and hurtled into the bushes, blindly pursuing what they never saw. They didn't catch it, of course – they never catch anything. They were too small to get over the wall which the rabbit had jumped; I had to lift them across. But they were very pleased with themselves and trotted home with tails high as though, for once in their lives, they'd actually provided their own dinners.

Crossing the iron bridge, going and coming, I couldn't see the goldfish. It wasn't there yesterday, either. But the moorhens make such a stir and palaver at my approach, perhaps it has fled downstream. I hope so. I want very much for it still to be there.

We spent that night and all the next day talking about writing. Charles thought both of my novels feeble, though the second, he conceded, was better than the first. It was a good thing, perhaps, that he hadn't read the third. I told him I was about to leave everything and go to Morocco to write a fourth – I wanted to avoid, if possible, the English winter, and I'd been told that Morocco was cheap, quiet and inspiring. He shook his head, not at Morocco, but at the speed of my production.

'You're too young to be any good,' he said. 'You'll write yourself out before you've got anything to say. You've quite a useful command of English, you can do the surface of a character pretty well, but you'll never write anything important till you're more mature.'

'I don't agree, and even if I did, what's wrong with perfecting one's technique? Isn't it better to learn one's craft while one's young, so that it's all there when one needs it?'

'Possibly. Though I suspect each work requires a new technique, or you'll find the technique you know may start dictating the novel you don't, instead of the other way round. You don't want it to become too automatic.'

'But craftsmanship is knowing how best to treat a subject, is knowing ten ways of approaching it, and choosing the right one.'

'I daresay. But that's no excuse for inflicting your juvenilia on the general public. You should burn it, so it won't even exist as a reproach. Then you won't have the temptation to rewrite it, either.'

'It's not that bad.'

'It's not that good, either. If you're going to write at all, there's no excuse for writing anything but masterpieces.'

'That's been said before.'

'I don't doubt it.'

Mercifully we left my contribution to literature aside after a while, and went on to the value of the novel in general. Charles was in favour of it now, in spite and partly because of what television and films had annexed from it. He felt it could explore aspects of life which nothing else could, that it was able, above all, to tell you how someone else felt and thought. It was an impure art-form, inextricably rooted in the real world; it could never go abstract, it had always to deal with basic human situations, whatever new techniques might be invented. I felt there was more to be said for it than just that. What art did, I argued, was present a particular form, image or situation in such a way that it had reference beyond itself to life in general; that it appealed from the experience of one man to the experience of mankind. Charles would have none of it; art belonged to its particular culture. Europeans might take a fancy to Indian sculpture or Chinese poetry, but they never properly understood it. The differences between cultures were far more important than the superficial similarities, and America provided a useful instance. American poetry and novels were largely misunderstood even in England where more or less the same language was used. How much, then, did we really appreciate of Tolstoy or Chekhov, reading them in translation or even (as he did himself, of course) in the original? The worth of a novel was to be judged by its contribution to the pleasure and understanding of the society which produced it.

Nonsense, I said; there were aesthetic standards which had nothing to do with a society's pleasure and understanding. Much very bad art had given great pleasure for a limited amount of time to particular societies – for instance, Pre-Raphaelite painting and verse. That didn't stop it being unspeakable. It was the aesthetic quality of a work which mattered, which determined its survival and assured it of an audience beyond the society in which it had been produced. It was possible to define aesthetic quality only up to a point, of course; you could discuss the technical means used to achieve the artistic end, but after that it was a matter of permanent disagreement as to why one writer survived and another didn't. Technically brilliant works could be failures, it was true; but few of what we could agree were great works of art were not technically accomplished to a very high degree. This was particularly true of music, though not perhaps relevant. What I was really saying was that what mattered was something beyond what gave the particular society in which the work was produced its pleasure and, possibly, understanding.

Charles wished I'd stick to the novel, and the contemporary novel at that. Now that philosophy had abdicated its traditional role as explicator of the mysteries of life, the novel had taken over. Novels were written and read for what sense they made of the world; that was their true importance. They were immediate; if they survived, that was because certain features of the society to which they were relevant survived also. Only an immense revolution, more sweeping than the French or Russian ones, could change everything overnight. But who still read eighteenth-century English novels? A few scholars and literary people: and they read only a tiny fraction of what was written, largely for its historical significance.

Such wild assertions, gleefully proclaimed, echoed through the beechwood and over the fields as we tramped about denouncing each other's views. It was wonderful – and terribly muddled. We kept switching positions, adopting ideas which we'd just ridiculed, not really knowing what we were saying or why we were saying it. I was very glad that none of my Oxford friends, with their minds full of logical scalpels, could hear us. But I was glad, too, to be out of the bleak intellectual operating theatre in which they felt at home. Charles argued very like me, leaping on individual points rather than maintaining a fixed position, preferring to lay waste the surrounding countryside than to settle to the patient siege of an idea. I think it may have been that weekend that, pausing for a moment, I suddenly realized that I wasn't and never would be a proper intellectual and that I didn't care. I felt, in fact, hugely relieved.

We made a bizarre pair, if anyone had known us. We were both twenty-seven, had never had serious jobs, had lived so far mainly on our wits and our parents, and had no idea what we were going to do next. At least, I knew I was going to Morocco to write my novel; after that my future yawned at its own featureless prospect. And as for Charles – 'I have another three weeks here. Then I shall do something, I suppose. Let's not think about it.' And we went back to the remains of the novel in our time.

When I left on the Monday morning, I said, 'Why don't you come to Morocco with me?'

'Perhaps I will.'

'I'm leaving in three weeks, just when your money runs out.'

'I'll let you know.'

'You can write a novel, too. Then you can burn yours while I publish mine.'

He grinned. 'Goodbye, Julian.'

Charles didn't let me know or come to Morocco, and I doubt if I'd ever have written *The White Father* if he had. I find it hard to write if there's anyone so much as in the same house with me, and even by myself I go to extraordinary lengths to avoid sitting down at my desk. I get terribly restless and think of people to phone, I read the papers, do crossword puzzles, anything rather than start writing. It is inconsistent and awkward and, if anyone else was ever with me and also trying to write, probably impossible for both of us – I don't know, of course, because I've never tried it, but I don't think I want to.

I ended up in a small, rather derelict port called El Jadida (once Mazagan), which had a Portuguese citadel with a *citerne* which Orson Welles was said to have used for his film of *Othello*. Otherwise it was a dreary town, and I worked without interruption except from myself. There was an endlessly obliging British Council teacher at the local *lycée* called Harry Sampson, and he and his French wife were my only friends, my one refuge, the certainty of which kept me sane. I found myself un-English in feeling little attraction to Arabs or Mohammedan culture; the town was very damp; it rained a lot; there was nothing to do but kick the shoeshine boys out of the way and go to the cinema. As a result the novel advanced at great speed, and I completed the first draft by Christmas. Then I went to Marrakech and caught flu. I decided I'd had enough of North Africa. I flew back into the coldest English winter for twenty years.

Battersea Park, on to which I looked from a friend's flat in

Prince of Wales Drive, was covered with snow, smutty from the smoke of the power-station. I put the novel aside and went house-hunting. Nothing in all my experience has ever been so lowering to morale. I trudged up and down frozen stairs, read endless advertisements, put my name on a hundred agents' lists. The secret squalor of middle-class London life revealed itself in that arctic weather with all the shamelessness of an Irish peasant woman I once saw in County Kerry, squatting to relieve herself in the full view of the crowd at a hurling match. I saw incredibly foetid two-room flats shared by six girls in Earl's Court; dripping 'garden apartments' in South Kensington which looked into blank walls and dustbins; 'penthouses' with clear views of the fourth floors of Marylebone skyscraper office-blocks; Chelsea 'maisonettes' of one room; Hampstead 'bachelor flats' to which no bachelor would dare introduce a girl – some were the size, it seemed, of Charles's Suffolk bathroom.

And then one afternoon I found, quite by accident, a terrace house in a quiet Chelsea street available on a six-year lease at a modest rent. The notice board had gone up that morning. I couldn't afford the premium, but I took the house all the same. For the next few months I was overwhelmed with the business of setting up house.

I'd sent letters and postcards to Charles from Morocco, but had no answer. I'd tried to find him again in London, but learned only that he was 'abroad'. It wasn't till I saw his sister Antonia, herself already married, at a wedding reception at the Basil Street Hotel, that I found out where he was.

Antonia didn't remember me till I told her my name. She was pregnant, her tiny waist gone, alas, for ever. She had a big black hat with an enormous brim under which I had to duck to speak to her.

'Oh, Charles is in Switzerland, didn't you know? He's in a bank, making pots and pots of money. Daddy's so relieved – we thought he'd *never* settle down.'

'Charles? In a bank?'

'Isn't it marvellous? It's a merchant bank, of course – whatever that is. I mean, he doesn't cash people's cheques for them or anything. I can't remember its name – it's something foreign. Jewish, I think.'

'Is he there for long?'

'Oh, a year at least. As soon as my baby's born, Leo and I are going to go and see him. I mean, after I'm up and everything.' She lowered her eyes with a little smile, as though to draw my attention to her swollen belly. She was obviously very proud of it.

'When's it due?'

'September. I was married,' she added hastily, 'on December third.'

'How marvellous for you.'

'Leo wants a boy,' she said. Then, dreamily: 'But I don't mind which it is. I want to have ten.'

If Charles was a difficult son, Antonia seemed to be an ideal daughter. Her husband, when I met him, was tall, dark, and made up for his lack of handsomeness by being in the Guards. I wanted to ask whether they'd call the baby Charles, if it was a boy; but somehow I knew they wouldn't, not unless Leo's father was called Charles, too.

Leo told me the name of Charles's bank, and I wrote to him again, crowing about the beauty of my house and how satisfying it was to know where I was going to be for the next few years. It was a pretty street, without being beautiful, and all the little houses on my side had small front gardens. I asked him facetiously to come and help me with the digging. He didn't reply. I assumed he'd put his old life behind him, and his old friends with it. I was both sorry and glad – sorry to have been dropped, glad that he'd come to terms with the world. I imagined him becoming immensely successful and rich, wondering at forty whatever could have got into him at twenty-five.

In the autumn of that year, at the suggestion of a friend who was a psychiatrist, I started to work for the Samaritans, a voluntary organization run by Chad Varah from the vestry of his city church, St Stephen's, Wallbrook. The Samaritans try to help people who are feeling desperate and suicidal, and my friend, who was then at St Thomas's, said he thought their work was invaluable, providing an essential link between the official organizations of the Welfare State and the individuals in need of help.

In spite of my house and the satisfactions of my work, I felt that I did nothing for anyone else, that mine was a selfish life and rather purposeless, that I wasn't a very productive member of society. Partly, I daresay, it was the depression which always follows the completion of a book – I had rewritten *The White Father* and had no idea what to do next. Partly it was the earnest, responsible, perhaps puritanical and guilty streak in my nature; I rarely allow myself to think my life satisfactory. Partly, too, it was curiosity, the novelist's wish to know more about the lives of other people. And partly it was two recent experiences with very unhappy people, one of which I'd handled with a disastrous incompetence, the other with some tact. I felt, in fact, that I knew something of the problems already.

I went one evening a fortnight. Sometimes nothing much happened, sometimes a great deal. I answered the phone, our lifeline to the desperate, I talked to people and let them talk, I made tea and gave sympathy, I learned how much more there was to it than doing just these things. It was not a job for intellectuals. It required one to give of oneself, to use the heart as well as the head. Previously, I had only really done that in my writing. I can't say how much, if any, good I was doing for other people; but I do know I was doing a lot for myself.

One evening in April 1964 we were especially busy. A mother with three young children was in the vestry, waiting while we tried to find her somewhere to spend the night. Two or three other people were sitting there, too, waiting to be seen, waiting, rather, to tell someone they'd never seen before the things they could tell no one else. We were very short of space then – the Samaritans operate from the crypt now, where there are more rooms for interviews – and we often took people out into the dimness of the splendid Wren church to listen to their stories.

I had just finished listening to someone in the church. He was a man of fifty who had done something foolish but unimportant, yet to him this one act blotted out the sky, looming in his mind like a terrible dark cloud of sin. He had lived with this cloud for months, till it had settled on him like an impenetrable midnight fog and he could see no way out of it whatever. He repeated his story seven or eight times; it was all he had to do, really, for the fog to lift and for him to see that it wasn't midnight or even dusk, that his life could go on again, not as though nothing had happened, but with the knowledge that what he had done was only silly and the hope that he wouldn't do it again. I hardly said anything. He did it all himself, for himself. When he no longer needed to tell the story again, he was absurdly grateful. He was a bad Christian, he said, but he wanted me to pray with him. I was not and am not a Christian of any kind at all, and I had a small struggle with my puritanical atheist's conscience before I could get down on my knees. But I did kneel, and I said 'Amen' to his prayers.

As I was seeing him down the steps of the church, back to life and light – it was eight o'clock and the sky was full of evening sunshine though the sun itself was hidden behind great slabs of Portland stone and glass – I saw a man standing uncertainly on the pavement. He had his back to us, but he looked from the nervous hunch of his shoulders as though he was trying to pluck up the courage to come in. I said goodbye to the man I'd prayed with. He thanked me profusely. He had wept with relief in the church, and I thought he might weep again when he got home.

'We're always here, day and night, if you want us,' I said. 'You know the number – Mansion House 9000.'

'I didn't mean to bother you,' he said.

'We're here to be bothered. We'd be no use if people didn't come, would we?'

'No, I suppose not,' he said. 'Well – cheerio.'

'Good luck.'

He went off to the Bank tube-station just up the street. I watched him go, then turned to the potential client outside the church. His whole body was shaking with hysterical laughter.

'Oh, no,' he was saying. 'Oh, Jesus bloody Christ! It can't be true!'

It was Charles. He threw his arms round my neck and cried like a child.

6

Once we made gods to give some meaning to our lives, and sometimes we make them still. But because we make them, we cannot believe in them for long, we cannot deceive ourselves with our own puppet-show. In our time the gods have become interesting cultural phenomena, anthropological specimens. We value their altars for their architectural settings, their images for their sculptural beauty, their myths for what they teach us of the myth-makers. Heaven has gone the way of hell into the history of ideas. We describe the natural processes which govern us, but we do not try to explain them. To the ultimate questions we have no answers, indeed we say the questions are not real ones, that they are based on a misuse of language. We have become a race of dandies, viewing life aesthetically, finding the purpose we crave in momentary satisfactions. Not to like our work, not to lead a full sex-life, not to love someone, not to respond sensually to everything about us, not to feel we contribute usefully to society, is to be a failure. For the only purpose in life which we can credit is to please ourselves in every possible way. And if we do not please ourselves, we are lost souls, we succumb to despair. Our societies, our clans, our families are no more than flocks and herds and murmurations, reproducing themselves for no purpose but further reproduction. There is no gratification in our lives for our hunger for something more. There is no reason to go on living.

That a man has not yet killed himself does not prove that he finds life worthwhile, for death is as meaningless as life to someone without a sense of purpose. And despair about the pointlessness of life is, I imagine, the rarest of all prime reasons for committing suicide, for there is usually some practical disaster underlying and creating the desperation, to which the abstract argument is secondary, a rationalization of an emotional, physical, social or economic problem.

In Charles's case the problem was clearly psychological, though its exact nature I do not know. Perhaps his psychoanalyst never discovered it, either. The possibility of suicide, Charles claimed, gave him a sense of power and purpose, allowed him to feel control over his own physical existence and, to a certain extent, over the emotions of his family and friends. But of course when the need to feel that kind of power is so demanding, it can be seen as the symptom it is of an emotional crisis. I'm sure that Charles's difficulties were caused originally by his parents' divorce and new marriages while he was still only an infant. But I am not a psychologist, and it would be foolish even to guess at the particular way he was affected. Now that he's dead, it is only of academic interest.

He had been coming to the Samaritans for several weeks before I met him there, not to be helped, he claimed, but to see whether anyone could argue successfully against him. He would kill himself, he said, when his death would give him real satisfaction; this might be next day or never. Meanwhile, could anyone give him a good reason for going on living? Many people tried and failed. He admitted that he had an emotional problem, but said that even if that could be 'cured', he would still have no reason to choose life rather than death, and it was a reason, not a feeling, that he wanted. He sat in the vestry, drinking tea, almost smug in his obstinacy. He was not, though, contemptuous; since he could find no reason for living, he didn't expect anyone else to be able to, either. When I asked him why he came so often – two or three times a week – he said he was interested in the motives of those who wanted to help others. He thought the Samaritans were probably more deranged and desperate than those they ministered to, and that was why, against the odds, they were actually quite helpful. He found the spectacle of two groups of people meeting in mutual need, in a church with virtually no parishioners, of genuine sociological interest, though sociology was no reason for staying alive. He said St Stephen's was like a house of assignation, only spiritual, not physical. When I told him I thought the Samaritans might be quite pleased by the comparison, he smiled and said, 'And why not?'

But that was all later, when he'd recovered himself. At first he wept uncontrollably. Then he broke away from me without a word and began to walk down Wallbrook towards Cannon Street. Naturally, I followed him. He began to run, so I ran too. I chased him all along Cannon Street, then right and halfway over London Bridge. There he suddenly stopped and stood laughing at me, harshly, horribly.

'Did you think I was going to jump?' he jeered. 'Did you? Did you?'

I had thought just that, but I said, 'I didn't know what you were going to do. Did you?'

'Oh, yes. I wanted to make a fool of you. And I did, didn't I?'

'Possibly.' I was out of breath, sweating and panting heavily. He seemed quite cool and calm.

'Look at you!' he said. 'An overweight young *littérateur* with a burning social conscience, no doubt, puffing over London Bridge! Of course you're a fool. You're a complete bloody idiot.'

'Perhaps.'

'Humble, with it! You've been cultivating humility! What's the matter? Have you suddenly felt a vocation? Are you taking holy orders?'

'Of course not.'

'Well, what the hell do you think you're doing with that gang of neurotic do-gooders, then?'

'Good, I hope. What were you doing there?'

'Having a thoroughly good laugh.'

'Well, I hope you enjoyed it. But I thought you were crying rather than laughing.'

'The ludicrous takes me that way. I'm never sure whether to laugh or cry, so I always do both.'

He was doing neither by then. He turned suddenly towards the parapet and I lunged at his coat.

'It's all right,' he said, pushing me away. 'I'm not planning to jump. I'm far too fastidious to drown myself in the Thames. It's too filthy. It wouldn't be elegant to be fished out with a pole.' There was just a note of friendliness in his voice.

I leaned over the parapet next to him, our shoulders touching. The tide was coming in, and for some reason I felt this was a good thing; we wouldn't be washed out to sea. The cranes on the wharves on both sides of the river pointed to the sky.

'Why drown yourself at all?' I said.

'It's said to be very agreeable, drowning.'

'Do you want to see your whole life pass before your eyes?'

'Christ, no. Anything but that.' He moved away from the parapet with revulsion. 'Well, Stetson, where shall we go?'

'Wherever you like.'

'You were supposed to say, "You who were with me in the ships at Mylae". Do I have to provide the pretentious literary talk as well as the drama in our lives?'

'Sorry. "A crowd flowed over London Bridge, so many, I had not thought death had undone so many."'

'Exactly. Very appropriate. But over the Bridge, you notice, not under it. Besides, my name's not Phlebas. You know the theory that *The Waste Land* is really all queer?'

'I have heard of it, yes.'

'Well, it's balls.' He took my arm like an Edwardian swell and we began to stroll back towards the City. 'It's a good thing your organization isn't near Westminster Bridge, isn't it? Imagine trying to persuade potential suicides that earth hath not anything to show more fair than County Hall and Scotland Yard – bureaucracy and the police! Where's St Mary Woolnoth?'

'I've no idea. Shall we try to find it?' The end of the bridge seemed miles away still. Perhaps the idea of a literary pilgrimage might hurry him up. He seemed deliberately to be dawdling.

'We ought to wait for the dead sound on the final stroke of nine,' he said. 'Then we could synchronize watches and jump together.'

'It's only eight-fifteen. Why don't we go and flow up King William Street?'

'Ah, you're getting the idea. Yes, let's, with our eyes fixed before our feet. Very peculiar, that, I've always thought. As though bodies were assembled in machine-shops, eyes first, feet second, arms third. Perhaps that's why he has that bit about death undoing so many. You can just see death, can't you, with a screwdriver in one hand and a wrench in the other, taking your body to pieces? Then he salvages the metal he can reprocess, and the rest – nails and hair – is crunched up in a big machine and – what do they do with old cars?'

'They litter the streets with them.'

'Ah, you're for keeping Britain tidy?'

'If people left corpses lying around, there'd be nowhere to park.'

'There could be corpse-meters,' he said.

I kept up with his whimsicality as we moved, unbearably slowly, along the bridge. Charles kept stopping to linger over some new grotesque fantasy, waving his free arm about and chortling at his own jokes. I was sure now that he was delaying us intentionally. At any moment he might try and break away from me and leap over the parapet. I kept his arm pressed firmly against my ribs, and answering brightly, I tried frantically to think whether it would be better to leap after him if he did decide to jump or to call the police. I knew nothing about how to rescue a drowning man, except that it was sometimes necessary to knock him out to stop him struggling. But how on earth did one manage to do that while trying to keep afloat oneself? It was a tremendous relief when we got off the bridge and he hadn't made a move to get away from me.

'Charles,' I said, while we were waiting at the traffic lights by the Monument, 'would you mind very much telling me what all this is about?'

'My tears and laughter? My running and not jumping and standing still? How should I know? A very expensive analyst is working on it. He's going to let me have an interim report in four or five years, if he's not gone mad himself by then.'

It was comforting to know that he was in professional hands, and I eased the pressure on his arm. But I tightened it again when I thought that perhaps it wasn't so comforting after all. A patient who sought out the Samaritans and then ran like a lunatic through the streets might be – well, a lunatic.

'You've had a breakdown, I suppose,' I said, trying to sound very matter-of-fact.

'How did you guess? Does it show in my face?'

I'd really been too anxious to look at him properly before. He seemed very healthy, though he was wearing dark glasses again. His hair was very long but recently washed – it looked very soft. He was wearing very tight white jeans, a red roll-neck jersey, and his old black leather jacket. He might have been a member of a pop group.

'What happened, Charles?'

'I broke down. I collapsed. I flunked the course. They found me weeping at my desk, all over the Burmese trade figures for December. Naturally, they assumed at first that I'd been stealing from the bank – they're like that in Switzerland, first things first, very practical. They were especially practical in getting rid of me just as fast as they possibly could. I was rather sorry, in a way. I've always fancied a month or two in a Swiss sanatorium. Very romantic, sanatoria.'

'I thought they were mostly for people with tuberculosis.'

'You're years out of date. Tuberculosis is completely out. Switzerland has gone in for mental health instead. And by God, it needs it.'

'And so you came home.'

'Yes, and so I did. About the middle of February. Since when I've been seeing my charming analyst, who's stupid, and generally getting everyone down. I think I'm going to try publishing for a while. I like the idea of reading all those hundreds of manuscripts of books which never get published. It must be very relaxing, knowing how hopeless they are, how pointless it is to read them, how all that energy has been uselessly, wastefully harnessed – I love the idea.'

'Have you any particular firm in mind?'

'Well, my stepfather is a director of a very large and mysterious business which just happens to own the odd publisher for what he calls diversification of interests. It saves tax somehow. That's really all books are for nowadays – saving taxes. And if you've got a crazy stepson, it's a great convenience to be able to put him to work of a sort in a business which is run at a loss anyway.' He was quite relaxed now, almost jaunty, as we walked between the huge office-blocks. It was dusk, and the street-lights were on. He slipped his arm out of mine. Perhaps he felt safer now, too.

I said, 'I don't think publishing can be all that relaxing, you know. My brother's in it, and he seems to work night and day.'

'But that's exactly what I want – something to occupy me every waking minute! So I don't have to think about how stupid everyone is, so I don't have to lie awake all night trying to find some reason to kill myself!'

I didn't, of course, then know what his immediate problem was, so all I said was, 'Wouldn't it be better to get some sleep?'

'I can't sleep. I could in Zurich. Not in bed, of course – at my desk. I only had to open a file for my hair to be full of paper-clips. I think manuscripts might do that for me, too. A huge pile of them by the bed for night starvation.'

'Charles, you don't have to tell me what's the matter if you don't want to. But I would like to know.'

'Who wouldn't? I would myself. My mind is so laboriously defensive, so labyrinthine in its evasions. Sometimes I feel that all these modern spy stories about people being double-counter-bluffed – they're exact images of my mental state. I never know whose side I'm on. And even when I think I do, I don't see why that side has my loyalty rather than the other. Life's so chaotic – there, that's what's the matter. But why should I find the chaos so much worse than everyone else? Every time I think I have an answer, it just leads to more and more baffling questions. And I can't – I'm not like you. I can't take two quick steps away from it all and give it a beady-eyed look and make sense of it that way. I'm too involved in the chaos. I can't manage a neat aesthetic detachment.'

'What on earth makes you think I can?'

'Your books. Their neutrality. Oh, I realize that it's quite difficult to be neutral, to stand aside, that the detached attitude isn't really detached, it's just a way of perceiving like any other – a tool, not an attitude at all. But it's not one I can use.'

'I'm afraid I can't quite follow you.'

'Never mind. I'll explain some other time. Perhaps you'll explain something to me. Why are you one of these Samaritan people?'

I tried, haltingly, to be fair to myself. I always seemed to see the unworthy aspect of my actions much more clearly than the worthy. Charles listened, then said, 'I see. Very interesting.' I asked him how he'd heard of the Samaritans himself. He said he'd read about them somewhere, and then he explained why he'd come and that he enjoyed watching them at work.

'Do you want to come back and observe some more? They must be wondering what's happened to me.'

'No thanks. I've had my little kick for this evening.'

'Can we see each other again? You've never visited me in Chelsea, have you?'

'No. I'd like to.'

We made arrangements to meet later in the week. He was living, he told me, in a bed-sitting room in Belsize Park, and had no phone. Then he walked to the Bank tube-station and said goodbye.

Just as he was about to go down the steps, he said, 'Purely as a matter of interest, you may like to know that, seeing you again there so suddenly, I felt a violent wish to die. It's a good thing you followed me. Perhaps.' Then he ran down the steps and left me.

I was too shaken to go directly back to the Samaritans. I'd preserved, I hoped, an appearance of calm and sympathy throughout my talk with Charles – except, of course, while actually pursuing him down the street. Now I began to tremble all over, and I thought I was going to faint. We are protected from the proliferating mass horrors of the world – concentration camps, gas chambers, electrical tortures, the knowledge of which would otherwise drive us mad – by the limits of our capacity to feel. But we are still vulnerable to the suffering of individuals. We feel the pain of our friends as our own; it makes us question the whole sorrow and suffering of the world. That we have survived while millions have hideously perished becomes almost intolerable, and we seek in however small a way to right this monstrous wrong.

I think one of the reasons that I found the work of the Samaritans so rewarding was that it was both personal and impersonal. I felt, as I have said, that I had disastrously failed someone, and doubtless I got some satisfaction from assuaging this continuing sense of guilt. But more than that, the work required me to give, but not, perhaps, to take much in return. It was quite a passive form of giving – sitting and listening and not giving advice, only one evening a fortnight; for several reasons I couldn't take part in the regular befriending of lonely and lost people which is perhaps the Samaritans' most valuable work. The people I saw remained 'other people', they were not genuinely part of my personal life. There was, in fact, a sort of selfishness in my giving, however absurd that sounds; because in a proper relationship one must accept as much or more than one gives, and I have always found it very hard to do that, as though I had to surrender part of myself to make room for what I was given. And by doing what little I did at the Samaritans I was, possibly, avoiding having to give in the rest of my life, and having to accept at all. My 'charity' was all to myself. In helping others to cope with the evil and misery in the world, I avoided having to think or feel about my own problems and inadequacies.

But Charles's sudden appearance made me realize that I couldn't go on dividing my life into neat, frightened divisions. The personal and the impersonal met in the client who was my oldest friend, the friend who meant more to me than anyone else had ever done. He had said that it was his function in my life to surprise me; but I felt, as I had a whisky in The Deacons just across from the church, that that was only superficially true, that the deeper reality of our friendship was that he was my conscience, moral and artistic. He prevented me from settling into definite attitudes, dogmas, the easy hardening of the mental arteries. And the more I failed him, the more he urged me on. It didn't seem to matter to me at that moment that of course he existed, had always existed, quite independently of me, had lived, in fact, by far the greater part of his life in no contact with me at all. We know people as we can, through the strange squints of our personalities, and I knew Charles as my conscience. What, then, was I to him? I didn't know – I still don't know. But it was that evening in the almost empty pub that I first regretted not having spoken that morning in Cambridge, having failed him at Maiden Castle and in Los Angeles and again and again and again. In an extraordinary way his desperate problems were mine; not because we were alike – we weren't. But because he had been right when he'd said that we loved one another inextricably. He needed to share the problems with me and me alone. I was necessary to him; and I had failed him, failed him utterly. Nothing I'd done or would do at the Samaritans could erase that overwhelming fact.

I can hardly say what I mean – I'm not even sure if I know. I don't understand our relationship any better because it is over, because he is dead.

Sometimes I wonder as I write this whether anyone else can possibly be interested. And I find I don't care. There isn't much more to tell.

The goldfish has definitely gone from below the bridge. I tell myself that its disappearance does not prove that it is dead. But I think it is. It will, of course, seem literary and artificial to some people to have mentioned the goldfish at all. I can't help that. Everything I see and hear I connect with Charles. Nature provides me with a thousand metaphors each day. And there was a goldfish in the pool below the bridge.

This village has a Saxon church. It is used now only once a month. The farmer is modern, he uses the latest machinery and techniques. He needs few labourers. Most of the cottages have been converted into weekend places for Londoners; there is a retired general, an Oxford don, a printer. The nearest pub is three miles away. A special bus fetches and delivers the village's two children of school age. It is the same all up and down the valley. It is a beautiful place, utterly peaceful. The church is full of flowers for the Harvest Festival. I walk about here, as through the ruins of a lost civilization. I am lost myself. Sometimes I feel that it is a holy place, and Charles is its deus loci. *But he never came here, and besides, all the gods have absconded.*

I saw a great deal of Charles that summer and autumn. He was wayward, difficult, violent; charming, relaxed, easy; himself and not himself. At the end of May he was taken on by his stepfather's publishers, but he wasn't in a fit state for regular work, and after six weeks, by mutual agreement, he simply read manuscripts for them. His room was grubby, but light. He looked over a few gardens to the backs of the houses in the next street, and there was a lilac just below his window. The house was full of foreign students and spicy cooking smells, and he used to say that he found extraordinary things in the bathroom, like horse-clippers. Though he saw his family from time to time, it was considered better for him to be independent.

He went regularly to his analyst. Sometimes he would be deeply depressed, and I would find him sitting in a sort of spineless apathy, as though his bones had been removed and the flesh plumped into shape like a cushion. Sometimes I could cheer him up, sometimes not. But his depressions didn't last long, and usually he was, if not lively, at least quite alive. Very occasionally he would seem completely his old self. But when I once congratulated him on it, he said, 'And why do you say one aspect of me is more real than another?' If he hadn't been himself, he wouldn't have asked the question, but it was hard to explain it to him. Even when he was at his best he showed no sign of a sense of purpose. He used to joke about it, saying that life was simply a business of emptying one bucket into another and then back again, was digging and filling ditches, and that so long as you kept fit for the job you could carry on happily till you got the old age pension. It was when you'd got the pension and had nothing to fill up your time that you started wondering why on earth you'd spent such a pointless life. And once you started wondering that, the tedium of it all got you by the throat and you turned your face to the wall.

'I love that phrase,' he said, '"to turn your face to the wall". Isn't it beautiful? It expresses the feeling so exactly, in such human terms.'

He talked about sex quite freely, as always, and was liable to stop and look at a pretty girl in the street with an affected connoisseur's air. Sometimes he raised an eyebrow at a particularly handsome or tight-trousered man, too. But he said that if he had sex with anyone it would over-excite his analyst.

'I'm waiting for the transference,' he said. 'But I think it's too late. I was transferred years ago, like a footballer, and now I've hung up my boots.' That seemed rather enigmatic, but he refused to explain himself.

He was never, like most analysees, tedious about his latest self-discoveries; he made rather a show, in fact, of emotional reticence. He appeared to treat analysis as an absurd manifestation of the failure of religion in our time, saying that just as some primitive societies demanded a ritual circumcision, so the decadent culture of twentieth-century western man required all intelligent people to undergo a symbolic castration, more painful and more permanently damaging than anything a mere savage could think up. 'I shall never be the same again,' he said. I asked if that wasn't the whole idea.

He laughed. 'You must realize that we're all Jews now, just as we're all working-class.'

'What's that supposed to mean?'

'What it said.' Then, with a characteristically swift change of mood, he said with great seriousness: 'As a matter of fact I think I am a Jew. My grandfather's mother was almost certainly Jewish. The family, naturally, denies it, but it's quite true.'

'That only makes you one-eighth Jewish. To be a Jew you have to practise the religion.'

'Like the piano, you mean? But that's just bigotry. All you have to do to be a Jew is to feel like one.'

I thought of the photograph of the concentration camp death-pit and said nothing. It was true, certainly, that many people felt identified with the Jewish struggle to survive – I did myself. But from listening to my Jewish friends discussing their Jewishness and the situation of the Jews in England, I knew that my feeling was quite different from theirs. It didn't matter that it was different, but it was important, I thought, to recognize that a difference was there.

After Charles's death I discovered that his great-grandmother was of the usual hybrid English stock. Her father was a Yorkshire farmer, her mother the daughter of a Leicester draper. There is no reason whatever to suppose that she had any Jewish blood. Charles's imaginary Jewishness was a rationalization, I suppose, of his intense feeling of alienation from family, class and country.

Throughout those months Charles attacked my ideas, my life and my books ceaselessly, at times almost feverishly, though never, I felt, maliciously. At the beginning of the summer I was writing theatre criticism for *Town*, a magazine of which Charles gravely disapproved. But he often accepted my offer of a free ticket, and after the play we would argue passionately about, for instance, Laurence Olivier's Othello, which I deplored and he found magnificent, rather on the same ground that I had admired and he disliked Richard Burton's Hamlet. I always went to second nights, where I regularly saw the literary editor of *The Sunday Times*. We used to drink together in the intervals. Charles said I was simply sucking up, and refused to join us in the bar. When I got back to my seat he would say, 'Well, *lèche-cul*, fixed yourself a few good reviews? You should spend the interval thinking about the play you're paid to see, not advancing your career in the bar.' Then he would come out with something he'd been thinking up while I was drinking, and I wouldn't be able to answer because the curtain would have risen again.

We argued a great deal about art, its general value, its particular importance in a non-religious society, and above all its practice. We discussed technique, craft, style, dissected plays, novels, poems, disagreed profoundly about almost everything. It was a way, perhaps, of avoiding talking about ourselves. There was a violence in our arguments about art which we couldn't have borne, I think, in personal matters. If art is sublimation, then so was our criticism. Charles could be very severe.

'Your novels,' he said one day, 'are piss-awful'. I had published four by then, and was thought by some to be 'promising'. 'You've deliberately excluded all feeling, all passion, all personal emotion. Your heroes are dim, wet little men who don't care about anything, and feel sorry for themselves because they can't. Why? You're not dim and wet yourself. You talk very well, you have strong feelings and you state them strongly. But as soon as you write anything down, all the guts goes out of it, all the energy drains away in self-doubt. If you're determined to write about the uncertainty in the world, and it's a perfectly good subject, I agree, you've got to do it from a definite standpoint. You're getting nowhere the way you're doing it now.'

I defended myself by saying that my own standpoint was implied. There being no such thing as absolute truth, I tried to show situations which seemed to me to have significance beyond themselves from several possible viewpoints. Obviously I couldn't show them from every possible viewpoint, but by choosing the ones I did, I was in fact showing how I felt about the situations myself. It was only stupidity on the part of critics not to see this. A writer shouldn't necessarily appear in his own work. I admired impersonality in art.

'That's all evasion,' Charles said. 'You're scared shitless of showing what you actually feel, that's all. If you do feel. Do you?'

'Of course. But I don't feel confident that my feelings are more important or intense than anyone else's. So I try to imagine how other people see and feel and –'

'You're a moral coward. All this phony classicism of yours, the detachment, the impersonality, even the bloody elegance of your writing – oh, yes, it's depressingly elegant – the whole lot's defensive. You daren't let yourself go.'

'Balls. And anyway, where am I supposed to go *to*?'

'Inward, Christian soldier! Inward and upward!'

He would veer away from a topic like that, making some sudden puncturing joke, refusing to go on with the argument. But over the months we kept coming back to the same subjects to wrestle for another half-hour or so over William Burroughs and his cut-ups or the lack of satisfying content in my fiction or the tediousness of Nathalie Sarraute, whom I rather admired.

One day, infuriated, I goaded Charles into saying, 'Yes, I am much cleverer than you, damn it!'

'Then go ahead and prove it! Write something yourself! Any bloody fool can criticize.'

'All right, I will!'

That must have been in August, I think, when I was already working on my first film-script with Stanley Price. Stanley and I were beating our brains out day after day, trying, like all other scriptwriters, to think of one new twist to a plot which seemed as old as man. I used to report our delusory, desultory progress to Charles. We were continually thinking up brilliant ideas which solved everything till the following morning, when they solved nothing whatever. We were being paid, by our standards, handsomely, but, as others have found, money cannot buy inspiration. We used to play squash to relieve our frustration: Stanley always won.

Charles said I had sold out at last, and when I pointed out that he thought I was no good anyway and had no integrity to sell, he said, 'Relatively no good, Julian, not absolutely. Now perhaps it *will* be absolutely.' All I could think of saying was, 'You don't believe in absolutes,' to which he smiled ironically and said, 'Good, good! Put it in the movie.'

He offered suggestions whose uselessness was unquestionably absolute. He asked me, for instance, why I didn't send the hero and heroine on a day-trip to Calais.

'Why should I?'

'So that you can have Maurice Chevalier singing mildly bawdy songs at a little bistro. Atmosphere! They can hold hands. Then – suddenly – a shot rings out. Gregory Peck is dead!'

'He can't be. He's got to rescue the phony prime minister at the airport, just about the time the day-trip sets off from Dover.'

'That's precisely what's wrong with your film – no flexibility, no imaginative use of time. Why don't you write the first ever comedy thriller in which the hero dies halfway through? Then Sophia Loren can have the rest of the picture to herself.'

'Peck wouldn't take the part.'

'Then get someone else.'

'Movies aren't like that, Charles. You get the stars first, then the story. I'm hired by the week to do what the producer wants. And he wants Peck and Loren to survive, I assure you.'

'So much for the bright young hope of the English novel! Sold to the movies, a Hollywood hack!'

'Well, what else should I do for a living? I have no rich stepfather to support me.'

'There are garrets, aren't there? What's wrong with poverty and integrity and a little total devotion to your art?'

'People who live in garrets don't get to move through the whole of society, and novelists must.'

'Rubbish. Do you?'

'I move through what I can afford.'

'That's simply not true. You can *afford* to go and live in the East End, can't you? But you don't. You simper away at your typewriter in Chelsea. Have you ever been east of the City except to give yourself a little thrill of danger, crawling round those picturesque, fashionable dockyard pubs? What about Birmingham? Have you ever been to Birmingham?'

'Well, no, actually I haven't.'

'There!'

'Have you?'

'Of course not! What on earth would *I* want to go to Birmingham for? I'm not a novelist. I don't have to "move through the whole of society", thank God. I can go mad all by myself.'

'I thought you were a novelist. I thought you were going to show me how it's all done.'

'Was I? Then I must be crazy, mustn't I?'

In fact he was writing, though he never showed me anything. I thought I noticed a moderation in the violence of his criticism once he'd started. Occasionally he would say things like, 'There's nothing to be learnt from James Joyce – he's *sui generis*, like Richard Dadd.' (Dadd, I discovered later, was a mad nineteenth-century painter who killed his father and spent the rest of his life in an enlightened lunatic asylum.) I took Charles's odd remarks about writers to mean that he was deliberately trying various literary models and rejecting them. I don't know what his analyst thought about it all – or even whether he knew about it – but it seemed to me that Charles began to show a marked mental improvement as time went on. What he was doing might not have been art, but it was pretty good therapy. Though he still mocked the vaguely artistic world in which I lived, he seemed to be quite interested in meeting painters and other writers. Perhaps it was vanity, but I felt that I had communicated my own absorption in the business of writing to him, and that he was beginning to escape from his intellectual despair. It didn't mean that his emotional problem was solved or even soluble, but it was something to weigh against the days of spineless blackness. I may have imagined it, but these seemed to be getting fewer.

That autumn I found myself glad for the first time in my life to accept what someone wanted to give me. I felt that Charles was offering me his life, and that in taking it I was making it worth his living. I was very happy, and my happiness was the more acute for being so perilous. At any moment I feared the blackness might come down irretrievably. And I sensed, too, that if Charles did survive his slow, inching, dizzying retreat from the abyss, our relationship would never be the same again, that the happiness could not last, and that I shouldn't even want it to. He needed me now, to inch along beside him. I mustn't falter for a moment. But afterwards, we might never need each other again. I would lose his friendship, as I had lost the friendships I'd enjoyed on my submarine. There we had all lived on top of each other, quite literally at times, and by necessity had got to know each other almost better than ourselves. But a posting could end such a friendship in a couple of months. I have never seen any of my naval friends again since I left the Navy. I can hardly remember exactly what they looked like. It was quite possible, I realized, that in ten years time Charles and I would not recognize each other in the street. But I didn't mind. I felt utterly confident that I was doing good. It is a dangerous feeling, but enormously satisfying.

At the end of the year I was due to leave England for three months to teach at Colorado State University, where, to my pleasure and astonishment, I had been invited to be writer-in-residence. I wondered whether I shouldn't feign illness and cancel or postpone the appointment in order to stay in London with Charles. But he seemed, by December, to be so much better that I could safely leave him. Besides, to my amazement he urged me to go, saying that though there was little hope for me as a writer, I might yet make a passable teacher. 'Even though you don't seem to be able to get your enthusiasm for things down on paper,' he said, 'it comes out quite nicely in your talk. So long as you don't write your lectures out, you should be pretty good. And you've got to reside somewhere other than Chelsea from time to time. No one should ever turn down patronage.'

He helped me devise my course on twentieth-century literature and politics. He was much better read than I was, particularly in modern fiction, and he had a genius for getting to the heart of a work and seeing its real value. With contemporary writing that is always difficult: there are local, superficial reasons why one writer is admired more than another. Charles was only interested in the qualities which would make a book last. He was very scathing about academic literary critics – not the scholars who produce variorum editions of poets and playwrights, but the men who write generalized essays for the sophisticated weeklies and monthlies. He particularly disliked the work of Leslie Fiedler, which he called 'supplement sophistication'. And his disapproval of FR Leavis was almost as moral as some of Leavis's own disapprobations. 'Lawrence,' Charles said, 'was a very muddled man who wrote one or two quite good but muddled books, and to argue so exhaustingly that he is a great writer is a deplorable waste of energy which could be used to illuminate someone who really is great. The trouble with all that kind of criticism is that it's so busy justifying itself. The justification becomes more important than the work discussed.' As a matter of fact, I don't think Charles ever finished a book by either Leavis or Fiedler, and I have a strong suspicion that this was because he found things in them which he couldn't help but admire. Perverse though he was himself, he couldn't bear what he felt to be perversity in others.

The night before I left England I sat up with Charles till two in the morning. He was extraordinarily gay, bubbling over with an excitement I'd rarely seen in him before. I'd only ever spent one day in Colorado, driving from west to east, but he claimed to know it intimately from a week's trip he'd taken to Denver with some of his beat friends from Los Angeles.

'It's terrific!' he said. 'Real frontier country, not like California a bit. I don't just mean there are cowboys, though there are – they're two a penny. I mean that you feel you're really living on the edge of civilization. The Rockies are hostile great lumps of rock. You can't tame them. You can climb them – but so what? The valleys may be inhabited, but not the cliffs, the gorges, the peaks. They're really threatening.'

'Isn't that true of Switzerland, too?'

'No. The feeling's quite different. In Switzerland you get the sense that man has turned his back on the Alps where he can't use them and that it's safe to do so. But in the Rockies, you never feel safe.'

He went on about the exciting feeling of danger that the Rockies had given him for quite some time. I felt he was wishing he was coming to America with me.

Just before we said goodbye he became very serious. 'Now you're not to spend your time being a bloody Samaritan to your students,' he said. 'You're supposed to be a writer. So write something. And make it a damn sight better than anything you've done before. I'm depending on you.'

'But, Charles, for months you've done nothing but tell me I'll never be any good at writing at all!'

'Consistency is like innocence, an admirable quality in others, deplorable in oneself.' He smiled, pleased with his epigram. 'Besides, I've only been trying to wake you up. Now – I don't want another of your social conscience novels like the last one, and if you've got to have a wet hero, make him someone else's victim for a change, instead of his own. While you're away I'm going to write a novel myself. For you. A positive statement, to show it can be done.'

'It can't. The world's too difficult.'

'It can, and I shall do it. We're in competition. Not for one of those chic little prizes you're always after, but for fame, for the future. And believe it or not, I want you to win.'

I didn't know what to say, I was so surprised and moved. I thought I might break down and cry – with relief and joy and for no reason at all.

'You look like a magistrate in a Turkish bath,' he said, and bundled me out of his room and down the stairs. Before he opened the front door, he put his arm on my shoulder and said, 'Hurry back, won't you?' The arm felt as stiff as an iron bar, and I don't know what Charles meant me to understand by it. I shall bear its weight for the rest of my life.

He stood shivering on the pavement as I got into my car. A street light threw the shadows of bare branches across his face. We had first met in January, we parted in December. The light emphasized the long lines of his nose. It was spitting with icy rain, and he took off his glasses to wipe them. Our eyes met and he smiled blindly, then raised his arm in a half-wave, half-shrug. I drove away.

Fort Collins, Colorado, was not quite what I was expecting. Although it was a mile high, it lay on the uppermost edge of the vast tilting plain which runs from the foot of the Rockies to the Mississippi, and its climate was remarkably mild. It was not a frontier town, even though there were genuine cowboys everywhere, and trains wailed mournfully down the middle of the streets, hauling vast loads of sugar-beet. The university was full of modern buildings, the town of modern suburban houses. Fort Collins was interchangeable with a thousand small towns between Wyoming and Oklahoma. I was rather disappointed.

The day that Winston Churchill had the stroke which finally killed him, I developed appendicitis. Sweating with pain, I drove myself to the Poudre Valley Memorial Hospital, listening to a radio bulletin about the old man's greatness. I wanted to cry, though whether for myself or for Churchill I couldn't tell. I was quite clear-headed in a strange way, and I remember feeling furious that I wouldn't be in England to see the funeral. I'd been waiting for it for years, wanting to see how the British would celebrate the death of their last genuine hero. Now I would never know how it felt to be in the crowd and see the old man go by for the very last time. Perhaps that's why I wanted to cry.

I wrote to Charles from the hospital, telling him I'd started *A Circle of Friends* as he'd instructed me, and that there were three seventy- and eighty-year-old men in the ward with me who qualified as genuine pioneers. He didn't reply. But then, apart from our correspondence when we were in the Navy, he almost never wrote me a line.

I was soon teaching again, but the scar was painful and I found it difficult, physically, to write. I got tired very easily. I was living in a grim hotel and read a lot and was rather bored. I wrote and told Charles that my progress was slow.

One day at the end of February I received a letter from Charles's stepmother, forwarded from my English address:

'Dear Mr Mitchell,
I know you will have been very grieved to hear of Charles's accidental death. I am hoping that you and some of his other friends will come to the memorial service we are holding for him at St John's Wood Church on Thursday February 25th at 3 pm. Perhaps you would invite anyone you think would like to come. Charles always said you were his very best friend.

Yours sincerely
Annabel Humphries'

7

Charles's family naturally did what they could to conceal his suicide from themselves. His 'accident' was carefully, considerately planned. He went sailing in his father's dinghy in Chichester Harbour at eleven o'clock one morning and never returned. There was a strong breeze blowing, and it grew stronger. Next day the dinghy was found capsized at West Wittering. Charles had not gone sailing by himself for more than two years. It was 'obviously an accident'. His body was never found.

It shows how much Charles kept his family life secret that I knew neither that he could sail nor that his father had a weekend cottage at Bosham. His stepmother told me that they had had it for fifteen years, and that Charles had started sailing when he was sixteen. He loved it, she said almost defiantly; and he was very good, he used to win races. There was no doubt at all that it was an accident. He was so much better, for one thing. Perhaps he had taken off his glasses to wipe them, and then a sudden squall had capsized the boat. There were so many sailing accidents.

Among his things in Belsize Park was a box-file sealed with sticky tape and marked 'PRIVATE – in the event of my death to be opened only by Julian Mitchell'. I had watched him write the words myself. He had made a joke of it. 'You're the only person whose literary judgement I trust,' he'd said, 'because I've had some hand in creating it. And I'm writing this novel for you, not for anyone else. If I got run over or something, my family might want to publish it in a pious memorial volume. People change their opinions of their relatives once they're safely dead. I rely on you to spare my memory that embarrassment.' I had a whole cupboard full of my own manuscripts at home, and he agreed to act as my literary executor, too. There was nothing portentous about it. I felt no tremor of disaster. If anything, I thought we were slightly ridiculous, being so solemn about our literary remains. But as soon as I saw that he'd sealed the file I was sure that he'd killed himself.

I have no other evidence to go on. Mr Humphries gave me the box when I got back from Colorado. He was a sick man, who had recently had a stroke. He died last autumn. He was extremely nervous as I pulled off the sticky tape. Both of us were thinking the same thing, that Charles might have left a posthumous booby-trap, a letter stating his intention of committing suicide. The tape was difficult to get off, and as I struggled with it I thought how scrupulous Mr Humphries was. I knew that under similar circumstances I would have been quite unable to resist opening the file to make sure for myself.

Inside was the manuscript of *A New Satyricon*. I looked carefully through it. There was no note.

'It's the novel he was writing,' I said. 'He didn't want anyone but me to read it. It was a sort of private joke. There's nothing else.'

Mr Humphries was tremendously relieved. 'Well, that's a load off my mind,' he said. There was no need to elaborate. 'You'd better keep it, if it was meant for you. If it's any good, we might publish it, don't you think?'

'I don't know if he'd've wanted that.'

'Well, it's up to you.'

I took the manuscript home with me and read it that night. It was uncanny, at first, hearing his voice elaborately muffled through the voice of his main character, and I found the book hard to follow. I thought that it was unfinished, a series of unrelated fragments. Then I realized that the fragmentariness was deliberate, that the point of the book was that it could never be finished in the ordinary way. When I realized that as far as Charles was concerned this was a completed work of art, I felt absolutely certain that he had killed himself and his death finally became real to me, as it hadn't when I'd first heard of it or when I'd talked to Mr and Mrs Humphries. There was a hole in my universe.

Sometimes I wonder whether Charles may not, after all, be still alive, whether he capsized the boat and swam ashore and made off somewhere into a new life all his own. He started again so many times. And his body has never been found. Did he weight it with lead? Or was it only the past that he drowned? Perhaps I have walked beside him in the street and not known him, have sat next to him on a bus, have halted for him at a pedestrian crossing. I keep thinking I see him – I run after strangers, pursuing the impossible. Because of course he is dead. He must be dead. If he reads this, he will laugh.

He wasn't quite thirty when he died, but he was no Shelley. He didn't even like Shelley's poetry. And his drowning wasn't an accident, like Shelley's. I don't want to make it sound as though he was a golden youth, cut off just as his flowering began. I don't know what I want to do. I didn't intend to write all this when I started.

He was six feet tall and his hair was black and his eyes were brown and his eyebrows met over the bridge of his nose. His name was Charles. He made me laugh and cry. He is dead. He used to astound me. He said I looked like a magistrate in a Turkish bath. I failed him, and he is dead.

This is no pious memorial volume, I hope, though I have decided that *A New Satyricon* should be published. I believe it is unique and immense. Perhaps my judgement is wrong – I am far too close to the book to say. I never showed it to

Mr Humphries, because I thought it would upset him too much. Antonia has read it, and insisted on some changes which she thought might cause unhappiness to the rest of the family if they were to see it. They are very slight alterations, involving a few small cuts and in one place the removal of a paragraph. Lawyers have advised the removal of one other paragraph; Charles's parodies of contemporary writers may cause offence, but only in this one case was there any libellous material.

I think it unlikely that I shall write another book of my own for a long time, with the fact of this one before me. Charles said that all art comes from an inner need. He said that I began to write because I wanted to be a writer, and that was the wrong kind of need. Perhaps he was right. I feel a need now to get away from books. Literary men are unlovely, unwanted and dying out, Charles said. I have nothing in my heart to say now except this, whatever it is – homage, memoir, love-letter. I have tried to commemorate my friend with all the love that is in me.

Part Two

The New Satyricon

Note

Some people to whom I have shown *The New Satyricon* have found it baffling to the point of illegibility. I have therefore added a critical introduction and a running commentary. I have tried to make the latter helpful without being obtrusive, but those who prefer to read the novel as Charles left it should ignore it.

Introduction

P oetry is not a turning loose of emotion, but an escape from emotion; it is not the expression of personality, but an escape from personality. But, of course, only those who have personality and emotions know what it means to want escape from these things.

TS Eliot, *Tradition and the Individual Talent*

A simple and effective way of discharging aggression in an innocuous manner is to redirect it at a substitute object.

Konrad Lorenz, *On Aggression*

The aggressiveness of artists has not, as far as I know, yet been a subject for either ethological or critical research, but when one considers the avant-garde writing of the twentieth century, one cannot fail to notice a distinctly hostile tone. 'Read this, if you dare,' many writers seem to be saying; 'You won't understand it, even if you can bring yourself to finish it. I am cleverer, more sensitive, wiser and nicer than you, you crass, dull, petty bourgeois, ordinary human being.' The sheer unreadability of many writers, not all of them French, their obvious concern to baffle and daze the reader, their private snickering and deliberate nonsense, have not always been seen for what I believe they are – gestures which are primarily aggressive and only secondarily artistic. Most avant-garde manifestoes, for instance, are a good deal more interesting as protesting social documents than the poems and pictures which subscribe to them are valuable as literature or painting. The aggressive escape from emotion does not necessarily produce art. Yet Eliot's 'objective correlative' – by which the poet channels his feeling about something through a neutral object – and Lorenz's 'redirected aggression' seem to be closely allied.

Satire is the most aggressive form of literature, and the one in which the writer's escape from his own emotions is perhaps most obvious. Descriptions of satire always use military language, for instance – 'volley', 'broadside', 'sniping'. Yet one feels anguish behind the anger, desperation in the derision. It is not for me to make high claims for *The New Satyricon,* but I believe that its real literary merit lies in its combination of these things. It is an escape from an intolerable emotion, and an aggressive assault on the world Charles knew.

The Satyricon of Petronius, on which it is based, is known to literary historians as 'the first novel' and to the general public as a classic of pornography. Neither of these descriptions seems to me quite accurate, but this is not the place to dispute them. Charles first read *The Satyricon* in William Arrowsmith's brilliant modern translation, an American paperback copy of which I gave him the weekend I spent with him in Suffolk in the autumn of 1962. Only a fragment of Petronius's original work has survived, and as Arrowsmith says in his introduction, 'its genre, its theme, its size, even its title, are in dispute'. The fragment we have is itself very fragmentary. But it seems to be agreed that it is satirical in three senses: it is 'a potpourri or farrago of mixed subjects in a variety of styles', it satirizes, in the modern sense, various aspects of life in Nero's Rome, and it is a 'satyr-book' – 'that is, concerned with satyrs, which is to say, lecherous, randy'. All these three elements can be found in Charles's modern version.

'*The Satyricon,* Arrowsmith says, 'is a satirical comedy based upon a fictional narrative both episodic and recognizably picaresque in nature. It also freely and gaily mixes and parodies half a dozen other genres, and these parodied genres are in turn central to the comedy at the same time that they provide scope to the satirist.' The central character is Encolpius ('The Crotch'). He has a running affair with a faithless boy called Giton, but every obstacle is put in the way of his achievement of any lasting satisfaction, and he is himself the butt of much of the satire. He is a crook, a lecher, a pervert, wicked, witty and delightful. Somehow he has offended Priapus, the god of lust, and he is pursued by divine anger from one calamity to another in a parody of the *Odyssey*.'

I don't want to go into details of *The Satyricon*, because they are not important to Charles's modern version. There is no direct correspondence of scenes or characters between the two books, and what Charles satirizes is very different from what Petronius attacked. But the general shapes and themes are the same, and it was presumably these which drew Charles to use the fragmentary classic as his model. The fragmentariness itself undoubtedly appealed to him. He once said to me that the traditional narrative line of the novel was of no interest to him. 'Why bother with all those boring explanations?' he said. 'Why tell people how A got from B to C? Why not just have characters and scenes?' When I protested that people would get lost or bored without some thread of plot, he agreed. 'Of course one must have connections between scenes,' he said. 'But if the same characters keep reappearing, that's all you need.'

There is, in fact, a strong, simple plot behind the vagaries of *The New Satyricon*. The 'hero', Henry, arrives in a new country, immediately sees and falls in love with someone whose sex, age and character are all quite unknown to him, and spends the rest of the novel trying to find her or him. His pursuit of his beloved leads him into ludicrous situations which give Charles an opportunity to satirize modern life. Like Encolpius, Henry seems to be hounded by an angry fate from one disastrous episode to another. He has been, one gathers, something of a satyr himself; the comedy springs partly from his being now a victim of lewdness rather than a randy aggressor.

I suspect that Charles began the novel with the intention of keeping it purely satirical, but that the second element – the furious pursuit of the hero – gradually became more and more important to him. Perhaps he felt a guilty need to punish himself for attacking so many other people. It would be wrong to see Henry as a self-portrait, of course; but it is true that Henry's persecution takes on more and more the shape of Charles's own destructive fantasies. The escape from personality of which Eliot wrote can never be entirely successful; Charles's attempt to escape was as doomed as anyone else's. Though it is also much more, *The New Satyricon* is obviously a psychological document of considerable interest; in a sense, it is a surrealist account of Charles's fantasy world.

But to see it only as that would be to miss a great deal. The central theme of the satire seems to me an important one. Everyone, everything, that is mocked in the novel is guilty of the same kind of error, of treating life like art, as something to be observed and criticized and compared rather than lived. Henry is himself particularly prone to this standing aside. He has obviously read a good deal, if not very deeply, in history, literature, philosophy, psychology, anthropology and criticism; he has travelled widely. But he is essentially an observer, and when he falls suddenly in love, his whole way of life is stood on its head. When he is finally compelled to acknowledge his love for what it is, he becomes almost blind in an effort to avoid seeing it. The end of this mixture of farce and parody and grotesquery can only be tragic – at least as Charles wrote it. Like *King Lear,* it could be rewritten with a happy ending, but that would be, I think, completely to miss the point. The key passage occurs very near the end:

'. . . ever seeking more knowledge and experience to compare with the knowledge and experience I already possessed in almost unmanageable quantities, but to no purpose that I could now see but this ceaseless business of comparison, which set me apart from my fellow beings and made it impossible for me ever to be part of any of the societies I studied, so that I was filled with unutterable despair as I stared with my blind eyes into a future which promised only a further series of expeditions and comparisons until my life should end.'

Henry is as much a victim of the attitudes he satirizes as anyone else. There is, too, a strong masochistic element in him, for which Charles clearly drew on his own experience. That this had something to do with Charles's relationship with his own father cannot, I think, be doubted. The dominating theme of the last part of the novel is the story of Abraham and Isaac, with Henry firmly in the role of Isaac and no ram in the thicket, alas. But I don't want to give the reader my version of the book, merely to suggest some of the strands which run through it. Less prejudiced readers may find both more and less in it than I do.

A word about Henry's style. This is itself a parody, though not, as far as I can make out, a parody of any particular book or author. It is florid, inflated, heavily 'literary'; perhaps Charles had eighteenth-century masterpieces of pornography in mind, like *Fanny Hill*. The point of it is that it allows absolutely everything to be said, without needing the four-letter words, while it keeps the events described at a deliberate, almost official distance. This distancing enables Charles to mock the whole business of writing. Literature is only fantasy, he wants us to realize, and both reader and writer are observers like everyone else. Through the style, he satirizes himself as a satirist.

We had many discussions about the relationship between art and life, fact and fiction, and Charles was always caustic about novelists' 'unscrupulous lying'. I used to argue for the illusion of realism through the elimination of the author from his work; Charles said that the only honest thing for a writer to do was to display himself in and through his book. 'I don't give a damn about stories,' he said. 'Not in themselves. But I'm always interested in the people telling them.' The style he chose for *The New Satyricon* certainly puts the narrator firmly between the reader and the narrative – at times so much as to overpower the story altogether. But it is true that the obvious delight of the writer in the style is a – very literary – compensation. Curiously, for me, the style fails to display the Charles I thought I knew; it is defensive rather than aggressive. But this was probably intentional, part of the counter-double-bluffing of which the novel is full.

The prose causes little difficulty if the reader imagines it being read aloud, as Arrowsmith suggests Petronius meant *The Satyricon* to be. Little is known of the historical Petronius, but Charles, who disliked most writers he met, once said that of all authors, he was easily the most attractive human being. He liked to quote two remarks from Tacitus about him (Arrowsmith's translation): 'Unlike those prodigals who waste themselves and their substance alike, he was not regarded as either a spendthrift or a debauchee, but rather as a refined voluptuary.' Charles would have liked to have been considered a refined voluptuary himself. The other quotation was this: 'So he severed his veins and then bound them up as the fancy took him, meanwhile conversing with his friends, not seriously or sadly or with ostentatious courage. And he listened while they talked and recited, not maxims on the immortality of the soul and philosophical reflections, but light and frivolous poetry.'

Petronius, condemned by Nero, had no choice but to commit suicide. Charles clearly felt he had no choice, either. Our modern Neros are even more tyrannical than the old ones, for they are in ourselves. Recently, I came on a doubtful fragment of Petronius, printed by John Sullivan in his Penguin version of *The Satyricon*. As far as I know, Charles never knew of it, but it sums up, in light and frivolous poetry, much of the dilemma from which *The New Satyricon* was an attempt to escape. If only it had succeeded!

Before my birth the gods, they say,
Discussed what sex I'd be.
'Boy!' said Phoebus; 'Girl!' said Mars;
Said Juno, 'I disagree'.
So I was born hermaphrodite,
But how was I to die?
The goddess was first with the answer·
'The sword!' Said Mars, 'The cross!'
But Phoebus decided on drowning,
So I had to die of them all.
A tree hung over a stream,
Wearing my sword, I climbed –
A slip, we were driven together:
My feet caught in a branch,
My head dipped into the stream –
Not woman, not man, yet both:
River and Sword and Cross.

[*The novel opens in the customs hall of an airport. While undergoing the usual examination, the narrator sees 'a creature of such extraordinary grace and proportion' that he at once falls passionately in love. His behaviour arouses the suspicion of the customs official, and he is taken away for a degrading physical search.*

This prelude to the novel introduces several basic themes: there is rather obvious satire on officialdom, there is Henry's first humiliation, and there is the first example of his delving, questioning, distancing approach to things – in this case his own falling in love. The very first paragraph suggests the endlessly repeated pattern of human behaviour: starting with an absurd catalogue of the world's contents (?), it ends with a powerful image of meaningless human activity. The whole section could be seen as a rationalized birth-trauma: Henry enters, in all innocence, a strange country and is at once met with hostility and humiliation.

I doubt whether Charles intended it to be read like this, but it is a hard interpretation to avoid.]

Customs

••• held up a small card which invited me to declare to the officer all agricultural implements, beachwear, cooking utensils, drinks vinous and spirituous, elephant guns, forceps, green vegetables, hacking jackets and other excisable objects, and which went on to draw attention to the grave penalties which could be imposed for any infringement of the many regulations then in force to govern the import of foodstuffs, metals, animals, materials and other goods both manufactured and raw, to enumerate all of which would be to throw valuable light on the country's economy, though only at considerable effort, for the list is continually changing, with parrots freed from duty as plasticine is taxed, so that any enumeration would be endless, as though one was a painter on a suspension bridge, committed for life to moving back and forth, up and down, in all weathers, in a regular, changeless pattern of progress which gets one precisely nowhere, for one begins always at one's end and ends ever again at one's beginning.

Mastering both my amusement and my impatience at the tedious familiarity of the pasteboard warning, I let my eyes appear to move slowly down it, while I focused, using the method I had been taught by the Brazilian optometrist, on the elderly Croatian who had so coarsely attempted to assault me as we passed over neutral waters during our flight. I was delighted to see that he was now suffering some humiliation at the neighbouring counter, for his interrogating officer tapped twice on the large, string-tied, yellow case in a bored but peremptory order to open up. Foolishly, I smiled – perhaps, even, I smiled foolishly – and a finger rapped fiercely on my own small leather bag.

'This is no joking matter!' exclaimed the officer. 'Do you understand this notice, yes or no?'

'Yes,' I answered, adopting a cringingly apologetic stance. 'It is not difficult to understand, thank you.'

'Open your case!' he thundered. 'I wish to inspect!'

I cursed my momentary lapse, inexcusable in a man who had so much experience of how a smile, a thoughtless blow of the nose or an idle scratching of the member could be taken as a twitch of guilt by such humourless St Peterkins. Indeed, I have heard them argue that a genuine sneeze is an illegal method of introducing livestock into the country, for nasal bacteria are, in a sense, livestock; and so all visitors should, if the law is strictly to be enforced, be baked to a high temperature before being admitted, and then only after a prolonged period of quarantine.

I opened my bag and stood respectfully back as the officer poked and pried, holding up for public ridicule the pyjama cord whose history I have already . . .

> . . . a creature of such extraordinary grace and proportion
> that I was immediately rooted to the spot, heart-struck,
> hoping for the small gesture, the quick turn of the head,
> which would allow the facial features to be as indelibly
> imprinted on my brain as the back of the head, the back of
> the shoulders and the back proper already were. I say
> 'imprinted', for no other . . .

Ridiculous? Of course. Absurd? How can I deny it? Grotesque? Certainly. Irresponsible? Unpatriotic? Undialectical? Yes, yes, yes.

But how else can I put it? It is the truth. I appeal to your experience, and ask you to consider with the complete and private honesty of your most midnight thoughts the following questions.

Question 1. Have you ever, while walking down a street, waiting to be served in a shop, watching a royal or presidential progress or a football match, stepping on or off a bus or train, conducting your usual business in your habitual fashion – have you ever seen, for a flash and moment, the most beautiful person on earth (gender, age, and physical characteristics determined by your own, and by the direction of your sexual fantasies)?

If your answer to this question is 'No', there is no need to attempt the remaining questions.

Question 2. What did you do about it?

If your answer to this question is, as I expect, 'Nothing', allow me to suggest why, and why nothing, in fact, was all you could, or wished to, do.

Primo, you were too astonished to act.

Secundo, the creature of inordinate beauty was in such temporal and spatial relationships to yourself that it was impossible for any communication between you to take place – e.g., the creature was alighting from the bus as you were stepping on, there was a press of people between you, you caught your glimpse only through an accidental eddy in the crowd and another haphazard movement ended it.

Tertio, even if you had not been incapacitated by astonishment or the physical and temporal situation, you would not have known what to do, being quite unprepared by upbringing and education for a situation whose only analogy would seem to be with the mystical experience of divines both christian and heathen. For the appearance of the beautiful creature in one's life is, truly, like an annunciation of perfect love by a tangible angel, the glimpse is literally blinding. And you do not credit angels and visions and the ecclesiastical claptrap which surrounds, and in most cases also begets, them.

You have no systematic method of dealing with such things, even when the annunciation is of flesh and blood. You are like an aborigine before a computer; you do not know what questions to ask, what knobs to press. Or rather, you are like a computer confronted with the logical but scientifically inaccurate systems of relationships devised by aborigines. You are not programmed to cope.

Question 3. Are you reconciled to the extreme unlikelihood of ever seeing the creature again?

This is the most difficult question to answer, since one cannot predict one's reaction to a second glimpse, any more than to a first. A second meeting implies dangers and difficulties, such as the immediate abandonment of wife and children, if they exist, in favour of the creature of total perfection – always supposing her or him to be willing and available. Furthermore, imagination may have altered the creature out of all recognition by subjecting him or her to intricate personal fantasies involving all the hopes and fears of which one is capable, so that the reality of a second glimpse might be practically dismaying rather than the expected occasion for joy, might indeed be positively unwelcome and . . .

. . . say is that it was as though a new element had entered the universe, and all the old ones had to shuffle round and adjust themselves to its powerfully radioactive presence.

And how can you believe me when I say that all this was achieved by the merest of back views, so that even the gender was indeterminable? That I saw only the black hair falling behind the upturned collar of the raincoat, whose anonymous whiteness and straight lines did not perfectly indicate either the wideness of hip which would assert femininity or the narrowness which might betray a man? Length of hair – and I could not even be sure how long the hair was – is no guide to gender in these ambiguous times, and the one ear which

I briefly saw was of medium size, neither distinctively male nor distinctively female, and without ring or jewelled stud to assist me. Had I been capable of reason at that moment I might have moved to left or right to obtain a different view, or have leaned forward across the counter to obtain a sight of the anatomy below the hem of the raincoat, but I was not capable of reason, and the problem of gender had not yet occurred to me, for I was struck dumb, motionless, overwhelmed by my vision of perfection.

The officer was speaking to me, but I was quite unable to attend his words. He became vexed.

'Answer me!' he cried. 'I am an official of the state! What is this object?' He placed his person between the exquisite creature and myself and waved my sponge before my face.

'It is my sponge,' I said, paying him brusque heed. 'For what did you take it?'

I endeavoured to peer past him, now taking those quick steps to right and left which I had earlier neglected, but the officer was determined to confront me directly and mimicked my efforts, so that to uninformed observers we must have appeared to have been engaged in some unsophisticated ritual dance, probably rural in origin, the counter between us like some primitive altar.

'A sponge indeed!' he jeered, dancing up and down as well as sideways. 'Here then, wipe your face with it!' So saying, he thrust the sponge into my hand. 'You are sweating and dancing about! Most suspicious behaviour! I must ask you to step this way for an examination!'

The purport of his invitation quite escaped me in my bemused state, though I was aware of some threat in his tone, and when he fllipped open the counter and stood aside with a sarcastic waiter's bow, I felt only relief and pleasure that he was no longer obstructing my view and that I should at last be able to see the beautiful creature from a closer and possibly, if all went well, from a different angle, with even the hope of a glimpse of the perfect features. However, . . .

Turning to catch a last glance, as I hoped, of my vision, I saw only the officer's face, remarkable for its evil expression of glee, the moustache small and clipped like a suburban hedge, a sure sign of obsessive neatness and puritanical aggressiveness towards the weaknesses both moral and physical of others, and I began at last to realize the possible extent of my predicament, which . . .

. . . in a most reasonable manner that I was extremely anxious to catch the regular airport bus into the city.

'We'll have to see about that!' he exclaimed. 'And whom have you arranged to meet on it, I wonder! Ha! Ha!' He flung open the door and pushed me roughly in. 'I know your sort!' he cried.

The room was an ill-kept antechamber with a few poorly designed chairs in which I was glad not to linger.

'Extremely suspicious behaviour!' he announced, as though such was my name. 'Sweating and not answering questions! Dancing about!'

It was then that I became suddenly aware of an urgent need to relieve myself, brought on, in part, by my dislike of airborne facilities, and my puzzlement and suspicion as to the methods of disposal employed in airliners several thousand feet above the earth's surface, and in part, doubtless, by the shock of my vision and the subsequent fear induced by the officer's hostility and his deliberate interposition of his person between myself and my vision. I therefore asked his superior, for such by the quantity of gilt tassels upon his shoulders I judged the clean-shaven man behind the desk to be, if I might be permitted to visit a lavatory before the investigation, if such was necessary, began. The two men exchanged a significant look.

'Unaccompanied, naturally! No one to watch you dispose of the contraband!' the junior officer burst out. 'We are complete idiots, of course!'

I at once denied any ulterior purpose and invited the officers to accompany me, if they so wished, to the washroom.

'I think not yet,' said the senior. 'First we will take your statement, if you please, as to your guilt or innocence of the charge.'

'I know of no charge,' I answered. 'I am no smuggler, captain, and to establish the truth of the matter, I invite you to search my baggage and my person. I shall make no resistance, for my conscience is clear. But I do beg you to make no more ado about it, for I am extremely anxious to take the bus into the city, if it is at all possible.'

'Thank you,' said the captain. 'If you will be so good as to remove your clothes, the business can be completed with expedition satisfactory to all parties.'

'May I not first visit the washroom?' I asked.

'No,' he replied, producing a porcelain chamber-pot illuminated with the country's coat-of-arms and placing it neatly on his blotting-pad. 'Remove your clothes, and then, if your need is really as urgent as you state, avail yourself of this receptacle. Let us begin, sir.'

His politeness was a relief after the exclamatory hostility of his minion, and I undressed myself with an alacrity encouraged by the literal pressing of my need and my passionate desire to be out of the place altogether. Very soon I was standing . . .

'Bend over, he said, donning an orange rubber glove and smearing the forefinger with some patent grease. 'Though this will not hurt, it may startle you.'

I found it, indeed, astonishing, and could not help reflecting on the irony of the situation, that one who had so lately seen an angel should now adopt the posture of a beast and be subjected to this crude veterinary examination!

'Surely,' I said, after a minute had passed, 'it cannot be necessary to repeat the insertion and exploration so often.'

'It will soon be completed,' the white-coated figure replied.

[*We next discover Henry at the hotel in which the rest of the action of the novel takes place. Typically, he speculates at length about a couplet he finds hanging above the reception desk. This is the first of several parodies of academic literary criticism, and its point is, if I've understood it correctly, that Henry completely misses the point. Though it is nowhere explicitly stated, it seems clear enough that the name of the hotel is ' The Western World', and that the couplet refers simply to the management's hope that it will satisfy its customers. Charles was perhaps afraid of appearing obvious, and so avoided making this clear. (Of course, my interpretation may be as absurd as some of Henry's are.) The couplet is taken from Timothy Dwight's 'Greenfield Hill' (1794).*

Henry then blunders into the wrong room, where an initiation ceremony is being held by the Encolpius Society, named after the hero of Petronius's Satyricon *and devoted to sex for sex's sake. This is the first piece of serious satire on contemporary attitudes. Henry is revealed as a satyr, as foolish about sex as his fellow Encolpians, though capable of greater athleticism and aestheticism.*]

The Encolpians

• • • red letters the following couplet, doubtless by some local poet, though no attribution or acknowledgement was made:

All hail, thou Western world! by heaven designed
Th' example bright, to renovate mankind.

It seemed an unusual and challenging distich to hang above the reception desk of so obscure an hotel, but I assumed it to represent the political feelings of the manager, perhaps an ex-officer in his country's now defunct colonial service, who remembered with pride the good work he had done, or believed himself to have done, in enlightening the backward tribes of his area as to the superiority of the civilization he was himself disseminating. Equally, I thought, the couplet could have an emblematic or religious significance rather than a political one, with 'thou Western world' standing for some divine spirit ('by heaven designed') which shone in such an exemplary fashion that 'mankind' (presumably not, in this interpretation, of heavenly design) would be made new, i.e. according to some superhuman, therefore heavenly, plan.

I did not feel it wise to question the manager there and then on so trivial a literary matter, for he appeared sleepy and none too pleased by my arrival, and might not have been the manager but a mere unlettered assistant to judge by the way he thrust several complex forms at me with a roughly phrased request to complete them without delay, which I did, with great care, not wishing to run foul of the country's laws again that evening. While I was thus occupied, another interpretation of the couplet occurred to me, in which I, as the guest, was welcomed in flattering terms as 'thou Western world!', i.e. a man of science and culture, who was bringing these valuable attributes with me to renovate the city, here personified as 'mankind'. But this exegesis raised formidable obstacles. First, the city, while by no means at the hub of western civilization, was certainly not by any ordinary interpretation of the words eastern, Asian or African, and would be showing excessive humility in referring to itself as 'non-western', even by implication; second, if 'mankind' and 'thou western world' were opposed, as they seemed to be, who or what were the latter? Were they perhaps angels?

The question continued to vex me as I handed the completed forms back to the manager who, somewhat to my surprise, at once requested me to deposit a considerable sum in advance of normal payment. I could only assume that it was the lateness of the hour and my somewhat woebegone appearance, the result of my altercation with the criminal and one-eyed taxi-driver, which raised suspicions. . .

. . . the numeral 6 may be inverted to read 9 and vice versa, and that I had therefore erred in supposing that the manager has misdirected me out of either malice or ignorance. The room adjoined a bathroom, and before proceeding further I took the opportunity of using its facilities. Though I would have enjoyed a prolonged immersion after all I had been through, I decided to make immediate use only of basin and bidet, feeling a particular gratitude, after the grotesque incident at the airport, that the hotel had imported the latter. My toilet afforded me much comfort after the day's vicissitudes, and I left the bathroom in good spirits, only to discover, as I entered what

I took to be my room, a most surprising scene, for the bed was already occupied by a man of middle years who was performing, as I supposed, his marital duties to a somewhat younger woman whom I naturally took to be his wife.

Apologizing profusely, I was about to withdraw discreetly when I observed that there were many other people in the room watching this socially desirable performance, one of whom tapped me on the arm and indicated an easy, though empty, chair, close to the head of the bed, which I refused in dumb show, not wishing to draw any further attention to myself. The man, however, seemed not to understand me, for he became insistent and tugged at my arm, until I felt obliged to explain my mistake in plain words. At this the couple suspended their business, and the woman said, 'Close the door, please; there's a draught.' Someone obliged her at once, and to avoid further embarrassment I resigned myself to the situation and took the chair which had been offered me, for I felt a distinct hostility towards my intrusion, as though I had disturbed a divine service. In order to become as inconspicuous as possible I pulled my raincoat about my face and put my bag on my knees, carefully copying the motions of the other spectators, an easy enough exercise in imitation for they were merely staring fixedly at the couple, who now recommenced their intercourse. The silence of the room was broken only by the rhythmical complaining of the springs, and I began, after several minutes of dull copulation, to feel drowsy and to think longingly of my omelette, lightly dusted with chopped parsley.

In order to keep myself awake, for I felt it would be rude to fall asleep, I began to reflect on the possible significance of the performance I was witnessing, albeit with a lacklustre eye. Clearly I had been wrong to assume that it was a mere marital conjugation upon which I had blundered and there was some, to me as yet hidden, serious moral purpose behind the surface bawdiness of the occasion, for the audience appeared to be rapt and unsmiling, in some instances actually frowning with the effort of concentration, and my wide experience of 'exhibitions' and similar displays led me to believe that this could not therefore be one of them. For instance, there was neither cheering on of the male performer, nor drunkenness, nor lechery among the voyeurs, who seemed more like medical students in an operating theatre than young men on a frolic. They were, however, all young or youngish, and all men, though of several hues and differing racial stock, and I wondered briefly if they might not perhaps be on one of the unenlightened government courses for converting sexual deviants to the classical postures which had made the country the laughing-stock of the civilized world. But this seemed, on a second consideration, far from likely in view of the recent change of government and the new administration's emphasis on almost any practical method of birth control, in spite of opposition from the expected Vatican quarters which had, on this occasion, earned themselves the local sobriquet of 'hindquarters'. Thinking of this frail joke, I involuntarily smiled, at which a man who appeared older than the majority of those present called out 'Stop!' and the couple on the bed, who had shown signs neither of enjoyment nor approaching climax nor even of interest in their work, stopped, disengaged, and lit cigarettes.

'You smiled,' said the man, addressing me.

'I must apologize,' I said. 'I was thinking of something else.'

'And of what?'

'Of the official spokesman in Vatican hindquarters.'

There were smiles among those standing near me, and the man who had spoken to me, and who was wearing, I noticed, a specially tailored jacket somewhat reminiscent of the blazer of a club I had once joined at school, though the buttons were much larger and came in pairs, allowed a small flicker of amusement to cross his face.

'You have raised mirth and are therefore permitted to continue with the initiation,' he said.

'I feel,' I replied, 'that I must take the opportunity of this hiatus to point out that I came here in error, looking for my room, which is number 6 or 9, I am no longer sure which, and where an omelette should by this time be awaiting me. I apologize for interrupting your revels, and I beg you to accept my assurances that it was in complete innocence and ignorance that I intruded upon them. Now, if I leave you, you will be able to continue them to your own satisfaction, while I will be able to break a long fast with my omelette. Gentlemen, good evening.'

'Not so fast,' returned my neighbour. 'We do not permit strangers to overlook our mysteries even in innocence. You must join with us or die. What is your name?'

I hesitated, as I had already given it to three people in this country who had mocked me for it immediately, and I did not wish to be mocked again, let alone by a man who had so casually threatened me with death. I decided therefore to give myself, as far as these young people were concerned, an alias, and the first name which came into my head was one by which I had been known in my cradle.

'My name,' I stated firmly, 'is Baba.'

'That cannot be,' said the man. 'That is the name of our chaplain. You must name yourself again.'

'Paddock,' I said, though why I should have chosen a toad's name I cannot imagine, unless the proceedings had put me in mind of the witches in Shakespeare's popular tragedy Macbeth.

There were frowns at this second suggestion and a man standing behind the club's president, for such I decided he must be, said, 'That will never do. That is my name.'

'You may try once more,' said the president.

I decided to risk the truth and said, 'Henry'.

There was a great shout of laughter, and the woman who still reclined on the bed slapped her bare thigh in exuberant mirth. The laughter quickly turned to calls for my prompt initiation into the society, and someone said, as though proposing a toast,

'Encolpius has need of him!' at which there was more laughter and some cheering. I pleaded that I might be spared any further rough-housing that evening, and explained shortly the unpleasantness I had already been obliged to endure. My relation won me much sympathy from the society's members, and I was assured that an early project of the club's executive committee would be to find out and severely to punish those responsible for my monstrous and undeserved treatment, but meanwhile I must, having begun them however unwittingly, consciously complete the ceremonies on which I had blundered, along with two other men of about my own age. When I begged on the grounds of starvation and faintness to be allowed first to consume my waiting omelette, the president replied that my eggs must first be broken, a statement which drew more laughter from my initiated brethren, but which caused me some alarm, though there was nothing for it but to resign myself to their boyish high spirits, and hope that no harm would come to me and that the ritual would not be too lengthily extended.

Before we began, I asked the president if he could explain one thing to me. 'I am a stranger in this country,' I said, 'and newly arrived, and every time I am asked what my name is and reply truthfully that it is Henry I am mocked and abused. I would be much obliged if you could explain to me why this perfectly ordinary name should induce such mirth in your fellow-countrymen.'

'That,' said the president with a smile which caused me some further alarm, 'is something you will discover during the course of this evening, for what in our country is called Henry is doubtless called something quite different in yours. But what we call Henry we never call anything else, and you will find it no handicap to have so frank and unblushing a name when you come to explore the byways of our land and to enjoy its cultural folklore.

'Let me now explain to you the conduct of our rites. This lady and gentleman who have been performing in so desultory a fashion, as you observed, did so in order to test the initiates' ability to ignore activities which though commonly thought to be sexually stimulating are not so unless artistically performed. As some societies are devoted to the tasting of wine, and to the scholarship of the nose, the expertise of cork and bouquet, so is ours dedicated to the scholarship of the sexual appetite, its refinement and sophistication, its ultimate gratification raised to the status of a major art-form. Just as the connoisseur of wine drinks for the pleasure of his palate, not to get drunk, so we perform sexual exercises for the maximum gratification of as many senses as possible, not simply to beget children. Anyone can produce children, but few can treat sex as the aesthetically satisfying experience that it should, that it was designed to, be. We are sexualists for the sake of sexuality. Anyone who had shown any sign of wishing to snigger, or worse still of any physical stimulation at the sight of the clumsy copulatory gestures which have just concluded, would have been automatically refused entry to the society, and his sponsor would have had to account for himself and give good reasons why he himself should not be expelled. Your own obvious lack of interest to the point where you were smiling in self-absorption at a crude anti-Catholic joke indicates the high standard of self-control which is an essential condition of club membership. Our motto is "Without shame, in exquisite taste". It is believed to be a translation from the Persian, though I myself suspect it to have been the invention of our founder. The club has been in existence, either above or below ground, since the year 66. We will now proceed.'

I was unable to take any interest in the series of postures, normal and abnormal, with which the novices now served, as with dishes from a fleshly kitchen, for though the positions were often prettily taken, none were new to me, and I felt that the club's standards were not, perhaps, as high as they should have been. When at last the postures ceased and the participants withdrew, covering their nakedness in defiance of the club's motto, and without, as far as I could judge, having given any pleasure whatever either to their audience or to themselves, we were invited to gather at a long table to eat oysters and drink champagne, while the president affirmed his pleasure that none of the novices had disgraced his sponsor. He then announced the next stage in the ceremony which was not, as I had hoped, a banquet, but a second and more subtle testing of our sophistication by a series of postures and performances, some of which we were expected to respond to with applause, some with enthusiastic participation and some with silence and contempt. The champagne and oysters revived me considerably, and I was surprised to notice that it was not yet midnight, but as my spirits rose, so did my longing to see again my exquisite vision and to escape from the tedious and boyish rites in which I had got myself so strangely involved. I decided, therefore, to make a plea for special treatment and somewhat to the consternation of my neighbours rose and delivered the following extempore speech.

'Mr President, gentlemen; as has been well said, a man who has to make a speech should do three things and three things only – stand up, speak up and shut up. Before I conclude, I would like to make a short personal statement, in the hope that it may move – and I sincerely believe and pray that it will move – the hearts of all those present, not to say their bowels of compassion. Speaking parenthetically, I hope that having made two bad, indeed despicable, jokes, the club will allow me to dispense with jokes altogether. I cannot believe that the searching and stringent series of couplings which the society deems necessary to detect any lack of refinement in its potential members need serve as a model for the construction of speeches – and I say this not in any critical . . .'

'. . . a creature of such perfection and beauty, a vision of such overwhelming splendour, that no one you can produce for my delectation and applause this evening can possibly obtain either. Not the muscular haunches of Ibo maidens, nor the pampered skins of Parisiennes, not the legs of Bedouin shepherds nor the rumps of American freshmen, the eyelashes of the Sinhalese or the yellow fringes of Swedes, the breasts of Californian swimmers or the smooth thighs of Javanese sailors, not all that every continent can boast can distract me now or ever, so long as I live, from my pursuit. And yet, gentlemen, I do not know even so much as the gender of this creature, I know only that he or she exists somewhere in this city of yours which has so rightly been named the bower of Eros. Believe me, my brothers, neither whips nor scorpions, the crescent nor the cross, can delay me now, can save me from the ceaseless search – not for an ideal, not that – I would not ask or want help merely for that – but for a reality, a walking, breathing, exquisite, attainable reality, somewhere quite close to where we are now gathered, perhaps even here amongst us, disguised from me by the face I have never seen.

'Will you help me to find it? It is the help of your hearts and hands that I ask, the assistance of your five senses, your eyes to peer, your ears to harken, your noses to scent, your fingers to feel, your tongues to taste, till we have found perfection, dwelling here in this golden city, mysteriously absent like the bubbles in champagne while it is caged within its bottle, but which yet burst forth in all their glory when the cork is drawn. Gentlemen! Draw the cork from my vision! Let it be found flowing in a stream of golden reality, more splendid than heaven, more beautiful than earth, at once human and divine, tangible yet needing touch to make it visible, my one desire, my hope, my future! Will you give me your aid? I ask it in the name of everything you hold dear!'

I sat down to tremendous applause, not wholly undeserved, for while my effect was calculated, I had spoken with such lucid passion that I had brought tears to my own eyes as well as to those of my . . .

. . . plank beds, on the first of which lay a young woman of great sexual attraction, and on the second a young man of obvious physical stamina. After we had been solemnly undressed, we were led to chairs behind the two beds and given a brief homily on the need for paying the closest attention to what would follow. Each member of the club was to demonstrate to climax a different posture with each of the young persons on the beds, and when these demonstrations were completed, we would be expected to prove our suitability by performing new postures of our own invention, which would be criticized for dexterity, originality, feasibility and artistry by the society's members, a committee of whom had been selected to test the male posture on its creator. The president would perform first, in reverent silence, the postures voted most conventional, and therefore requiring the greatest art, and he would be followed by the other twenty-two members of the society in an order drawn by lot. A variation on an existing and demonstrated posture would not count as a new one, we were warned, and our attention was drawn to the grave penalties which attached to any use of artificial aids.

The lights were extinguished, except for the heavy billiard-table lamps which hung over the two plank beds, and the president demonstrated postures 'A male' and 'A female', which were, indeed, conventional to the point of being academic, though the president performed them with masterly fluency. Having calculated that my own knowledge was not likely to be exhausted by the few postures the club could command and that little if any invention would be required, I sat back and watched the members with an eye rather to the intelligence of their performances than to the details of their persons, for I knew I should soon need a lieutenant of no common ability, both physical and mental, to aid me in my search. Three of the members impressed me considerably, and I was wondering how best to approach them, not wishing to cause any jealousy or schism in the society by appearing to seek out a favourite, when my eye was caught by a figure in the gloom of a far corner of the room, standing by a door which led, I assumed from the drink and food which occasionally emerged from it, to the kitchen.

The figure appeared to be wearing a dressing-gown, and I guessed that he or she was probably one of the demonstrators in the series of test postures which it had been decided to forgo. The light was extremely poor and the person, whom I had at first taken for one of the pieces of sculptural portraiture in examples of which the room was rich, seemed to be watching the members' demonstrations with keen interest, though with one hand held to the brow, thus throwing the face into complete darkness. Yet I felt sure that I knew the face, if only I could see it, and I waited for a telltale gesture or a sudden shaft of light to help me identify it, though none was forthcoming. I was, naturally, at the same time keeping an attentive eye on the demonstrators, for it would have appeared boorish if I had advanced proudly on to the stage and performed a posture which had already been given by an initiated member, so my glance was able to travel only occasionally to the puzzling, and probably servile, figure by the door.

The twenty-three male and female postures having been completed to the satisfaction of the members, though not, as far as I could judge, to that of the young woman and her companion, whose appetites showed no sign of abating, I set myself to preparing a particularly flamboyant pair of positions, while first Pym, then Graffety, did their somewhat unimaginative best, reminding me, so that I was hard put to it not to smile, of the nightclub chorus-girls of my own country who give earnest pastiches of genuine arabesques. I realized that something remarkable was expected of me, and I was determined not to disappoint the members by falling in any way short of the high standard of performance, rather higher, indeed, than they achieved, to which they attained, but I was confronted with a problem which at first seemed insuperable, namely that neither the young man nor the young woman was able to arouse in me the physical enthusiasm which is obligatory for male sensualists, though they would both undoubtedly have done so some four hours earlier. I was reduced therefore to imagining the ideal creature of my vision as participating with me in the acts I wished to perform, even though such a subterfuge was repugnant to me. Using the Korean disciplines of mental control which Mr Abberley had taken such pains to inculcate in me, I mastered the parts of my body with such success that when I was at last called upon to illustrate my fitness to join the society and rose to do so, there was spontaneous applause, which I briefly acknowledged, before approaching the young woman to demonstrate what would, if the society accepted me, become position 'Z female'. There were some exclamations of surprise as I indicated what I required her role to be, and she appeared at first somewhat taken aback, though her genuine pleasure in the posture, once she had mastered it, was plain for all to see in the eagerness with which she encouraged every member of the test committee to try it out upon her. The real test, however, was posture 'Z male', for this was the one which the committee would try out upon my own person, and I had seen, from its efforts with Pym's not very original position, that the committee was not very quick to grasp new concepts and rather blundering in its execution of them. Nonetheless, I felt I must risk its clumsiness by doing something so extraordinary that the entire membership of the society would be willing to accept me as a grandmaster, or black belt, and follow my instructions without hesitation when we began to search for my vision of perfection.

I deliberately staged this posture with the maximum amount of drama, first pacing slowly round the young man whose curiosity was gratifyingly plain, then inviting him to stand beside me, as though I was obliged to compare measurements in order to decide upon the feasibility of my idea, and finally raising my eyes to the darkness of the roof, as though in prayer, of which I had no need. Having inflamed the entire assembly with these dispensable preliminaries, I then demonstrated the posture itself with a deliberately conscious artistry which not only made as plain as a diagram what it was that I was actually doing but also convincingly attested the extreme sensual gratification both of myself and the young man.

When I had completed my demonstration, the young man shook me warmly by the hand and embraced me fervently, and there were three cheers led by the president himself, which I modestly acknowledged. The test committee was in a fever of impatience to try the posture's validity, and quarrelled furiously among itself as to who was to have the honour of first learning it from the master, so that the president was obliged to settle the dispute by allowing me to choose my own partner, to my great relief and pleasure, and I was able to select one of those members whose flair and intelligence had already caught my notice. He proved every bit as pliant and adaptable as I had hoped, and the posture was recommenced, with my position of course reversed, but with no qualm on my part. The members crowded round to watch, everyone being anxious to get the details precisely correct and to overhear my quiet words of command and advice, for the appalling dangers of erroneous performance were manifest. All proceeded smoothly, and the trial was just about to end in a triumphal verdict for myself when I happened to glance over the heads of the absorbed members and see the quite unmistakable though now dressing-gowned back of the creature of surpassing beauty whom I had seen at the airport. My shock was such that it saved me from what might easily have been a most painful accident, for I was quite unable, for several moments, to move so much as a finger, so totally unexpected was this second vision at such a most inopportune moment. For imagine that you are involved in a complex and sophisticated engagement with a complete stranger for whom you have no especial feeling, and are able to maintain and complete that posture only by imagining your partner to be the most beautiful, heart-stopping creature in the world; that you raise your eyes, shortly before climax, to observe that very creature stealing quietly away from your side, having never known how much that frame and those features were at that precise moment replacing in your mind the barely tolerable ones of real life; and you will agree that Priapus himself would have been at a loss for a moment.

Fortunately the moment was enough for the substitute to complete his work of demonstration with a cry of achievement which rang through the room and brought immediate clamours from the entire society for private instruction. As I rose in haste from the springy planks of the bed, the president poured a bowl of some chrism over my head, temporarily blinding me, and declared . . .

I threw open the door to discover a room full of peasant women dressed in black hats, skirts, blouses, stockings and shoes, seated round a fine eighteenth-century Bavarian porcelain stove. At the sight of my still throbbing nakedness, they began to shriek and cover their heads with their voluminous aprons, and not wishing to cause them embarrassment or shame, I seized a dishclout which lay upon the table, pulled it over my head like one of their aprons and invited them to tell me if they had just witnessed someone in a dressing-gown pass through the room. I could see through the thin muslin of the clout that my ruse had succeeded, for the women peered out from behind their cover like birds from their nests, then, clearly believing me unable to see, picked up the knives which they had dropped on my entry and continued with their work of opening oysters, at the same time giving contradictory answers to my question. I repeated it slowly, for I did not wish to begin my naked pursuit along a false trail, and the oldest woman present replied that there had been so much toing and froing that evening that though the general answer to my query could only be 'Yes', for many dressing-gowned figures had passed through the room, yet the particular answer must be 'We cannot tell you', for the women for whom she spoke were good workers who received a special bonus for their speed and skill and who concentrated on their work to such an extent that they neither knew nor cared what else might or might not be happening in the same room, and would immediately cease work and proclaim an official strike if anyone suggested otherwise.

Seeing the futility of further discussion, I thanked the elderly spokeswoman and passed on through the room, returning the dishclout to the table as I went, to the consternation of the ladies whose absorption in their work was not, I thus determined, as absolute as they would have liked it to appear. Finding myself in a long corridor, off which many doors gave, though none of them showed any sign of having recently been opened or closed, I decided to follow it to where it turned abruptly . . .

[Henry fails to find his beloved. He is rescued from some unexplained disaster by the Encolpians, and adopts Milo as his lieutenant in the methodical search of the hotel which takes up the rest of the novel. Logically, the search begins at the top and works its way down. On the roof a dance is being held, which gives Henry an opportunity to exercise his limitless faculty for academic criticism on the pop songs.

I think it possible that Charles, who rather enjoyed pop music, got carried away writing Tarn Callow's ballad 'I didn't ask to be born.' Henry admits to being moved by it, and the words may express Charles's genuine feelings. (It is not unknown for bashful poets to slip their verse into prose works under false aliases.) One of the difficulties of Charles's satire (and of Petronius's) is that in the pot-pourri real feelings are sometimes expressed in grotesque situations, leaving the reader unsure quite how to react. There are other uncertain moments later in the novel.]

Popular Music

My friends bandaged my wounds and begged me to advise them on three or four small but essential points of detail on the maintenance of the postures I had taught them, from attempting which with too much zeal two members had injured themselves so seriously that stretchers had had to be sent for. I was not wholly sorry to learn that one of these unfortunates had been the society's president, for I felt that his absence would give me a good opportunity to assert my supremacy over the other members of the club, and I was more than pleased when the leader of my rescuers proved to be none other than the youth with whom I had demonstrated the posture some time earlier. I asked him his name, and why he had come to search for me, and he replied that he was called Milo, which I took to be a good omen, for though my Latin, as I have said, was weak, I knew enough to recognize the word 'miles' in its debased form, and though Milo's form was very far from being debased, a soldierly spirit was precisely what I sought in my lieutenant. To my second question he seemed at first reluctant to reply, but at last he admitted that he had formed a deep personal attachment to me, although he had known me for so short a time, and could not join the rest of the society in its innocent pleasures until he had made sure that my disappearance betokened me no harm. I was much moved by the manly but modest frankness of this answer, and though I explained that, as he well knew, my affections of the deepest kind were irremovably engaged, I added that there was room in my heart for a brotherly love such as he had shown me, and to prove that this was so I suggested that when I had corrected the postures of the society's members, an intensive search of the hotel should at once begin under our joint direction, a scheme with which he eagerly agreed.

The hotel was very large and ancient, he told me, however, with many rambling passages and corridors, and its administration had virtually collapsed, so that many independent hostelries, or inns within inns, had been set up, between whose staffs there was much hostility and intense rivalry for custom, leading to the creation of virtual frontiers between them, heavily defended against intruders. When I expressed amazement at this state of affairs, he said that in recent weeks a form of economic warfare had replaced the earlier civil broils which had followed the breakdown of the central administration, caused by a militant rising among the kitchen staff, who had erected barricades in the traditional style and defied the management, while the rest of the staff had bargained from positions of greater or lesser strength to assert their independence. The main centres of organized power remained the kitchen and the head manager's office, and the rest of the hotel could be roughly divided between these spheres of influence, though the garage attendants and the wine-waiters preserved great freedom of action, and refused to accept the general leadership of either. The kitchen and the management were mutually interdependent, of course, for neither could exist without clients whom both were obliged to satisfy, but they remained on speaking terms only through the good offices of a ceasefire commission largely manned by hall-porters, while extremist factions on both sides – washers-up on the one, and barmen, who were in no way connected with wine-waiters, on the other – continued to urge a once-for-all civil, or war to end all, war, for which wiser heads were not at all anxious, contenting themselves with the erection of prohibitive tariffs and the minute regulation of all the usual commerce.

Pondering on these things, after thanking Milo for his information, and with the recent sightings of my beloved to aid my performance, I demonstrated the posture for which the Encolpians were clamouring on two or three of them, who expressed themselves extremely satisfied. Then, to secure the devoted loyalty of the remainder, I supervised Milo and these new initiates while they satisfied the rest. When these lessons had been concluded, we adjourned to a banquet which awaited us in an adjoining room, and there, amidst many toasts and pledges of friendship, I was able at last to calm the by now urgent demands of my system for nourishment. As soon as I had eaten my fill, I turned to Milo beside me and outlined my detailed suggestions for . . .

Coloured spotlights moved over the dancers in a garish . .

. . . the bandstand. No one was paying any attention to these clearly reprehensible activities, or endeavouring in any way to prevent them, and when I called Milo's attention to the extreme youth of many of those who were swallowing these free stimulants in handfuls, he said that no policeman dared to enter this roof-top dance-hall, for the last who had attempted to make an arrest had been summarily thrown over the parapet, landing, by an accident which had much delighted the ejectors, on top of a small conclave of his colleagues who were in the process of being paid their weekly bribes by the management, killing all concerned, and thus freeing the management from their obligation to continue the expensive and wasteful bribery system, and enabling it to abjure the agreement to permit one arrest per week which had been drawn up by a committee of social workers, policemen, drug-traffickers and dance-hall operators after a public outcry following the discovery of the bodies of forty young children at the bottom of a well in the courtyard of the mansion of a well-known noble addict,* who had on previous . . .

Tarn Callow then appeared, a man of some twenty-eight or thirty years who had made obvious but not altogether unsuccessful attempts to make himself look considerably younger. He wore black trousers of so tight a fit that only many concealed zips and buttons could have made their entry feasible, and even then he had found it difficult satisfactorily to arrange the false phallus which was intended to arouse the admiration and envy of his fans, for it was plain to the most casual observer that while a very large phallic object jutted at an acute angle upwards from his fork, another smaller one hung below it in a more natural position and was in fact his real member, while the first was a patent and rather unskilful forgery. Above these ludicrous nether garments, which made his buttocks, when he turned them, as he frequently did, to the public, look like a split, shiny, black potato, he wore a spangled shirt, through whose white silk had been shot many threads of gold, or imitation gold, and whose open neck revealed a bare chest, perhaps shaven, and a prominent Adam's apple.

His arrival was greeted by several minutes of hysteria, and his person, already at such great peril from its garb, seemed likely to be assaulted at any moment and from all sides. However an electrified fence had been erected around the bandstand against which the shrieking adolescents pressed in such numbers, and though one or two of the youngsters seemed to receive minor burns from its current, Callow himself was safe. After some minutes a platoon of thickset men in blue uniforms began to clear the mob back with electrified cattle-prods so that first-aid might be administered to the fallen, and the din

* [A reference, I think, to the celebrated fifteenth-century murderer Gilles de Rais.]

somewhat abated, though not sufficiently to enable me to convey to Milo my utter distaste for the whole proceedings.

The abatement of noise was short-lived, for while the last casualties were still being cleared by stretcher-bearers Callow began to sing, or rather his instrumentalists began to play and he to utter into a microphone words which were totally incomprehensible when they emerged from the many amplifiers about the dance-hall, though a girl of eleven or twelve who stood beside me sang to the tune in a pleasing treble and with a gratifyingly innocent freshness of tone.

> Get thee behind me, baby,
> Baby, baby, baby,
> Get thee behind me, baby,
> We're gonna go, go, go tonight.

Though the rhythm was insistent, the melody of this song was not inventive, and it did not seem to me likely that a collector of folk music would find the evening stimulating, though paederasts of both sexes might have been better entertained, for the average age of the dancers could not have been more than ten, and I saw several tots of three or four jigging to the tune with apparent bliss and showing no fear of the probability of their being crushed in the enormous throng. These jolter-headed juveniles pranced and sang in idiot fashion about my knees as I advanced in line abreast with my comrades across the floor towards the bandstand, from which Tarn Callow continued to recite the words of what Milo informed me was his signature tune, which became more intelligible to me as I adjusted my hearing to the appalling volume of sound.

> Get thee behind me, baby,
> Baby, baby, baby,

Get thee behind me, baby,
We're gonna go, go, go tonight.
Get thee behind me, baby,
That's where I like you best,
Baby, baby, baby,
Hug me to your chest.
We're gonna go,
Don't say no,
Let her rip, rip, rip!
We're on a trip, trip, trip!
Bang, we're away,
Hold me tight, night and day,
Get thee behind me, baby,
We're gonna go, go, go tonight.
All the stars we pass
And the cars we pass
On our racing hot machine,
We're both so gay,
It's a holiday,
And all the lights are green.
Get thee behind me, baby,
Baby, baby, baby,
Get thee behind me, baby,
We're gonna go, go, go tonight.

Although my eyes were naturally occupied in searching the crowd for my beloved, and this was not easy, for there were many adolescents of about his or her height, and several adults, perhaps mentally retarded, my mind was also busy attempting to analyse this song as I moved through the dancers. The words immediately conveyed a vigorous masculine image, and the 'racing hot machine' was clearly a motorcycle, probably of a special design for competitive hill-climbs and cross-country runs. The singer was urging his 'baby' – an appropriate term for many of the youngsters present – to climb upon the pillion and embark with him, in holiday mood, when 'all the lights are green', on a night journey whose ultimate destination, though not stated, was probably some remote and private haystack, for the phrase 'All the stars we pass' unmistakably suggested the experience of orgasm. This simple and surface interpretation, however, left much to be desired, for there were also strong hints of religious overtones in the frequently repeated exhortation to the 'baby' to 'get thee behind me', which, in its archaic use of the second person singular, and its deliberate echoing of the ancient admonition 'Get thee behind me, Satan', seemed to suggest a diabolic cult, and that the devil was being invited to appear on the motorcycle as an incubus in the shape of 'baby', there to indulge in sexual intercourse while the operator of the machine continued to drive it at speed past both stars and cars. The song required, therefore, considerable further study, and my earlier notion that it would prove of no value to a collector of folk music and literature clearly had to be revised.

My reflections on this interesting subject were further stimulated by Tarn Callow's next song or 'number', as he inexactly called it, which was, he stated, a 'ballad', for the ballad form had died out of the popular literature of my own country some hundred years earlier, and I was surprised and delighted to find that it still lingered here. My cohorts and I had by this time combed the hall to no avail from east to west (taking our bearings from the pole star, for it was a warm and cloudless night) and were realigning ourselves for a further sweep in line abreast from north to south, after which we would know for certain that my beloved was not on the dance-floor. The words of Callow's 'ballad' were clearly audible, for one of the definitions of 'ballad', Milo informed me, was that it must be sung slowly and comparatively, though by no means absolutely, softly, so that as we began our second drive through the mass of writing and cavorting children, I was able to pay close attention.

> Oh, they told me life was sweet,
> Yes, they told me life was beautiful,
> They said love was like a dream
> And that living it was wonderful.
> But it's not so, but it's not so,
> Say goodbye and let me go.
> I didn't ask to be born,
> I didn't ask to be alive,
> Tie brass weights around my neck,
> For I'm going to take a dive.
>
> Oh, they said that to be young
> Was the best thing that could happen,
> There was nothing else on earth
> Brought you quite so close to heaven.
> But if that's so, but if that's so,
> Say goodbye and let me go.
> I didn't ask to be born,
> I didn't ask to be around,
> Put pennies on my eyelids,
> For I'm going underground.

I found this lament extremely moving, though the simple dignity of its words and the sad, appropriate melody seemed to leave the young people through whom I moved quite untouched, for they jerked and twisted to the slower rhythm much as they had twisted and jerked to the faster. I could not help reflecting on the excitement which the two songs I had heard would cause in my own country among academic researchers, and on the irony that I, who had no interest or vocation for such investigation, should nonetheless be in the position of one of those early explorers who returned from unknown and savage parts to write casual, conversational reports of their travels, with no thought of scientific exactitude, yet whose accounts are of far greater value to modern anthropologists than the more elaborate and self-consciously scientific efforts of those who followed them, who intruded their presuppositions into their observations, thus making them useless. For it is the ignorant man who most often ...

[*From the high plane of scientific truth Henry now descends to the lower one of theatrical fantasy. Having lost touch with the Encolpians, he is mistaken for an actor in a school play. There follows a very funny and quite unfair parody of avant-garde theatrical theory and practice. The theatres of cruelty and absurdity are made to look cruelly absurd. The play being rehearsed is a mixture of* Everyman, Samuel Beckett *and* Shakespeare, *and Henry is ironically cast as Infidelity. I don't know if Charles had ever read about Marinetti's plan for a Futurist theatre, whose sole object was to infuriate the audience by putting glue on the seats, issuing the same seat to several different people, throwing sneezing powder about and similar japes, but if he had, he improved on it.*

He never, so far as I know, had anything to do with any professional theatre, though he appeared, as I have said, in school plays and at Cambridge in the Footlights. I would like to think that the headmaster had his origin in Mr Bradley; but I'm afraid the connection is too tenuous.]

At the Theatre

••• had disappeared in pursuit of what I now realized to be a chimera or unfounded conception, leaving me uncertain as to whether it would be better to follow them, and so risk my beloved slipping unintentionally and all unaware through the net which we had now spread so carefully over two floors of the building, or to stay where I was in the hope that they would soon recognize their error and return to their starting-place. I felt somewhat as I imagine a huntsman must feel when his hounds have vanished in the degraded pursuit of a cat, mistaking it for an otter, and I bitterly regretted that I had no horn upon which to blow an urgent summons for my pack's return.

It was as I stood in this uncertainty that a woman in a loose housecoat, her lips bristling with pins, came mewing excitedly down the passage, her natural speech impeded by the stainless steel. She seized me warmly by the hand and at once attempted to make me accompany her, and when I explained that though I was honoured and flattered by her interest I had enjoyed sufficient intercourse for the immediate present, she shook her head so vigorously that pins showered upon the carpet. Spitting out the two or three which stayed loyal to her lips, she said, 'Come along, Infidelity, everyone's been looking for you high and low.' When I continued to resist her blandishments she began to rail at me, saying that I was letting the whole side down, and asking me what I thought people would think of me when they heard how I had behaved; to which I answered that it was no concern of mine what strangers might think, that her words were so many soap-bubbles to me, that is to say without substance or intellectual nourishment, that I was and had ever been on no one's side but my own, and that I deplored the tendency of people to take sides on every possible occasion of contention and on many matters which were, properly considered, indifferent. At this she made a show of smelling my breath and exclaimed, 'I knew it! You've been at the wine-cup, haven't you, you naughty boy? Just wait till the head hears about this!'

All was instantly made clear by this discovery, and I began hurriedly to explain that I was not, as they thought, Infidelity, but merely myself wearing, in all ignorance, Infidelity's costume, which, if they would look closely, fitted my body no more accurately than the abstraction fitted my character. But there was a loud shushing from all around me, and the man with the lugubrious eyes announced the start of the dress rehearsal.

Seeing that there was nothing for it but to continue in the obnoxious role which had been so suddenly thrust upon me, I looked urgently for a prompt-book so that I might discover what I was expected to say and do. Enjoying an almost photographic memory, I knew I would have no difficulty with the lines, though the movements, at this late stage of the production, would call for the instinctive sense of theatrical fitness which I believed myself to possess, for I had wasted much of my youth in amateur theatricals, and had been used to pride myself on my ability as an arranger of dramatically effective tableaux. Finding a script on a table in the wings, I began hastily to turn its pages, discovering with a relief which was not unmixed, I must acknowledge, with some small disappointment, that Infidelity did not appear until halfway through the play, and then uttered only a few bathetic lines, which I quickly memorized before beginning to study the rehearsal itself in the hope of there finding some indication of the style in which I would be required to perform.

There was neither scenery nor action on the stage at that moment, for the play or masque had been halted almost before it had begun by a man who, unusually for an *homme de théâtre*, wore clerical garb.

'Now this will not do, it will not do at all,' he was saying to the actors. 'It's too bad, really too bad. I won't award any house colours at all if we go on at this rate. And if I have one more giggle out of you, Furnival, I shall cancel the whole thing and tell the parents – regretfully –why I have done so. I shall not spare them the whole, bitter truth. That you have deliberately, consistently, maliciously, attempted to undermine the work of those who know what is good for you and for the school. Stand up straight! Pull your shoulders back! That's better. Now listen to what Mr Bund has to say and do what he tells you without argument and without delay. I shall not warn you again. Look to it!'

Giving the actors a last, rather uneven, look, he then left the stage, stopping to pat one of the girls on the cheek, and causing the man with the lugubrious eyes to draw in his breath and mutter, 'He shouldn't do it, not the head. He really shouldn't. Not in public.' From all this I deduced that it was a school performance, and that the headmaster's authority had been called upon to quell some small outbreak of high spirits among the youthful mummers, both boys and girls, though I erred in assuming that those dressed and painted as girls were girls, for I soon realized that they were boys, their sex giving an added significance to the mutterings of the man with the lugubrious eyes, it never being happy for the reputation of a school when a master, least of all the headmaster, takes an open fancy to one of the pupils, patting him or her upon the cheek or cheeks. Bund, who now revealed himself in the stalls as the director of the play, followed the headmaster's departure with a few admonitions of his own, said that he hoped his troupe had paid careful heed to these and then launched into a fierce criticism of the brief scene that had been acted.

Not finding his tirade of interest, I returned to the script to discover, if I could, what precisely the action of the play portended. The main character, I learned, was a woman of middle age who was much grieved by the course of her life, which a mysterious messenger informed her was about to end, for no clear reason and to her intense chagrin. Various characters, such as the one I was to play myself, approached her from time to time and reviled her for various moral slips which they claimed she had made in the past and for which they insisted it was now too late to make any amends. The text caused me considerable puzzlement, for it was of no clear or consistent style, combining passages in an archaic dialect which I found impossible to understand with others in many later manners which were more comprehensible, the whole being something of a ragbag or anthology. The woman herself spoke in rhymed couplets, many of them bordering on sense, though some of her expressions were unfamiliar to me:

> Now would I fain be in your company
> And have ado to be so hardily,
> For of my reckoning I am behind,
> And Death, thou comest when I had thee not in mind,
> And wended not to die, nor blind matter knew,
> But muddled bad advisement and the true.
> Verily, grammercy, Idleness,
> I thank thee for thy gentleness,
> But now I must my count-books set aright
> In figure of this heavy night.

To the woman's obvious anxiety, Idleness replied, astonishingly and not at all helpfully, in a form of prose:

> 'Speaking thus thus arbitrarily arbitrarily speaking taking speak
> to mean utter utter depravity utter chaos utter hell which our

grammarians notably Minow and Pawn quaqua-qua philosopher etcetera etcetera taking taking quaquaqua the day on the lake when the sun came out between the clouds etcetera and shone on the water etcetera and you rowed past the castle of Chillon and opened your legs etcetera below the thwarts below the thwarts one more effort was it wasn't it try again no all gone gone utterly so to speak yes gone now all gone all gone I don't remember.'

Though it was possible to find some scraps of sense embedded in this speech I did not feel that either it, or the extraordinary collage of literary styles to which it belonged, was likely to prove theatrically viable, and I considered that the more traditional language of Greed was more suited to dramatic purposes, both of monologue and dialogue:

Greedy I am, and greedy aye shall be,
And those that skimp their meat to slim their sins
Shall brown with me in hell; aye, chestnuts all!
We'll roast ourselves there, not the sucking-pig,
And chew our own fat's crackling, like the fox
Gnawing his maimed paw in the iron trap.
The world's a pudding, we but sixpences,
Old buttons young girls keep to polish
Into husbands; and so die, crying
For more; and more; until the middle air,
That stomach set between the earth and stars,
Bursts with the surfeit of its appetite.
Death turns his everlasting spit, and lards
His supper with salt lamentations,
Nor, till the last trump, shall we sup again
This side the banquet-house of heaven.

I much regretted that I was not myself playing Greed, for this seemed a fine speech to which I could have given considerable emotional power, moving the audience perhaps to weep for its own uncontrollable, natural, but mortal, appetites. Imagine my dismay and disgust, therefore, when I heard Bund directing the actor who was taking the role to say the lines with no regard to their rhythm, but rather as though they were prose, for, he said, no one cared to listen to verse and if people realized that it was in fact poetry to which they were being subjected they would cease at once to pay attention. This lunatic desecration was made still more unacceptable by Bund's conception of Greed as a pig who was to pause in the middle of sentences and lines to grunt and go through the motions of rooting about in the earth for acorns, thus creating a pantomimic effect of humour and utterly destroying the sublimity of the poetry.

'You've got to remember,' Bund said, 'that the audience has come to be amused. They're not going to laugh at the lines, so they've bloody well got to laugh at you lot. And besides,' he continued, perhaps aware that his attitude towards the text went against its own moral seriousness, 'you must remember we want the audience to laugh because this is a very serious play. They've got to go home disliking it, knowing they've had their easy bourgeois values criticized. If they're forced to laugh when they want to be moved, that's good. They'll forget the poetry and get the message, and that's the whole point of this production, isn't it?'

'Please, sir,' said Greed, formulating a question which was on my own lips, 'would you mind explaining what the message is, sir? I mean, again, sir?'

To my surprise Bund seemed pleased rather than angry that the significance of his effort had been overlooked by one involved in it, and answered, after a ponderous pause, with the following speech:

'This play is about a woman. The first thing we do to stop the audience identifying with her is to have the part played by a boy. It's always embarrassing, that. No one knows quite how to react. And why do we want to stop the audience identifying with the woman? Because identification leads to emotional sympathy, and emotional sympathy leads to people not thinking, and the audience has bloody well got to start thinking, because that's the only way we can get the world changed, isn't it?

'Good. Now – as the woman goes over her past life before she dies, the various characters come on and either try and comfort her or tease her or tempt her or something, don't they? And each of these characters has got something pretty intelligent to say – intelligent, but immoral, by our standards. And we can't risk the audience not getting the point that they *are* immoral, these characters, so we have Greed, for instance, coming on like a pig, on all fours. And Idleness coming in on flies, wrapped up as a mummy – so that he's inhuman, so that the audience won't sympathize with him. Because quite frankly, it's jolly hard work stopping people sympathizing with someone in a play. They *like* sympathizing, it lets them know where they are, the ignorant sods.

'But we can't possibly allow them to feel sympathy in our theatre, can we? That's why I have the woman spitting into the front row all the time and blowing her nose on the curtain and farting. That's why, at the end, when those bloody angels come on, they're stripped to the buff. By that time the audience will be crazy for something to enjoy, someone they can *like*. And when they see these angels, they'll think 'At last! How beautiful and lovable!' So that when the angels start peeing over the balustrade of the gallery on to the people below, all hell will break loose.

'Incidentally, I hope you angels are knocking back all that lemonade. I've paid for it out of my own pocket, and I don't want a single drop left in the bottles – get to work on it, won't you? Drink up!

'Now finally, the whole point of the play is that it's not really a play at all, but a political speech. The point of it all is to confuse and irritate the audience, and the ultimate result should be to bore and infuriate them so much that they'll rush out and demand censorship and police prosecution and all the rest of that right-wing stuff. And then we'll have a real political issue to fight about – the freedom of the artist. But none of this'll happen unless the audience really *loathes* the play. So to make quite sure of that I've prepared a big surprise for the end. You see that sort of sheet up there above the auditorium? Well, it's full of rubbish and filth of the slimiest kind – old vegetables, dead rats, that sort of thing. When the woman gets taken up into heaven at the end of the play, I'm going to pull a secret little string and all that shit's going to fall all over the audience. It probably won't be necessary – it shouldn't be, not if you do your stuff properly – but just in case things aren't going badly enough, I think this should do the trick. OK? Does that answer your question?'

'Yes, sir, thank you, sir,' said Greed.

Bund's perverse and sadistic speech immediately determined me to have nothing whatever to do with his production, in spite of my earlier resolution to assist, and I made haste to find the dressing-rooms so that I could rid myself of the offensively inappropriate costume of Infidelity – seamanlike, I assumed, from the old legend of sailors' sexual incontinence – and don some more suitable and innocent garb. Pretending to an urgent physical need which I did not feel, I made my way off the stage and began to open doors at random until I found what I sought, a large changing-room, empty of actors but full of their everyday clothes. At once I was met by a problem I had not foreseen, for all the clothes were of similar design and shape, though of different sizes, being the uniforms which the school doubtless required all its pupils to wear at all times so that any miscreant or escaping scholars might at once be recognized for what they were and apprehended. The uniform consisted, to my chagrin, of . . .

[*There now follows an elaborate parody of a James Bond thriller, witty in itself, but with serious undertones. The Bond character is a Jew, and the villain is an ex-henchman of Hitler's. The horrors of fascism and the nightmare of Jewish persecution obsessed Charles; this literary joke has a very bitter taste.*

The theme is elaborated further, for the Bond parody turns out to be a religious lesson, and in a ludicrous sermon Bernie (the James Bond figure) is compared to Christ and Isaac. This is the first appearance, grotesque but significant, of the Abraham-Isaac theme which is central to the novel. Charles was guying the new godless Christianity here, of course. What is most striking to one who knew him as well as I did is the implication that Christianity should be taken a good deal more seriously than it is by some contemporary apologists.]

The Lesson

' ... of "Pavlova", setting off the high ping of a mental danger signal. His brain whirred through its meticulous files and came up with the answer in less than three seconds. SALOME! And Q had ordered him to walk into this adder's nest clean! Not so much as a Wilkinson razor or a Rolex Oyster!

Deliberately slowing his pulse-rate, Bernie fondled her cupped breast with his left hand, while the right crept slowly down her spine, stroking and testing each vertebra for the tell-tale tremor of a radio transmitter. It was at the coccyx, as he'd expected. He smiled to himself in the darkness, letting his hand continue the fondling further down. She mustn't suspect he knew.

'You've been to Japan?' she murmured into his hair, then bit his ear-lobe till he could feel the blood run.

'Vampire,' he whispered. There was nothing for it but to play it straight. For the next few minutes he allowed himself to be carried away on the waves of sensual enjoyment. It might, he thought as he went under, be the last time. Afterwards they fell apart and he lay on his back, gazing up at the ceiling, where the wide-angle lens had doubtless recorded every thrust from somewhere behind the acoustic tiles.

SALOME! Société Anonyme de Lyons, Orange, Marseilles – et Egypte! Ever since Napoleon, France had had a thing about the Nile. Disraeli saved us last time, Bernie thought. But now all the waters of the Nile, the Tigris and the Euphrates couldn't save the world unless he could bluff his way past Zeno. And Zeno held a royal straight flush in spades!

Suddenly the light snapped on, and as Bernie sat up the two Carpathians stepped out of the fitted Norwegian pine closet.

'Genug,' said the one with acromegaly. 'Kommen Sie mit!'

'Mind if I put on my pants?'

'That will not be necessary.'

He looked at the girl, but she had turned on to her pretty stomach. Was the little shake in her shoulders a suppressed sob? Or was she laughing at him? If he ever got out of this mess alive, he'd make it his business to find out.

The two Carpathians frog-marched him down the passage to the gymnasium and handed him over to the eunuch and his simpering boys. They strapped him over the horse and emptied two jerry cans of aviation spirit over his torso and legs. Helicopter fuel! Bernie saw from their intent, absorbed, utterly inhuman faces that they, too, were products of Zeno's hellish workshop, incapable of any emotion, automata. He closed his eyes and thought very hard about Miriam. What would she be doing now? Having gefilte fish for her tea, probably. His bonds were professionally tight – no hope there. Squinting down his chest he could just see the tip of the murder nipple, tantalisingly close. But it was a one-shot weapon, no use against this gang of zombies. What were they waiting for?

Zeno came into the gymnasium, and the boys sprang to attention at a high-pitched word of command from the eunuch.

'Where is the acetylene lamp?' he demanded.

There was a pause. Then the bandaged face of the master criminal loomed over Bernie. 'Well, Levi, I see you are one of the circumcised. One of the chosen people.'

'I didn't choose to come here,' said Bernie, 'if that's what you mean. I was forced to come.'

'Do you imagine I am a complete fool, you schmuck?'

Bernie felt the jet of flame parting his hair like a thick comb. Zeno's hand must be very steady not to singe the scalp, Bernie thought as he screamed.

'Liar!' In Zeno's voice was all the contempt of one who believed himself to belong to a master race. 'That did not hurt you! But you are going to die, my non-Aryan friend, so that you will feel it indeed. Whether you tell me how much you have reported or not. But I will give you this choice: if you tell us immediately, my eunuch will light the petrol, and death, though extremely painful, will not take very long. If you do not, I shall cut off your limbs one by one and burn them in front of you till you do. I'm sure you can guess where I shall start. How sad for you that there is no foreskin to go first!'

He was insane! A puritanical pyromaniac, who wanted the whole world to go up in flames like Joan of Arc, the Achilles' heel of the English armies in France! And all because he and his psychopathic pals had failed to get their way! Bernie knew that if he died now, it would be with no regrets, that the cause was a good one. How lucky he'd not had a stamp for that letter of resignation! Zeno might kill him, but enough was known now, the world would be safe from this insane incendiary, who didn't care if he blazed up with everyone else. Bernie could feel the sweat trickling out of his armpits. Not quite the stuff, he thought grimly, to dowse high-octane spirit.

Zeno put the acetylene lamp on the floor, to the right of Bernie's head, then brandished a knife over him. A Kikuyu machete, blunt and rusty, the blade nicked – on purpose, of course. And with blood on it. Poor old Nicholas.

'I'm afraid this may take some time,' said Zeno through the black hole in the bandages. 'I fear my butcher has been using the knife to chop wood – or perhaps bones?' Was that a glimmer of amusement in the mad eyes?

There would be a split second in which Zeno would have to pass within the sights of the murder nipple. It was the only hope – and a slim one. Bernie fractionally shifted his collarbone. Yes, the safety-catch was off.

Zeno stared down at him. 'Well?'

'You're crazy, Zeno. Out of your mind.'

The eyes definitely flickered this time. Anger.

'Very well. As you insist. This will hurt you far, far more than it will hurt me, you dirty Jew.' He gloated for an instant, then took two steps away, as though to size up his task.

He stepped forward. Bernie turned his head sharply to the left, and the deadly nipple exploded. As Bernie threw his whole weight to the right and the horse toppled to the floor, he saw Zeno start back with a terrible scream as the acid melted the bandages like a flamethrower going through butter and seared into the hideously scarred flesh beneath. Zeno's hands went to his face, tearing at the dissolving pulp in a nightmarish frenzy, as his scream rose higher and higher. Then it shut off like the whistle of an engine as the windpipe dissolved. The acetylene lamp was just where Bernie had hoped it was. With a gigantic effort, he twisted himself and the horse so that the flame burned through his cords in an instant. Lucky his hands had been underneath the horse when they'd soaked him with petrol!

Bernie leaped to his feet. The eunuch was standing over the writhing mass of blubber and blood which had once been Hitler's right-hand man. The boys simpered, thinking it was all part of the fun. Orders! That was all they understood –orders!

'Get to the wall-bars!' Bernie rapped out. 'Jump to it!'

The grey-haired ecclesiastic ceased his reading and put the book down, much to my relief, for I do not care for cheap thrillers, and did not wish Vaux's gang to be inflamed to still greater sadistic inventiveness by the crude sentiments of this particular specimen of a worthless genre.

' "So Crist woundid the feende and his foulle assembling,
And led seints out of helle til eternale feding" ',

quoted the reverend benignly, and immediately began a moral disquisition to those before him, who were constrained from expressing their obvious distaste by the menacing presence of the brutal Nazis.

'Dearly beloved, the passage of scripture which I have just read out to you is the lesson set for today, but its message is for every day of the year. You may have heard people say, "Oh, I don't believe in heaven and hell any more". You may have heard them doubting the existence of God and the divinity of our Lord. You may have heard the whole of our religion, sanctified though it is by centuries of devotion, mocked and ridiculed. And sometimes it will have seemed to you, the mockers have had a point. What has all this old-fashioned stuff got to do with life as we live it? What, indeed? Before we can answer, we've got to take a jolly close look at the question, and if we do that, we'll see that there really is something in it. Many of those whose faith is greatest are at the same time the most doubtful about the validity of the whole shebang. Take me. I don't believe in God, not as such. I don't believe in miracles. I think saints are men and women much like us, and the Lord was too, only more so. Let's cut out all the cant about mysterious virgin births, shall we? Let's drop all the claptrap about resurrection! Let's not look at the facts as facts – they won't stand investigation, not for two ticks. So let's look at them as something else – as allegories, symbols, whatever you want to call them. And let's, for God's sake, not take them as literally true. Good Lord, if there really was a God like the one people worshipped for nearly two thousand years, he wasn't very hot stuff, was he? And he certainly doesn't seem to have paid much attention to prayers and incense and all the rest of it, does he? I should say not!

'No, what matters is that people are people, and that they've had pretty much the same sort of needs down the ages. And what are these needs I'm talking about? Well, they're for love, of course, and security, and all that. But, far more important, they're also for hatred and violence and destruction. It's no good pretending it isn't true. That's what the Christian myth teaches us – the need for violence. Look here, it's based on a pretty damned violent Judaism, isn't it? What about Abraham and Isaac and the destruction of poor old Sodom? What about the Flood, for God's sake? It certainly wasn't for man's sake, was it? And if you don't believe me, take a look at the gospels some time when you've got a minute. What happened the moment Christ was born? A slaughter of infants! That was a pretty good start, wasn't it? And what happened at the end? First scourging, then a rigged trial, then nails and ropes and spears in the side – if that's not pandering to man's need for violence and destruction, I certainly don't know what is.

'Which brings me to the point. That chapter I read to you – what's it all about? Why do we call it a 'lesson'? Well, I'll tell you – it's simply a reworking of an old, fundamentally Christian story. Remember Abraham and Isaac I mentioned a moment or two ago? In case you don't, I'll remind you. Abraham, if you can believe it, was about to kill Isaac – his son, mind you – as a sacrifice to God, a burnt offering. He was going to kill him, then set fire to the body. Sounds like a detective story, doesn't it? Well, why do you think all that aviation spirit gets thrown over poor old Bernie? Why do you think he's a Jew? Because he's Isaac, of course, tied down, all ready to be sacrificed. Pretty nasty business. But then along comes God – Q, in this case – who's had the wit to fix him up with a murder nipple. In the old story, that nipple's a ram, actually, caught by its horns in a bush. But that's not relevant to us today. What matters to us is just the connection. Abraham, of course, the killer, is Zeno –and this ties in with the whole Alpha and Omega business, which I won't bother you with tonight. But listen to this –what's happened between the time that old story was written and today? Well, Freud, of course. In the old story, Abraham gets away with it, which goes against the whole grain of the Oedipus myth. It's a terrible old muddle, that story. In the new one, our one, Abraham catches a packet, as is only right and natural. He's got to die so that Bernie can live.

'Of course this isn't the only level that Bernie's story is operating on. You'll probably have seen for yourselves how Bernie is also Christ, of course – tied down to that horse in the gymnasium in an obvious parallel with the crucifixion. He has come to harrow hell – and he does a fine job, you'll agree. That's why there's all that fire imagery about. And of course there's a direct reference here to Auschwitz, too – Bernie stands for all the Jews who went up in smoke. Zeno's the devil – and Hitler. You get it? Why is Zeno the devil? I'll tell you. And listen carefully, because this is the real nub of the whole thing. He's the devil because he's dehumanized those poor simpering boys. And Christianity, modern Christianity, is pure humanism. Christ was human, Bernie is human, I'm human. Some of you look almost human, too! That's all there is to it. That's why I'm a Christian – because I'm human. Next time you hear someone mocking your religion, you tell them that and see if it doesn't shut them up. It's not so old-fashioned, Christianity, after all, is it?'

Stupefied by this incredible twaddle, I soon ceased to pay it heed and began to wonder how and when I would be able to effect my escape without notice, for in spite of the severe punishment I had received from my captors ...

A colleague was busy erecting a screen in front of the altar, while another set up a cinema projector in the nave and a third strung cables between it and two large amplifiers, the choir continuing to chant obscenities to the tune of a well-known and much-loved hymn.

Thinking that boldness might now prove my best friend, I approached this shape and shouted above the appalling din, which resembled the firing of machine-guns in an echo-chamber, that I considered *Religion Vérité* to be a genuinely revolutionary advance in ecumenical practice, and that Vaux was a man of genius who deserved not only beatification but immediate sanctification. To this the shape replied in a soft voice, for there was a brief lull in the cacophony to allow Vaux to ring a number of assonant hand-bells, that he or she, I could not tell which, regarded the service as a monstrous imposture, and had only entered the chapel to discover the cause of the blitzkrieg, and to call the fire-brigade if that was necessary. Heartily agreeing with these sentiments, I admitted that I was in fact attempting to find the exit, to which the shape, whose candid criticism had very much cheered me, answered that it was exactly behind me, and that he or she would join me as I left.

'But,' the voice went on, 'we will have to leave with great speed and dexterity, for this insufferable nonsense is about to end, and from what I know of previous services here, there will be blood spilt. The door opens towards you. I will position myself to dash through it at the moment you pull it open, and will close it smartly behind you as you follow me.'

'But is it not locked?' I asked.

'It is. But I am employed here, and have a key which fits every lock in the hotel. Come, let us move with expedition. I will unlock the door, and when we are both in the passage I will lock it again from the outside, thus delaying our inevitable pursuers.'

The figure, whose practical approach to the problem more and more impressed me, brushed past, unlocked the door with great stealth, and then took up the agreed position. The fury of aerial bombardment booming from the amplifiers drowned all the sounds we made, and in any case the audience seemed engrossed in studying the close-ups of the daily work of an abattoir which appeared on the screen.

'Now!' said the almost invisible partner in my escape, and I pulled open and saw – but you will have guessed what I saw – my exquisite vision, revealing once more only the back view, but now only a few inches before me, and, turning to push home the key into the lock, affording me a glimpse of brown eyes, smooth brow and straight nose, which so stunned and paralysed my sense that I could not follow. A ruthless hand seized me by the collar of my blazer and hauled me, even as I gasped out the words I longed above all others . . .

[*Henry now finds himself at an Ideal Mother competition, where, apparently, the contestants are presented with maternal problems to solve against time. National servicemen will be reminded of the methods of the War Office Selection Boards for army officers, and Commissions and Warrants Boards for naval ones. Charles, of course, appeared before one of the latter.*

This section is rather baffling, for though it starts as a fairly straight satire on such absurdities as 'Mother of the Year' awards, it soon switches to the chairman's hideously perverse notions of child-rearing and then goes into a homosexual variation on Aristophanes's Lysistrata. *The ground puzzlingly keeps shifting. But it is the last part which requires most comment. Here Henry gives an account of his own birth.*

He begins with a paragraph about perception and different kinds of knowledge, which so continually cuts the ground from under its own feet that one is left uncertain whether one is meant to accept its conclusions or mock it. He then describes 'birth-trays' and their use in his country. There actually are such things as birth-trays, for Charles and I once discovered some Florentine ones in the Victoria and Albert Museum. He laughed at them then, but they clearly caught his imagination and inspired the whole fantasy. We gather from it that Henry was born with an acutely developed critical sense, illustrating what I have already suggested is his fundamental weakness: he is given to judging rather than experiencing even the most basic events of his life. His birth trauma was an aesthetic one. Obviously aware of the implausibility of his story, he then launches into a diatribe against psychiatry. This is followed by a discussion of the innate personality of babies, and his own relationship with his mother.

What is the reader supposed to make of all this? It seems to me that Charles was here both guying his hero and stating his basic thesis. It is the telling of the birth story which is important rather than the story itself. Henry's enormous capacity for adding footnotes, parentheses and subclauses to every remark is a symptom of his over-rationalization. He protects himself from life by thus distancing it, but there is, I think, a distinct note of desperation, the elaborate style is self-defensive. Henry is talking in order not to have to listen to himself. His feelings about his mother are too ambiguous for him to face them. Like Charles, he knows how much truth there is in psychiatry and psychology, and so he assails them; he doesn't want to know. He wants to believe that he was born as himself and that no environmental factors have changed him.

The doubts and fears and ambiguities of this section are characteristic of Henry and his creator. They are essential to the novel as a whole and explain much of its complexity.]

Ideal Mothers

• • • shape of an English bowler and would, had it not been for a gauzy veil, have looked very like an English businessman as portrayed in the humorous magazines of my own country, though there was nothing in the least comic about the way she attempted to mother, almost indeed to smother, the wretched boy whose duty it was to submit himself to embraces, enfoldments and engulfings in those fleshy, powdered arms. Having mussed his hair and combed it, kissed him and looked behind his ears, felt his temples for dryness and his fork for moisture, she sat down and took him to her capacious lap where she began to sing him lullabies in a tuneless drone, at the same time holding his head so firmly to her protuberant bosom that I feared the child must soon suffocate, an end which he appeared devoutly to desire, for he soon began most pathetically to weep and wail in spite of his promised reward for stillness and smiling, and the woman was obliged to discontinue her mothering, at which she showed peevishness, though she had kept the infant's tears at bay for eleven minutes and thirty-seven seconds by the chairman's stopwatch, a figure by which my colleagues and the audience seemed much impressed.

The next contestant was younger by five years, and had won her way to the final, we were told, through sixteen rounds of extremely fierce competition in the 50–55 age-bracket, a story I could well believe, for despite the efforts of her milliner, dressmaker, haberdasher, hairdresser and cosmetician, she looked not less than seventy, having a lined, aggrieved face, and hair too white to be genuinely grey. For this woman a different, but to my mind equally foolish and humiliating, situation had been devised, and she was informed that her sixteen-year-old son had just been expelled from his school for attempting to rape the senior gym-mistress, and that his psychiatric report gloomily credited him with a hysterically aggressive psychopathic personality, a perfectly possible background, I considered, for the lout who slouched in to enact this dramatic role and who, I hoped, would quickly demonstrate his aggressive traits in so hysterical and psychopathic a manner that the Ideal Mother competition would come to an immediate halt, for though I bore no resentment towards my own mother and had nothing against ·mothers as a class, the thought of enduring a whole series of these preposterous . . .

. . . breasts like waterwings and gave thoughtful suck, while . . .

. . . incest, for she clasped him to her and in her eagerness to satisfy his need tore off her skirt, scattering fasteners like confetti on their criminal bed, for which she was at once disqualified, much to the fury of her trainer, a stout woman in a pinstriped, double-breasted blue suit, who attempted to read from a recent paper in a learned journal which recommended the deliberate breaking down of interpersonal taboos within the family unit and suggested that many neuroses might thus be prevented, a theory which brought execrations, as well as handbags and umbrellas, down upon its proponent's head.

To calm the hubbub the chairman launched upon his own ideal of motherhood, claiming to speak, as indeed seemed the case, frankly and from his own experience as a son, husband and father.

'What,' he began, 'is the ideal mother? I don't know. I only know about my own dear mum and my own dear wife as she's been a mum to my children by her and my previous dear wives. There are sixteen in my family, not counting the dogs and the guinea-pigs. And there's another on the way, which is one reason why my wife can't be here tonight.

'When I look back on my childhood, what do I see? The nursery – with tea laid and Nanny making toast by the fire. Dear Nanny, how I loved her! While my parents were away for seven years, and they were long years for all of us, she brought us up and wiped our noses, saw that we cleaned our teeth and brushed our hair and prayed for our sick brothers and sisters – none of us was ever very healthy – and then, at six o'clock every night, she locked us in so we wouldn't get up to any mischief. Promptly at ten next morning she let us out again for a run round the garden, then chained us up till lunch-time, while she sat by the fire, clicking her knitting-needles and darning her own socks. After lunch we always went for a run round the parade-ground – then it was back for tea and an hour with our toy in the basement – how we loved that unbreakable steel bar! – while Nanny got on with her jobs, locking the door behind her so that we wouldn't feel frightened of burglars. And then bed. How good it was to get the shackles off our feet! How hateful the monthly bath-night! We loved Nanny, and we do still, though she is dead and gone.

'When my parents returned from their long journey abroad, we hardly recognized them. And to this day, when I happen to meet my mother in the street, I have to think quite hard before I remember who she is. And that, I truly believe, is how it should be. A boy must get away from his mother as soon as possible. That's why I'm so passionately opposed to breast-feeding and the twaddle of so-called psychiatrists. That's why I invented Universal Mother, the plastic substitute, which sells now in its millions, second only in our total business to our many lines of contraceptives and spermicidal jellies. If you can't stop the blighters coming, I say, at least you can keep them off you! My wife agrees. As soon as we have a child, we send it off to my country estate till it's ready for boarding-school. I'm proud to say that my children have never met their parents, and I hope they never will. Universal Mother, the plastic substitute with built-in homogenized milk, fills every child's need. The monthly servicing charge is negligible, and our men come to you to do the work, you don't have to do anything at all. Buy one today! As advertised on television and radio! Universal Mother!'

The audience received this astonishing mixture of autobiography and sales talk in silence, too stunned, perhaps, to comment, though comment seemed to me urgently called for. After a short silence, a man of forty-five or fifty rose hesitantly to his feet and asked to be allowed to speak, and though the chairman said that it was really time the competition continued, permission was eventually granted.

'I don't know quite how to begin,' said this man, who had an elaborate silver coiffure and baby-soft cheeks, 'but I really do feel, don't you, that someone should put in a word for the dear, good, old-fashioned mummy? I mean, I just adore mine, and I always have. And I want to tell you a little story to show just how good and dear she is.

'You may remember that last year there was very nearly a most ghastly strike. Well, I'm a coiffeur des dames by profession, and do you know, I'm not a bit ashamed to say that it was our union which started the whole thing off. It's too exhausting, fidgeting about with madam's lilac rinse all day long, you've no idea. You're on your feet from nine to five, and it's rush, rush, rush the whole time, with the ladies telling you all their naughty little secrets and expecting you to remember which silly little bitch of a daughter it was that married the master of otter-hounds, and really! It's a nightmare, I don't mind telling you, and Friday nights, when we're open till eight, it's more than flesh and blood can stand, sometimes, though I love my work, and so does Honoré, my partner.

'Well! We all decided, we coiffeurs des dames, that we really just couldn't go on, I mean it was impossible, unless we got just a teeny bit more reward for our labour, though it's not labouring work, of course, more of a vocation, I always think, even if we do literally have to use our hands. And do you know, some jumped-up little parvenu in the government said that no one was to have any more money because the economy was all to pieces or some such nonsense. Well, of all the cheek! As though it was our fault they couldn't make their horrid little books balance! We'd been washing and setting and drying and dyeing as hard as we possibly could, hadn't we? And then along comes this really very lower class little man and tells us we've got to lump it, just like that! Oh, I know that sort – they're all the same, these politicians, with their little silver wings brushed over their blushing great ears. Butch as Samson, you'd think, wouldn't you? But just you get them with their hair down and you'll see! They're all just Delilahs at heart, roll over like those funny little clowns at the circus and not a peep out of them! You try cruising the cottages down by the Senate House tube-station and you'll see what I mean. Nasty, dirty-minded lot they are, not fit to lead a troop of boy-scouts, though most of them do, of course.

'Well, at first we just didn't know what to do, we were so surprised. I mean, we're respectable, decent people with respectable little businesses, the salt of the earth, I call us. And those ghastly little parvenus would be trying to nationalize us next, we could see that. Packing us all off to the National Stud, I wouldn't be surprised, not that I'd've minded, though in my own time, if you don't mind, and at my own speed, please, nothing rough. So what we did was call a special meeting of all the members of the union, an extraordinary general meeting they called it. Extraordinary! You should have seen us! Some people have *no* sense of occasion, fluttering their eyelashes, I was quite upset. And do you know, the whole strike committee had put on their drag and was sitting up on the platform like a lot of common little tarts. I was disgusted, I don't mind telling you. I mean, that sort of thing may be all right in the capital for the New Year's Eve Ball when everyone gets a bit frisky and we all have a giggle, but it's just common down by the seaside at eleven o'clock in the morning, and I don't hold with it, and I said so. I said to Honoré, Honoré, I said, really! And he agreed with me, he always does, the dear lamb.

'But do you know, we'd got it all wrong! They're very sharp the boys on our strike committee, really very sharp indeed, and they'd put on their drag because they'd decided to appeal to all the queens in the country to come out on strike with us! Now wasn't that daring? And clever! There's millions of us, you know, millions. Why, I could tell you the names of some very well-known people who you'd never even suspect – very well-known they are indeed. And of course we've always been around, much more than anyone thinks. Honoré says we're like the Jesuits, we've got so much secret power – Honoré had a friend who was an acolyte once, you see, so he knows all about these things – but then I say most of the Jesuits are, too, aren't they? Practically everyone you've ever heard of liked it better than that other thing, you know. Kept it quiet, of course, but usually there was a cosy little love-nest tucked away somewhere, and not just for a common little tart, either. Pythagoras, Paul, William the Conqueror, Louis the Fourteenth – him specially. I've got an American friend who says that George Washington's wife was a boy in drag. No, really. That's why there weren't any children, you see. And of course all artists and writers and musicians and those sorts of people. What you know about is only the tip of the iceberg.

'Well, where was I? Oh, yes. So our union made this general appeal, and the response was fantastic, quite fantastic. The whole country would have come to a stop – I mean it. No light or water, no buses, no trains, no aeroplanes, nothing. All the shops shut. Complete chaos. We're really very powerful people.

But the silly faggots in the cabinet – closet, I call it, they're just a lot of closet queens, if you ask me – they went quite mad and said, No, they were sorry, but they'd made their stupid law, they said, and they couldn't go back on it now or the foreign bankers would lose all confidence in the economy, as though they ever had any. Did you ever hear such nonsense? And then they said that if we didn't all go back to work they'd call out the army. Well, I mean to say, have you ever heard anything so ridiculous in all your life? Practically all my most intimate friends are soldiers, and one or two of them, just between ourselves, are very good customers, too. The army's just stuffed with us, from field-marshals on down, though there's nothing like a colour-sergeant, I say. It was as silly as threatening to call in the navy, though they did have the common sense not to do that. And anyway, imagine having your hair done by some common fusilier, with his great, fat, beefy hands! Or a lance-corporal from the cookhouse! It was just stupid, and everyone knew it.

'Well, after that there was a bit of a pause, while everyone agreed not to meet to discuss the problem, and then my mother came up with the most brilliant idea. She's a lovely woman, my mother, and she's always treated me as her favourite son – my brother's a dustman, nasty common profession, married with two horrid little girls, Gail and Lorraine, if you please, and his wife's just a common little tart, even if she is my sister-in-law, and she's dragged him down, when he could have had a decent life running the nappy-service with his friend Harold. It broke Harold's heart when my brother got married, really it did, and my mother's, and mine. And Harold couldn't run the nappy-service all by himself, could he? So of course he had to find someone else, and there was no call for my brother to speak to him like that, no call whatsoever. I was quite ashamed.

'Anyway, as I was saying, my dear old mum suddenly had this perfectly marvellous brainwave, which was that if we could only keep the strike going another ten days or so every lady in the country who was a lady, and a lot who weren't, would be on her knees to us and do whatever we wanted, and by that I don't mean what nasty common parvenu people think I mean. Of course I saw what she meant right away – you could see the roots as clear as daylight on half the women you passed in the street, and home-perms or no home-perms there wasn't an elegant head of hair to be seen. It was a choice between common little headscarves or complete disaster, poor things, which just goes to show what an essential industry ours is, as I said to Honoré, and he agreed. In fact he saw my mum's point right away, which surprised me – he's not very bright, to tell the truth, though he's a genius, an absolute genius, with his fingers – and he said – Honoré, I mean – oughtn't we to organize a petition or something, because women being what they were, all backbiting and gossip and reading silly magazines, they'd never get together unless someone pushed them.

'But dear mummy! She'd thought of that already – she's a remarkable woman, really she is. You see, some years ago now, when she saw there was really nothing she could do about me – I think she was secretly a teeny bit pleased, actually – weren't you, mum? Well, anyway, she started a Society for Mothers of Different Sons, which was meant to be for the mothers of you-know-whats, only it turned out that practically every mother in the country thought her sons were different in one way or another – if only they all had been, Honoré said! – so the Society quickly became gigantic, and my mum was permanent president and able to make all those lovely mothers eat out of her tiny hand. So she called an emergency meeting, and the evening before, Honoré and I spent making her hair look simply terrible – I was ashamed of her, really I was. I said to Honoré, if anyone knows she's my mother, we're ruined! But mum went on saying, "Make me uglier, darlings, much uglier, really hideous," so we did, we made her look just dreadful, and when she stood up next morning at the meeting and took off her headscarf, the whole executive committee burst into tears. Well, it was hardly even necessary to do anything after that, of course, but she really gave it to them all the same, straight from the heart, all about how the whole thing was a dirty plot by nasty *ordinary* men with nasty *ordinary* sons to humiliate their wives and stop them looking nice, and the strike had got to end for these poor women's sakes, and the government must give in at once, and till it did, no one was to cook or sew or clean or let her husband put his dirty thing near her, otherwise the entire lady population of the country would end up looking like her, just ghastly.

'Well, of course the government gave in almost the next day, *and* we got a special tax concession, which is why coiffeurs des dames are now able to offer such marvellous reduced rates, and everything was due to my dear, sweet, young mother! And now I've got a little special request to make, if you don't mind. You see, that was the only time the poor thing's ever been on television, and she looked an absolute nightmare from some science fiction programme unsuitable for children. And we've all teased her about it so much, and told her that's how she'll go down to history, that she's got quite upset about it. So as we're all on television here tonight, I want her to stand up and show everybody how gorgeous, how lovable, how sweet and how young and beautiful she really is – my mum! Upsy-daisy, darling!'

The hairdresser took the hand of the woman sitting on his right and encouraged her to rise, which she did, to a height of some six feet seven inches, her simperingly Amazonian features being crowned by an enormous green hat which was shaped like an ostrich egg and added another eight or nine inches to her overall stature. She was a powerfully built woman, broad of shoulder and hip, and she was wearing, I thought incongruously, a very short skirt of some shiny purple material which was clasped to her by a wide striped belt originally designed to be a saddle-girth for a hunter-chaser of some seventeen hands. Her hair was unconvincingly red for one of her late years and hung down over her shoulders in a tumble of improbable curls, the whole effect being ultimately and obscenely girlish, though above her diminutive skirt she wore a tight purple sweater against whose pearl-stitch thrust two adult breasts which gave the impression that, far from having given milk themselves, they had only reached such zeppelin proportions by being regularly and grossly milk-fed, and whose nipples, from where I was sitting, looked as large, fragile and pointed as the stones of apricots.

The television cameras now trundled forward to electrify the insulted ether with this grotesque image of maternity, and I could not help reflecting on the poverty of popular entertainment in the country if such a ludicrous and tedious occasion was considered suitable for the popular screen, when in my own country there would have been an indignant outcry if the perpetual diet of melodrama, music and old jokes had been interrupted even for so much as a news flash of such a competition. This reflection led me to ponder other significant differences between our two cultures, and I began to think that an account of my own childhood might perhaps be of interest to those present, for I could honestly say that it was in all respects an average one for a boy born into my particular stratum of society, and that my mother and I typified in many important respects the virtues and vices of the maternal-filial relationship, even though my father's role in family life was frequently ambiguous. When, therefore, the cameras began to move away again from the hairdresser's mother, I rose and made the following remarks:

'It has occurred to me that it may intrigue those of you who have come here tonight to judge your ideal of motherhood to hear how this natural, but always difficult and sometimes dangerous, role is viewed in other inhabited parts of the world.

Though I have travelled a great deal and examined the social systems of many countries, I will confine myself to the system which I naturally know best, that is to say that of my own country, for my knowledge of other countries is of course only external knowledge, obtained by rational deductions from sensory apprehensions notoriously unreliable and subject to subconscious interferences, while my knowledge of my own relationship with my own mother, while admittedly subject to subliminal censorship and perhaps even to alteration in the light of later external knowledge, is fundamentally internal, self-generated knowledge, of a kind which though it can be rationally analysed remains quintessentially the subject-matter of all ratiocination as it is not falsely felt through an imposed system of thought, but always experienced directly on the senses, so that however we try later to define it systematically, it influences our formulation of systems quite as much as, if not more than, those very systems influence our apprehension of it, and it may therefore be considered as pure, almost abstract, and certainly unique and unrepeatable knowledge.

'In my own country, it is the habit of mothers of my social class to give birth, if possible, in their conjugal beds, on the side on which the father usually sleeps. Elaborate birth-trays, decorated with scenes symbolic of the triumph of women over men, and laden with cakes, biscuits covered with icing, candied fruits and sweet liquors, are brought to the woman as she labours, so that she may both choose a few token gifts of food and wine for the emergent child and herself take nourishment during her sometimes protracted ordeal. Those which she sets aside are placed on a smaller birth-tray, sometimes known colloquially as a 'welcome mat', decorated with mythological scenes in which infants tyrannize over adults, and this tray, with its offerings, is placed at the appropriate moment so as to receive the hatching child, who is thus welcomed into the world with ceremony and symbolic gifts so that it may not feel quite at a loss in its unfamiliar and apparently hostile surroundings, or be frightened by the rough, though often humorous, attentions of the midwives and doctors, who are privileged actually to eat the sweetmeats after the child is safely delivered.

'Thus it was that my first experience of post-uterine life was an aesthetic one, for I was born head-first and with my eyes open, and thought for a moment that life would, after all, be tolerable, for the birth-tray depicted a putto seated on a canopied throne of mid-eighteenth-century French design, resting his feet on the prostrate bodies of his father and mother, imagery which was naturally pleasing to one who had had no wish to abandon the upholstered comfort of the womb. But if the symbolism of the tray was satisfactory, the design was poor and the execution of the painting was so amateurish and slapdash that my pleasure was short-lived and I felt obliged to make an immediate critical protest, thus entering the world flourishing, as it were, a long and bad review, though my furious, if thin, wail was in fact uttered before my knees had so much as poked their caps out, and technically, and perhaps also legally, I may quite well have been still part of my mother, so that the cry should perhaps be credited to her, even though I distinctly remember it as my own. A similar, though not identical, problem of when to adjudge a child an entity independent of its parent has caused, as I am sure you are all well aware, great theological difficulty in recent years.

'This incident of the birth-tray is by no means as insignificant as several psychiatrists I have consulted have tried to make out, for their claim that it is impossible for me either to have remembered my own birth or to have been born with a highly developed aesthetic sense is flatly contradicted by independent witnesses, notably two of the surviving midwives, who later confirmed every detail of my account without having been in any way previously influenced by me to do so, thus demonstrating that a psychiatrist is only as good as his limitations, and that these are in the majority of cases so gross and obvious that only other psychiatrists would fail to comment upon them, for it is, to say no more of this aspect of the matter, totally unscientific to refuse to accept as genuine those human experiences which one happens not to have experienced oneself, indeed it is positively solipsistic, and once psychiatrists, psychotherapists and psychoanalysts become solipsistic it is time for the whole uningratiating trade to be exposed for the charlatanry it so frequently is. That I entered this world with an aesthetic disappointment is clearly established, besides, by the evidence of my mother, who has always taken my side in this dispute against that of the psychiatrists, even though she was paying for my alleged 'analysis', 'therapy' and 'treatment', none of which were necessary, but taken, or rather endured, in the interests of scientific truth, by one wishing merely to establish whether or not these quacks were quacks, which many, though not all, of them were.

'The significance of the birth-tray incident lies, I believe, chiefly in the clear indication it gives both of my independence from and attachment to my mother. The first is illustrated by my innate aestheticism, for my mother is a woman of no artistic sensitivity whatever, thus proving that an embryo may have attributes correctly called, innate and clearly not even psychologically dependent on the structure of the harbouring body; and the second by the fact that even while I was acting with such marked independence, I was still physically joined to my mother in an embrace more intimate than any I can ever hope to repeat with her or any other woman, even if I wished to do so, and even though my mother was, of course, at the time spasmodically attempting to free herself in a literal sense from my ceaseless demands on her energy and time. Such, basically, has been our relationship ever since that first traumatic moment, a close distance or detached attachment, and as an immediate example of this curious mutual interindependence, let me briefly describe to you an incident which took place only this morning as I said goodbye to my mother at the air terminal, to which she had accompanied me not out of an obvious sentimentality but in order to share with me the taxi-fare, as she was planning to spend some hours in an emporium close to the terminal choosing a new carpet for –'

Barely launched though I was into my description of my mother's day, I was at that moment obliged to stop, for with wild yells and war-whoops a gang of what I took to be Mexican revellers burst in on the competition, cracking enormous coachwhips and letting off blank cartridges from sawn-off shot-guns to the manifest alarm of the sons there present with their mothers, though the mothers themselves remained commendably calm, and indeed seemed to treat the Mexicans' entry as part of their evening's entertainment, which it doubtless was, for the banditti wasted no time on the audience but made straight for the platform with blood-curdling cries and lassos. Quite soon I was pinioned and carried off in triumph from the room, despite my efforts to resist my own abduction, but as soon as we were outside I discovered that . . .

. . . death, for at the end of this hideous rite, Milo said, the sons were stripped and paraded before the mothers, then sacrificed on the naked belly of the Ideal Mother herself, after which the judges were blinded, their tongues cut out, their hands lopped, and their . . .

Then, for the first time in my life, I gave solemn thanks to the inventor of television, whoever he may have been, a matter on which there is still, I believe, some international contention.

. . . a familiarity which I could not explain, for I felt at once a stranger, as of course I was, and yet also an old inhabitant, perhaps one who, having lived here many years earlier, was now returning to his native place, though this was naturally not so, for it was my first visit to the country, and the manners and customs of the people, in some ways superficially similar to those of my homeland, proved on closer inspection extremely strange and baffling, so that I felt almost as though the walls which I had taken to be solid might in fact yield to my touch if I pressed them with my fingers, and I found myself walking with exaggerated care along the corridor, keeping studiously to the dead centre of the thick pile carpets whose colours changed from bend to bend.

I mentioned this sensation to Milo, who threw a comradely arm about my shoulders and said, 'My dear friend and captain! Would indeed that you had been here before, so that I might have known you in the days before my powers began to wane! Had I but known what the human form was capable of, what knots and postures, how I would have been the terror of this land, bringing joy to all and laying waste the barren fields with fecund seed!'

I pointed out the self-contradictions of this elaborate figure, and he answered that his joy was too great to be cribbed within mere sense, and that his sole regret was that he was now twenty-two and so, according to the most advanced scientific opinion, past his physical prime. To this I replied that the mere ability to ejaculate with great frequency was nothing, that man does not live by bread alone, and that the true prime of the adult male was that often never achieved moment when he reached perfect psychological equilibrium. Such a balance, I argued, was unknown to adolescents, however great the variety and trajectory of their emissions, for the very splendour of their inchoate physical powers brought with it more frustration than satisfaction.

'Consider,' I said, 'my own case. I am older than you, Milo, and only capable of marginally improving my performance aesthetically, yet that equilibrium I am far from having obtained. Even when we have at last found my beloved, I will not necessarily be made whole and stable, for he or she may well take no fancy to me, and even if she or he does, a mere fancy will not even begin to satisfy my urgent longing for a total mutual interdependence. Only a response as immediate, deep-striking and irreversible as my own can meet the overwhelming demands of my passion. It is my ambition,' I concluded, 'to enjoy with my beloved the most basic posture as it has never been enjoyed before, to discover in that crude and outworn engagement the very highest ecstasy. For aesthetic and technical mastery must finally give way to pure living. The very highest form of abstract thought is not to think at all.'

We continued our discussion with Milo arguing against me with all the youthful intemperance with which I had myself once argued with my masters, until we came to the end of the corridor and spread out again to renew our search. As I heard my fraternal comrades' voices grow dimmer and dimmer, I could have sworn that I had heard that sound of . . .

[*Henry dresses as a woman, and promptly turns into one, to his intense bewilderment. This change of sex allows Charles to alienate him still further from his 'normal' self. Charles's own bisexuality is not, I think, particularly relevant. In a 'Satyricon' anything can and should happen. For a modern Petronius the change of gender was almost obligatory.*

To avoid rape by a gang of Lesbians, a sort of less amiable and feminine version of the Encolpius Society, Henry borrows the tactic of Scheherezade and sends everyone to sleep with a story about some extinct ducks.

This fable or parable is an extraordinary tour de force, far and away the most finished section of the novel. It can be interpreted in several different ways. Though I have read it many times, I am still not certain if I have grasped all its meanings. But it haunts me. I feel as though it contains some message from Charles specifically for me. I can't explain or justify this feeling – I wish I could. I also wish I had written the fable. Perhaps that is all there is to it. Charles could certainly have guessed how much I would like it.]

Though this was very far from being the first time that I had donned feminine garb, or indeed the last, I was somewhat more anxious than usual as to my disguise, for if, as I hoped, my beloved fell for me with the same utter and reckless abandon with which I had fallen for her or him, there would inevitably be a period of confusion before my real gender became clear, for I was wearing my new clothes with style and conviction. But even as I was debating what course of action would be most appropriate, an extraordinary sense of loss began to overwhelm me, only partially compensated by a separate sense of gain.

. . . vanished utterly, and their proud place now gaped with an astounding openness, even though I could not even then help noticing that there were certain advantages as to the arrangement of . . .

I touched them surreptitiously, as though smoothing my white blouse's dainty frills, and found them to be as much a real and conjoined part of me as had once been my unbending member.

. . . anguish at this loss may be . . .

It may seem strange to those who have never experienced an abrupt change of gender that the matter which chiefly occupied my mind was not my new status as such, but the problem of the correct approach to my beloved if he or she should prove also to be female, for though I had ample experience of approaching both men and women as a man, I naturally had none whatever as a woman, and though I had frequently observed women performing together and knew, or thought I knew, what actions and reactions would be expected of me in most of the usual postures, I had never experienced these with or upon my own person, and I was most anxious not to disappoint my beloved by falling in any way below the extremely high standard of performance which I had always set for myself as a man.

The door of the lift opened as I was turning to push away a particularly pressing frotteur of some fifty-eight or -nine, and I felt pressure of another kind upon my shoulder, apparently that of a well-intentioned hand, though I doubted very much whether its intentions were in fact free of selfish and aggressive motive. Turning back in order to repulse this new attack, I was obliged to allow the frotteur to resume his assault upon my undefended flank, which he did with a small cry of gratitude and delight, which I scarcely heard in my astonishment at discovering that the hand belonged not, as I had supposed, to the chargé d'affaires, but to my beloved, who was now using it to beckon me to follow him or her, I still could not say which, from the elevator. Rooted once again by the violence of my surprise and love to the spot on which I was being assaulted, I watched the exquisite figure disappear slowly through the throng, the eyes casting as they went a glance of such galvanizing perfection behind them, begging and pleading with me to follow even as I was silently but passionately begging and pleading with them to wait till I could free my limbs from their inhibiting torpor of joy, that I was at last able to throw off the now open and ecstatic clasp of the frotteur and resume my pursuit with the highest hopes I had yet had.

It is of interest to note, I believe, that at this time I had the very firm impression that my beloved was a man, though whether or not this was due to my own femininity I cannot say. As I thrust my way through the packed ranks of travellers, following my beloved's ever-retreating back, I was overwhelmed with bliss at the thought that he or she was now clearly as attracted and fascinated by me as I was by her or him, and I congratulated myself even as I pushed and shoved on my boldness in having gasped out my love, even so briefly, at our dramatic parting in the chapel. I had not then been certain how my words had been received, though it had always been my belief that if it was true that all the world loves a lover, then a lover is probably wise to declare himself to his beloved at the earliest possible moment, so that he or she, who must, after all, be part of that world which already loves him for being in love, may return the love without any tedious shilly-shallying and delay. Now that this thesis was so happily confirmed I . . .

When I recovered my senses, I found myself lying in a comfortable four-poster bed of late seventeenth-century provincial Spanish design, quite naked and still female, attended by a number of well-built women, equally naked, but not in all cases so decidedly womanly as myself, who were fighting with some mirth over my coffee-soaked clothing for the right, as it seemed, to wash out the stains. I sat up with a start, clutching the bedclothes to my breasts in a gesture with which I should never have troubled myself in my alternative incarnation, though I was in no fit state to make this observation at the time, for my head ached and my right hip seemed painfully bruised, though these trifling discomforts were as nothing to that of finding myself in such strange and unexplained circumstances. Seeing that I had made at least a partial recovery from my fall, the women now gathered about me, questioning me as to my name and occupation, roughly removing the covers from my body and firmly insisting on giving me an elaborate and prolonged physical examination, despite my repeated requests to be left alone until I had been able to take some stock of my new surroundings.

'We are doctors,' announced a bespectacled woman of some thirty-seven or -eight, with short hair and neat rather than nutritious-looking breasts, 'and our time is extremely valuable. We see you when we wish to do so, or you sicken without the benefit of modern medicine.'

'I,' said an older woman, laughing shrilly till her companions shushed her, 'am Miss Wonder Drug, and you are the bacillus I love! Come, let us fatally entangle!'

A third woman, of much greater maturity, with a kindly, maternal expression on her face and with breasts to match, gave me a friendly kiss on the cheek and said, 'It's much better to have it done first time by experts, dearie. They know what they're doing.'

Seeing that there was only one frail hope for me against this coven of medicinal witches, I ceased to struggle and gave myself to tears. 'I am,' I sobbed, 'a virgin, and on my way to my first assignation with my first lover. Spare me, I beg you, out of charity and respect for my condition.'

As I uttered this moving appeal, I realized with horror that the first part of it was, in a sense, true, though it was incredible that I, who had loved so industriously for so many years, could still technically be chaste. Yet such the gossip of the women indicated that I was, though I had as yet had no opportunity to check the fact for myself and was indeed only now for the first time viewing my new naked limbs and still had no knowledge of my facial appearance.

The gaggle of maldames showed no sign of sympathy with my plight, indeed they poured scorn on any woman who had reached my age with a hymen yet unbroken, though mine apparently gave their lust a greater than usual incentive to brutality, for they were not, I gathered from their exclamations, merely lovers of their own kind, but ones especially devoted to the initiation of virgins, a fetishism I had previously only encountered among men of advanced years, who had often told me that hymens were collected in their youth by gentlemen of distinction, much as small boys in my own time collected the corks of wine-bottles of rare vintages. My appeals thus fell on deaf ears, and when I saw that my captors showed some signs of impatience at my continued unwillingness to give myself to their pleasure, and began to threaten me with violence, I realized that there was nothing for it but to yield, though I asked that a mirror and a comb might first be brought to me, so that I might at least make myself comely for their debauch, though my real motive was to obtain a long look at my maiden face before it became that of a mature woman. The mirror was somewhat grudgingly brought, and I was most pleasantly surprised to discover that I was a strikingly beautiful girl of eighteen or nineteen, with large blue eyes, elegantly shaded by long lashes, naturally rosy cheeks, a small, slightly tilted nose, full lips, good cheekbones, small ears and long, silky hair of a blondeness so radiant that I appeared almost to be haloed.

Enraptured by my own appearance, I gazed at it for a long moment, watching the tears roll prettily down my cheeks as I thought of my immediate ravishment by these vicious surgeons, if such they were, and wondering if there was not some ruse by which I might defend myself against their capering lust. For it seemed to me a tragedy worthy of a great dramatic poet that I should be denied the ordinary maidenly pleasure of preserving my perfect beauty for the one for whom I longed, and it even occurred to me as I wept and pondered, running my comb through tresses which had no need of grooming, that the life of a woman was indeed different from that of a man, as so many writers have said, for whereas I had managed without difficulty or sense of loss to give pleasure to the Encolpians, while still preserving my undying devotion to my beloved, I knew that shame and dishonour would soon utterly overwhelm me, and that the damage done me would be irreparable, whether or not I fiercely imagined my assailants to be, one after the other, my beloved.

At last my feelings became too much for me, and words broke from my lips without my conscious control. 'Is there nothing that can persuade you to break off your revels? Does the abject misery of your wretched sacrifice not waken any emotion in your granite breasts? Have none of you ever loved, as I now love, and wished to give yourself only to the object, whatever it may be, of your devotion?'

'No,' answered the biggest of the women, with an ugly chuckle. 'Never. But we will give you the opportunity to preserve your rag of virtue, as we always do under such circumstances, compelled by the rules of our organization. If you can tell us a story so titillating and stimulating that we are obliged to exhaust our lusts upon each other before you have finished, then we will leave your initiation to whomever you may choose, and much hurt may it bring you. I must tell you that no maiden has ever yet succeeded in narrating such a tale to us, and the delay you cause us will only lead us to treat you with the greater brutality.'

Although I was familiar with the pornographic literature of many lands, I paused for several moments before deciding how best to fulfil the conditions which the woman had so precisely outlined, for it is not always easy to know which postures, and which descriptions of those postures, will most excite to frenzy a group of strangers, and it had often been my experience that those who achieved satisfaction only through, for instance, the contemplation of high-heeled ladies' shoes, were stimulated not by descriptions of their particular fantasy but rather by banal narratives of the simplest and least original conjunctions. At last I resolved to adopt an unusual and risky tactic, which was to tell a fable I had learned at my mother's knee and which contained no matter which could by any stretch of the imagination be considered lewd or inflammatory, in the hope that the women, obliged to resort to their own imaginations, would create satisfyingly debased interpretations of the simple story and so exhaust themselves. Bidding them to sit comfortably about my feet, I began the following relation:

'Once upon a time, in a gloomy swamp in central America, not far north of Panama, there lived the last surviving members of a species of wild duck which ornithologists believed to have been extinct for several hundred years, which they were not. These birds lived modestly and contentedly in their swamp, the occasional prey of alligators and snakes, but preying themselves only on various waterweeds and their parasites. Though they did not increase in numbers from year to year, neither did they decline, and having reached a state of satisfactory equilibrium with the ecology of their environment, it is probable that they would have continued to live there to this day, had it not been for the overweening ambition of Senator Gomez.

'Senator Gomez was the owner of vast acres of the desolate and backward province in which the ducks happily survived beyond the ken of explorers and scientists. Sixty-five, white-haired and with golden earrings in his large, fleshy lobes, he came of much-debased Spanish stock and represented mainly pure-blooded Amero-Indians in the Senate, though only a minority of these knew of his existence, and of this minority less than a quarter knew that there was a Senate, for little social or educational progress had been made in the area since the fall of the Aztec Empire, though many political changes had been made in the capital since those early days.

'Senator Gomez was not an unkindly or cruel man, nor was he hostile to the advancement of others, provided that they were members of his family and the advancement was not to his own financial loss, but though he had been Senator for forty years, since the very month in which his father had been shot by mistake for another politician in the barbershop of the Senate, he was not, as his senescence began, content. "I have not done anything by which I shall be remembered," he told his fifteen sons on his sixty-fifth birthday. "But before I die, I mean to." No one ever dared to disagree with the Senator, and his sons did not question the first part of his statement, much to his disappointment. His sense of failure deepened. "I shall do something so tremendous," he said angrily, "that my name will never be forgotten." His sons agreed enthusiastically.

'At that time much financial aid was being poured into the country by two rival foreign powers, and many schemes for the construction of roads, railways, airports, banks, offices, churches, presidential palaces and even schools were being mooted by influential Senators, for it was clear that the money had to be put to some flamboyant public use or the two rival foreign powers would lose interest and take their aid elsewhere. Senator Gomez pondered the problem for many weeks, and at last put forward a scheme which would be flamboyant and practically valuable to the country, and yet would bring him everlasting renown. His project was for the construction of two great state highways to run north and south, east and west, across the entire country and serving every province.

'The idea was quickly supported by the other Senators, for the great profits to be made from its building would be widely distributed, though it was clear even at a cursory glance that Senator Gomez would profit most. After anxious debate, during which the routes of the roads were frequently altered, and only after one of the foreign powers threatened to withdraw its grants of aid altogether unless a decision was soon reached, the plans were agreed, and it was seen that Senator Gomez had lost none of his old political cunning, for while many alterations had been made to his original scheme, none had been made to his province's part of it, and the whole of the east-west highway was to be named The Golden Miles of Senator Gomez.

'Now it so happened that the final route for The Golden Miles lay through the middle of the swamp in which the unknown ducks survived, for Senator Gomez considered that though glory was what he most wanted, it would be foolish to allow someone else to pocket all the gain. And thus it came about that bulldozers, lorries, caterpillar tractors and giant excavators invaded the peaceful dankness of the swamp, and strange, almost European faces were seen where only a few diseased Amero-Indians had passed before.

'After many months of sickly work, of tree-felling, swamp-filling, concrete and noise, and after many deaths among the diseased Amero-Indian construction workers, this section of the great highway was at last completed – the first to be so, for Senator Gomez was anxious lest the foreign aid should cease before his own property had thoroughly benefited from it. During the construction the ducks avoided the noise and kept well away from the new road. But once the ancient peace had settled again over the whole dismal area, they came to examine this strange new feature of their environment. Cautious at first, they grew only slowly bolder, but at last they came to like the straight white road down which no traffic ever passed, and were often to be seen, if there had been anyone to see them, parading up and down the concrete.

'But there was no one to see them. The road ran from one side of Senator Gomez's domain to the other, but near no town, for the Senator lived on a ranch many miles to the north, and the area was virtually uninhabited by Amero-Indians because of the poisonousness of the swamp. Nor was it of any attraction to tourists. An occasional alligator-hunter came in a jeep, a few Indians walked along the edge of it, but that was all, and on the occasion of these very rare visits the ducks had plenty of time to fly away before anyone reached them. Thus they remained quite unknown to civilization.

'Senator Gomez died before the rest of the roadway was completed. The project was halted. Senator Gomez's sons quarrelled amongst themselves. There was a revolution in the capital. The foreign powers ceased their aid. Then there was a further revolution and they resumed it. A new trans-continental highway was planned to be named after and to pass through many miles of the property of another Senator. The Golden Miles of Senator Gomez sank slowly into the swamp.

'One day, a party of scientists from one of the foreign powers was permitted to explore that region of the country in return for still more aid and still greater capital investment. They came to the swamp and decided to make an ecological study. They built themselves a camp and constructed hides for bird-watching. Although the ducks were extremely shy at first, they found that these new visitors were not noisy like their predecessors. Furthermore, they left large quantities of new and delicious foods for the ducks to eat. Being of an essentially amiable disposition, the ducks soon made friends with the scientists and after a few weeks were literally eating out of their hands. The scientists took many photographs, in colour and in black and white, and within a few months the ducks were famous. Believed to be as dead as the dodo, the species was shown to be astonishingly alive. Ornithologists came from all over the world to see them and photograph them. The ducks became self-conscious and learned to pose. Soon the ornithologists were followed by tourists, for the country was now prosperous, owing to the discovery by a second party of explorers from the rival foreign power of a valuable mineral in another part of the same province. Comfortable hotels sprang up in several nearby towns, themselves only recently upsprung. It was possible for tourists to obtain passable beds and meals within half a day's journey of the swamp. In certain over-developed parts of north America and Europe, not to have visited the ducks was to be uncultivated, untravelled and clearly unrich.

'Now it so happened that the country's new prosperity, though as crookedly managed as the old poverty, was so great that the new east-west highway was actually completed, its final section running some thirty miles to the south of the old route through the swamp. As a result, new tourist areas with new tourist attractions, such as shark-fishing, pederasty and gambling, were opened up many miles away, and visitors to the ducks ceased almost overnight. The comfortable hotels in the new towns were no longer comfortable enough. There was not enough nightlife. Ducks were, after all, only ducks. Besides, the old road, thanks to the inferior materials used by Senator Gomez's builder at Senator Gomez's express and secret instructions, the profit from which was almost but not quite equally shared – the old road sank below the surface of the swamp in two or three places. It was hard to reach the ducks without an amphibious craft and there was none in the whole province. Quite soon the ducks had been forgotten by all but a handful of professional ornithologists.

'But, alas, the ducks had not forgotten the tourists. By now completely tame, and used to attention and petting, they were bored and dissatisfied at the return of their old, uneventful life. A movement began among the younger ducks, who did not even remember the days of their obscurity, to move south to the new road, which they had spotted on occasional flights to escape the tedium of home. It was tiresome, these young ducks said, to have to find one's own food when there were people willing to give it to one free; the tourists were thoroughly worth looking at – they enlivened the dismal scene; it was foolish to imagine that any species could go back after it had made a great evolutionary step forward. Quite soon, there would be nothing of the old road left, and then where would they be able to strut up and down as they all so much liked to do?

'The older ducks were not convinced until the argument had gone on for many days, but then they told themselves that it would be wrong to go against the spirit of adventure which their juniors were so praiseworthily showing, and they agreed that the whole tribe should make the short migration. Only one old drake refused to go with them. "I will not leave my old haunts at my time of life," he said firmly, "to go on a wild-goose chase. I shall expect you all back here tomorrow evening." But he was laughed to scorn, and the assembly agreed to set off at first light on the following morning.

'It did not take the ducks long to reach the new road, and it was still very early when they settled on its smooth white surface and began to preen themselves. The younger ducks were in ecstasies. "Look!" they cried. "Our new road is whiter and smoother far than the old! When we waddle across it to be fed, it will give an extra sheen to our feathers." And the older birds agreed that the new road was in every way an improvement, for among other things it had a row of hard, glinting lumps which ran down the middle of it in both directions as far as the eye could see. These lumps were comfortable places on which to sit, and many of the ducks, tired by the unaccustomed exercise of their morning's flight, sat on them and went to sleep.

'Quite soon the first of the day's travellers appeared, Amero-Indians on bicycles and on foot, who passed the ducks without paying them much attention, though after one of them had stopped and discovered how tame they were, two young drakes mysteriously disappeared. The leaders of the ducks, squinting up at the sun, decided that the hour was almost at hand at which visitors with cameras and food might be expected, so they called all their people together and told them to make themselves neat. After a short delay, they held a general inspection, tidied away a few loose feathers, and marched the entire gathering out into the middle of the road to await developments.

'Sure enough, the first bus of the day was approaching, and expecting it to stop and disgorge eager photographers, the ducks began to jostle each other for front positions. They were so busy quarrelling amongst themselves that they failed to notice that the bus was not even slowing down. All the ducks, without exception, were killed. Thus the only remaining member of this almost extinct species was the drake who had stayed behind in the swamp, and he, growing lonely and depressed, wandered off into a gloomy cane-brake where he was at once eaten by an alligator.'

There was a profound silence after I had ended my tale, and I saw to my great delight that its narration had worked even more satisfactorily than I could have dared to hope, for the women had long since fallen asleep, lulled by the tedium of the story, and now lay about the room like crumpled bath-gowns, the last dregs of their lust wrung from them, only the soft movements of their breathing indicating that life still continued in their flaccid forms.

I rose quietly from the bed and dressed myself in what I could find, then went to the pier-glass to satisfy myself that my remembrance of my own beauty was not at fault, which it was not, for I looked as delectable in clothes as out of them, and my hair looked even softer against the white of my blouse than against the faint pinkness of my shoulders. Stepping lightly over the exhausted . . .

[*Having escaped from the Lesbians, Henry at once falls into the hands of the Encolpians, who, though they are searching for him, quite fail to recognize him now that he is a woman. He is subjected to a mass rape, then falls into the hands of a rubber fetishist. As he is getting away, Henry discovers that he has again changed sex – now he is a hermaphrodite. He runs straight into his beloved, who tells him that he or she is as deeply in love with him as he is with her or him. Waiting for her to reappear from a banqueting-hall, Henry composes a poem.*

Henry's sexual aestheticism is here severely punished, and the Encolpians are seen for what they really are – a brutal gang of irresponsible hedonists. After them, the interlude with the rubber fetishist is simply comic. (Incidentally, Charles once showed me a rubber fetishist newspaper not at all unlike The Rubber Sheet. *Some things are too absurd to be parodied, and the letter quoted here may easily be a real one.)*

Henry's hermaphroditism, which lasts till the end of the novel, is the physical expression of his true psychological nature. As he himself observes, 'true hermaphroditism is extremely rare', but I think we can take it that his is the genuine article. Apart from that, his uncertainty about the sex of his beloved leads him to want to be ready for all eventualities, though not even hermaphroditism prepares him for the final revelation.

I find his poem charming and characteristic, combining, as it does, his earnest seeking after truth and scientific spirit with his high romanticism. That he never questions his own passion as he questions everything else is fundamental to the comedy. His love is ridiculous. Yet I suppose it is the logical outcome of a certain type of western idealism; we would all like to imagine that we are capable of such a total devotion.]

Hermaphrodite

'Milo!' I cried in real distress. 'Do you not know me? I am Henry, your captain and friend! Under this disguise of widow's weeds, I am your comrade and brother!'

'As to that,' he answered, quite failing to recognize me, 'we shall soon see. Take him into the pink bedroom.'

Against my continued protests and appeals, I was carried into the room, which was misnamed, for its walls were not pink but blood-red, and the canopied bed, which seemed to me probably of early American design, perhaps from Baltimore, was covered with a magenta bedspread, on to which I was roughly cast. The Encolpians, in grim silence, then stripped me and discovered my feminine nakedness, which I could scarcely deny, though I attempted to explain to Milo what had occurred. He paid me little heed, however, and answered brusquely that if I had any knowledge as to Henry's whereabouts I should instantly divulge it, for he had lost him, and was anxious not to continue his search without my (or his, Henry's) assistance. Thus it was that I came to see how loyalty, such as that which Milo now undoubtedly displayed, was even at its highest not always so useful a quality in a lieutenant as some moralists have suggested, for it tends to stint imaginative sympathy and to lead to grave errors of judgement, such as the one Milo now committed, for he believed that I had deliberately and maliciously misled him with my true account of what had happened, and to punish me he ordered my immediate rape by the entire membership of the Encolpius Society there present, myself of course excluded. This rape lasted many minutes, and taught me much which was afterwards to be usefully incorporated into my knowledge of womanly pleasure, but at the time I could only weep for my innocence and reflect bitterly on the irony of the situation, for it was I who had taught the Encolpians much of what they now practised, and practised well, though only to my sadness and chagrin. Our bodies are, it is true, but cottages of corruption, yet we do not therefore cause them to be tumbled carelessly down, rather we shore up the tottering chimney, fly buttresses against the bulging wall, preserving what we can for as long as we can, for the corruption is dear to us, and when these our only abodes are invaded by hostile visitors, when the door is battered down and the window broken to afford unlimited ingress to ruthless brigands, when even the chimney is not safe from unwonted, unwanted descents, then we may weep indeed, for we do not mind the dirt on the carpet in the hallway when we have trodden it there ourselves, but we protest most strongly against those strangers to the cot who do not wipe their feet on the mat we have provided for the purpose, and we feel an unutterable sense of violation when burglars root among our possessions like sows after acorns.

When the Encolpians had finished their sad work of destruction and left me to the sorry silence of my desecration, I lay for some minutes too tired and oppressed by despair to move, for it is always, each single time that it occurs, disheartening when reason is unable to make itself heard against unreason, or when truth is drowned out by the tintinnabulum of falsehood, and it is wrong to say, as some ignorant men do, that women enjoy being raped, for they do not, preferring the gentle approach of true love to the randy brutality even of expert thieves and vandals. Yet I could not wholly blame my erstwhile comrades for their errors either of mind or of body, for I was comely, and my story, though true, was not easy to credit, though if Milo had only allowed me time to give him that certain evidence of uniquely shared experience which would have . . .

. . . rubber, a purpose for which I could not at first imagine, though after we had entered the cupboard I was left in no doubt, for he thrust it into my mouth as though bridling a refractory mare, then tied my hands tightly behind my back with what seemed to be mackintosh thongs. Wearied as I was by the continual and often successful efforts of strangers to assault me, I adopted an apathetic attitude and closed my eyes in preparation for yet another battering by one of these insatiable rams, only to open them again in some surprise when I felt my shoes removed and replaced by new ones. Bidding me stand up, which I did, he capered about me in great lechery and delight, for the heels of these shoes were at least nine inches high and steel-tipped, and his pleasure, he quickly informed me, lay in having certain tender parts of his anatomy trodden upon by women so gagged, tied and shod, a taste which I myself had never shared. Obliging him as rapidly as I could, I tottered above him to his entire satisfaction, after the fulfilment of which I hoped I would be freed to continue my search. But such was not to be the case, for my captor was not so easily gratified and would not let me go until I had read to him, after the gag had of course been removed, passages from his favourite reading matter, a cyclostyled monthly bulletin entitled *The Rubber Sheet*, which consisted almost exclusively of letters from readers such as the following:

Dear Ed, I think your fans may be interested to hear of how my girlfriend and I amused ourselves last weekend. We're neither of us very strict disciplinarians, but we both love rubber, and our only quarrels are about who's going to wear what! Sometimes I have to take a piece of rubber-tubing to her, to get my own way! And I think she loves it – because it's rubber!

After work on Saturday morning, we met at my flat (rubber underfelting – with nothing on top of it!), and we gave each other an hour's bondage, though I didn't mind one little bit when she let me have an extra quarter of an hour while she vacuumed me from top to toe several times. Then we put on our rubber and went for a ride on my bike – not forgetting the motor-oil, of course! There's nothing like a pint of lubricant *inside the rubber* (put it in at the front of the neck for the best results) when you're doing a ton, at least I don't think so. We stopped in a wood and I tied her to a tree with some barbed-wire which was lying around, and I laughed like anything when she said she was afraid her rubber might get torn. She was really hooked, I told her! Get it? ['We *do* – Ed.] But I didn't want to rub'er up the wrong way ['*Thanks, we got that one, too!*' – Ed.], so I soon let her go and we went home via the mudflats, where we had a tremendous half-hour of rolling in the wet mud – terrific! Seriously, rubber fans should try it – it's great! ['*I have tried it! And it is!*' – Ed.]

Then we went back to her place for some more bondage till bedtime – only I left her tied up all night, on the rubber sheet! She loved it, and begged me not to undo her, but it was time for church, so we put on our long rubber underwear with our Sunday suits on top and listened to a terrific sermon on degeneracy. If only people would be a little more disciplined, the vicar said, they'd be a lot happier. We both agreed! He's a good chap, the vicar – rides a bike! Then it was home for Sunday lunch with her parents – the dumplings were smashing – just like rubber! Afterwards we put on our macs and went to the local fleapit to see a documentary on rubber plantations in Malaya – it made us want to emigrate right away. Then we went for a last spin on the bike, only this time she drove and I poured – sounds like a tea-party, doesn't it? Well, it was and it wasn't –

if you know what I mean! And so to bed, after a really rubber weekend.

We enjoyed ourselves – did you? Hope so!

FG (Name and address supplied.)

[*Yes, we did! Do other readers want to share their weekend hobbies with us? We wish you would! And thanks for the tip about the motor-oil, FG! – Ed.*]

After I had read a number of these tiresomely improbable letters, my hands were untied and I was allowed to go, though not before I had securely fastened my abductor inside his skin-tight rubber clothing and left him roped in a painfully foetal position inside the cupboard, with the door locked from the outside, and with an all-rubber gag securely clamped to his mouth so that he could not attract passers-by with cries for help. There I left him, throwing the key to the cupboard, on his express instructions, out of the window, and there, for all I have since heard, he still may be, for I doubt whether anyone can have been aware of his hiding-place until the inevitable stench of his corpse revealed it.

It was as I was resuming my normal footgear, or rather that which had come to seem normal to me as a result of the extraordinary transformation which I have described, that I became aware of a new biological change, or retransformation, or at least partial retransformation or restoration of old tissue, for, apparently as a result of my promenade over the tender parts of the rubber maniac's body, my own had begun to resume its normal appearance, though not wholly, for while I discovered with not unmixed feelings that I was once again fully capable of taking masculine postures and leaving no doubt in my partner's mind as to my fitness to do so, my breasts remained as they had been, full and enviably proportioned, and though my legs were once again, perhaps because of their brief exercise, covered with manly hair, my face remained hairlessly feminine. If I had earlier felt bewildered to change from one gender to another, imagine my amazement on now discovering that I belonged at once to both and neither, for true hermaphroditism such as mine is not only extremely rare but very puzzling for its possessor, since it is impossible for him, her or it, except from moment to moment, to know to which side of this complex nature to tend in the infinitely variable chaos of chance acquaintanceship.

My immediate problem, once I had overcome my first sharp shock of surprise, was to decide whether to go forth as a man or as a woman, for if I dressed as a man my well-developed upper part would certainly cause curious comment, even if I were to cut my hair, which I was reluctant to do until some definite tendency had established itself in my relationships with members of both genders, while if I were to proceed as a woman, how could I explain my hirsute legs, whose obvious maleness only thick stockings or tights, neither of which were then to hand, could conceal? There was nothing for it but to don the motorcycling outfit which lay upon the bed, for that effectively disguised me below the neck, even if it meant risking unwelcome attentions from those whose inclinations chimed with those of the fetishist I was now robbing, at his wish, and leaving to an apparently painful and prolonged death. Thus garbed, I believed that I could continue my pursuit of my beloved without any further let, and I even experienced a small sensation of relief that my present halfway status was halfway in the way it was, for to have been male above the waist and female below would have been, I thought, to enjoy the best of neither world, while to be female above and male below might well prove, in some circumstances at least, no handicap whatever.

I had scarcely closed the door of the room than I came face to face with my beloved in the corridor, and received for the first time the full force of that exquisite beauty which once again quite literally stunned me with its perfection, and though I was still unable to say whether she or he was a man or a woman, it seemed of no great importance while my own status remained so intransigently ambiguous. She or he was carrying a large tray of victuals, which, with a composure I could in no way begin to match, he or she informed me were for a banquet being held in the next room, and which must at once be delivered.

'But,' said this divine, this sublime, this incomparable, indescribable creature, 'as soon as I have delivered the tray I will return for though I do not know who you are, nor what your name or profession, I know that I love you, and that you in turn love me and I have spent the last hours searching for you throughout this cursed, refractory hotel, for I must love and cherish you all my life long, whatever may befall. Wait for me here, my beloved, and I will return in a trice, and then we will give ourselves to each other for all eternity.'

With these words my beloved passed by me and entered a room from which I could hear the sounds of knives and forks against gold plate, and smell the wafted scents of a private, possibly clandestine meal, suggesting small but brilliantly cooked dishes, so enticing that my mouth began to water, though in my heart I longed only for my beloved's promised return, and my head was busy composing the following verses to celebrate our fortunate reunion:

TO MY BELOVED

My love is a branch of knowledge,
Like philosophy or biochemistry,
And its blossoms
Are as learned articles in technical journals.
Its leaves are covered with strange symbols.
I cannot read them,
For love has made me blind.

My love is an arcane science, like alchemy,
But like chemistry, its compounds are real.
Oh for the white coats and sterilized instruments,
The complex arrangement of tubes and jars,
The whole laboratory of love!
I am my own professor,
I work without grants from the government
Or stipends from famous foundations.
My only assistants are my own two hands,
My heart and my soul,
For what I discover
Can never be shared.
The secrets of my love
Will die with me.
But my love
Will never die.

While I composed this little compliment to passion, waiting each instant for my beloved's return, I was continually accosted by people of both genders who apparently assumed that I was standing in such provocative garb in a main highway, as it were, of the hotel only in order to solicit advances, than which nothing could, of course, have been further from the case, which I told my accosters in no mistakable terms. Finding their ceaseless importunity insupportable, I at last decided that it would be wiser to enter the dining-room in which my beloved was so long detained than to continue drawing the unwelcome attentions of every lewd pedestrian in the corridor, so I boldly opened the door through which he or she had passed and went in, having no intention of staying, and being motivated perhaps most strongly by anxiety as to my beloved's person, for she or he had definitely stated that he or she would almost at once return to where I had been waiting, but this promise had not been fulfilled, and many minutes had passed while I worked on my poem, for I am a slow composer even of free verse, and after its completion I had delayed some considerable further time before venturing into the dining-room.

[*Henry joins the banquet, an elaborate gourmet affair, and listens to an appallingly inhumane speech about the starving nations from his own father.*

On the surface, this is a straightforward satire on the wine and food snobbery of the Sunday colour supplements and glossy magazines. But Henry's father's speech is clearly meant to imply the inhumanity of this form of sensual aestheticism. Charles was no gourmet himself. How can anyone, he asks, indulge himself while millions are starving for lack of basic sustenance? The answer is, only by adopting Henry's father's repulsive point of view.

He is a violent and sadistic man, we learn, given to drunkenness and wife-beating; he is to prove an Abraham without any tenderness. From now on the father-son conflict comes to dominate the novel.

Incidentally, the Tastebud Club's menu is a series of dreadful jokes. I haven't been able to recognize all the references, but 'Consommé Est' is presumably a play on 'Consummatum Est'; 'Rougets au thésaure' refers to Roget's Thesaurus; *'Raie à l'homme' to the artist Man Ray; and 'Boeuf en daube à la phare' to the dish whose aroma fills the pages of Virginia Woolf's* To the Lighthouse. *Charles took great delight in excruciating puns, and there is no particular significance in these, as far as I can make out.*]

The Tastebud Club

To my amazement I discovered an enormous banquet in progress, with many hundreds of diners assembled at long tables, and not, as I had supposed, a small supper party of two or at the most seven or eight people, and I quickly saw that my error was due to the almost total silence in which the meal was being consumed, for in spite of the great number of people present, only one person at each table was actually eating and that extremely slowly and with the most careful mastication and ingestion, after which he spoke in low tones to his immediate neighbour on his left, who listened intently, then made copious notes before himself taking a small portion of food and treating it with the same elaborate, almost religious deference. Thinking that it was indeed some rite upon which I had unwittingly stumbled, I determined to look rapidly for my beloved and then withdraw, for I had no wish to intrude upon so obviously reverential an occasion, and I was in fact closely examining the faces of the servitors about me when one of these approached me and said in a whisper, 'Have you brought them? Are they absolutely ripe?', questions which I was quite unable to answer, for I did not understand them.

'I have brought nothing,' I answered in similarly low tones, and was about to continue with some queries of my own when the man, who seemed to be of some seniority, bowed in the most servile manner and apologized quite unnecessarily for having mistaken me for a special messenger from a fig-farm, which I was not. Compounding his error, and before I could protest, he ushered me to a vacant place at one of the tables, under the false assumption that I was a late arrival to the feast. After a brief initial resistance I allowed myself to be seated, for I believed my beloved to be still somewhere in the banqueting-room, and I thought that I should take advantage of this opportunity to investigate yet another curious custom of a country which was clearly full of them while I continued my search for him or her.

In front of my place was a large printed placard, which I took to be some form of advertising matter until I closely examined it and found it to be a menu, which read as follows:

The Tastebud Club

Annual Dinner

· · ·

Consomme Est
Crème de la Crème

· · ·

Oouf en cocotte coquette

· · ·

Barbue a la Durand Ruel
Filets de macquereaux de Paris
Rougets au thesaure
Raie a l'homme
Filets de sole justification

· · ·

Hommard Fahrenheit

· · ·

Boeuf en daube a la phare
Carre d'agneau a la visonti
Le Fricandeau feydeau
Rognons sautes tobago
Les hommes de terre musclemen

. . .

Interval

Though by no means hungry, I was a little peckish after all my untoward experiences, and I was glad to see that my fellow diners had got no further than the rougets, a dish of which I have always been fond, though too many chefs remove the entrails or 'trail' of this 'woodcock of the sea', which should always be left in to impart the extra subtlety of flavour which raises this distinguished fish to at least a barony in the aristocracy of taste. My plate being empty, I was about to summon one of the many unoccupied waiters when my neighbour, a dilettanteish young man, sporting a buttonhole of the common vetch known as eggs-and-bacon, turned to me and said, 'I think the oeuf en cocotte was a mistake, don't you? I mean, one should not attempt to mingle so early in a meal the hot and the cold. Much though I like brown-bread ice-cream, the idea of it with an egg, at least with an ostrich egg, is happier on paper than on the palate. I think the menu committee is becoming a little too fanciful in its efforts to amuse. My taste, for one, is not yet so jaded as to feel the need for violent extremes immediately after the soup.'

I agreed with him that the best cooking tended towards a middle path, as Aristotle is believed to have recommended in his treatise *The Domestics,* though it is lost, and references to it may have been misinterpreted, for they are few and ambiguous and may well refer to some quite different book or books of the great *chef de philosophie,* as he has been called. But I was naturally unable to comment on the cocotte coquette as I had not had the good fortune to taste it, and so I informed my new friend, who answered that he thought it sensible of me to have arrived after the opening courses, for in his opinion soups were so much greasy bilge-water from the great liner which was gastronomy, and he could not understand why anyone liked to start a curious meal with such tepid stuff, however warming and nourishing it might be for the abjectly poor on winter nights, or for the rich between drives while out shooting pheasants on cold mornings; though why, he added, anyone wanted to slaughter birds so aesthetically pleasing to look at and so unyielding in their lack of interest to a sensitive palate, he for one could not think, indeed he was prepared to go further and say that of all game-birds only the quail was really satisfactory, particularly as cooked in the Auvergne, stuffed with wrens and baked in wafer-thin papillottes. I agreed with him as to the pheasant's toughness and lack of flavour, but never having tried the quail was unable to confirm his latter judgement, though I had heard it said that there was at least one passable kitchen in the Auvergne, at the Château du Père Henricourt, and I asked if it was here that he had found the dish he so much recommended.

'Indeed it was,' he replied, 'for the cuisine there is in the hands of a true master – not, I need hardly add, a Frenchman, for the French are mostly poor cooks and prefer the hamburger to any masterwork of their own native cuisine, though it is true that those Frenchmen who have spent time in the African countries which were once part of France can brew a more or less drinkable pot of coffee. As to Père Henricourt, he is second to no one in the old world for mushrooms, though I believe there is a Bolivian in Indonesia who is his equal in the new. He gathers them himself at dawn each morning, and will allow no hand but his own to prepare them, though he has myriad scullions. Myself, I consider the picture of this devoted craftsman rising in the dark and setting out on foot to find the ripest and choicest fungi on the steep sides of his adopted hills one of the most moving pieces of evidence I know to confound those pessimists who call our age decadent. For what moral seriousness is there displayed! What loyalty, what hardiness, what passion!

'The last time I dined there I wept openly, for his masterpieces were being consumed by oafishly hungry ignoramuses, his works of high art were being demolished like so many television dinners served on cardboard trays, straight from the vulgar supermarket! What loss, what irreparable loss, there is in our society! How much that is truly valuable, truly worked for, honestly achieved, is thrust to one side of the plate by the new suburban man, as though it were the burnt jacket of an overbaked potato!

'A culture may be judged by what it eats – thus we call cannibals savages, for we do not care to eat human meat ourselves, and we scorn vegetarians because we are carnivorous, just as they scorn us for not abstaining from flesh. But it would be wiser and truer to judge a culture by how it serves its food, by the tenderness of its meats and the firmness of its vegetables, by its sauces and sallets, its garnishes and use of garlic, and above all by the variety of these. For civilizations can be absolutely valued only by the width of the range of sensations available to their common citizens, to the humble men at the bottom who must always, however technologically advanced their society, work with their hands in simple drudgery, shelling oysters or mending drains. It is the variety available in the kitchens of the slums, the different dishes which even a sluttish housewife will be expected by her gross, labouring husband to provide out of the basic provender of the people, the ability to experiment and to enjoy experimenting with food, so that today's corned beef is tomorrow's hash, yesterday's kippers today's fish soup, that we can truly call the final measuring-rods of a civilization.'

I was much impressed by this argument, to which I had paid the closest attention while continuing to search the hall for my beloved, and which struck me as original, even if certain points were unclear. As I was about to ask my friend to clarify these, our attention was called to a diner at the highest table, which stood on a dais above tables which themselves stood higher than my own, and was clearly reserved for the officers of the club, of which I was not, of course, a member, though I was suddenly overwhelmed yet again by a sense of familiarity, as though I had sat at that table and watched the same elderly, grey-haired man rise to address an identical assembly, and not long ago, which was naturally impossible. I could not help reflecting, as the diner began to speak, on the strangeness of the recurrence of this sensation, which seemed to grow stronger as I descended floor by floor towards the foundations of the building and knew with increasing certainty that whatever might still befall me I should at last obtain my beloved and see all that had happened in the true perspective of love.

This reflection occupied me but a moment, and all its implications were at once forgotten as I studied the distant speaker, for with a shock greater than any I had yet experienced in an evening that had been full of amazing revelations, I saw that he was, or seemed uncannily similar in appearance to, my own father. My father had been presumed dead for many years, though had he still been living, he could not have more exactly resembled, feature by feature, the present orator, all allowances being made for the years since I had last seen him, on the occasion of his final departure from the home, after a particularly prolonged drinking-bout and savage beating of wife and children which had only ended with the fortunate summoning of the police by a neighbour who feared, as we did ourselves, for our lives. Gaping in astonishment, I missed his opening remarks, and even when I began to pay attention to his words, they at first conveyed little to me, for his voice was unmistakably my father's, every intonation, down to the slight affectation of hesitation before the choice of words, being entirely his own, so much as to fill me with an entirely explicable nausea.

'So,' he was saying, when I had at last mastered my amazed disgust enough to pay him full heed, 'it must be answered as it has been asked in – sober – seriousness.' There was some laughter at this, which my inattention prevented me from comprehending, though I smiled as though I had fully understood the joke, just as I had been used to smile at my father's small witticisms in the nursery, fearing that if I did not I should be chided and smitten. 'The problem is, I think,' he went on, 'fundamentally, like so many problems, one of definition. For what these people call starving in one country, may well mean having an unusually – extended – belly in another. Take our little supper here tonight, for instance. None of us, I think I can say without fear of contradiction, is grossly – corseted. We all have fine, manly figures. None of us would want to eat more than we are going to eat between now and the time we rise from this – snack – tomorrow evening. We are not greedy. We do not over-indulge ourselves – though the temptation, I think it's only fair to say to the menu committee, is great. We eat not to get fat, as some savages do, but to develop our bodies – by which I don't mean our bellies but our – sensitive – buds. We are gourmets, not gourmands.'

There was some applause for this remark, in spite of its hoary apologetics, and although it seemed to me from my reading of the menu, which was, of course, only a partial one, quite untrue. But as an uninvited guest it would have been rude to say so, even if the speaker was my own father, which I was more and more certain that he was.

'What nonsense it is to talk of starving people in – contemptibly – backward – parts of the world, as though we were responsible for their mismanagement and ill judgement! Are we to blame because they will not work, will not use modern methods of food production and contraception, will not limit their ceaseless – spawning? Must we deny ourselves just because they won't? Must we go hungry because they do? Must we be stinted of our natural development because they are under developed – in mind as well as body? Must we undermine the very basis of our – tremendous – civilization, because theirs is so puny? I think not. I think, too, that you think not. I think we are all sick and tired of the – drivelling – and – masochistic – talk we get night and day from so-called – humanitarians. I think our motto should be – Eat, drink and be merry, for tomorrow, *they* die!'

There was a storm of applause for this repugnant battle-cry, in which I recognized one of my father's oldest saws, first used to me as a child on the eve of one of our national holidays, at which it is the custom of our people to eat a roasted wild rabbit with burgundy jam sauce. My father, whom I then still partially respected and ambiguously loved, in spite of his long absences from the home and frequent insobriety when he did remain with the family for any length of time, was strolling with me past the cramped hutches of my pet rabbits, Balthazar and Marilyn, when this foolish witticism occurred to him, causing him much amusement and me none, for I was devoted to my pets and could not bear to think of them skinned and gutted, cooked and eaten. I was so disturbed by the casual cruelty of his jest that I struck him with all the force I could command upon the upper thigh, the most available target for one of my petty reach, to which he reacted by opening the door of Marilyn's cage, extracting the enchanting, twitching creature, and slitting her throat from ear to floppy ear with the boy-scout knife he always carried 'against policemen in the night'. He then daubed my cheeks with gore, saying, 'That will teach you to try and emasculate your father, you bloody little rat.'

The memory of that hideous occasion caused me to break into a sweat, and I missed my father's next words, which doubtless contained further elaborations of his detestable theme, for when I listened to him again he was saying, 'There is no such thing as starvation – but there are lazy beggars! Some people would rather waste away than work. I say, let them die! If we go on pandering to these – trivial – mendicants, these blackmailing – ne'er-do-wells, we shall most surely decline as a world power. And I make no apology for saying that we are one, and repeating the word – power! Power is not something that can be put aside like a walking-stick, to be picked up again when it's next wanted. No. It has to be exercised – every minute of every day. You have to use it, or give it up, and you have to use it with confidence in your ability to do so. It's no good, telling people you've got it, but you won't use it because you feel sorry for a lot of people who are too damned idle to earn their bread, who would be too lazy to grind corn if you sent it to them, who must have not merely flour, not merely bread, not merely cake, but summer-pudding and – fancy biscuits! If you do that, you're done for. They won't believe you've got the power at all. And when the time comes that you've really got to use it – and that time will surely come, as night follows day – you'll find it isn't there. So – let them starve! Don't send them so much as a lump of – barley-sugar. Tell them we're the boss, and if they want barley-sugar they'll have to work for it, and if there isn't enough work for them in their own country, then let them start a war. There's always a demand for men in wartime!'

After the tremendous cheer which followed this remark, my father concluded his oration with these words: 'You may feel that I have travelled a long way from our – elegant – repast. But I haven't, you know, not really. There's a whole world in alphabet soup. And since our little get-togethers have been so maliciously and ignorantly attacked, I thought someone should put our simple, homely philosophy to our opponents and see if there wasn't just a – morsel – to be said for our point of view. Food is our religion – as religion, alas, cannot be said to be our food.' (Laughter.) 'I believe most sincerely that in devoting ourselves to the highest possible development of our tastebuds we are doing no less than what those sages do who contemplate their own navels. Anyone for an orange?' (Laughter.) 'But seriously, my friends, I do believe that man exists on this – dumpling – of a planet to fulfil himself to the utmost of his capabilities.' ('Hear, hear!', and applause.) 'Those who criticize us do so in a spirit of such perverse meanness, such ultimately – anti-human – puritanism, that we can take heart and indeed congratulate ourselves. For unless our almost spiritual discipline outraged their frankly animal susceptibilities, they would leave us in peace. We can afford to ignore these malignant – snoops. Let us do so.' (Prolonged applause.) 'Now, Mr President, I think the Vice-Presidents in charge of the raie à l'homme may take their first mouthfuls. I've certainly said mine!'

To renewed cheers my father resumed his seat, and when they subsided I saw again that the reason for the quiet which I had misinterpreted as indicating a small party was that a very high degree of gourmet appreciation, such as almost to deserve my father's epithet of spiritual, was demanded of the banqueters. I did not feel that this expertise was beyond me, of course, for I had spent part of my youth in the kitchens of a great chef, learning at first hand how to create the dishes which earned him the plaudits of both hemispheres, but though I was still peckish, the idea of joining with any society to which my father was permitted to make speeches filled me with such nausea that I was barely able to check an immediate uprushing of bile. Making a hurried excuse I left the table, though no sooner had I done so than I at last saw my beloved, standing directly behind my father with a platter of the fish which I would gladly have seen him or her empty over his glossy head. In appalled horror, I watched my father help himself to the ray, and then, with a gesture which brought back sickening memories, tweak my beloved's right buttock between the thumb and forefinger of his left hand, so that I was quite unable to prevent myself from giving a loud cry of 'Lecherous and degenerate libertine!' and then precipitating myself violently towards the table where my obnoxious parent sat. My loud taunt caused all eyes to turn upon me, including those of my beloved, who dropped the platter in his or her delight at seeing me, though not, to my grief, upon my father, who looked at me without recognition and ordered my immediate expulsion from the banquet, which was accomplished without delay by . . .

[*Ejected from the banquet, Henry ponders on the extraordinary resemblance between his beloved and his immediate family. While he is pondering, a civil war breaks out, following the announcement of the assassination of the king. Henry is captured by extremists from the kitchen and given a medical examination, during which no interest is shown in his hermaphroditism. He becomes rather confused. The Encolpians appear and capture his beloved.*

The resemblance between Henry's family and his beloved is perhaps a matter more for psychological than literary comment, but in a key paragraph we see Henry strenuously resisting the idea of any subconscious influence. He becomes positively moral about the necessity of love being conscious and rational. This refusal to accept the strength of his own subconscious perhaps leads to the confusion of mental images which he can't quite make out. The civil war, indeed the whole hotel, is an outward expression of his inner conflicts. His determination to believe in a logical explanation for everything is a kind of madness.

The account of the king's assassination seems clearly drawn from the confusion which followed the death of President Kennedy. Without wishing to press my interpretation too far,

I wonder if the king/Kennedy figure may not stand for reason overthrown. For Charles, as for many other people, Kennedy's murder seemed to mean the end of all hope for a sane international politics.

From Charles's hilarious description of the Venereal Diseases Clinic which he was once obliged to attend at a London hospital, I can safely say that that is where Henry's medical examination takes place. It is, I believe, one of the last customs posts on Henry's odyssey. The images in his mind which won't come clear are beyond this outlying symbol of civilization.]

Civil War

It was only then that a strange truth dawned upon me, one which I at first could neither credit nor comprehend, for it filled me with much anxiety and distress and no pleasure, though it explained at least in part my persistent sensation of having been in the hotel before. The more I thought about it the plainer it became that my beloved very strongly resembled my elder sister and brother, the twins who had given me a deep sense of isolation in my earliest childhood, for they had been so engrossed in one another's company that far from feeling and expressing the usual rivalry of siblings they had scarcely noticed my appearance with all the demands it made, to their deprivation, on the affection of my mother, demands which I myself considered excessive when my younger brothers and sisters were born and similarly deprived me. Yet as I pondered still more closely on the matter, I realized that it was not only the twins that my beloved resembled, but also my mother, whose features were easily traceable in those of her offspring, and might indeed be said to have given the whole brood of us our individual stamp, for if we resembled each other we certainly resembled no one else either in looks or personalities.

Thus preoccupied with memories and facial comparisons, I for a time forgot the hideous business of the banquet and my father's typically libidinous gesture, only to recall with a start that as my beloved had stood by him to serve the fish, their faces had inevitably come into some proximity, though not mercifully into anything which could be called contact, and that as they did so they appeared precisely as those of father and child, for their features were not merely like, but the one the exquisite counterpart of the gross other, down to the last details of eyebrow and ear-lobe. Astounded by this remembered image, I fell into a complete bewilderment, for my father and mother in no way resembled each other, yet my beloved, I had now established, closely resembled both, which was not possible in nature and never has been. The more I worried over this puzzling business, the less I understood it, and the more urgent became my desire to find my beloved and see for myself how much of this speculation was valid, for I had to take into account the fact of my brutal treatment by the obese head-waiter and his loathsome henchman the sommelier and its possible effects on my usually clear and logical processes of thought, which seemed now at a most unusual impasse which could perhaps be explained as hallucinatory, though I believed myself to be suffering from neither confusion nor concussion, thought contusions were everywhere apparent.

My sorry bewilderment was made still sorrier by the sudden announcement over loudspeakers of the death of the country's king, a man of no great age and considerable good looks, who represented many liberal hopes and did much valuable work on such domestic issues as the ending of slavery in the agricultural provinces, though his foreign alliances were not always so happy or well-conceived, for they had entangled him in one disastrous war from which he had been obliged to secure a humiliating peace, and in many foolish economic ventures which served only to impoverish the people over whom he ruled. Though he had been a popular monarch to the poor and to certain intellectual circles, the announcement of his death brought a great cheer from the banqueting hall, until a further announcement made it clear that the king had not died a natural death, but had been assassinated, apparently by a member of an extreme right-wing party, who had himself immediately been shot down by palace guards, all of which, said the serving men who frequently passed by me, clearly betokened a plot by the extreme liberals to seize power, for they were anxious to get the king, who was by no means a left-wing figure, out of the way, and if they could successfully charge his murder to a right-wing fanatic, then they would seem to the populace to be the more level-headed of the two parties, and might, with some skilful manipulation of the information services, be able to claim the dead monarch as a martyr in their cause, though he, had he still been living, would have been the first to deny that he was any such thing.

I was naturally much interested to see how far these speculations by on the whole ill-informed minions would prove to be correct, but the true situation only became more and more confused, for the announcements which had continued for some minutes, interspersed only with solemn music, were suddenly interrupted by a burst of gun-fire in the studio, which was itself followed by a short silence and then an entirely new version of the murder, in which the assassin was said to be a well-known member of the party of the extreme left, though in this new guise he was again described as having been himself promptly assassinated by the palace guards, who were perhaps, I could not help thinking, the key to the whole situation and even possibly themselves responsible for the death of the king. The passing and repassing waiters now prophesied that a civil war was about to be fought in order to establish the true motive behind the assassination, and barricades of tables, chairs, beds and other domestic furnishings were hastily erected across the corridors at all strategic points, much to my consternation, for I knew that they would still further hinder the meeting which I craved with my beloved. As though the situation were not already sufficiently complicated, new problems at once arose, for as Milo had told me, the hotel was itself already in a state of almost open anarchy, and the various factions took immediate advantage of the prevailing uncertainty to extend their fields of influence, so that appanages of varying stabilities were quickly established, between which flourished numerous bands of écorcheurs, mostly drawn from among the guests, who treated the property of the hotel with a disdain which considerably surprised me, for they seemed on the whole respectable people, and to come from a social class which puts a high value on the protection of personal property.

It was no situation for a neutral observer, for missiles flew in all directions, and it was with a sense of something like relief that I allowed myself to be captured by a roving band of extremists from the kitchen, who threatened in no minced words to make pâté of me with their meat-axes if I made any effort to resist them, which I did not.

. . . though couched in the simple and moving language of reason, fell on deaf ears, and he replied that if I would not remove my garments myself, he knew of two fellow-guards whose daily task it was to dismember sheep and bullocks in the butchery department and who would be only too happy to rip them from me, for they had often expressed a desire to practise their surgery upon a man, first flaying, then dissecting him. Seeing that there was nothing I could do, I unzipped my motorcycling suit and stepped from it with all my unusual appendages displayed, at which my captor looked carefully and without emotion, saying only, 'I see nothing peculiar. I would not laugh at you myself.'

He then picked up the suit and went away with it, telling me under no circumstances to leave my booth, a superfluous instruction, for I had no desire even to so much as draw back the curtain which concealed me from passers-by and their possibly less friendly lack of interest in my rare state. While waiting for the doctor whose duty I assumed it to be to interrogate me, I examined myself with great care, and came to the conclusion that though my physique was too original to be properly described as beautiful, for true beauty is the perfection of the norm rather than something apart from it, it was by no means unhandsome, and I need have no fears as to my beloved's continued interest in me once he or she had ascertained the truth.

Where, I wondered, now was the delectable creature? With what band of guerrillas or regular army brigade did he or she now rove the barricaded corridors in search of the only love in life which had ever truly moved her or him? Was he or she happy in the knowledge that I could not be far away, as I was happy in the certainty that she or he was near at hand? Or was he or she in tears of agony at the thought that I might be dead? Whatever might be the case, I knew with the knowledge of true love that she or he was thinking of me even as I was thinking of him or her, and I took great comfort from the thought, continuing meanwhile to puzzle over the strange business of resemblances.

I was, of course, well-read in those writers who argue that all our emotional lives are dictated by the patterns set up in earliest childhood, so that we are for ever seeking surrogates and substitutes for our mothers, fathers, siblings and nurses in our later lives, and that what we mistake for love of other human beings is in fact no more than love for those first objects of passion sublimated without our conscious knowledge. But I could not credit these scribblers or their thesis, for I believed that it would be outrageous and unendurable if an emotion so central to normal human relationships as love were dictated to us without our conscious wish, and that it would be quite wrong for the human mind not to take due stock of all important emotional influences or to allow itself to be hurried and harried hither and yon at the whim of an often irrational and illogical subconscious. And so I determined to find the rational and logical connection which I knew must somewhere exist to link my beloved and my immediate family, however deviously, and I was deep in thought when a man whose breast pocket bristled with thermometers both oral and rectal entered my cubicle, pushing aside the curtain with a brusque gesture, and saying in boorish accents, 'Shut up, and show me what you've got,' which I did at once, expecting him to show some greater interest in my hermaphroditic state than the rather slow-witted if kindly guard, for it was, though I say it myself, of considerable scientific value. But the doctor seemed unimpressed by my blatant ambiguity of gender, and after minutely examining me without any more comment than an occasional 'Bend over' and 'Stand up' left the cubicle with the words, 'Stay where you are. The proctoscope will be along shortly, after which smears will be taken and a blood test made. You seem, however, to be free of disease, if that is any consolation to one in your captive state. I advise you to remain so.'

Somewhat taken aback by his indifference to my condition, I did as he bade me, resuming my seat upon the low stool and giving myself once more to thoughts of my beloved, though these thoughts were curiously intermixed with anxious promptings of a mysterious nature from my memory, which, usually so reliable and accurate to the smallest detail, now merely hinted and suggested, and instead of producing clear mental pictures for my contemplation provided only dark and smoky ones, in which I could dimly discern shadowy figures in a whirlpool of rapid motion, like horses on a merry-go-round without music, or characters in an early motion picture projected with a failing bulb and at many times its proper speed. Though I strained to recognize these figures, I was quite unable to do so, for their faces seemed always to be turned from me, and the only clear impression I could gain was of frenzied activity, which seemed quite without purpose, mere motion for motion's sake.

It was as I was contemplating these baffling images and reflecting on their significance, if any, that I suddenly heard a great tumult outside my cubicle, as though an invading mercenary band was laying waste the interrogation room, which indeed it was, for when I dared at last to peer through a chink in the curtains in order to survey the broil, I saw that my dear, if sometimes misguided, Encolpians were boldly releasing kitchen prisoners from all the cubicles at the far end of the room, while themselves capturing those guards and doctors who had not fled towards the end in which I was myself a captive. A fierce battle for possession of the middle-ground was in progress, with hand-to-hand fighting, the kitchen party being armed with surgical instruments intended for more humanitarian use, and the Encolpians with stout, symbolically shaped clubs which they attempted to bring down with mortal effect upon the heads of their opponents. I felt that it was advisable in my uncovered state to remain where I was until the issue of the fracas became more evident, for I had no armour of any kind, and no weapon, and I was in some doubt as to which side I should most properly support and encourage, for my recent brutal handling by the Encolpians gave me little confidence that they would recognize me in my latest transformation, and, rather than again be subjected to their violent loyalty to myself and my cause, I thought I might do better to remain, at least until I was once again the man I had been, a kitchen prisoner.

I continued therefore as a spectator or neutral voyeur of the furious conflict, until I saw the Encolpians make a sudden rapid sortie on the left to capture a figure dressed from head to toe in the costume of the operating-theatre, complete with cap, mask, gloves and a long green smock, who, as he or she was born triumphantly away, gave a great cry of 'Peace! Peace! I am a member of the Red Cross performing exclusively humanitarian work!', upon which I recognized the voice of my beloved and sprang all naked as I was from my cubicle and attempted with all the energy of love to go to her or his rescue, in which I was frustrated, for fighting a skilful rearguard action, the Encolpians withdrew, carrying my beloved with them, though not before he or she and I had managed, for a brief moment, to exchange a look which told both of us all we wished to know. In the chaos which at once followed upon these abductors' departure, I rapidly clad myself in the curtain of my booth, twisting it round my body to form an elegant sari, and then . . .

[*Henry hurries after the Encolpians. He passes through the butchery department of the hotel, then joins a hunt hall. There is a symbolic cabaret, and Henry's beloved is nearly killed.*

The brief scene in the butchery department illustrates better than anything else Henry's elaborately defensive mind. The image of the turkeys with their beaks linked to their anuses by steel hooks is a vivid and disturbing one, with direct significance for Henry himself. But he is reminded of other things, of the phoenix, pelicans, a piece of literature; in a few hundred words he moves from a physical fact to the comfortable safety of literary criticism. Nothing could be more characteristic.

There is no need to underline the significance of the events which take place at the hunt ball; but I wonder if the symbolic fox-hunt may not, among its other references, refer to Henry's own pursuit of his beloved.]

The Hunt Ball

••• the butcher's shop, in which rows of fat plucked turkeys hung by their scrawny legs from long steel bars, their gross nudity and prickly flabbiness repugnant to the eye, for each had its head twisted back and up, the closed beak spiggered by one end of an S-shaped steel hook whose other spike rested in the bird's plump anus, intake and exhaust here joined to close the circle of life and death, beginning and end, *per os et per anum*. The pope's noses, as they are called in non-Catholic countries, hung uselessly down, exposing the recta, into which the hooks sank without trace, swallowed in some private pleasure, discharging steel semen, red hot droplets of iron and carbon, tempered and stainless, a hideous necrophilia.

I could not help reflecting on the riddling phoenix, and wondering whether it did not, as is always supposed, burn alive, reproducing itself from its own hot ashes, but rather achieved the perfect vanishing trick, gliding up its own irresistible arse, an example of self-love equalled only by the pelican, whose pecking of its own breast to feed its hungry offspring with its own blood has been so ludicrously misconstrued by generations of moralists, who see in it an example of self-sacrifice and perfect parental love, whereas the truth is that the pelican's sole concern is for its own survival through its children, so that in preserving them it may itself be preserved, its motive being not selfless but entirely, devotedly selfish. And I could not help remembering, as I passed through the long lines of dead birds, the words of the great novelist who, in his excitement and inspiration after seeing a similar display in his native city, broke from prose into a kind of verse, which is not an easy or a common transition, or one popular with contemporary writers, so I will reproduce it here:

How like a human's are the orifices of a fowl! How rounded and dark, how flinged with hair! How abused and abhorred, how loved, how cosseted, how driven to strange shapes! Accommodating like a lock

> The urgent passage of their daily trade,
> Riding the downward stream towards the sea,
> And coming up, the salt still on their prows,
> The pleasure-boats, the squat, flat-bottomed punts,
> The slim canoes with Cupid at the helm,
> Leaving a frothy wake of bubbling cream
> Where love ascends to bless the flowing stream.
> The black banks tremble with this teeming white
> Which searches vainly for an answ'ring light.
> And when the boats at evening must withdraw,
> The lock-gates weep and cry for more, still more!

Though the novelist was in error in thinking that canoes have helms, and the rhyme of 'withdraw' and 'more' would not be permitted in an age less lax than his, there is genuine feeling in this unusual passage, and the imagery is suggestive and original, for though we have no wings, and fowls have no arms, there is much that men and birds . . .

It was while I was trying to distinguish the now audible music of the band, for band it was, from the rapidly vanishing sounds of Encolpian triumph that I was suddenly given new heart by the thought that my beloved would be quite safe in the hands of my comrades, for they had doubtless sallied forth to capture her or him not for their own spoliation, as I had been so fearfully imagining, but for mine, or rather for my delectation, for the whole object of their and my search of the hotel was of course his or her apprehension, and what I had so recently criticized as the headstrong and uncivilized violence of the Encolpian Society was nothing of the sort, for Milo had clearly led his troops with dash and authority, and there was no need to suppose that he would offer my beloved anything but proper respect and obedience. Delighted with this seemingly unanswerable deduction, I saw that there only remained for me too to be captured by the Encolpians for our long separation at last to be concluded, and I gave thanks from a full heart to my foresight in appointing Milo to be my lieutenant, for he had held the place well, and who could have said what might not have . . .

The orchestra, which played, I thought, badly, now broke into a plaintive old foxtrot, and many couples took the floor, confident that the rhythm would not prove too strenuous for their advancing years, and in some cases humming the tune or crooning such of the words as they were able to recall, for it was a melody which had been popular, the red-faced man told me as he urged another brandy into my willing hand, in his, and therefore their, youth. There is something inexpressibly moving in the sight of people past their middle years shuffling their feet in time to sentimental music, for it seems to suggest that love is possible beyond the usually accepted limit of twenty-five, and that after the frenzy of youth a maturer, perhaps less ecstatic and more contented, love can be relished and savoured as that first sweeping, pulsing passion by its very nature cannot, for it is imperious in its demands and insists upon conclusion with all the finesse of an uncivilized savage. Gazing on the dancers, I remembered my own parents, and thought with a small twinge of nostalgia of the way in which, on rare but charming occasions, they would embrace before their offspring as though we were not there, and this memory led on to others of a similar peaceful and familial kind, all of which momentarily lulled my senses, in spite of the fact that I had always felt nothing but black detestation for my father.

Thus it was with the shock of a sudden and midnight wakening that I saw my parents indisputably foxtrotting with elegance, if not distinction, past the bandstand. They were visible to me only for a moment, but it was enough for me to know with complete certainty that it was they, though it could not be, I told myself, for they were long divorced after a most acrimonious court case in which many details of their married life were revealed which it would have been wiser and kinder for both parties to have suppressed, and they had both, on the occasions on which I had separately seen them since, expressed an unyielding contempt and loathing for each other, with which I thoroughly sympathized at least on my mother's side, for theirs had been a marriage neither of love nor convenience, but rather of sheer misjudgement. Yet though their dancing together was clearly incompatible with their genuine feelings, there could be no doubt, as I have said, that it was they, and I was rooted to the spot with an astonishment almost equal to that with which I had first encountered my beloved, and to which was added an inexplicable feeling of both sadness and happiness, the one for the misfortune of their marriage, the other for their present impossible conjunction, which became the more conclusively real even as it became the more incredible and beyond reason.

So amazed and disconcerted was I by their appearance and my own emotion at the sight of it, that they had disappeared into the vast concourse of dancers before I could bring my powers of rational analysis to bear, and by then the orchestra had ended its old melody, lain down its instruments and moved off the bandstand. The cabaret at once began with the entry of a masked and booted, spurred and riding-cropped chorus, whose leader held a long pole from the top of which grinned the mask of a dog-fox. After chanting to much applause what appeared to be the hunt song, the chorus stood aside to allow the formal and processional appearance of a giant figure, of the stature of a character from myth or advertising, who carried an axe and was masked not as a hound, like the chorus, but as a hangman or executioner, and whose sole clothing consisted of a black loincloth, over which there dangled in a symbolic manner the brush of a fox, perhaps belonging to the same dead creature whose head smiled so macabrely over the stage and into the delighted audience. This figure of death led upon a pigskin leash a man or woman dressed as a fox and on all fours, so cleverly disguised that though from its size alone a countryman would have known that it was not a real fox, a townsman might have been deceived, though it was of course plain to all those present that the action of the little drama, which had obvious religious overtones, was entirely symbolic, for the mock-fox was unleashed and symbolically pursued round the tiny stage by the chorus, which bayed the following jingle:

> Follow up, follow up, whipper in!
> Gone to earth, tally ho, to the kill!
> Master, huntsman, hunter, hound,
> Catch him quick or he'll go to ground!

This part of the action was much applauded by the audience, some of whom blew hunting and coach horns and gave tongue with incomprehensible cries, apparently to encourage the symbolical dog-pack in its endeavours, though the chorus paid no attention to these offstage noises, and the symbolic master-executioner figure angrily cracked his whip and called, 'Hold hard, there! Hold hard!' The fox-surrogate at last feigned weariness of the chase and allowed itself to be captured by the hounds, who leaped upon it with excited howlings until the

stage seemed to boil with panting and seething bodies, and the
master was obliged to wade into the doggy maelstrom, beating
about indiscriminately with the bone handle of his riding-crop,
to drag out the limp and bloody body of the symbolic victim.
Seizing his axe, he lopped off the brush and threw it into the
audience, who fought greedily for its possession. He then
prepared to cut off the mask, at which point the actor or actress
inside the symbolic victim gave a great shout of 'Help!', a cry
which wrung me to the very heart, for it was uttered in the
unmistakable accents of my beloved, who, though hampered by
her or his disguise, attempted to leap into the audience,
thinking there to find safety, but was frustrated by the hounds
who fell once more upon him or her and began ferociously to
tear her or him to pieces, causing much consternation in the
audience, part of which declared that some mischief was afoot
and that the symbolic drama should at once be halted, while
another part openly expressed the view that if the blood was
human, so much the better, for it was high time that the
hunting of men was again made legal as it had been in the days
of their grandfathers.

As I struggled through the press of watchers towards the
stage, I saw that in the scuffling and skirmishing there taking
place the mask of the huntsman-hangman had become
displaced, revealing the familiar features of my erstwhile
lieutenant Milo, and I realized with a dread which filled me to
the very depths of my soul that I had entirely misjudged him
and the whole of his Society, for far from respecting and
obeying my beloved or capturing her or him for my sake, they
were treating him or her as a mere plaything in their terrible
pageant, and were engrossed in their parts to such an extent
that they could no longer tell fantasy from fact, and were on the
point of actually murdering her or him, either with Milo's axe
or with their own bare hands, while the watchers through
whom I pushed to almost no effect cheered and screamed and

whooped as if they too had lost all contact with the reality of the situation, which was only saved, and in the nick of time, by the arrival of a rabble of militant plongeurs, who swept on to the stage brandishing plastic bottles of liquid detergent which they sprayed with remarkable and devastating accuracy into the eyes of their opponents, uttering at the same time and at the tops of their voices such slogans as, 'Down with the bourgeois hyenas, death to the capitalist warmongers!' and, 'Long live the people's revolution, strengthened and fortified by the Marxist-Leninist-Stalinist-Maoist teachings of our revered leader, the chief washer-up!'

The confusion which followed the irruption of these hard-line revolutionaries was indescribable, and I shall not attempt to describe it except to say that much real blood was shed and all notions of play and aesthetic significance were forgotten in the pandemonium of battle, and that just as I reached the spot where the limp and bedraggled body of my beloved lay in what I profoundly hoped was a state of unconsciousness and not of death, all the lights were switched out and . . .

[*The cabaret is not a parody of the 'theatre of cruelty', it is that 'theatre' itself. The subconscious is appearing in nightmare forms.*

Henry is next being cross-questioned by a communist tribunal, though the case against him has been decided in advance. Charles avoids comparison with Kafka by being explicit. Such trials are an all too real part of modern history. Henry's devotion to logic is turned against him. He is now the subject, no longer the objective, neutral observer. The list of clubs he gives is a catalogue of failed identities, it is the story of his life. It shows not only how much he has always wanted to belong, but also how dependent he has always been on organizations, and so, by implication, on rules and regulations, law and order. Now he is being deliberately excluded from society. His own fraternity, the Encolpians, has turned against him. He has only himself.]

The Trial

'Your name?' asked the chairman.

'Henry,' I replied.

'Do not mock the tribunal,' said the washerwoman angrily, 'or you'll get yourself into trouble, you mark my words. Now tell us your real name.'

'I have spoken the truth,' I answered in a cringing tone. 'I am a stranger to your country, a guest of this hotel, and my name is, as I have told you, Henry. By all means change it if you wish, for it has brought me nothing but contumely ever since I have been here. I will answer to any other name you choose.'

'Let us call him Class Traitor,' said the thin boilerman.

'A good idea, comrade,' said the chairman. 'Very well, then, Class Traitor, so you admit that you are a spy!'

'Certainly not!' I cried. 'I am an ordinary innocent tourist!'

'But you have admitted to the tribunal that you are a foreigner and a guest of the hotel,' said the boilerman. 'If you are a foreigner, then you must be a spy, for it was decided only a few minutes ago that all foreigners must leave the hotel at once or be arraigned before tribunals such as this on charges of espionage. You have not left, therefore you must be a spy, and a stupid one to imagine that we will be taken in by what you will undoubtedly say next – that you did not know of the order to leave.'

'But I didn't!' I cried.

'You see, comrades?' said the boilerman. 'And now I will show that he is an imperialist, bourgeois, capitalist, reactionary spy as well. All guests of the hotel are rich, or they would stay elsewhere, in proletarian lodging-houses. All the rich are imperialist, bourgeois, capitalist reactionaries. Class Traitor has admitted to being a guest of the hotel, so –' He shrugged at his brilliant logic, with a smile on his face like that of a man who has held up a bucket to demonstrate that it has a hole, but who has not yet realized that the proof of his assertion requires water.

'You stand condemned out of your own mouth,' said the chairman. 'But we will continue the trial, even if it can be no more than a formality. Justice must be seen to be done. What are your political views?'

'I believe in liberty,' I answered with some bitterness, for it seemed plain that these charlatans meant to deprive me of mine.

'Liberty, Class Traitor?' said the washerwoman. 'And what do you mean by that? Liberty for whom to do what?'

'Liberty for all,' I replied recklessly, 'to do whatever they like within the limits of personal freedom as established by the laws of the particular society of which they are democratic members.'

'I do not find that definition in the printed works of our leader,' said the washerwoman, brandishing a small pamphlet. 'And what is not in his works is not correct theory. Have you no better answer?'

'No,' I answered, 'though I am fully aware of the philosophical and practical difficulties of the one I have given you.'

'So you believe yourself to be a better philosopher than our leader?' said the boilerman. 'You must then be very intelligent indeed!'

'Or very stupid!' said the washerwoman.

'Or perhaps without an intelligence at all,' said the chairman. 'Have you ever belonged to any organization, social, sporting, artistic or political?'

'Yes,' I replied, 'my life has been, in a sense, a series of elections and resignations from such organizations.'

'Name all of them to which you have ever belonged,' said the chairman, 'in chronological order of joining and at dictation speed.'

'The Under-Three Play Therapy Unit, The Four-to-Five Kleinian Kiddy Klub, The Drum Gang, The I-Spy Association of the Inner Urban Authority, The Society for the Protection of Circus Animals, The Vermin Men, The Bumble-Bees, The Dando Fan Club, The Gene Autry Society, The Tintin-Abula, The Babar Black Sheep, The Masters of Ballantrae, The International Union of Infant Male Ballet Dancers, The –'

'Ah!' exclaimed the washerwoman. 'A proscribed organization!'

'Continue,' said the chairman, making no effort to disguise his lack of interest.

'The Junior School Debating Club, The Young Idea, The Young Men, All The Young Men, The Young Club, The Young People, All The Young People, The Young Fellowship, The Young, The Young Young, The Lester Young Fan Club, The Young . . .'

'. . . The Freudian Fellowship of Ex-Analysees, The Jungian Home for Lost Children, The Adler Association of Teenage Delinquents, The Wye Valley and Uttoxeter Fishing Club, incorporating the Fisherman's Association of the Upper Yonne, The Real Madrid Fan Club, The Elvis Presley Fan Club, The Marilyn Monroe Fan Club, The Charles de Gaulle Fan Club, Le Club Des Sans-Club, The Lawn Tennis Association of Jutland, The Schleswig-Holstein Question-and-Answer Pen-Pal Association, The North-East Swedish Timber-Tops Club, The Ancient and Honourable . . .'

'. . . The Pink Banana, The Yellow Canary, The Ox on the Hoof, The Blue Door, Sally's, Prue's, Jane's, Jimmy's, The Last of the First, The Franco-Bulgarian Friendship Association, The Anglo-Brazilian Friendship Association, The Association of Hispano-Swiss Friendship, the Italo-Chinese Association, The International Brigade Old Comrades Association (Junior Branch), The Democratic Party of Western Bavaria, The Social Democratic Party of Eastern Baden, The Socialist Democratic Party of Northern Westphalia, The Democratic Socialist Party of Southern Württemberg, The Free Social Democratic Party of Mid-Nuremberg, The Munich Free Democratic Socialist Party, The Free Social Democratic Socialist Party of –'

'Why did you spend so much money on the membership of so many Fascist political organizations?' asked the boilerman.

'I was engaged on writing an article for the Press Association of Central America,' I replied with a small sense of triumph, 'on the infiltration of those new parties by old Nazis.'

'Was the article published?' asked the chairman.

'No.'

'Continue.'

'The Free Association of Mental Patients, The Discharged Prisoners Aid Association, The End of the Matter, Recividists Anonymous, The New Start, The Old Story, The Same Again, The Pedestrians Association, The Fresh Air Guild, The Association of International Air Pilots, The Way to the Stars, The Union of Aeronautical Maintenance Men, The Tail Spinners, The Near Thing, The Daytona Beach Boys, The Deep Sea Divers Association, The Union of Pressure-Chamber Operators, The Closed Shop Society, The Green Valley Orange-Growers Association, The Last Post, The Ford Madox Ford Fan Club, The South Wilts and East Dorset Yeomanry, The Staffordshire Hikers Club, The –'

'I think we have heard enough,' said the chairman.

'More than enough,' said the washerwoman.

'Your masters have provided you with material for many cover stories,' said the boilerman. 'But it was foolish to send you here without at least one which was not palpably revisionist.'

'Can we speak of revisionism in one who appears never to have held the original doctrine or to have been a party member?' said the chairman.

'Of course we can,' said the washerwoman. 'I've never heard so much revisionism in all my life. It sounds as though Class Traitor has never had time to sit down and get the weight off his feet. Like a pea on a hot plate, he is.'

'The unsettled life, the lack of a permanent home, the adaptable loyalty, these are the natural hazards and trade-marks of the secret agent,' said the boilerman. 'And are all quite contrary to the teachings of our leader, who clearly states on page 47 that comrades should not rush about the country looking for a little more food or wages, but should only move at the direction of the party and in the direction the party points.'

'What have you to say to that?' said the chairman.

'Nothing,' I replied, 'but what I have said before. I am a stranger here, wishing only to view your historic and artistic monuments and to study your social arrangements. I understand almost nothing of the arguments which you have advanced against me. I am a simple man, and –'

'It says here that you're nothing of the sort,' said the washerwoman. 'It says you're a hermaphrodite.'

'A case of revisionism, perhaps?' said the chairman, giving a dry chuckle.

'What is a hermaphrodite?' said the washerwoman. 'Have they used the chopper on him, poor thing?'

'Rather the opposite,' said the chairman. He leaned over and explained my condition in a lengthy aside.

'Oh,' said the washerwoman. 'Really? Let's have a look.'

'A good idea,' said the boilerman. 'Perhaps a People's Artist or Cameraman should come in and take a picture of this symbol of biological and dialectical revisionism, so that comrades may recognize others and bring them to this tribunal for judgement and punishment.'

'Oh, let's leave that till later,' said the washerwoman. 'I just want to have a quick peep, that's all.'

'Remove your clothes,' said the chairman.

It was a request with which I had so often in the last hours complied that it came as an almost welcome note of familiarity into the bizarre and ludicrous proceedings of this kangaroo court, whose authority to question me I would myself have questioned if I had not, I believe correctly, judged that to do so might have jeopardized my unhappy situation still further, for I detected a murderous look in the eye of the washerwoman, whose elevation to the position of tribune seemed to have filled her with a zealous desire to wring blood from the mangling of my political past, and to whose brawny arms I would not have trusted so much as the rinsing of my underwear, for they looked as though they were made rather to rip and to tear than to knead and soap the delicate materials of which these garments were made, though of course I wore none at all beneath my impromptu sari. I therefore undressed in haste and soon stood naked before my judges, who leaned forward in interest and even descended from their podium to poke at me with their fingers and to pry into my most private parts with their eyes, though they seemed disappointed with what they saw, and argued amongst themselves as to its dialectical interpretation.

'It is a classic case,' said the boilerman, 'of capitalist rapacity, for here is either a man who has made a successful takeover bid for femininity, or a woman whose anti-party attitudes have led her to a similar seizure of masculinity. In either case, Class Traitor stands before us as an antisocial element who must be purged before he or she corrupts the innocent proletariat.'

'Oh, shut up,' said the washerwoman. 'The poor thing can't help being all mixed up. I feel sorry for her myself. Or him.'

'Already,' said the boilerman, 'this bourgeois abortion has succeeded in moving the simple heart of one of the people. It is the first step towards revisionism.'

The washerwoman looked annoyed. 'I told you to shut your trap,' she said. 'How can Class Traitor be an abortion when he – she – is standing in front of us? You don't know what you're talking about. You don't even know what an abortion looks like, I can see that.'

'Now she attacks a member of the tribunal,' said the boilerman grimly, 'thus taking the second step towards counter-revolutionary activity. You'd better think carefully about what you're saying, comrade, and to whom. I shall not allow my personal friendship for you to prevent me from reporting your decadent sympathies to the central committee. The tree of revolution cannot grow strong if it is strangled by the poisonous ivy of subversive elements.'

'Oh, go and boil your petty-bourgeois head!' cried the washerwoman, striking him upon the side of it. 'The proletariat can tell a skunk by its anti-party smell, and you stink!'

'Comrades,' said the chairman, 'we are forgetting our duty to the revolution and allowing personal considerations to interfere with the course of working-class justice as interpreted by the popular will enshrined in this tribunal.'

But the washerwoman, whose bloodthirstiness was now apparent, paid him heed only to strike him, and quite soon the courtroom was an undignified spectacle, with the three tribunes trading fraternal insults and blows before myself and my impassive guard, whose eyes never lifted from her knitting-needles, for she was stone deaf.

[*Henry seeks refuge in the traditional chapel, and by implication in religion, the traditional comfort of those in despair. He is taken for a new member of the choir and at once required to take part in a marriage service at which his father escorts the bride and Milo is the groom. After a sermon on the ephemerality of love, it is revealed that the bride is none other than Henry's beloved.*

The key passage here is the sermon, which not only reduces the role of women in marriage to one of total servitude, but also proclaims that love is only a passing sensation and should be cherished purely as such. 'The life of the spirit is a life of pure sensation,' says the preacher. 'Love gives us perhaps our greatest number of spiritual insights simply because it doesn't last.' The doctrine of pure aestheticism, which has been held in one form or another by everyone in the book, is here expounded in its most absolute form.

It is almost immediately followed by a series of desperate and unanswered questions about the meaning and purpose of life. 'We are fallen into a decadence of feeling from which no recovery seems possible,' Henry says. 'We have sensation to live by and nothing to live for.' It is the crux of his problem; it was the crux of Charles's. In this passage I hear Charles's own voice ringing out in a terrible agony of doubt. It is a voice from the dead.

The continued emphasis in the marriage service on sacrifice prepares the way for the conclusion of the novel.]

The Religion of Love

Stepping from among the stifling robes, as a vision might appear to holy men, I said to this quartet of religion-mongers, 'Good evening, my name is Henry, and I have sought sanctuary in your church from the blows, buffets and brutality of my enemies. I beg you to allow me to shelter here, for I am innocent and cruelly persecuted, and I am willing to perform any ecclesiastical chore which you may choose to thrust upon me. But name the task and I will gladly set to it, if you will only permit me to rest here awhile in peace and safety from the arrows of my adversaries, for I am a veritable Sebastian or Sebastiana, and have been much shot at in these last hours, to say nothing of having been beaten, though it is true that I have not yet been pilloried or crucified, and that I am hoping to avoid these further punishments, for I have done nothing of which I feel in the least ashamed. But there comes a stage in the practice of turning the other cheek when one is at a loss which cheek next to turn, for the blows have rained so heavily on both that the whole cuticle is bruised almost to insensitivity.'

'This must be the new choirboy,' said the cleric, whose eyes were lowered out of that humility which so distinguishes men of the cloth, while at the same instant the choirwoman said, 'This must be the new choirgirl,' for her eyes, after a nervous skittering, had settled on my upper part.

'Get some robes on, then,' said the choirman. 'There's a wedding in five minutes. Are you alto or tenor? I take it you can't be treble or bass, looking like that.'

'He's a she,' said the infant, itself of dubious gender.

'I am a counter-tenor,' I said truthfully, for such indeed I was and had always been since the breaking of my voice, for though I had many times attempted to carry tunes in lower registers I was quite unable to do so, and yet was able to reach high D sharp or E flat without any difficulty in my normal singing voice, and had once performed at short notice at the Fenice opera house in a role originally written for a castrato, though I was of course not one.

'I told you so,' said the child.

'A counter-tenor, eh?' said the cleric, beaming upon me. 'How very pleasant! Such a strange, almost unnatural range! It suggests such angelic potentialities. For angels, you know, are of no gender and yet of both. When I hear a counter-tenor solo, I always feel myself very near to heaven.'

'Can you do "My soul is a bird with wings of fire?"' asked the choirman as I donned cassock and surplice.

'Indeed I can,' I replied. 'But I am also a perfect sight-reader of music and will be happy to render any solos you wish, whether they are familiar to me or not, for I am so naturally musical that the notes on the page transform themselves into song almost without my conscious knowledge, and I have, on occasions in the past, been able to sing mere blots of ink on lined white paper, Rorshach tests, and schizophrenic drawings, making one and all aesthetically pleasing to the ear. My head notes regularly break glass, I should warn you, and it is dangerous in a place with such splendid acoustical properties as this chapel to wear spectacles during my singing, though I have never yet cracked plastic contact lenses, which is one reason, and a good one, why I always wear them myself, another being that my sight is extremely poor, and without the assistance of optical devices I should be but a poor stumbling creature in the half-dark.'

'I shall pray for your sight to be made whole,' said the cleric compassionately, 'for you are yourself a sight for sore eyes,' with which ecclesiastical pleasantry he pinched me first on the cheek, then on the buttock, murmuring so that the others could not hear, though from the expression on their faces they knew well enough what it was he was saying. 'Stay behind after the service, and we'll have a little parlez-vous about your problems, shall we?'

'I shall go and switch on the carillon,' said the choirman. 'The service is due to begin.'

As he departed, the choirwoman took me aside and whispered, 'Look out for the brat, he's put bubblegum under most of the choir-stalls, and he tries to make us laugh during the sermon.'

I thanked her for this useful warning, and listened to the unpleasant jangling of the electric bells, which soon mercifully ceased, for the choirman returned and said to the cleric, 'Not a bad crowd, Fatso. Should be quite a decent collection.'

'The Lord giveth,' said the reverend, 'and the Lord taketh away. Too damned much,' he added under his breath, pretending he did not wish us to hear, though deliberately allowing us to do so, so that we felt in duty bound to acknowledge this feeble sally with wide smiles as we lined up to make our entry into the chapel. As we solemnly proceeded up the aisle, I was struck by the great number of wedding-guests who, from the backs of their heads, seemed young and male, the few women present being handcuffed to these men, indicating that they were prisoners, perhaps there to celebrate the nuptials of one of their fellow unfortunates and allowed out only for the ceremony and under guard. After we had taken our places in our stalls, and I had removed the offending gum of which I had been warned and arranged my music to my satisfaction, I began to look round the chapel. With a feeling of hideous inevitability I saw that the heavily veiled bride leant on the arm of none other than my father, and I wondered in a fever of dismay what could have induced him to leave the ball at which he had seemed so to be enjoying himself, to attend in so formal capacity at this gaolbird's marriage. Why, too, did he seem to be pursuing me down the hotel from floor to floor, he whom I believed to be dead? Could he be a ghost?

These were questions which I could not readily answer, and in my flurried state I did not at once go on to observe that the male guests in the congregation were all, without exception, Encolpians, and stood on the groom's side of the aisle. I was still further taken aback by my discovery that the groom himself was Milo, for he now stepped into my line of vision from behind a pillar to take his place in the ceremony. I thought it wisest, even in my confused state, not to draw attention to myself by making any movement of recognition towards him or his comrades, but rather to stay where I was, sing what was set down for me to sing, and only greet them if I saw that there was some real chance of our previously very amicable relations being restored, which seemed to me from the evidence of the handcuffs and shackles unlikely, for though no shotgun was visible, the atmosphere in the chapel was tense, as though one or more shotguns might at any moment be produced and fired, and in fact would be if things did not go exactly as planned.

As the bride's progress, on account of her leg-irons, was slow, I had plenty of time to pick out the faces below me, and it was, by this time, with no surprise that I recognized my mother sitting entirely alone on the bride's side, though I could not imagine what she or my father were doing there, for all my sisters were married, and I had no other relations, legitimate or bastard, whose marriage might explain my parents' prominent and isolated position. Puzzling though all this was, it was as nothing to my bewilderment on feeling yet another recurrence of the sensation of having been where I was before, this time even more potent and demanding, as though some urgent memory clamoured to be admitted to my conscious mind, which frantically tried key after key in the great lock of its door, yet could not find one which would turn it, however much it strained and wrenched, and though each key was tried three or four times. I had a dismaying feeling that the locks had been tampered with or changed by some unknown agency, so that I could no longer wander freely in the great mansion and demesne of my past sensations, and surrounded as I was by sense impressions which I found it impossible to credit, I was on the point of nervous panic, if not of breakdown, when the booming of the organ announced a psalm, and I was obliged to sing, which I did, finding some relief in so natural and pleasurable a physical labour after the terrible mental turmoil which had possessed me, though the psalm was one with which I was not at all familiar:

When the Lord spoke in the thunder: when his voice was heard in the great calm;
When his name was over the firmament: and his great name over all the earth;
Then said they among the nations: the Lord God is angry, we have much offended him.
How shall our sin be punished: how shall he mangle the bones of the wicked?
Hear ye, hear ye, O my peoples: the Lord shall smite the evil-doer;
Yea, though he hide in caverns: he shall pluck him out like snakes.
Go ye up unto the temple: and prepare a sacrifice;
For the Lord your God is angry: ye have much offended him.
Go ye up unto the altar; and choose among yourselves;
A maiden whose heart is pure: a young girl from among the righteous.
Bring me a snow-white bride: prepare me a virgin decked with flowers;
Let her hair be braided with pearls: and her neck bear a collar of gold.

Lay her upon the altar: lay her upon the altar stone;
For I the Lord am angry, my wrath is exceeding great: and the
blood be upon your hands.
Bring forth knives and incense: let the fire be kindled with
cedar;
Lay her upon the altar: the sacrifice is acceptable unto the
Lord.

After this gloomy and deplorable opening, the service continued with many unfamiliar features, such as the bride's kissing of the groom's hands and feet, and the priest's sprinkling of both of them with what seemed to be blood, though it may have been an unusually bright red wine, or ink, both of which rituals were quite unknown to me, though my sensation of having partaken in some such rite before grew ever more insistent, to the point where I began to search my memory for evidences of the weddings at which I had sung as a child, in the hope of finding some point of reference which might explain it, but in vain, for all my recollections were sweet and of a traditional and happy service in which there was no mention of bloody sacrifice, but much of the virtues of love and enduring personal relations, neither of which now received even a passing reference either for or against. I regretted the absence of such references, for to me the idea of marriage was redolent of a different kind of sacrifice, that of self for one's beloved, of independence for mutual security, of lewdness for love, of one for two, of freedom without limits for the greater liberty within them, and it seemed to me strange and even lowering to regard the union of two people as though one was divine, irrational and implacable, and the other little more than a kid or a calf whose throat was to be cut and carcass to be burned. Such, however, appeared to be the outlook of this country, and it was confirmed in no uncertain terms by the address which the cleric soon delivered to the couple, the bridegroom standing with one hand on the shoulder of his kneeling bride and the other on the handle of his dress-sword, while the bride's right hand lay symbolically under his left foot.

'All flesh is grass,' the clergyman began. 'That is the meaning of the ceremony which we celebrate here today. Men are born, and then they die. They achieve nothing. Their flesh is one with the earth, above which the common graveyard grasses flourish. Once in a hundred years a man is born whose name may survive five thousand years by some trivial accident. For the rest of us, obliteration is swift, is total. And so it must be. How could we live burdened with a jostling past of relatives, heroes and villains? We don't want the whole human race pressing at our backs, whispering advice, gossiping, hectoring, sneering at the way we do things. We don't want back-seat drivers. That's why it's right and proper that all flesh should be grass. And that's why, in the wedding service, we emphasize how much, how very much, the bearer of seed matters rather than the flesh which receives it and transmits it in the form of children. Being so much more of the flesh than men, women are so much more like grass. They breed, they put down roots, they are fecund, they are never out of the earth. While men, scattering their seed, fertile and million-fold, are never quite in it. Men treat the flesh of women as they might a lodging-house, indifferent to the landlady's name or character. Our religion teaches that this attitude is correct. We are recommended to abjure the flesh, to be spirit. Man can sometimes be spirit, pure spirit. Woman can't. That's why it's so important that the woman should be entirely subservient to the man, why the bridegroom is at this very moment crushing the hand of the bride, in a symbolic representation of the triumph of spirit over flesh.

'A final word to the groom. You have to make several promises here tonight. But don't feel you have to keep them, any more than God keeps his. The life of the spirit is a life of pure sensation, of detached, isolated experiences. That's another of the meanings of "All flesh is grass". Just as we're all ephemeral in the long run, seen in the perspective of history, so too, in the perspective of our own lives, all that matters is the fleeting moment. All the things, and the only things, that make for the spiritual life are ephemeral sensations. You may well feel now, as you stand there with your foot grinding her hand, that you will love your bride for ever. That's a splendid feeling, a real, spiritual moment. Enjoy it, cherish it. Because, take it from me, it won't last. Love gives us perhaps our greatest number of spiritual insights simply because it doesn't last. That's why great poets write about it. It's a tremendous feeling. It's a major impulse in all our lives. But its real importance is its ephemerality. Remember, while you're actually loving, to store up the memories of what it's like. You will need them later. For love is like flesh, love is grass.'

At this moment an undignified tussle began on the chancel steps between bride and groom, the latter trying to prevent the former from utterance, but without success, for she gave a great cry of 'My beloved!', rooting me to my stall and making me forget all speculation in the terrible yet wonderful certainty that it was my own beloved who had uttered the cry, and who now tore back her veil to reveal those features which had so obsessed and driven me since . . .

Why are we here? To what end do we trudge our weary stint on the treadmill of life? What wheel do we turn, what ox do we roast? Are wheel or ox there at all? Are we treading simply in order to tread? Is it for its own sake that life lashes us on?

What questions! But who will answer them? We are a race of technicians – whether financiers, horse-trainers, doctors, plumbers, teachers, train-drivers, artists, road-sweepers, lawyers, electricians, we are all mechanics, but do not know what purpose our machines serve. We are told to find satisfaction in our work, to do our jobs, live our lives, for their own sakes. But why should we? Why must we? We are fallen into a decadence of feeling from which no recovery seems possible. We have sensation to live by and nothing to live for.

Or so they say, the intelligent, sensitive, cultivated men and women who lead our society. But at no point does their intelligence, their sensitivity, their cultivation, relate to the ordinary life of the people they lead, or even to their own lives. Do they in fact lead? Or are they behind? Are they labouring earnestly backwards, literally going downhill? Why else is their bread all stone, their wine all chlorinated water? Why else do they never laugh?

Let us have a revolution! Or have we had too many? Why can we only ask questions, never answer them? What would we have a revolution for – its own sake? For the blood and the sensations?

It is very hard to believe, but harder still not to, for the temptation of faith is that it makes life reasonable, and we should like it to be that. Now that we have successfully resisted the temptation, however, what are we to do? We have no alternative scheme, only explanations of why what is behaves as it does, never why it is there at all.

I cannot. . .

Old King Cole was a merry old soul.

When he heard he should live no more,
Then he laughed, but never ere!

[*Henry reaches the Turkish baths at the very bottom of the hotel. He has to remove his contact lenses, and as a result can scarcely see anything. After successfully resisting a final sexual assault, and avoiding the wrath of the Encolpians, he at last finds his beloved.*

Henry's blindness in this final section is symbolic. He can see clearly enough at the end. The Encolpians' appearance as fanatical

Red Guards was a clever piece of anticipation, though Charles was obviously thinking of the Hitler Youth. The steam-room is also a gas-chamber. The masked faces which Henry sees peering down at him are those of the men who put in the capsules of poison. The fragments of verse which Henry sings to himself are all taken from medieval English Corpus Christi plays on the subject of Abraham and Isaac.]

The Beloved

I was therefore obliged to remove my contact lenses, though it seemed at first as though I was stone blind without them, for the light was very dim and I thought, with a strange longing for the countryside of my native land, how grim and baffling life must be for the scurrying mole, who, though he freckles whole fields with his little volcanoes of rich earth, and scampers down his long corridors at surprising speed, sees almost nothing, but scrapes and burrows in a perpetual night.

Wrapping my towel about me, I passed again through the great hall, its many statues now invisible to me, though I stopped and peered up at the vast central pillar, wider than any tree-trunk that I had ever seen, trying to descry the group of philosophers, Socrates, Alcibiades and their well-wined companions, which had so much moved me before. But all was a dimness, a flicker of shadow upon shadow, and I had to proceed towards the baths without another glimpse of this masterwork which had given me so profoundly to think, though I of course continued to ponder those matters, and to develop as best I could the many lines of speculation as to the ultimate purpose of. . .

All now depended on chance, for it was improbable that I would be able to identify him or her without my normal visual aids, yet I was not disheartened, for it was unlikely, I considered, that the baths would be much occupied so late in the evening, and I knew that my beloved would find me even if I myself was

capable only of being sufficiently present to be found, for he or
she was in the baths, and they were, the attendant had assured
me, at the very bottom of the hotel, with nothing below them
but drains and foundations, for the hotel had been built before
the need for atom-shelters to be incorporated into public
buildings, and no attempt had been made to modernize it so as
to include one. In order to assist my beloved to discover me, I
resolved to sing quietly as I blundered my way up and down the
many steps between the rooms of various heats and humidities,
for I knew that my voice had revealed me to her or him before
and might do so again. Thus it was that, feeling my way
cautiously forward, I entered the general area of the baths with
these tender words on my lips:

> She was wont to call me her treasure and her store,
> But farewell now, she shall no more.
> Here I shall be dead and wot never wherefore,
> Save that God must have his will.

Hardly had I begun this moving lament than an angry
attendant bid me cease my music, for there were those present,
he said, who were trying to sleep, and others were reading and
writing, playing chess, studying foreign languages and
memorizing trade figures, for the baths were like a university
library, to which students go in order to escape the noisy
jollifications of their comrades, and in spite of the difficulties of
writing with sweat streaming from hand and brow to the paper,
many theses and dissertations had been composed here by
young men and women who had afterwards gone on to great
triumphs in the field of scholarship. Groping my way with this
man's assistance to a seat by the wall, I screwed up my right eye
and was able to make out that the ante-room in which I sat was
indeed full of nearly naked young men, ridgels and women,
who were poring over learned tomes, and when I expressed my

wonderment in a low voice to my bookless neighbour, she replied that it was only possible thanks to the original research into waterproof ink and paper conducted in those very baths by a brilliant young scientist whose dislike of low temperatures amounted almost to a mania, and who spent his entire university career shivering over his books, clad in thick sweaters and trousers, in the very hottest room in the place, a well-known sight at that time, pointed out by old customers to new ones and even mentioned in a guide-book to the city, though this was perhaps a reference paid for by the hotel, who charged the student a very low rate, hoping his extraordinary behaviour would attract new bathers, which to a certain extent it undoubtedly did.

'I see,' she continued, 'that you are yourself a stranger to these beautiful walls and floors. Have you yet examined the exquisite designs in encaustic and mosaic tile which surround you? They are well worth a look.'

I confessed that I was too blind to see anything more than a vaguely coloured blur, except when I screwed up my right eye, which I preferred not to do, for it was a painful business, and my oculist had advised me most strongly against it on the grounds that it might still further distort and weaken the already feeble and ill-shaped muscles. 'But,' I went on, 'I take it that you have your eyes about you, and that they are sharp ones, and so perhaps you can tell me whether you have seen amongst the students and bathers a certain person whom I will describe to you as best I can, though my evidence is biased, and not based, alas, on an intimacy as deep as I hope it will one day become.' And I gave what details I could of my beloved's appearance, neglecting nothing, and confessing my continued ignorance of his or her gender.

'I think,' answered my friend, 'that I have indeed seen someone of the description you have given me, and that she or he – I confess I thought him or her a woman – went towards the dry rooms. But before you go to try to find your friend, let me describe to you the beauties of this place, for they are many, and worthy of your attention.

'Thank you,' I replied, 'such information would under normal circumstances be of the very greatest interest to me, for I am a student of your country, its people, economy and arts, but I must for the moment decline your kind offer, for it is vital that I find the person whom you think you have seen as quickly as possible.'

'Let me at least accompany you part of the way,' said this obliging woman, 'for it is time that I myself moved into the baths proper.'

So saying, she took my hand and led me towards the area from which dampness and heat were exuding, making the floor slippery and dangerous even to those wearing the footwear provided by the management, so that it was only narrowly that I avoided a tumble which might have rendered me incapable of further search and pursuit of my beloved. Making my slip an excuse to put an arm about my shoulders, my guide helped me to maintain a fair rate of progress across the antechamber, and I was about to express my gratitude when she opened a door and thrust me through it, saying in a low whisper which trembled with uncontrollable lust, 'At last! I thought you would never yield!' She pushed me quickly down upon a bed, from which, in my surprise, I had no time to rise before she herself was upon it with me, indeed rather upon me than it, and was covering my body with kisses, her design having been all along thus to assault me and not, as I had innocently supposed, to render me the assistance due from all kindly disposed persons towards the near-blind. Though handicapped by my dimness of vision, I was not otherwise physically weaker than my rapist, and I fought against her with all my strength, surprising her by the violence of my resistance and succeeding at last in throwing her to the floor, whereupon she rose in anger and, better able to attack than I was to defend, began to pummel me about the head, while I punched hopefully in the general direction from which her blows seemed to come, finally striking some bony projection and causing her to cry out and cease her attacks, for I had knocked her out. Stepping cautiously over her unconscious body, I felt my way towards the door and made good my escape, though once outside I did not know quite literally which way to turn, and only after long experimentation decided to move to the left rather than to the right, for the air from the former direction seemed appreciably less moist than that from the latter, and the woman had said that someone resembling my beloved had gone towards the rooms of dry heat, though her statements could no longer be taken at their face value and she might either not have seen my beloved at all, or have deliberately misled me as to his or her whereabouts. Shuffling along, I hummed gently to myself, partly as a ship will sound a horn in thick fog to advertise its presence to other navigation, and partly for the reasons I had entered the baths with a song upon my lips, that is to say in the hope that my beloved might recognize my voice even pianissimo. And as I hummed, I occasionally broke into a low crooning, repeating again and again as chorus to my tune these moving words:

> But, good father, tell ye my mother nothing,
> Say that I am in another country dwelling.

This couplet seemed ironically appropriate to my case, and I could not help reflecting, as the air grew hotter and drier, on the extraordinary ability of simple poetry to carry its emotional charge down the centuries, growing richer and richer as new associations are accreted, quite unlike the rolling stone of popular proverb, for its moss grows ever more abundant, providing a fertile subsoil for other less primitive flora to flourish in, and as its language grows less familiar its original simplicity seems ever more complex, so that at times one can feel that only poetry written many centuries before one's own era can speak directly to one, the works of contemporaries being too finished and new to speak with anything more than their glinting surfaces.

It was as I was thus reflecting and probing slowly towards my goal that I heard the sound of marching feet, as though a platoon of soldiery was coming up behind me, and I crept into a doorway to let it pass. As it drew nearer I could hear that it progressed to the shouting of crude slogans, some of which formed a sort of marching song which went as follows:

> The teachings of Henry are sacred!
> The words of our leader are gospel truth!
> Death to Anti-Henry elements!
> Death to the murderers of Henry!

In spite of my defective vision I had no difficulty in making out that the shouters were none other than my old friends and enemies the Encolpians, and I wondered if they would so easily recognize me, or even recognize me at all. Shrinking against my door I tried to make myself as inconspicuous as possible, for I had only one purpose left in life, which was to find my beloved, and I did not wish to become entangled in any further complications of any kind whatever, least of all with a troop of undisciplined irregulars such as I knew the Encolpians to be. But I was not to avoid them, for as they came abreast of me I heard Milo give the order to halt and the thunder of their slippered heels as they obeyed him.

'Who are you, old person?' demanded Milo roughly.

'A poor blind creature, going for a bath,' I answered, adopting a suitably senile tone, though why Milo considered me old I could not tell, unless, as seemed improbable, my body had suddenly sagged and wrinkled without my knowledge, my hair and teeth fallen and blotches appeared on my skin, none of which I believed to be the case.

'Are you pure?' Milo next wished to know.

'Not entirely,' I returned. 'That is why I am going to take a bath.'

'No insolence!' he shouted. 'Be respectful! Do you not know who I am?'

'Alas!' I answered, 'I can see nothing but a dim shape before me. Forgive me if I have committed an unpardonable blunder.'

Milo seemed to believe that my blindness was genuine, for his voice was softer as he explained that he was leading a clean-up campaign of the baths, for they were notoriously the haunt of libertines, he said, and the teachings of Henry, by which the Encolpians now lived, having changed their name to the Henricians, clearly stated that all lewdness must be rooted out so that men might concentrate on their spiritual welfare, a doctrine which, I need hardly state, astounded its alleged proponent, for I had never said anything of the sort and found any form of interference with individual liberty utterly repugnant. Henry, Milo continued, had been foully done away with by rakes and lechers and his body smuggled away he knew not where or by whom, for the Henricians had minutely searched the whole hotel without finding him, and had now abandoned all hope of doing so, though they were not allowing his memory to die. 'For,' Milo concluded, 'he was as pure in body as he was in soul, devoted to the very highest ideal of spiritual love and repulsed by the sordid practices of the randy whom we are now expelling from this vile place. May he find peace wherever he may be!'

I echoed this last sentiment fervently, and, seeing the sincerity of my feeling, Milo kindly advised me to turn about and head for the steam rooms, for, he said, they had already been thoroughly purged, whereas the dry rooms were still uncleansed hotbeds of corruption and vice, and much blood would undoubtedly have to be spilled there before a truly Henrician paradise could be established within the purlieus of the hotel. Thanking him for his good advice, I made haste to follow it, hurrying away as fast as I dared from the bloodthirsty crew of puritanical maniacs who had once been my boon companions and to whom Milo gave the order 'Quick march!' Their hearty young voices slowly faded away as they sang:

Henry teaches the doctrine of pure spirit!
Long live the clean-living followers of Henry!
Death to the lewd and lecherous!
Let the murderers of Henry be publicly executed!

When I at last felt myself to be safe from the furious righteousness of these storm-troopers, I sank upon a convenient bench and gave myself to reflection on the irony of my situation, than which few in the history of mankind can have ever been more ironic, for it was I . . .

. . . ever seeking more knowledge and experience to compare with the knowledge and experience I already possessed in almost unmanageable quantities, but to no purpose that I could now see but this ceaseless business of comparison, which set me apart from my fellow beings and made it impossible for me ever to be part of any of the societies I studied, so that I was filled with unutterable despair as I stared with my blind eyes into a future which promised only a further series of expeditions and comparisons until my life should end.

Blind though I was, I was at small disadvantage to those of acute vision, for the steam was so thick that they could scarcely see their own feet, or so one of them informed me, going on to say that the heat and humidity were too much for him, and that he must leave me to my own devices, which he did. I sat down on one of the long marble benches and crooned softly to myself another of my singing teacher's favourite melodies:

> Alas, gentle father, why put ye me in this fear?
> Have I displeased you anything?
> If I have trespassed, I cry you mercy;
> And, gentle father, let me not die!
> Alas, is there none other beast but I
> That may please that high king?

. . . great rubber tubes and protruding goggle eyes, which much alarmed me, for these grotesque figures seemed to be pointing at me and jeering in a most hostile manner. But after dropping some small objects, perhaps coins, into the steam-room, these monstrous apparitions closed the trap-door and . . .

. . . through the dense hot fog, and as it loomed nearer, I started from my seat, for it seemed some ghostly visitant who wished to approach me, and there was only one person from whom I desired or expected such an approach, namely my beloved. I screwed up my right eye and the pink shape seemed to take on the form for which I so much longed, and believing it to be none other than the one for whom I had panted and suffered, searched, groaned, endured insult and assault, but whom I had never ceased to love, I threw off my towel and opened my arms to receive that exquisite creature whose coming to me at last made all that had occurred seem as insubstantial as a spider's web at noon.

'At last!' I cried. 'Come to me, my bride and groom, my beloved!'

The form came on as I had bidden it, taking more and more surely to my passionate eyes the shape I desired above all others to behold, and folding me in its own arms whispered endearments into my ear so that my blood, in that steaming, foetid place, turned to ice in my veins, for the voice was not that of my beloved, not that of a friend or a stranger, but the voice of the man I most loathed in all the world, my own father, who had pursued me to this ultimate rendezvous, this last hiding-place on earth, to press upon me that love or hate or . . .

. . . even to protest against the feel of his gross flesh against my own . . .

I let him pick me up and lay me on the marble slab like a ram on an altar, let him draw from beneath his towel a gleaming blade, let him hold it, as though to bless, above me. As he did so I became aware of many familiar faces about him, though how in my blindness I knew . . .

. . . all whom I had ever loved, rank upon rank of them like angels, each with the face of my beloved, and my mother, praying at my head, and my brothers and sisters at my side, and all the company of . . .

. . . mixing pity and love and detestation, pride and humility, indifference and care, the face of my beloved never changing as the hands raised the knife, nor when it fell with great force upon me, to the sweet lamentation of my abandoned loves, who . . .

. . . suspended between life and death, changing from gender into gender, no longer mine but the fluid shape of their imaginations, as they followed that first mortal assault with their own grave and loving farewells, each and none my beloved, my expiring self ready at last to give what . . .

. . . coughing and sighing . . .

... no trumpets, no clarinets, neither trombone nor bassoon, nor any singing ...

... black ...

        ... black ...

                ... black ...

      BLACK
      BLACK
      BLACK

also available from
CAPUCHIN CLASSICS

These Charming People
Michael Arlen. Introduced by Anthony Lejeune
Michael Arlen, best remembered for his highly successful novel *The Green Hat*, continued in the same compelling ruthless vein, with this strong interconnected collection of short stories.

The Conclave
Michael Bracewell. Introduced by Anthony Gardner
Martin Knight is a suburban aesthete with a dangerous attraction for the beautiful, for whom the boom years of the 1980s have served to heighten aspirations and to persuade him of the incontrovertible link between good taste and high finance. For Knight, a 'privileged customer', beauty is cash, and cash beauty – until his edifice comes tumbling down…

Incandescence
Craig Nova. Introduced by William Boyd
Stargell had it all – a prestigious job at a think tank, a beautiful wife and money enough to indulge his expensive tastes. Then one day he lost his job and his life started to take a very definite turn for the worse. In the midst of all this danger and chaos, however, the resilient and darkly comic Stargell is sustained by those rare moments of redeeming grace when every experience feels vital and valuable, when even the darkest moments and the most soiled landscapes seem to glow with a burning incandescence.
'A novel of great power, deadpan humour and uncanny beauty – and one of the finest American novels of our times.' William Boyd

The Green Child
Herbert Read. Introduced by Graham Green
First published in 1935, Herbert Read's only novel is a strange, powerful and original work: a sustained piece of political and philosophical fantasy. Widely debated when it came out more generations ago, *The Green Child* is truly a masterpiece, a rare blend of fantasy and reality.